MEDICAL
Pulse-racing passion

Risking It All With The Paramedic
Janice Lynn

Pregnancy Surprise With The Greek Surgeon
Luna DaRosa

MILLS & BOON

RISKING IT ALL WITH THE PARAMEDIC
© 2024 by Janice Lynn
Philippine Copyright 2024
Australian Copyright 2024
New Zealand Copyright 2024

First Published 2024
First Australian Paperback Edition 2024
ISBN 978 1 038 91765 2

PREGNANCY SURPRISE WITH THE GREEK SURGEON
© 2024 by Luna DaRosa
Philippine Copyright 2024
Australian Copyright 2024
New Zealand Copyright 2024

First Published 2024
First Australian Paperback Edition 2024
ISBN 978 1 038 91765 2

MIX
Paper | Supporting
responsible forestry
FSC® C001695

Published by
Harlequin Mills & Boon
An imprint of Harlequin Enterprises (Australia) Pty Limited
(ABN 47 001 180 918), a subsidiary of HarperCollins
Publishers Australia Pty Limited
(ABN 36 009 913 517)
Level 19, 201 Elizabeth Street
SYDNEY NSW 2000 AUSTRALIA

Cover art used by arrangement with Harlequin Books S.A.. All rights reserved.

Printed and bound in Australia by McPherson's Printing Group

Risking It All With The Paramedic

Janice Lynn

MILLS & BOON

USA TODAY and *Wall Street Journal* bestselling author **Janice Lynn** has a master's in nursing from Vanderbilt University and works as a nurse practitioner in a family practice. She lives in the southern United States with her Prince Charming, their children, their Maltese named Halo and a lot of unnamed dust bunnies that have moved in after she started her writing career. Readers can visit Janice via her website at janicelynn.com.

Dear Reader,

I had the privilege of volunteering for a legacy flight during the summer of '23. Meeting the WWII veterans on the trip and the people of Normandy was life-changing. With the powerful emotions evoked, it only made sense that I'd want to write a story set around the event. Only truly special characters would work, though.

Dr. Ivy McEwen had volunteered as the medic for the Smoky Mountain Veteran Foundation to honor her WWII hero great-grandfather, not to add another dating mistake to her already-long list.

After an injury ended his military career, army paratrooper Caleb Rivers found new life meaning by becoming a paramedic to help others. Filling in for his buddy's volunteer spot on a veteran legacy trip was a no-brainer. But when he meets the doctor in charge of the medical team, it's his heart on the line. He's been burned before. Can Ivy accept him as he is?

I hope you enjoy their story and the glimpses into the beauty of Normandy, France, and the very special people who live there and stole my heart.

Janice

DEDICATION

To Honouring Veteran Legacies, the Best Defense Foundation and Veterans Back to Normandy. Thank you for all you do to honour those who served.

CHAPTER ONE

"I WAS AFRAID you'd change your mind about going."

Dr. Ivy McEwen paused from wheeling her luggage beside her at the Knoxville airport departure terminal area to smile at the seventy-year-old daughter of one of the World War II veterans she'd be with almost nonstop over the next two weeks. Ivy had changed her mind a dozen times. That had been just in the past hour. How could she be so excited to be a medical volunteer for a veteran legacy flight to Normandy, France, and so emotionally devastated at the same time?

"Gramps wanted me to go." She fought to keep her emotions checked. She'd cried enough tears the night before while inspecting her medical supplies one last time. The trip was something she had to do for the greatest man she'd ever known. She'd forever regret it if she didn't follow through on the plans they'd made prior to her great-grandfather passing two months ago.

"You're right. Leon would want you watching

out for us." Mary gave an empathetic look. "Dad and I sure feel better knowing that you'll be taking care of us."

Not that Mary knew anything about Ivy's medical skills other than what Gramps had bragged to the Smoky Mountain Veteran Foundation.

Bless him.

He'd set the bar high, but then, when hadn't he? Ivy had spent most of her life making sure she not only met but exceeded his expectations. She'd wanted to make Gramps proud. Always.

"It's an honor to be on the medical team." With D-Day having occurred on June 6, 1944, there wouldn't be many more WWII legacy trips to honor those who had helped liberate Europe.

"Speaking of the medical team…" Mary waggled her penciled-on reddish brown brows that perfectly matched her dyed hair cut in a trendy bob. "Have you met the paramedic who took Stan's place? He makes this old gal want to call 911."

Ivy appreciated Mary's subject change to lighten the conversation. She'd instantly liked the woman when they'd met months ago at one of the few planning meetings Ivy had been able to attend while she'd been finishing her medical school out-of-state residency.

"I haven't." Stan had canceled last minute due to a family emergency. Regardless, Ivy and Lara, a nurse from Maryville, should be able to handle most medical situations that might occur while traveling with five almost-centenarians. Ivy grinned at how Mary dramatically fanned her flushed cheeks. "Mary, do I need to check your blood pressure?"

Mary laughed. "Probably. He's a handsome one. Linda asked him if he was available."

"Linda isn't available," Ivy reminded of the married fifty-two-year-old granddaughter of one of the veterans.

"No, but you are." Mary waggled her brows again. "He's single and a real hottie."

"Not interested." Ivy hoped the women weren't going to play matchmaker. The only thing she could imagine worse than having to get on an airplane would be getting into a new relationship. Luke had left her with a terrible aversion to another relationship. Blech. No, thank you. "Besides, looks fade, Mary."

Grabbing hold of her suitcases' handles, Ivy rolled them toward the departure terminal counter. As much as she dreaded the flight, she needed to check in. Maybe the knot in her stomach would ease once she'd taken that step.

Mary kept pace. "True, looks fade. But some men are classically handsome throughout their lifetime. You can see their beauty no matter how much time has tried to ebb it away."

Ivy knew exactly what she meant. She'd felt it every time she'd looked at her great-grandfather.

She'd always known why her great-grandmother had been besotted with the paratrooper when he'd returned from Europe in 1945. Later in his life, Ivy had thought he'd hung the moon and soaked up every moment she got to spend with him. Why didn't they make men like Gramps anymore? Men who were honorable, brave, skilled, loyal, *faithful*, and not threatened by a woman's success? Today's men just weren't of the same caliber.

"Caleb is that kind of handsome," Mary continued as they walked toward where the others waited near the group meeting point. "Stan did us right by asking him to join us. When we got here, he jumped right in to help with our luggage. I haven't heard so many 'Yes, ma'ams' and 'No, ma'ams' as when I was talking with him. Mark my words, he's a keeper." The woman's gaze went beyond Ivy and she grinned like a Cheshire cat. "Oh! He and Owen are back from the restroom now. Have a gander, and it may be you needing to have *your* blood pressure checked."

"You're a funny lady, Mary, but I'm not interested." Three strikes and she was out. She'd thought Luke, aka Heartbreak Number Three, was different, but he'd been cheating for months with an undergrad student he'd first met at a Christmas party he'd attended with Ivy. To top it off, he'd blamed Ivy. Just recalling his unjustified attempts at shifting the blame for his unfaithfulness had her fingers curling into her palms. If he'd felt inadequate, it had been because he was. Too bad it had taken discovering he'd been sleeping with Little Miss Coed for Ivy to finally admit that she'd been blind because she'd wanted to believe in their relationship. Not so long ago, she'd dreamed of having what Gramps and her great-grandmother had had. She forced her fingers to relax their tight grasp on her luggage handle. She wasn't letting Luke, or any man, sully this trip to honor Gramps's legacy.

"You should keep an open mind," Mary sighed dreamily. "Or maybe I should say an open heart?"

"No, thank you." She'd be keeping her heart to herself.

Mary had the audacity to laugh.

That's when Ivy spotted Caleb Rivers. Although she'd never met him or even seen a photo, the man walking beside Owen had to be whom Mary went on about. She hadn't been kidding about that blood pressure check. Despite Ivy's aversion to the male species, her pulse did a wild dance, proving that she was still a young, healthy female who wasn't as oblivious as she'd like to think.

Younger than she'd been expecting as she'd imagined someone closer to Stan's age, Caleb wore his dark hair cropped short but not quite in a buzz. Long lashes fringed intense amber eyes. A slightly crooked nose hinted that it had once been broken. Rather than detract, the imperfection added to his manly appeal. He was tall, probably six-two or three and thick-chested but not in an "I'm on steroids" way. He was easy on the eyes, but ultimately what did that matter? With Ivy's dating history, good looks were a detriment as they made a man a more appealing target for other women. With as much as she'd been cheated on, maybe it really was her fault the men she dated had all betrayed her.

"Caleb." Mary waved at where he stayed close to Owen. "Come here. I want to introduce you to Dr. Ivy."

Mr. Ruggedly Handsome shifted his gaze toward Mary. Ivy's breath caught. Okay, there was something about him that turned her insides to goop.

Pheromones, Ivy. That's what's about him. Pheromones wrapped in a gorgeous package. You're used to academic types, not someone so...physical. She was over relationships, but not physically dead.

A woman might have to be dead not to notice Caleb River's manliness. An aura clung to him that assured he could take care of business, whatever that business might be, and yet, when he'd turned toward Mary, his smile was warm and genuine. Right up until his gaze met Ivy's. At that point something flickered that made her want to spin her luggage around and hightail it out of the airport. Or maybe just spontaneously combust right then and there because warm had shot to *hot*.

Not once could she recall having had such an instantaneous reaction. She'd dated Luke during residency because he'd been intelligent, attractive in a scholarly, dependable way and she'd thought they shared the same values. Luke had replaced Beau who she'd dated during medical school, but who had rekindled a relationship with his high school girlfriend during a trip home to visit his family over the Christmas holidays. Only, he'd forgotten to mention that tidbit for several months and had been stringing both women along until the girlfriend back home had gotten pregnant. Beau had replaced Kenny from undergrad. Kenny had said he loved Ivy, but she'd eventually learned that he'd "loved" lots of women. Yea, her track record wasn't so good when it came to men. Forcing herself to stand as tall as her five-six would stretch with her heavy backpack weighing her down, Ivy straightened her shoulders. Gorgeous Caleb Rivers had probably broken so many hearts he made the men of Ivy's past look like child's play.

He said something to Owen, then they crossed the twenty or so feet to her and Mary. Caleb kept his pace matched with Owen's slower, but steady one, not touching him, but aware of every nuance. Good for him for realizing that the proud veteran would have been insulted if he'd attempted to unnecessarily assist him in any way.

When they joined where Ivy and Mary had stopped just feet from the counter, Owen grinned. "Glad to see you, Doc."

"You, too." It was true. She'd fallen hard for the veterans she'd met during the information sessions she'd attended, especially Owen. There was something dapper yet tough about him. When he'd talked about his late wife, Ivy had gotten goose bumps at the love in his voice. Sometimes, she thought she'd been born in the wrong generation.

"You've not met Caleb?" Was there an extra twinkle in Owen's pale blue gaze that hinted he and Mary were on the same page? Ugh. She really hoped she wouldn't be dealing with a bunch of wannabe Cupids the entire trip.

"No, sir. I haven't." She shifted her gaze from Owen to the paramedic and swallowed. She might need to send her hormones a memo that she was not interested even if they had blossomed to unexpected life.

With a friendly smile cutting dimples into his cheeks, Caleb stuck out his hand. "Caleb Rivers. Nice to meet the infamous doctor who Owen keeps telling me about." His eyes danced with a mischievous gleam. "You have a lot to live up to, but so far, he was right on the money."

Interesting. What had Owen told Caleb? And

why were her lips curving upward in such a huge smile? Puh-leeze. Had she learned nothing? Apparently not, because when she gripped his outstretched hand, every nerve ending in her body started and ended where their skin touched.

Hello, lightning bolt.

Goodness. Obviously, her lack-of-sleep brain was playing tricks on her.

"Dr. Ivy McEwen." Determined to shake off whatever insanity was gripping her, she pulled her hand from Caleb's, marveling at how her hand threatened to rebel and return to the warm, firmness of his callused grasp. "Don't believe a thing this ancient coot tells you." She kissed Owen's cheek. "Are you ready for this?"

Owen's eyes sparkled. "I'm always ready for traveling the world with a beautiful woman." His expression turned serious. "It's been a long time since I've set foot in France."

Ivy's heart squeezed. He and Gramps had instantly clicked when they'd first met. Ivy had devoured the stories the two men had shared in between the organization's coordinator running through the proposed trip itinerary.

Owen gestured toward Caleb. Pride shone on his weathered face. "This guy was in the Eighty-Second, too, just like your great-grandfather and me."

Surprised by Owen's revelation, although not sure why since she knew very little about Stan's

last-minute replacement other than a few shared
group text messages and what Mary had told her,
Ivy glanced toward the paramedic. Her gaze collided with his as he'd apparently been watching her rather than looking at Owen. Her breath
caught. "You were a paratrooper?"

Ivy would swear he grew a few inches taller.
"Yes, ma'am."

Mary nudged Ivy at his good manners, as if to
say, *See what I mean?*

"Much to my mother's chagrin—" Caleb
grinned "—jumping out of perfectly good airplanes is all I ever wanted to do."

She could tell it was an auto-response he must
give often, because it flowed so smoothly. Yet
there was something in his eyes that hinted there
was more to what he was saying.

"I hear your love of jumping. But you're working as a paramedic. Should I ask why the career
change?"

He shrugged. "Being a paratrooper is a job for
the young."

"I've seen your trip health form. You're not that
old," she pointed out, then felt her cheeks go hot.
Maybe she should point out that she'd intently
reviewed everyone going on the trip's forms to
proactively plan for any potential issues.

Owen chuckled. "That's right. He's barely old
enough to need to shave."

Ivy took in the strong lines of Caleb's jaw, surprised by how much she wanted to run her fingers across the smooth-shaven skin. She'd put money on his having shaved that morning, and it wouldn't surprise her if he had stubble prior to their reaching their host family in France. She'd never been attracted to stubble, preferring a clean-cut appearance, but she suspected that Caleb could pull off most looks.

"Just barely." Caleb chuckled at Owen's teasing, then focused on Ivy. "My career change is a long story. Let's get your bags checked."

Ivy was disappointed that he hadn't given her an answer. She had a natural curiosity about people, about all aspects of life, really. Caleb Rivers intrigued her more than most, which wasn't necessarily a good thing.

Ivy didn't need help with her two roller bags and backpack, but Luke's insults echoed about how she refused to allow a man to be a man, citing her heftier income as making her too independent. Ivy pointed to the suitcase she planned to check. "If you put that bag on the scale, you might prevent me from toppling over."

See, that hadn't been that difficult. Then again, she didn't want Luke being the voice in her head that dictated future actions.

"No toppling. You're not allowed to get hurt."

That would be a travesty since she was there to take care of others. How her heart fluttered at

Caleb's eyes crinkling in the corners was enough to have her knees buckling, though.

Cheeks warm, she pulled her gaze from him to the duo watching her curiously. "Mary, you and Owen behave while I get checked in."

With a twinkle in their eyes that suggested they might purposely seek trouble, they laughed. Mary linked her arm with Owen's and they walked to where her father and the others waited. Owen's great-granddaughter Suzie tried to get him to sit in one of the empty wheelchairs near the bench. If looks could kill, Owen would be facing time. He patted the girl's hand then, continuing to stand, started talking to a send-off volunteer.

Having watched the exchange, Caleb grabbed the handle of Ivy's largest suitcase. "He's probably hoping that thing disappears to where no one suggests he sit in it again. He sure wasn't happy about my suggestion I push him in it when he had to go to the restroom."

"None of them are going to want to use a chair any more than they absolutely have to. I'm glad. It's good for them to move as much as they can before we get on the plane. Knoxville to Paris is a long way for them to travel."

It was a long way for Ivy to travel. Logically, she knew all the reasons why flying was safer than driving, but her aerophobia was impervious to logic. Always had been.

Caleb nodded. "True. I'm going to struggle

with trying to protect them to the point of annoying them."

"No worries. They'll set you straight." She moved to the check-in point and fought nausea. Why couldn't she love flying the way her parents did? People flew all the time and were just fine. She would be, too. If the flight to Paris was too bad, she'd take a boat back to the States. Which wouldn't work since she'd never abandon the veterans in her care. One way or another, she'd endure the round-trip flights. With what the veterans had once endured, she could handle a few hours of discomfort.

Ivy gave the woman at the counter her passport and ticket information. When Caleb put her bag upon the scale, Ivy held her breath. Her bag came in just under the weight limits.

"That was close." Caleb grinned. "Does this one go?"

She shook her head. "That one stays with me. It and my backpack are full of medical supplies."

Smiling, Caleb gestured toward where the others from their group were. Amongst the various luggage items were a camouflage backpack and a sturdy black hard-case bag. "I feel ya."

Ivy's face heated. Ha! Her whole body heated. Which was ridiculous. What was wrong with her? She blamed Mary's earlier comments.

As distracting as he was, Caleb would not be "feeling her" short of her suffering a heart attack on the plane brought on by her anxiety and his needing to perform cardiopulmonary resuscitation. With the way her heart pounded, his needing to revive her might not be such a far-fetched possibility.

From where he sat across the aisle from her while they awaited their plane's turn to take off, Caleb Rivers studied the brunette bombshell whose eyes were closed. He'd heard so much about her from everyone he'd met in connection to Smoky Mountain Veteran Foundation. They all adored Dr. Ivy McEwen. Several had mentioned her beauty, including the ninety-nine-year-old veteran in the plane seat next to him. Caleb had worried that he'd be dealing with a prima donna, but was reassured that Ivy was willing to lose her personal items over her medical supplies.

The moment his gaze had connected with hers, the same headiness had rushed through him that he got when free-falling through the sky during a jump. It had been a long time, too long, since he'd experienced that sensation. From a jump or a woman. Ivy's long shiny dark hair was braided. Faint freckles kissed her lightly tanned skin across her nose and cheeks. Her lips were plump and rosy. Her eyes were what had sucker punched him, though. Big blue irises shaded by lashes so perfect he wondered if they were extensions like TransCare's receptionist wore. Ivy was a knockout, no doubt about it. That she was intelligent was a given, but something in the way she'd looked at him seemed to see beyond the surface, too.

Her eyes opened and met his. "Everything okay?"

He'd like to ask her that because of the fatigue showing on her facial features. Had she not slept well the night before? For all he knew, she'd worked and headed straight to the airport at the end of a shift.

"I'll make sure the guys get up to walk in an hour or so, if you want to grab a nap," he offered, hoping she'd feel comfortable as long as she knew their veterans were being taken care of. The foundation had purposely requested that the medical team be in aisle seats so they could more readily get to anyone who needed them. Lara was toward the front of the plane near part of their group. Near the rear, Ivy sat in the left side row, with Owen sandwiched between her and his granddaughter at the window. Caleb sat in the middle row section with Roy next to him and Mary in the opposite middle section aisle seat.

Looking alarmed, guilty almost, Ivy shook her head. "I hadn't planned to sleep."

"No?" He arched a brow. "It'll be morning in France when we arrive. We should all rest while we can."

Her fingers white-knuckled the seat belt strap.

"I'm fine. You can nap. I'm not much for sleeping on planes, but even if I was, I'm not tired." It was early morning in Tennessee, but the six-hour time difference would catch up with them at the end of their flight, especially if Ivy hadn't slept much the night before. Did she struggle just with takeoff or flying in general? Although he loved flying, he empathized with those who did not. Maybe he could distract her during takeoff enough to ease some of her anxiety.

"We've been cleared for takeoff," the captain said over the loudspeaker.

The plane moved onto the runway strip. The skin stretched across Ivy's knuckles as she gripped her seat belt strap more tightly.

Caleb fought the urge to reach across the aisle to place his hand over hers. If he could do it without being so obvious, he would. Ivy's fear was real, but he knew she fought to hide it and wouldn't appreciate his doing anything that pointed it out to others. "You've got this and you're going to be fine," he encouraged in a low voice.

Her gaze met his and she tilted her chin ever so slightly. "Residency has me well prepared to function on little to no sleep."

Stan had mentioned that she'd just finished her residency. He suspected she knew he hadn't been referring to napping, but he went with it.

"It's been a while, but the army did the same

for me." Memories assailed him, good and bad, but he forced his focus toward the good. "It also taught me to sleep whenever I got the chance, so I generally do."

She narrowed her gaze. "You're one of those annoying people who can nod off anywhere, aren't you?"

He grinned. "Guilty. How did you guess?"

"Just a hunch," she admitted, her fingers flexing, then smoothing over the seat belt strap as if she'd like to put it back in a death hold but was forcing herself not to as the plane increased in speed. Taking a deep breath, she rushed on. "That's never been me. I'm not a napper and usually don't try to sleep if I don't have at least four hours. Less than that, I feel worse than if I'd not slept at all."

He wrinkled his nose. "That must have been rough during residency. With the long hours, I'd have thought you'd sleep whenever given the chance."

"If only I had an on-off switch to make that happen. I wanted to be a doctor, so I did what I had to do regardless of how much sleep I did, or didn't, get." Another forced smile, then she failed to do anything other than hold her breath as the plane lifted off the ground. Sighing, she met his gaze with a warning in her blue depths not to point out what had just happened. Her chin was lifted in that show of defiance, causing something to stir deep within him. Empathy, he assured himself. No one liked seeing someone else suffer and takeoff had certainly not been a pleasurable experience for Ivy.

"What made you want to be a doctor?"

She took a deep breath, as if she really didn't want to be talking but to focus on what was happening to the plane.

"My great-grandmother was a doctor." She glanced toward the window two seats from her. "She was a pioneer, since at the time most physicians were male. She died when I was young, unfortunately. Gramps told me stories about her and how she loved taking care of others. I wanted to honor her legacy."

"And ended up in Knoxville?"

"Gramps's farm is just outside Knoxville, so Knoxville has always felt like home." She grimaced, her face going pale, then corrected herself. "He passed a couple of months ago."

"I'm sorry," Caleb said. He'd been told that, originally, she'd been going on this trip to accompany her great-grandfather, who had served in World War II.

"Me, too." She gave a tight smile, then obviously unable to keep her hands still, she tightened her seat belt again. "You should get one of those power naps you were bragging about while you have the chance."

Rather than continue their conversation, Ivy

turned from him, saying something to Owen, which the natural-born talker jumped all over. Caleb wasn't used to being dismissed but that was what she'd done. The opposite sex usually found him attractive. He'd taken advantage of that to the fullest in his younger years until he and Katrina had started dating, but since his accident he hadn't had time for frivolous encounters and wasn't interested in anything more. Maybe his reaction to Ivy was his body's way of telling him he'd been on hiatus too long.

Even without Katrina's rejection of his life choices, women hadn't been a priority. Healing his ankle had consumed him. He'd moved on, had a different life now. It wasn't the one he'd planned on, but he liked to think he still made a difference in the world even if those closest to him didn't agree with his choices.

Frustrated by his own limitations, he stretched out the best his economy seat would allow while keeping his feet out of the aisle so he wouldn't trip anyone. Maybe he'd get lucky, doze off for a while, and, hopefully, not dream of the life-altering event that had robbed him of his greatest joy.

Otherwise, it might be Ivy having to reach across the airplane aisle to calm him.

CHAPTER TWO

HAVING TRULY DOZED off and fortunately not experiencing any nightmares, Caleb awakened when about an hour into the flight a stewardess came over the public address system.

"Are there any medical personnel on the plane?" she asked. "Would any medical personnel on board please come to the back of the plane? Thank you."

Coming fully alert, Caleb unsnapped his seat belt. When he stepped into the aisle, Ivy was already out of her seat and headed to the back.

"You're medical?" a stewardess asked as they reached the back of the plane.

"I'm Dr. McEwen and Mr. Rivers is a paramedic," Ivy informed the woman, whose face immediately filled with relief.

"Great. A passenger isn't feeling well and is having trouble breathing. Come this way."

A flush-cheeked female in her late forties hunched on the other side of the back galley. Several people crowded around her. With her expression panicked and tears flowing, she shook her head at whatever someone had asked her.

"Step back," the stewardess told the other airline employees and the man huddled around the distressed woman. "This is a doctor."

All except the man who had his arm on her shoulder, perhaps the woman's husband, stepped back, giving a grateful look toward Caleb and Ivy.

"Hello, I'm Dr. McEwen." Ivy stepped forward. "Is it okay for me and my paramedic acquaintance, Caleb, to examine you?" The woman nodded and Ivy asked, "What's your name?"

"Bella…" The woman's name came out with a bit of a croaking sound. The woman coughed to try to clear her throat. Her scared gaze cut to her husband, obviously pleading with him to do something.

"So that I can best help you, tell me what's going on, Bella." Ivy refocused the woman's attention on her.

"I…can't…breathe," she managed, sounding more and more hoarse. She glanced toward the man with her, again, and he took over speaking for her.

"I'm Bella's husband, Tom," he said. "We were sitting in our seats, and she started feeling funny, saying she felt tingly and itchy. Then she started breathing funny. We weren't sure what to do so I pressed the stewardess button. They had us come to the back of the plane."

"That was the right thing to do," Caleb assured while Ivy stayed focused on the woman. He reached for Bella's wrist. Her rapid pulse bounded beneath her clammy skin. Glancing at his watch, he counted for fifteen seconds, then multiplied the number by four. "Tachycardic at 120."

"Bella, I'd like you to open your mouth as wide as you can and stick out your tongue," Ivy advised as she turned on her phone's flashlight and shined it into the woman's mouth. She didn't grimace exactly, but Caleb could tell Ivy didn't like what she saw. "Your throat is swollen. Are you allergic to anything? Peanuts, maybe? If so, do you have an epinephrine pen to counter the reaction?"

Looking more and more panicked, Bella shook her head.

"She's not allergic to anything," Tom assured them. "No medications, foods, nothing."

"She's allergic to something and is having an anaphylactic reaction." Ivy turned toward Caleb. "I have an epinephrine injection pen in my backpack. Go get my entire bag, please, and bring it here."

Although his instinct was to stay with the patient, Caleb immediately fast-walked across the crew area then back up the aisle to where Ivy's backpack was stored beneath the seat in front of hers. Grabbing it and his own bag from the overhead bin, he returned to the back section of the plane as quickly as he safely could.

Bella was now sitting on the floor and was actively wheezing and holding her chest. Ivy knelt beside her and was reassuring her that she had the appropriate medications to stop the reaction. Ivy held Bella's wrist, no doubt keeping a check on her pulse. The poor woman's husband looked a mess and one of the flight attendants, appearing almost as harried, was on the phone with the pilot, advising him of what was happening.

"The doctor says we have to land the plane," the stewardess was saying into the phone.

Caleb agreed. The sooner, the better.

"Thank you." Ivy took her bag, unzipped it and pulled out a pouch where she quickly found what she was looking for.

Kneeling beside them, Caleb opened his own bag and found his pulse oximeter. He slipped the oxygen saturation monitor over the woman's fingertip. "Eighty-nine percent oxygen saturation and a 128 heart rate." He glanced toward another of the stewardesses. She held a pen and paper and was making notes. "It's probably what you're doing, but, if not, I'd appreciate you writing down vital signs, along with the time, as Dr. McEwen or I say them. Same goes with medications given. That way we can reference them if needed. Thanks."

The stewardess nodded. "Got it. I have to keep a record of what happens anyway for our report."

While Ivy jabbed the epinephrine pen into the woman's thigh, releasing the medication, Caleb reached for his blood pressure cuff to get diastolic and systolic readings.

"Bella, this was epinephrine." The woman barely reacted to the injection and seemed oblivious to where Caleb was wrapping the cuff around her arm. Her gaze jumped back and forth between Ivy and her husband. "It's a medication to help with your allergic reaction. It's what you'd be given if you were at a hospital emergency department," Ivy continued, her voice calm, steady, confident. "Initially, it's probably going to make you feel shakier, sort of like you are overcaffeinated, but that's okay. It means the medicine is taking effect."

Still clutching at her chest, Bella nodded. She coughed in between her ragged, wheezy breaths. Her face had a purplish hue, appearing slick with sweat and tears and now having raised red whelps.

"The epinephrine should start taking effect quickly, but I'm going to give you an injection of diphenhydramine, too, since I have it and I only had the one epinephrine pen to give you. That should be enough, but we're on a plane, so it's better to be overly cautious." Ivy looked directly into the woman's eyes. "Diphenhydramine is something you may have taken in the past. It's over-the-counter for allergies in a capsule or tablet form as it's a common antihistamine that's been around for many decades. I'm doing the injection because I don't think you could swallow a pill right now."

"Couldn't," the woman choked out between trying to clear her throat with another wheezy cough.

Taking his stethoscope from his bag, Caleb completely agreed with Ivy's decision process and admired how she worked efficiently while trying to keep Bella calm and focused on her. At over thirty thousand feet in the air, they needed to hit Bella with everything they could to get her reaction under control. While Ivy dug through the medication vials in the pouch she'd pulled the epinephrine injectable pen from, he paused in taking Bella's blood pressure and instead reached into Ivy's bag for the plastic packet stuffed with syringes and needles. He got out one of each, along with an alcohol pad, and handed them to Ivy just as she found the vial she sought.

Ivy took them. "Thanks."

While she drew up the diphenhydramine, he finished taking Bella's blood pressure.

"Eighty-four over sixty-two," he said out loud for Ivy's benefit and so the stewardess could record it. He glanced down at the pulse oximeter.

"Pulse is 134. Oxygen saturation is at 87 percent."

"Is that good or bad?" Bella's husband, Tom, asked. "The medicine is going to help, right?"

"Her blood pressure is low." The decreased pressure was from her anaphylactic shock. The epinephrine Ivy had given the woman should cause the vessels to vasoconstrict to increase the pressure quickly, though. The sooner the better. Hopefully, the medication had been given in time to prevent fluid from leaking into Bella's lungs from the reduced blood flow pressure. He didn't know what all Ivy had in her bag, but dealing with pulmonary edema on the plane would be challenging under the best of circumstances. Too bad Ivy didn't have IV supplies in her medical bag. Pumping fluids into Bella would be helpful to quickly increase her plasma volume.

"Low?" Frowning, Tom's expression grew more panicked. "Her blood pressure is usually too high. Why is it low? Is she dying?"

"No," Caleb said with great force, hoping he told the truth. With the epinephrine, he hopefully did. Either way, the last thing anyone needed was full-blown panic setting in.

"She normally has elevated blood pressure?" Ivy asked, then to Bella, "I'm going to put this injection into your hip. It's the diphenhydramine I told you about." Ivy moved to where she could readily pull the woman's elastic banded pants down to expose where she wanted to put the medication.

"Well, she used to but not recently." Tom cringed as Ivy administered the shot. "She takes blood pressure medicine. It usually works well, but not like this. She's never had a pressure this low."

"It's the release of so much histamine that's causing her blood vessels to dilate and drop her blood pressure," Ivy explained from where she was pushing the safety device on the used needle into place to prevent an accidental stick. When done, she handed it to Caleb to do something with and went back to digging through her bag. "The medication I just injected into her should counter the release of more histamine. That and the epinephrine should have you breathing easier soon, Bella."

"I hope so." Tom was starting to look a little pale himself to where Caleb worried the man might be going to pass out. They didn't need him doing so, possibly hurting himself in the process.

"Hey, Tom," he said loud enough to get the man's immediate attention. "What's the name of Bella's blood pressure medication? Is she on anything else? Prescription or over-the-counter?"

Tom took a deep breath. "I have a list of her medications in her bag that's at our seats. She has thyroid disease and takes a few vitamins, too."

"Get them," Caleb ordered. "I'd like to see her entire list."

Bella reached for her husband's hand, clutching it to her and not wanting him to go.

"I'll be right back." He pulled free to head toward their seats to fetch the list.

Glad Tom was not on a rapid descent to the plane's cabin floor, Caleb glanced at the pulse oximeter reading on Bella's finger. Her oxygen saturation was at 84 percent. She was dropping. Not good. Her tissue wasn't being properly perfused with oxygen. They needed the epinephrine and diphenhydramine to reverse her reaction fast. They also needed to get her feet elevated to help with blood flow to vital organs. Gently, so as not to topple her over, he lifted her feet, then motioned to one of the stewardesses. "I need you to hold them or for you to get me something to prop up her feet so I don't have to hold them. I need my hands free." He didn't say in case he needed to do CPR, but the thought sure rang loudly through his head.

The flight attendant took over holding Bella's feet and another went to see what she could find to keep them elevated. Ivy was still digging through her medication vials, glancing at each one, then quickly moving to the next. "I have dexamethasone with me."

Great. The steroid would help with the reaction, too.

Bella's breathing was coming hard, fast and ragged with audible wheezing.

"Bella, look at me." Caleb noted how her heart rate had spiked even higher. The woman's mascara-streaked eyes shifted to him. "It's going to be okay. Dr. McEwen and I are going to take care of you. Dr. McEwen had the right medications to give you and you got care much quicker than you would have at most places even if you'd been on the ground, rather than on a plane. Thanks to Dr. McEwen having what you needed, you're going to be okay."

What he said was true. Not that what was happening with Bella wasn't serious and even life-threatening. But with as quickly as Ivy had gotten the epinephrine into her and then the diphenhydramine, his gut instinct was that the woman was going to be okay once the medications started fully kicking in and the plane landed so they could hand her over to ground emergency services. Just so long as fluid hadn't leaked into her lungs. He wasn't going to go there. Only a minute or two had passed from their becoming aware of the incident, but every second was vital during a medical emergency.

Ivy pulled out the vial of dexamethasone. Swiping the top with an alcohol pad, she filled a syringe. "Sorry, Bella. I have another injection.

This one is a steroid. It'll help stop the inflammatory process and open your airway so you can breathe easier." Ivy glanced at the attendant holding Bella's feet. "I need the plane's medical box so I can see what's there. Sometimes there's IV fluid on transoceanic flights. Let's hope this is one of those times."

Another stewardess moved to the compartment above the last set of plane seats and retrieved a medical kit. She handed the bag to him. He set it on the floor, intending to go through it, but Ivy immediately undid the fastener and began searching through the bag. She outranked him, so he didn't resent her take-charge attitude. If anything, he liked it.

"Yes! This may come in handy." Excited, she picked up a vial of epinephrine and showed it to him. Good. They had backup adrenaline.

Pulling a five-hundred-milliliter bag of normal saline from the kit and supplies to start an IV, Ivy smiled. "Now, we're in business."

As a paramedic, Caleb dealt with life-threatening situations on a regular basis. Enough so that he wasn't even sure his own adrenaline got up much these days when working a call. However, Dr. Ivy McEwen's smile had just gut punched him with a dose so huge his breath caught, and he almost felt dizzy from its impact.

The next two weeks were going to be interesting to say the least.

* * *

Ivy double-checked that she had everything she needed within reach so she could start Bella's IV. *Saline bag, tourniquet, antiseptic, insertion catheter, tubing, gauze, tape, gloves*, she mentally ticked the items off.

She quickly swabbed her hands again with a disinfectant packet, then gloved up, opened the packaging around the bag of saline, attached the tubing and filled the line with fluid, making sure she'd cleared out air bubbles.

"I'll hold it," Caleb offered, jumping to his feet and taking the bag from her. "Or if you want me to start the line, I'll do that. Either way, I'm good."

"I've got it," she assured. She hoped she told the truth. She was usually a great stick, but she'd never started an IV on a plane at over thirty thousand feet.

Lord, please don't let them hit any turbulence.

She put the tourniquet on Bella's arm and cleansed her antecubital space, trying not to wince at what she felt. Bella wasn't going to be an easy stick.

"This is going to be interesting," she mumbled under her breath as she opened the catheter. "Keep your fingers crossed," she told no one in particular as she readied the catheter, then slid it into the woman's vein. Holding her breath, she released the tourniquet and was thankful blood filled the clear cylinder chamber. She sighed a relieved breath that she'd gotten the needle into the vein on the first try. After feeling Bella's weak veins, she'd definitely had her doubts that was going to happen. "Thank you, Jesus."

She slid the catheter forward, but not the needle. Once she was happy with placement, she removed the needle, leaving the catheter, then attached the end of the tubing Caleb held out to her. Checking to make sure it looked right, she taped it down to prevent the catheter from slipping out of place. She watched closely to make sure the fluid went into the vein and not the surrounding tissue, and then she undid the lock mechanism and let the fluid go at wide open.

"Nicely done," Caleb praised from where he handed off the IV bag to a flight attendant and moved next to Ivy. He reached for his blood pressure cuff to check the woman's vitals on her free arm again.

"Here's her list. I had trouble finding where she had put it, but I finally did." Tom held out a piece of paper. Taking in that his wife now had an IV going, his eyes widened. "What's happened? You said she was going to be okay. Is she worse?"

"No, she's not worse," Ivy assured. "Look, the rash on her arms is already slightly improved." Not from the IV fluid, but from the epinephrine, diphenhydramine and dexamethasone. "She should be breathing a little easier and continue to improve as the medication continues to work."

Bella's still frightened gaze went from watching what Caleb was doing to looking up at her husband. She motioned for Tom to sit down next to her, and he did so and clasped her hand in his.

"Her pressure is starting to come up a little already. She's ninety-four over sixty-eight," Caleb told her. "Oxygen saturation is at eighty-six. Pulse is 122."

"Her pressure and O2 sats should continue to improve." Ivy hoped. If too much fluid had leaked into Bella's lungs from the histamine reaction, getting her oxygen saturation back to normal on the plane might prove impossible. And fatal.

Over the next couple of minutes, they continued to check Bella, looking in her mouth to monitor her airway, listening to her lungs and heart, and keeping a check on her vital signs. Other than her wheeze, which didn't sound nearly as noisy as it had initially, Bella's lungs remained clear other than the sob she couldn't seem to control every few breaths. No doubt she was terrified and understandably so.

"I know it's scary, but just know the medicine is working." Ivy patted her hand. "Look at your arms. The red splotches are fading. The medicine is going to keep you feeling antsy, but you are improving. As scary as it is to feel jittery after having a reaction, that nervousness is expected from the treatment and the stress of what you've been through. You are getting better, Bella. Whether you feel it yet or not, I can see it. You are going to be okay."

If Ivy said it enough, it would hold true, right? As long as fluid hadn't leaked into Bella's lungs, everything would be fine. If it had, well, it was going to take more than what Ivy had access to on an airplane to clear the woman's symptoms. Bella would drown on her own body fluids and there wouldn't be a thing Ivy would be able to do to stop it from happening. She didn't think that was going to happen. They'd gotten to Bella quickly, given the epinephrine and other medications in time.

Hopefully.

Kneeling next to his wife, Tom made an appreciative sound.

"Take slow, deep breaths through your nose and blow them out of your mouth. Slow and steady," Caleb encouraged, keeping a close check on the pulse oximeter readings. He'd done a great job keeping a check on Bella's stats while Ivy administered medications. He'd talked with Bella and Tom with admirable kindness and compassion that seemed to make up who he was since he'd interacted with the veterans and their families in a similar manner. "Inhale through your nose," he repeated, his voice calming, a little mesmerizing even. "And blow out slowly through your mouth."

Ivy automatically fell into the breathing pattern of his words and felt some of her own tensions ease. Realizing what she'd done, she almost smiled. What a blessing he must be to his patients.

Sniffling, Bella did as Caleb said. Her breathing was still noisy, but there was an audible improvement in air movement. Excitement that what they were doing was working had Ivy doing a mental fist pump and thinking, *Yes!*

"You're doing great," Caleb encouraged in a tone that had Ivy thinking she might nickname him the Breathing Whisperer, as she was pretty sure everyone in the back galley was now breathing in sync. "Again, breathe in through your nose and now, out through your mouth. Good job, Bella. Your vital readings are looking better and better."

The stewardess who was recording the incident had been on the phone several times during the episode and currently was again. "I'll let the captain know she's improving. He wants to know what we need to do. Do we need to divert our landing still? Or can we keep going?"

Making sure she left no doubt of the seriousness of what happened to Bella, Ivy looked directly at the stewardess and said in no uncertain terms, "We have a medical emergency. Bella should be fine, but we need to get her on the ground as soon as possible so she can get continued care. We need to land."

Holding the phone to one ear, the attendant kept her gaze on Ivy. "Even though she's getting better?"

"Yes, the medications are taking effect, but we aren't crossing the ocean with someone who is having an anaphylactic reaction." She didn't want to further upset Bella or her husband, but she wasn't going to make light of what had happened. Bella could have died. She still could. "We don't know what triggered the reaction, what's going to happen when the medications start wearing off, if the worst has passed or if she'll start swelling again. We need to land. The sooner Bella gets out of this confined environment that might be providing her trigger, the better. We have to land."

The flight attendant glanced to Caleb for confirmation. Ivy fought saying something. A plane making an emergency landing was a costly big deal, and not taking anything away from Caleb, because she appreciated his help, but did the woman not think Ivy's opinion was enough?

"The pilot needs to land the plane," Caleb agreed. Perhaps sensing Ivy's irk, he added, "Dr. McEwen's quick actions and medications saved Bella's life. We're all lucky that she was here and got Bella appropriate care so quickly. But she's right in that we don't know what's going to happen when the medications wear off and whatever triggered Bella's reaction may still be a threat. Dr. McEwen knows what's best for her patient. We need to land the plane."

Warmth at his easy praise spread through her. Luke would never have made it about her but would have puffed out his chest and come up with some slightly different recommendation to elevate himself while punching holes in what she'd said. For the longest time she'd not acknowledged that was what he would do, and she'd let him mentally beat her down without her even realizing. Never again. If she ever dated again, it would only be with someone who was her superior, who wouldn't feel the need to belittle her emotionally and mentally.

"Okay," the stewardess replied, then relayed the message to the captain on the other end of the phone line.

Ivy met Caleb's gaze and although she didn't say the words out loud, she knew her face expressed her gratitude, because he gave a slight nod of acknowledgment. Maybe her surprise had showed, because his eyes held a curiosity that she didn't have time to dissect now, but suspected she would later. He was definitely what she'd label as a "manly man," and yet, he'd readily let her take control of the emergency and praised her efforts without any attempts to minimize what she'd done. That might be his most attractive quality yet and that was saying something because Mary had been right in calling him a "hottie."

Taking a deep breath, she ran her gaze over Bella again, letting everything register: her pallor, her breathing pattern, her fading rash and the pulse oximeter reading on her fingertip. "How are you feeling? Breathing any easier yet?"

"Maybe." Her voice was still hoarse and crackled with the word but was more readily understood than previous speaking efforts.

She definitely was. Her wheeze had significantly calmed. Maybe, just maybe, the worst had passed. It sure seemed that way, but Ivy knew better than to get ahead of herself when it came to the human body. Anything could happen and often did.

The pilot came over the PA system to let them know that the plane would be making an emergency landing in about twenty minutes.

Even as her stomach clenched at the thought of landing, Ivy let out a sigh of relief. Now was not the time for her aerophobia. She'd be fine.

"Did you hear that, Bella? We'll be landing soon."

"We have to have you in seats with your belts on," the stewardess told them. "For landing, we all have to be buckled in. No exceptions."

Ivy got that. She wanted that. Ivy turned to an attendant. "Can you clear out the back seats to let us sit there? I'm going to want to be close until we have her safely off the plane just in case anything changes."

The stewardess nodded and moved to talk to the passengers in the back row, then returned. "The flight is full, so they're moving to sit in your vacated seats until we're landed."

"Perfect." She glanced at Caleb. "Let's get her moved to the seat. I'd like her in the middle of us. Tom, we want you close, too."

They got situated into the back row, with Ivy taking the window seat, Bella in the middle and Caleb to the aisle. The stewardess had a passenger trade so Tom sat at the end of the aisle across from Caleb's seat. Eventually, the pilot came over the PA system to let them know that the plane was making its final descent.

Even as her stomach clenched at the thought of landing, Ivy let out a sigh of relief. "Did you hear that, Bella? We'll be on the ground soon."

Ivy's throat tightened as the words left her mouth. Now was not the time for her aerophobia. She'd be fine. Maybe.

Bella had drastically improved as her hives were almost gone and her wheeze had greatly subsided to where Ivy could only hear it when she held her stethoscope to Bella's chest. That was good, but with her patient's situation less urgent and landing imminent, moisture dampened Ivy's nape as her own fears took hold.

Her stomach roiled as the plane got lower and

lower. Now was not the time to get all panicky. Bella needed her and she sure didn't want Caleb seeing her have a meltdown over the plane landing. She'd managed during takeoff. She'd deal with landing, too. Those were always the worst parts for her, but she'd manage.

Fortunately, Tom asked Caleb something, so he turned his head toward the man, answering his question. Ivy spoke to Bella, hoping to reassure any concerns the woman might have and to distract herself with her patient, who seemed over the worst of her reaction. Thank God.

Ivy used every mental game she'd ever learned to distract herself as the plane touched ground, then roared down the runway, slowing to a stop. As soon as they'd come to a stop, they moved Bella to the back of the plane to get her ready to be transported.

Within minutes, the ground paramedics were onboard. Ivy and Caleb handed off Bella's care to them, assisting as they moved the woman off the plane. Tom followed closely with their carry-on items.

After Bella left, Ivy let out a sigh and silently told her body that it was okay, the plane was on the ground, and there was no longer need for alarm.

"Great job," a flight attendant told her, then smiled at Caleb. "Both of you were wonderful.

We were all so glad you were on the flight. Thank you so much."

"You're welcome." Ivy was a little embarrassed at the woman's gushing.

She and Caleb made their way to their seats and Ivy's embarrassment grew when the passengers clapped as they made their way through the aisle.

"You're a hero," Caleb said from behind her, causing Ivy to turn to frown. He knew they'd only been doing what they were trained to do. Nothing heroic about that. Not really.

She paused at where she'd been sitting as Lara stood from Ivy's seat.

"I went to the back of the plane to see if I could help, but you and Caleb had things under control. I'd have been in the way," the young nurse explained. "So, I stayed here to make sure these guys didn't make trouble while you and Caleb were occupied. I figured I had a better view of all our guys from back here than up where I had been sitting with the others. Oh, and, Caleb—" she looked past Ivy at where Caleb stood behind her "—Roy wanted to sit by Owen. Hope it was okay that I told him I didn't think you'd mind swapping seats. Those two have been talking nonstop. Well, mostly Owen has been talking nonstop and Roy has been listening."

"No problem," he assured.

Maybe not for him, but that meant Caleb would

now be in the middle seat of Ivy's row. Maybe Roy had just meant temporarily during the chaos, and he'd want to swap back for the actual flight. Not that Ivy minded sitting by Caleb. He seemed like a nice guy. Just…just, sitting next to Roy felt safer. Which was silly. Caleb hadn't done anything to make her feel threatened. Well, other than be in the running for Sexiest Man Alive, and on that, he unnerved her a bit.

Rather than have Caleb take the middle seat, Ivy took pity on him and his long legs. "Do you want the aisle?"

He grinned. "If you're willing, that would be great."

If there were additional emergencies on the plane, Caleb would be jumping to action as well so the few seconds lost by sitting in the middle seat shouldn't slow things much. Hopefully, they wouldn't have any other emergencies. Or be on the ground too long. Because the longer they sat, the longer she had to anticipate takeoff.

Reaching into the seat pocket in front of Caleb, she pulled out her phone, turned it off airplane mode and scrolled through messages, struggling to focus on any of them. She answered a message from her best friend, letting Jenna know that they'd had a detour but should be back in the air soon. She started to mention Caleb but didn't since she didn't want to field the questions her bestie was sure to ask.

Ivy couldn't say she was disappointed when the pilot came over the intercom to say they'd be on the ground a couple of hours to refuel and then to get worked into the takeoff schedule. The delay meant that much longer before she'd have to deal with that horrific tightness in her chest.

"You okay?" Caleb asked from next to her. He'd pulled out a book—a book she recognized as one she'd been wanting to read—and she'd thought he was engrossed in the pages. Instead, he was watching her. Perhaps in a fight-or-flight response to his presence as much as her fear of flying, she needed to move.

"We should get these guys up and moving while we don't have to worry about turbulence. We're going to have a few extra hours onboard and can't have any of them getting a blood clot. Can I get out?"

Sliding his book into the seat pocket, Caleb stood, and she jumped up, then smiled brightly at Owen sitting on the opposite aisle where Caleb had previously sat. "Come on, Owen. You and I are going for a stroll. Gotta get your blood flowing and keep those joints from getting stiff. You've got a lot of walking to do the next couple of weeks."

Owen stretched, then stood to walk around the seats. Caleb joined with Roy. Soon, most of the group fell in, looping around the middle seat section.

"We're conga dancers." Owen gestured to where the line curved around behind them.

Hearing him, Caleb began to sing an old Gloria Estefan tune.

Ivy glanced back to see him gently touching Roy's waist and dancing to the beat in conga line fashion. Something inside her eased and wound tight all at once. No. No. No. Just because he'd come across as pretty much perfect so far, he wasn't. He definitely didn't meet her criteria of making more than she did. It wasn't that she cared about the money. It was that she couldn't bear another man in her life who might feel the need to tear her down. Caleb was Heartbreak Number Four waiting to happen. She needed to steer clear.

His gaze met hers and he grinned and she felt herself weakening.

Think Luke.

"Come on, Ivy. Roy and I are showing you and Owen up back here," Caleb teased. "Come on, shake your body, baby, do the conga."

Owen chuckled, swaying his shoulders a little. "Can't have them showing us up. My dance partner is way prettier than his."

Ivy gently nudged Owen. "Ha! You just be careful you don't fall, Mr. Ninety-Eight-Years-Old-and-Dancing-in-an-Airplane-Aisle. No face-planting allowed on this trip."

The older man just laughed and waved one

arm, then the other, as he continued to slowly move forward. Although not fluid, his movements did stay with the beat. She couldn't help but smile. She loved his generation.

From behind her, Roy poked her ribs. "Do the conga."

"Why not?"

Meet a man who has me all a flutter. Save a life. Practically have a panic attack over the plane landing. Dance in the aisles. Makes sense to me. Ivy joined in their very slow conga dance, telling herself that if nothing else it gave her a good reason to hold on to Owen. She wasn't surprised when a few more passengers joined in their circle around the middle seats, and they were soon curving around from one side of the plane's aisles to the other. Younger folks danced in place while older folks inched forward while participating with a smile. Even the flight attendants who'd propped Bella's legs joined them. Several were singing along with Caleb to the lively tune.

When they'd gotten the guys back to their seats and everyone was settled to wait for the captain to let them know when they'd be able to take off again, Caleb said, "You've got to admit, so far this trip hasn't been dull."

"When it comes to being a medical volunteer, there's something to be said for dull," she reminded, causing him to chuckle. The truth was, in the cramped airplane seats, he was way too close to her for anything to feel dull. His arm brushed against hers and her stomach dived as if they were back in the air and had dropped a few thousand feet at once. She repositioned, trying to safely tuck her arm out of reach, but that was pretty much impossible in the limited space. How was she supposed to keep from accidentally touching him during the flight to Paris? What did it matter? Accidental touches were just a part of sitting next to someone on a plane, right? But that brush of his arm had been an electric jolt to her system. Ugh. So he was a gorgeous man with an overabundance of pheromones and her young, healthy body was responding to all that attractiveness. She was just human, after all. She really didn't like that she found him physically attractive, but that was life and didn't mean anything. She scooted over the remaining inch of her seat toward where Mary had put on headphones and was watching a movie. Any further and she'd be in the older woman's lap. "This 'dull' start makes me nervous about what's in store for the rest of the trip."

"Whatever happens won't be anything you can't handle." His tone was confident, full of flattery, but not facetiously so.

Turning, Ivy met his gaze. Her breath caught at the light there. Or maybe it was more at the heat that flashed through her insides at seeing desire.

He didn't bother trying to conceal his interest, but instead seemed okay with revealing that he was attracted to her.

Uh-oh. Her finding him attractive was one thing. His returning that attraction, another completely, and had her wondering if he was wrong, that she might not be able to handle everything in store during the remainder of this trip.

CHAPTER THREE

DR. IVY MCEWEN was a fascinating woman. She was also not easy to figure out. Get her to talking about something that interested her and her entire persona sparkled, but afterward she'd rein in her excitement and go back to being überprofessional.

For someone who'd just finished the long hours of residency, she had a great knowledge of the Tennessee Volunteers sport's program. Despite living in Knoxville, he was an Alabama fan.

"How is it that you know so much about local sports when you've been bogged down with residency in another state?"

"People keep up with things that are important to them, no matter how busy they are."

He arched a brow. "The University of Tennessee football team is important to you, even during offseason?"

Her gaze lowered a moment, staring at the seat back in front of her, then she shrugged. "I bleed orange 365 days a year."

"So, you get a day off every four years to roll with the tide?" he teased, referencing leap year and his favorite home state team.

She glared. "If I were you, I wouldn't count on me sporting any team color other than orange regardless of the day."

"A shame. You'd look great in black-and-white houndstooth with a big *A* across your chest."

Her gaze met and searched his. He could see she was trying to read him, trying to decipher if he was flirting or just being friendly. Both, he realized. He liked Ivy. Despite his family wishing otherwise, he wasn't in the market for a relationship, but maybe meeting Ivy would be an added bonus of the trip.

The pilot came over the loudspeaker. "Folks, I've turned the seat belt sign back on. You'll be happy to know we've been cleared for takeoff. Crew, ready the cabin."

Ivy sucked in a deep breath, then checked her already tightened seat belt. Rather than letting go of the clasp, her fingers white-knuckled the metal as if trying to make sure it stayed attached.

Caleb made sure his own seat belt was securely fastened. "I take it you're not much for flying?"

She didn't meet his gaze. "It's not my favorite thing."

"Bad experience or lifelong?"

She didn't hesitate. "Lifelong. I can't recall a time where I didn't dread flying. I hated it so much that when my parents traveled, they would drop me off to my grandparents'. Mom and Dad were schoolteachers—professors at a university in Nashville—and they spent their summers exploring the world."

Unlike his family who worked 24/7 and thought the world revolved around the almighty dollar. He supposed it could be argued that in some ways it did, but life was short and, beyond basic necessities, Caleb didn't get caught up in the things they did.

"Sounds exciting. You didn't want to go with them?"

"Not if it meant being in an airplane, but even beyond that, I'd rather have been with my grandparents." The plane started moving, slowly taxiing away from the gate where they'd been for several hours. "I know I should be glad that we're on the move, but…"

"But you're not because you like being stuck in a plane next to me? Understandable," he teased, waggling his brows. "I get that reaction all the time."

"Since you put it that way, maybe takeoff won't be so bad." Her gaze shifted to his and despite her anxiety, she half smiled. "But seriously, thanks for not making fun of me and making me feel worse than I already do that I can't conquer this silliness. I've even tried hypnosis. Nothing has helped, unfortunately."

"No reason to feel bad, Ivy. A fear of flying is common, so it's not as if you're being irrational." Rather than look reassured, her eyes squeezed shut, her long lashes peeking out from where her face squished together. A longing to trace his fingers across her face to smooth the tense lines hit so strongly that he curled his fingers into his palms. "Tell me how I can help."

Her expression remained tense. "Pray."

"Asking for divine intervention, eh? Not sure how much sway I have with the Big Guy." Probably not much. Otherwise, Blake wouldn't have died and Caleb's ankle would have healed to where he could jump again. "I'll do my best, though. Anything else?"

Both her hands now gripping her seat belt, she shook her head. "Quit talking." She sucked in a deep breath. "No, talk because I want you praying. Just, I can't have you distracting me from my misery."

He chuckled. "You're a funny lady, Ivy."

Her eyes were clenched so tightly that her cheeks practically met her eyebrows. "Good to know that if medicine doesn't work out that I have a backup career in stand-up comedy."

Wishing he could ease her discomfort, Caleb studied her profile. She really was stunning, but it was the excitement of being near her, of talking to her and hearing what would come out of her brilliant mouth next that intrigued him the most. From the moment Stan had asked him to go in his place, Caleb had known this was going to be a great trip. Meeting Ivy had certainly upped the ante.

"Medicine will work out for you."

Her eyes opened. Curiosity shined in their blue depths. "You know that after seeing me work a single patient? Maybe I was just having a good day."

"I stand by my initial assessment." Why did he get the feeling there was more to her question? That she was testing him? As if she expected him to say something that would undermine what she'd done? "You handled yourself well, with confidence, and skill," he pointed out. "Your competency and calmness saved Bella's life."

Pink tinging her cheeks, she shrugged as if his words were no big deal. He wasn't buying it. That he'd complimented her skills pleased her. He was sure of it. Her reaction did funny things inside him. Or maybe it was that the plane was rolling. Unlike her, he loved the exhilaration of taking off and soaring through the air.

"If I hadn't been here, you'd have done the same thing. It's what you do every workday," she reminded him. "I didn't do anything out of the ordinary that any other health care professional couldn't have done."

"Other than be completely prepared for any emergency that came up while thirty thousand plus feet in the air?" he countered, knowing that he could argue that she'd done a lot of things out of the ordinary. Everything about Ivy McEwen was out of the ordinary.

She humphed. "I like to be prepared. Sometimes to the point that I drive those around me a bit crazy. Be forewarned." Her eyes challenged him, urging him to keep pushing. He told himself it was just because her tension lines had momentarily eased during their plane's taxiing to the runway.

"Were you a Girl Scout?" he teased.

"I was," she admitted, half smiling. "But just for a couple of years during early elementary school."

"Never sold cookies?"

She made a scoffing sound. "I sold cookies. Lots and lots of cookies."

Caleb liked that she was distracted from what the plane was doing. "That sounds as if there's a story there."

"I sold the most cookies of anyone in my troop."

He grinned. "Competitive much?"

"Maybe." Her eyes sparkled. "I like to always do my best. That's why I prep so much. I try to plan for success no matter what comes up. That I wasn't fully prepared for what happened with Bella is a bit frustrating."

"It's not as if you can travel with a full emergency room inventory. You impressed me. And it wasn't just me who was impressed. Everyone on this plane was grateful you were here, especially Bella and Tom." Despite how she white-knuckled her seat belt, Ivy's smile appeared genuine. Hoping she'd further relax and that maybe he truly could distract her through takeoff, he continued, "Comedy will have to be a side gig. Medicine is your calling."

She let out a relieved-sounding breath. "Phew, I was worried that I'd wasted all those years on med school."

Joy filled him at her teasing tone, and he laughed. "It's always good to have a plan B, but you're right where you're supposed to be."

Beside him.

The thought caught him off guard.

Not beside him.

Sure, he was attracted to her, but he was getting way ahead of himself. They'd just met. She was the kind of girl his mother would like him to bring home. These days, she'd settle for him to bring any girl home because, after his last split with Katrina, she claimed to have given up that he would ever settle down. He found that odd since he was only in his early thirties, but she'd been known to be dramatic in the past. In regard to his dating life, or lack thereof, was no exception. Then again, after Katrina, he'd certainly never given his mother a reason to think he'd ever "settle down."

"Thank you," Ivy said. "I like thinking I made the right choice when I chose to go into medicine."

Curiosity got him again. "What would you have chosen if not medicine?"

Before she could answer, the pilot came over the PA system, letting them know they were next in line, and they'd soon be on their way to Paris again. Ivy grimaced.

"Not a pilot or stewardess or paratrooper," she assured, grimacing. "I really don't like flying."

"Seriously? I never would have guessed," he teased, hoping that doing so would help. He'd thought he'd been semi-achieving distraction, but her face had lost all color.

Still, she frowned. "Be nice. Not everyone is crazy—I mean, *brave* enough to jump out of airplanes."

He'd never thought of jumping as being brave. Jumping was a passion, a pure happiness, a rush of adrenaline like no other. Nothing he'd ever done or experienced made him feel as alive as he did when he was free-falling through the atmosphere. Nothing was so quiet or so peaceful. Jumping put all of life into perspective. He missed that sensation so much he ached with it.

The plane moved into position to where they'd begin their ascent.

Ivy sucked in a deep breath, her throat visibly working as she swallowed hard.

"Are you dating anyone, Ivy?"

"What?" She sounded almost as surprised by his question as he was. He sure hadn't been thinking of asking the question. It just popped out of his mouth.

He went with the question because she certainly looked distracted. Plus, he found himself really wanting to know her answer. "Are you dating anyone?"

"Now is not the time to be asking me about my dating life."

"Because the plane isn't going to lift off if you aren't completely focused on it and intensely gripping your seat while squeezing your eyes closed?"

She narrowed her gaze. "Smarty-pants."

"Sometimes," he agreed. "You didn't answer. Is there someone special who is missing you while you're in France? Someone who makes your heart go pitter-patter and feel as if you're on top of the world?"

She snorted. "Not hardly and I'm planning to stay single." Turning to him, she frowned. "I know what you're doing, Caleb, and it's not working. I'm well aware that we're gaining speed and— Ooh!" She grabbed his arm, squeezing as they gained momentum.

"I must be doing a terrible job distracting you.

Let's see if I can do better." He leaned toward her and, eyes wide, she jerked back, but didn't let go of where she clenched his arm in a death grip.

"I don't think so, buster."

"What?" he asked, innocently, lips twitching. "What did you think I was about to do, Ivy?"

"You know exactly what I thought," she countered, her grip on his arm tightening as her eyes squinched together.

"I was just going to whisper an ancient Chinese proverb into your ear."

"Sure, you were." The wheels lifted from the runway, and she had another sharp intake of breath. "Tell me. Tell me now."

"That you're quite lovely when your face is pinched up like that?"

Her eyes shot open and her brows formed a V. "Are you making fun of me?"

"Only in the sense of teasing you, Ivy. People are afraid of different things. I'd never make fun of someone for something they were afraid of. Fear is an emotion real to all of us. It's just what triggers the fear that varies."

"What are you afraid of?"

Caleb thought back to the times in his life he'd been afraid. There had been many, such as the time when two of his buddies had collided midair, leaving one of the guys unconscious and in a free fall at seven thousand feet. As he'd guided his own body through the air toward him, he'd been scared that he was going to watch his friend die. Essentially, he had, but not that day. Blake's automatic activation device should have gone off if he hadn't regained consciousness and deployed his chute by the minimum feet. Caleb getting to him and deploying his reserve chute had bought him four thousand feet to regain consciousness. Thank God the chute opening had snapped Blake awake so he'd been able to safely get to the ground, then go out for a few days' hospital stay with a concussion. Blake should have gotten out after that, but had lived to die another day.

"Why do I get the feeling that the things running through your mind right now make my fear of flying seem paltry?" Relaxing her hold on his arm, Ivy interrupted the dark rabbit hole he'd been falling in to. A rabbit hole he sometimes struggled to claw his way back from. Yeah, much better not to go there as he couldn't change the past. He couldn't bring Blake back, nor take his place.

"We all have our demons to face."

"I agree with that in principle, but I'll go on record as still finding my fear of flying irrational considering statistics and things I do that aren't nearly as 'safe,' yet I never give them a second thought. I mean, I'm more likely to be struck by lightning than to be in a plane crash, yet I don't get panicky during storms." She looked directly into his eyes, and he knew her next words weren't going to be about herself. "Were you deployed during your time in the military?"

"Yes. Several times."

"I'm sorry."

Her soft words had him meeting her gaze. "What are you sorry for? No one forced me to enlist, Ivy. I volunteered for high-risk missions. That doesn't mean I never experienced fear." He'd just learned to keep fear secondary to logic and the will to survive.

"Whatever you were thinking... I shouldn't have sent your mind there. That's what I meant when I said I was sorry."

"I have no regrets regarding my time in the military." Other than that he wasn't still there, proudly serving his country. His ankle tweaked, reminding him of why he wasn't. Frustrated, he flexed his foot back and forth.

"That's good." Taking a deep breath, she glanced around the plane. Concern and a deep sense of responsibility showed in the way her big blue eyes noticeably touched on all the veterans within her visual field. "They're braver than I am. I feel so weak that I hate flying so much."

He suspected that her admission was a rare one and probably due to the fact that they were in the midst of her trigger. "There are a lot of folks on this plane who found you brave while you were saving Bella's life. Not everyone can remain calm during a crisis. People have different strengths and weaknesses. It's what keeps humanity going."

Her gaze met his and she gave him another one of those smiles that had firecrackers going off in his belly. "Thanks for not thinking me wimpy for something that even small children do without it bothering them. Sorry if I caused permanent damage to your arm."

He cleared his throat and repositioned within his seat. "No problem. I'll send you a bill if I have to see an orthopedist."

"You do that." Her lips twitched. "You should also tell me that ancient Chinese proverb."

He shook his head. "Nah, the moment has passed. I'm going to save that one for the flight home."

"Ugh, don't remind me." She glanced around the plane again, then pressed the screen on the seat in front of her. "I'm going to watch a movie. Why don't you see if you can get some sleep?"

Caleb would rather talk to her, but she was obviously done. "You'll wake me when you want to rest?"

Although she nodded, he doubted that she'd wake him. He got the impression Ivy had to be tough. What had happened to make her feel that way? That she always had to be strong and not reveal any vulnerability? Then again, who was he to judge? Not that he was really, just more of a curiosity about the beautiful woman sitting next to him. He closed his eyes. He'd rest while she watched her movie.

Caleb had always been able to fall asleep readily. He'd also always been able to remain somewhat aware of what was going on around him. It was something he'd appreciated during his service days. While on a plane next to a woman he found more attractive than he'd found anyone in a long time, if ever, being constantly aware of her was distracting from being able to let himself drift into sleep, though.

Especially when a couple of hours later, her head rested against his shoulder.

Something deep within him relaxed as he focused on the rhythmic in-and-out of her breath, on the sweet vanilla scent that he'd caught a whiff of earlier, but now would forever remind him of her. His peace felt so at odds with the tumult that gripped his stomach at her body against his.

Suspecting that if he stirred, she'd awaken, he kept still, wondering why having a stranger resting upon his shoulder felt so right, so simultaneously dangerous, and why keeping her there felt so imperative.

CHAPTER FOUR

"COME ON, ROY," Ivy told her veteran. "Let's walk around the restaurant." The convenience center was more like a high-end commercialized rest stop than a single restaurant. There were multiple dining options, a general store, a fancy coffee shop and a refueling station. Truly, a one-stop shop for travelers and locals alike. There were even picnic tables out back and a small playground for children to stretch their legs. "Slade, if your grandfather is finished eating, get him to walking, too. Between the flight and the bus ride, we all need to move as much as we can prior to the rest of our drive."

They'd landed in Paris, been met by a local veterans' group and were being bused the four hours to Normandy. Halfway there, they'd stopped for a restroom and food break. And to get everyone moving. She couldn't have them getting stiff from travel and then not being able to enjoy the rest of the trip. As horrific as why they'd originally been here many decades before was, this trip was about honoring their legacy in freeing France from the occupation and helping them find healing.

"Okay, Owen. You and Suzie have finished eating, too. Let's get to moving," Caleb encouraged, standing and sorting his trash to put into appropriate recycle bins. "Do I need to start another conga line?"

Laughing, Owen's great-granddaughter did a little upper body shimmy. "I mean, if you want to, I'd be happy to dance with you."

Uh-oh. The young woman was staring at Caleb with stars in her eyes. Or were those hearts? Caleb needed to be careful not to encourage her. She was barely twenty and still at university.

Hello. Who was Ivy to think Suzie didn't need to be encouraged? Ivy had been the one all up in Caleb's business when she'd awakened on the plane. Her face had been smashed against his shoulder. How could she have gone to sleep like that? Ha. It wasn't even the going to sleep that was the biggest issue. It was how she'd been snuggled against him that had her internally cringing. Even worse was the knowledge that he knew. He'd made sure the guys walked and went to the restroom at some point during her snooze. She hadn't slept well the night before in dread of the flight, but that was no excuse for zoning out. The veterans had all been fine, but still, she wasn't one to shirk her duties.

Caleb hadn't said a word, not to point out that she'd been slacking and he'd had to take over, nor about her using him for a pillow as Luke would certainly have done. Her ex always made sure she knew anytime she failed to live up to expectations. Maybe Caleb had just assumed that invading your seatmate's personal space was natural airplane behavior. For Ivy, there had been nothing natural about sleeping against him.

His shoulder had been strong. He hadn't seemed to mind, but Ivy hated that she'd done so. She prided herself on her self-reliance and didn't want to lean on anyone. What must he think about her? How embarrassing!

Soon, they were back on their bus and moving down the road. As each veteran had a family member that they sat by and Lara sat next to a board member, Ivy supposed it was natural that she had ended up next to Caleb on the twenty-person minibus. Short of supplanting someone's family member from next to one of the veterans, she was stuck with Caleb. Owen's granddaughter might volunteer for the swap.

"Did you notice Paul stumble on the curbside on our way out to the bus?" Caleb drew her gaze to him from where she'd been staring out at the French countryside. "He refused to use his cane. Slade stayed close but Paul didn't want any help. He almost fell."

"Yeah, I caught that and tried to stay a little

closer, just in case. Pride is in no short abundance." Her biggest worry was that something preventable might happen to one of the veterans.

Caleb nodded. "It's what's gotten them to this point in life. They all impress me. When Stan asked me to go, I'll admit, given their ages, I wasn't expecting such ambulatory, sharp-as-a-tack men. Most of the ninety-five-plus folks we transport at the ambulance service are bedridden and may or may not remember who they are. For that matter, most of the eighty-plus-year-olds are."

"You're right. These guys are amazing in their zest for living life and refusal to sit down and 'act their age.' My grandfather—" Her stomach took a dive as surely as if they were still on the plane and had hit turbulence. "He knew how much I hated flying and teased me about how he was going to hold my hand like he did when I was a little girl. Honestly, if it weren't for how he loved being a paratrooper, I'd think he felt the same about flying as I do. To my knowledge he never flew again after his discharge from the army. He always said there was nowhere else he'd rather be than on his farm with my grandmother."

His face held empathy. "Sounds as if it was a big deal for both of you that you were planning this trip together."

"We were looking forward to it and dreading it at the same time." Ready for the personal conversation to end, she twisted to peer through the space between the window and seat. "How are you doing, Paul? You and Slade good?"

The former Higgins boat driver nodded, as did his great-grandson. Paul had been back to Normandy once, a couple of years previously, but this was his first time with his grandson. After a minute of light conversation about the beautiful French hillside and the minibus's robust air-conditioning, Ivy straightened in her seat and closed her eyes.

After they traveled the remaining two hours to their first stop in Sainte-Mère-église, the bus parked. French host families where the veterans would be staying during the trip greeted them. Introductions were made, and, travel weary, the guys and their family members took off with each of their hosts.

"I feel weird now that they're gone." Ivy glanced around the now vacant area, then smiled at her and Caleb's host family. Another had taken Lara and the board member. "We can drive to them if they have any issues, but part of me wants to keep them all within sight."

"And well cushioned with some bubble wrap?" Caleb teased.

"They are in good families' homes," Phillipe, their fiftyish host said in excellent English. Most of the local veterans group who'd met them had spoken at least some English. Most had been fairly fluent, like Phillipe. Phillipe had thick salt-and-pepper hair, warm brown eyes and a quick smile. "Come. I will show you where I live."

Phillipe insisted upon helping with Ivy's bags as they walked the two blocks to his home where he and his wife ran a bed-and-breakfast. Once at the close-to-the-road home, with its stone walls, steeply pitched slate roof and gorgeous red geraniums beneath the street side windows, his bundle of energy wife, Delphine, greeted them with cheek kisses. "Bonjour. Welcome."

Delphine's short wavy hair was streaked with gray, and her lovely face was lined from years of too much sun. Dimples dug into her cheeks each time she smiled, which was often. Ivy instantly adored her.

The home's inside was a mixture of stone and timber. The furniture looked sturdy and comfortable. The scent of something delightful, perhaps fresh baked bread, filled the house and had Ivy's stomach grumbling although it hadn't been but a few hours since their food stop. Apparently, there were two sections to the home's upper levels. The bed-and-breakfast's other guests were in one section and Caleb and Ivy in a smaller section.

They were shown their respective rooms. Caleb's was closest to the stairs, and Ivy waited in the hallway as Delphine led him into the bedroom with an antique bed. Their hostess pointed out where the shared bathroom was in the hallway, then showed Ivy a charming room with a heavy brass bed covered with a handmade quilt. Similar to Caleb's room, there was a lovely wardrobe and chair with an extra quilt draped over its armrest. The rooms could have looked the same a hundred years prior save the lighting and electrical outlets.

"Everything is beautiful, like stepping back in time," she told Delphine. Her hostess looked pleased that she liked the rooms, then headed back downstairs, leaving Ivy to unpack.

The remainder of the day had been set aside for getting acquainted with one's host family so all the veterans were fully occupied, leaving Ivy out of sorts as she felt she should be checking on them. She unpacked and settled into her room, used the shared bathroom and then went downstairs to where Delphine was in the process of preparing a meal. Delphine refused help, insisting that Ivy was her guest, and it was her honor to feed her.

In the living area, Phillipe was showing Caleb his collection of World War II memorabilia. The Frenchman very proudly told of veterans his family had hosted during previous D-Day anniversaries, proclaiming great honor in the privilege. Ivy couldn't help but wonder if the couple felt cheated by hosting her and Caleb rather than a veteran.

Regardless, the couple were wonderfully friendly, charming in their accents and happy looks at one another. There were three other guest

couples. Two American and one British. All were
there for the D-Day events. Their dinner was excellent and the company entertaining. Phillipe
had pulled out a 1944 wine to commemorate their
arrival. Ivy didn't usually drink, but her hosts had
been so proud of the special bottle, she'd taken
a small glass of the woodsy red liquid and was
slowly sipping the delicious vintage.

"You're a couple?" one of the American women
asked. Trista and her husband were in their late
fifties, as were the other two couples. They all
seemed to be well acquainted.

Even though she knew it was a natural assumption, Ivy's cheeks heated. "No. We just met this
morning at the Knoxville airport. We're medical
volunteers for a veteran group."

"Ah, that's wonderful on the volunteering.
We've been here for a week. We volunteer an-
nually at one of the reenactments. Fred looks forward to our time here more than anything else
we do during our retirement."

"That's great. How many years have you been
coming?" Ivy was grateful that the conversation
hadn't lingered on Caleb. Odd to think they really had met less than twenty-four hours prior.
Then again, it had been a long, eventful day of
constant togetherness.

"This is our twenty-fifth year coming for the
D-Day anniversary. We visited for a vacation one
year early on in our marriage. The first time we

came, we became good friends with some people who were involved with the reenactments. Most stay in tents on-site. We usually do a few key nights, as well. But I prefer Phillipe and Delphine's. This gal is over sleeping on an uncomfortable cot," the woman laughed, obviously being hit with memories.

"We love having you and Fred visit each year." Delphine topped off Trista's wineglass.

The two women chatted about past stays, the other female guests chiming in as they were apparently also repeat guests. Fighting fatigue and perhaps the wine catching up with her, Ivy listened, smiling frequently. The men were in a hardy discussion regarding whether or not the paratrooper jump at the end of the week would end up being rescheduled as rain was predicted for the scheduled date. The two American men were both retired military, as was the British gentleman. Although he was young enough to be their son, Caleb still fit right in with his military background. Head tossed back, he laughed at something one of them said.

"He's quite handsome, your fellow."

"Truly, we just met this morning," she reminded, cheeks on fire. "He seems a great guy, but I barely know him."

The women exchanged a look and just smiled. "Paris may be the City of Love, but it is because the country of France opens one's heart to the possibility of *amour*. You'll see, Normandy is no different."

Mortified at the conversation in case the men were paying even the slightest attention to what the women were saying, Ivy shook her head. "Nope. Not interested in *amour*. I just finished my residency and moved back to Tennessee to start working at a hospital's emergency department." Plus, she had to figure out what she was going to do with her grandfather's farm. She didn't have the heart to sell it, but she didn't want it to deteriorate. So much love and sweat and tears had gone in to working the land over the years. It was a part of who she was. But what was she going to do with hundreds of acres of farmland? She didn't want to think about that right now. Or ever, really. She wanted Gramps there, working the land and adding his own sunshine to the world. Tears prickled her eyes, and she fought swiping at them. She couldn't and not have Delphine and Trista convinced that their love conversation had brought her to tears. If it had, it would be for the time she'd wasted in the name of "love."

"Which hospital will you be working for?"

A fresh heat wave spread across Ivy's face. Caleb had heard the women's comments. Had he been internally laughing at her emphatic denial of interest in him? Yep, she was mortified. Then again, he'd been the one to ask if she was dating anyone. Of course, that had probably just been an attempt to distract her during takeoff rather than any true interest in her relationship status.

"Knoxville General."

He grinned. "Our paths are destined to cross again after we return home."

Curious, but trying not to look too much so under the ladies' watchful eyes, Ivy arched a brow. "Do you make emergency calls? I thought you worked for a private ambulance service."

"I do, and one of the places we transport patients is to your hospital. Nonemergency trips, but we seem to be in and out of the ER frequently." He grinned. "I look forward to continuing our new friendship after we return to the States."

She couldn't see them being BFFs, but she enjoyed talking to him and had she not embarrassed herself by falling asleep on his shoulder, she'd say it had been a great experience.

"One can never have too many friends," she said for the benefit of their curious audience. "It'll be good to see a familiar face from time to time." Other than those she'd met during the hiring process she knew very few people in Knoxville. She'd met a few of her grandfather's friends, but most of them were her parents' age or older. And, then there were those she'd met through SMVF that she likely would remain friends with. Why would Caleb be any different from the rest of the group with whom she'd already bonded?

The meal lasted over two hours and was still going strong when fatigue won over Ivy. Her eyelids had grown too heavy to keep fighting them.

"Sorry to call it a night so early—" which it was by the clock "—but the traveling is taking its toll and I'm ready to get some sleep. I will see you all in the morning, sooner if any of our guys or their families need anything. Night."

The men, including Caleb, all stood, showing their manners. The women bid her goodnight. Ivy used the restroom she shared with Caleb, cleansing her face, brushing her teeth, then returning to snuggle beneath the covers of the antique bed. Her room was small by American standards, but well decorated with beautiful antiques that had been in Delphine's family for many decades.

Thinking of the furniture at the farm that had been her great-grandparents', Ivy sighed. Someday, if she did meet someone who could lift her up to their level rather than try to tear her down, got married and had children, she'd want them to walk the land her great-grandparents had. She'd want them to play in the creek her grandmother, mother and herself had once caught crawdads in and swam in the deep spots to cool from the hot Tennessee sun. She'd want them to sleep in the bed that had belonged to their family for over a hundred years.

But, oh, the thought of how lonely she'd be on

the farm without her beloved Gramps beside her, to hear him moving about the kitchen, making his coffee at the crack of dawn before heading out to check on the cattle that no longer belonged to him, but rather a neighbor who leased the land. Ivy would need to talk to Mr. Griggs to see if he wanted to continue doing so after his current lease expired. She'd want all the help she could get in paying the taxes on the place. Then again, there was the trust her grandfather had left, as well. Her mother wasn't too happy that Gramps had, for the most part, bypassed his only living child, and left his worldly goods to his sole great-grandchild. Ivy wasn't sure of his reasons and certainly had never encouraged him to do such. In some ways, his leaving the farm to her mother would have been easier, although heartbreaking as her mother would have had no hesitations in selling the place.

Ivy couldn't do that. Perhaps Gramps had known and that's why he'd made the decisions he had. Ivy would live there and keep the land he'd loved for as long as she had breath and ability to do so. The farm was in her blood, a part of her past and a part of who she was.

She couldn't help wondering what Caleb would think of the white farmhouse that's walls had seen such love, and the land that had provided for her family for multiple generations. Why was it that she could imagine him there, at the house and walking the fields with the Smoky Mountains off in the distance? Would he hold the rich soil in his palm and feel the soul of the land? Would he understand or think her crazy for keeping something that would be a lot of work to maintain even with leasing the farmland?

What was wrong with her? Her thoughts were insane ramblings of a woman too weary from travel and too much wine. Just the one glass, but when she usually didn't drink, those were the things she was blaming for her thoughts. Blaming for her dreams.

That, and that alone, was the reason she drifted to sleep with the image of walking hand in hand with Caleb Rivers, a man she'd just met, across the fields at her great-grandfather's farm, and a sense of peace at his being by her side.

CHAPTER FIVE

"Good morning," Caleb greeted Ivy as she came down the narrow steps leading into the living area of Phillipe and Delphine's bed-and-breakfast. She wore black pants with side pockets and a navy T-shirt with the SMVF logo across the chest. Her hair was in a fresh braid and her cheeks were rosy as if she'd just washed her face. "Coffee?"

She smiled as if he'd offered her a great treasure. "That would be amazing."

He got a bowl from where Delphine had shown him. Ivy glanced at it in question.

"Bowls, not mugs. It's so you can dip your bread in your coffee." When she still stared at him, he grinned. "Just go with it. Cream? Sugar?" he asked as he filled the bowl, hiding his surprise when she shook her head. He would have guessed her to be a cream and sugar partaker. "Phillipe headed out this morning to deliver some of Delphine's goodies to a few other bed-and-breakfasts. He should be back any moment. Delphine is outdoors cutting fresh flowers for her bouquet. She has a garden out back. She said to tell you to help yourself to breakfast if you came down prior to her coming back indoors."

"Her flowers are gorgeous. I noticed them out my window." Taking the steaming mug he handed her, Ivy took a tentative sip, then sighed her pleasure. "I don't eat much bread, much less dip it in my coffee, but Delphine's smells heavenly."

"The bread is wonderful, but I'm with you on dipping it in my coffee. I recommend using the butter and jam. Delphine cans the jam and the butter comes from the same neighbor where she buys her milk."

Ivy placed her coffee bowl on the table, then went to Delphine's morning spread. "Wow."

She looked like a kid on Christmas morning. He grinned. "Just wait until you taste."

When she'd applied butter and jam to her bread, she licked her jam spoon and her eyes widened. "Yum. That *is* good."

Watching her put the spoon in her mouth, Caleb fought to rein in his gut reaction to the innocent action. "I told you."

"Good thing we're only here for two weeks or I'd have to buy a new wardrobe." She took a bite of the doctored bread, then her face relaxed with pure joy. "Mmm… I may have to anyway. This is worth it."

Ivy's sigh of pleasure did funny things to Caleb's insides, like twist him into knots. He gulped back the one that formed in his throat and reached for the bread. "You make that look so good I'm going to have a second slice."

"You better hurry. If you don't, there won't be any left," she teased. "For real, I may hide what's left in my room."

Caleb chuckled. "Apparently, she does this every morning for their guests and sells loaves to other hosts in the area as an income supplement. Delphine says the communities in the area are very interdependent upon each other, buying from local farmers and vendors and supporting each other."

"I love that. With everything being so fresh, no wonder it tastes so wonderful." She took another bite and moaned. "This reminds me of when I was small and would visit my grandparents. The flavors are so rich."

Almost choking on his bread, Caleb cleared his throat. "Um, yeah, Phillipe should be back so we can head to the school for our first program."

Still enjoying her bread, she glanced at her watch. "Did I run late? It's just after seven and I thought we had plenty of time."

Caleb slid his fingers into his jeans pocket. "We do."

Her brow lifted. "Is the school far away, then?"

"Not far. We should arrive in plenty of time since we're not due until ten. The board purposely didn't schedule anything early this morning so that the veterans could have a later start in case any of them experience jet lag. Or if we did. Or, well, you know." What was wrong with him? He wasn't one to ramble, but that's certainly what he was doing. He felt like an awkward teenage boy talking to the homecoming queen. "The other guests won't be here for dinner tonight and Phillipe thought we might enjoy dinner with him and Delphine at a friend's who lives along the coast."

Ivy took another bite of her bread. "I don't want them to go to any trouble."

"I got the impression he hoped we'd say yes. Paul and Slade are staying there, and they've invited Owen and Suzie, as well."

Ivy's gaze met his, but she didn't say anything.

"What?" he asked, knowing something was on her mind.

"I was just trying to decide if that's why you wanted to go."

Confused, he asked, "If what was why I wanted to go?"

"Suzie."

Shock filled him. She thought— Seriously? "You're kidding, right?"

She studied him a moment, then a slow smile

spread across her face. "Oh, I don't know. She's beautiful."

"And young."

"As long as both parties are of legal age and of normal mental capabilities, then age is just a number."

"I agree up to a certain point." He noted how her gaze never shifted from his as she took a sip of her coffee. "Would you date someone a lot younger or older than you, Ivy?"

She considered his question, then shrugged. "As long as my conditions were met, I would if I was attracted to him. Maybe I even should since dating men around my own age hasn't worked out too well."

Curious, Caleb started to ask her to elaborate on what her conditions were and what had gone wrong with the men she'd dated, but Delphine came in, her hands full of colorful flowers.

"Oh, the zinnias are beautiful," Ivy praised, eyeing the blooms. "And, Delphine, this bread is the best I've ever put in my mouth. The texture and flavor are perfection. It literally melts in my mouth."

Placing her flowers on the counter, Delphine beamed. "*Merci*. I've been making bread since I was a little girl. It was my *grandmère*'s recipe."

Caleb watched the two women chat, helping himself to more bread as he did so. When Ivy had finished eating, she offered to assist Delphine, but the Frenchwoman shooed her away, just as she'd done to Caleb earlier. He'd be sure to leave a generous tip and in-depth review online as a way of saying thank you.

Phillipe returned, asking if they could be ready to leave within the hour. Ivy disappeared upstairs for about fifteen minutes, came back down with her backpack. Caleb had grabbed his, as well. He doubted he had anything Ivy didn't other than his defibrillator, but as they'd learned on the plane, one never knew. They headed for the middle school where the veterans would be speaking that morning. They left early, so Phillipe drove them by Brécourt Manor, stopping to look at the 101st Airborne memorial at the edge of the private property. Other than the memorial to the brave paratroopers who'd taken out the four-gun battery aimed at Utah Beach, the area appeared like ordinary farmland. It would be easy to drive past without realizing unless one knew its history. Caleb knew. The brave men of Easy Company were legendary and had fueled his desire to be a paratrooper. The 101st no longer jumped, so joining the Eighty-Second had been a no-brainer. They were all his brothers-in-arms.

Caleb dug through his medical backpack, found a package of wipes and cleaned the yellowy-green pollen film from the top of the monument.

"Much better." He turned back toward where

Ivy stood with Phillipe. Appreciation for what he'd done shone in her gaze. A gaze that burned so blue it shamed the sky above them.

"Yes. It is," she agreed. "Thank you for doing that."

Caleb shrugged but was pleased at her sincerity. She understood where they were, what they were seeing. Perhaps she just recognized the area from the television series from several years prior, but she seemed to hold true empathy for the men whose names were on the stone. With having been so close to her great-grandfather who'd been a WWII paratrooper, perhaps she did.

Phillipe returned to the car, but only to lean against it.

Running his gaze over the land, images filled Caleb's head. Images that transformed from the men who were there into Caleb's team from—Yeah, it was time to leave. Spinning, he moved toward the car.

Back in the car, Ivy eyed him, then to his surprise, she touched his hand. When his gaze met hers, she gave him another one of those empathetic looks.

"This place can really get to you, can't it?" she whispered.

"There were voices on the wind, as if those men who died were calling to us from the past."

Her eyes shone with surprise. "I felt it, too."

They arrived at the school, joined the others

who were just arriving, and were welcomed by the French children and the school's staff. Then the veterans were set up at the front of the cafeteria.

When they were done, Caleb spoke with one of the teachers and every so often glanced around, taking in where each of the veterans were and how the children surrounded them, asking questions, some having to be interpreted, and the ones who owned phones wanting to take selfies with them. Ivy stood close with a bottle of hand sanitizer which she shared with the children and frequently with veterans, obviously determined to do all she could to keep the guys from picking up germs. Smiling, she chatted with the children, asking questions and praising their efforts to speak in English.

After the kids had gotten a chance to meet the veterans and get photos with them, a few gave a tour of the school and how they'd prepared for the veterans' visit. Ivy and Caleb fell to the back of the group.

"What amazing children and teachers," Ivy whispered, echoing his thoughts. "This place makes me want to go to school here."

"None of my schools had a garden or chickens." This one had both.

A commotion at the front of the crowd instantly had him and Ivy rushing to see what was happening.

A long verbal string of French, doubtful that it was cursing given none of the children reacted, came from an older woman sitting on the floor. She shooed the students back with one hand as her other grasped at her leg. Blood stained her fingers.

"Here's Dr. Ivy and Caleb now." Mary waved them closer. "This retired teacher volunteered today. She tripped and fell against Dad's wheelchair. I'm not sure what she cut herself on, though, as there's not anything sharp."

The teacher said more in French and another interpreted. "She says it's just a scrape. No big deal. She doesn't want a fuss." The interpreter eyed the injured teacher's leg. "That's a lot of blood, though."

Ivy already knelt next to the retired teacher and was unzipping her backpack.

"Tell her that we won't make a big deal of it, but I want to check her leg and clean the area for her." Ivy donned a pair of gloves and grabbed some supplies. "Here, let me see what's causing the bleeding."

The woman removed her hand from her leg. Whatever she'd hit had avulsed the skin, possibly from tension, and peeled it to a crinkled bunch at the wound's edge. Caleb knelt and put on a pair of gloves, too. Ivy had already started cleaning the wound. One thing he'd learned about Ivy was that she preferred being in charge and dived right in when there was a medical issue. Was she that way in other aspects of life? He didn't think so. If anything, he suspected she overthought everything.

Ivy carefully smoothed the pushed back skin into place. "Tell her that fortunately the injury isn't too deep. I'm going to use adhesive strips and then will cover the area with a protective dressing."

Serving as her "clean" hands, Caleb got the items from her backpack.

"She'll have a scar," Ivy continued. "But I suspect it will barely be visible a year or so from now."

One of the other teachers translated for the injured woman, who then shook her head and said something back. "She says she is a clumsy oaf and is embarrassed at the attention."

"Assure her that there's no reason to be embarrassed. Anyone can trip." Smiling her appreciation, Ivy took his offerings. "Will you ask if she is allergic to anything? Adhesives or latex bandages, specifically?"

The interpreter asked, then advised there were no allergies.

"Good. We've had enough allergic reactions this trip." Caleb opened the packet of the adhesive strips and gave them to her.

"Thanks." She glanced up just long enough to meet his gaze, sending his pulse into hyperdrive.

"Help me keep the skin pushed together while I apply the strips?"

"Sure thing, Doc." Caleb kept the wound edges together while she removed a strip then pressed it on the torn skin. She meticulously repeated the process until she had the wound closed. After she'd pressed the last one into place, he covered the area with a dressing. He secured his work with a self-adherent wrap.

"Good as new," he proclaimed when he finished.

"*Merci*," the woman thanked them. "*Merci beaucoup.*"

"Yes, *merci beaucoup*," Ivy repeated, causing Caleb's gaze to go back to hers. She smiled and, in that moment, something stirred deep inside him that made him want to kiss her.

Although, if he were honest with himself, he'd admit that he'd been wanting to kiss Ivy from the moment he'd met her gaze at the airport and recognized something in those blue eyes that he still didn't quite understand.

After they'd finished the morning's events at the elementary school, Ivy and Caleb traveled back to Sainte-Mère-église with Phillipe. They met with the others from their group at the courtyard in front of the Notre-Dame-de-l'Assomption. As Phillipe and Delphine lived in the village, they'd passed the famous church with its "paratrooper" hanging from the bell tower several times. The chute's white material flapped in the wind, a reminder of the events that had once taken place there.

Goose bumps covered Ivy's skin and not for the first time that day. After they'd repaired the teacher's laceration, Caleb had made her goose bumps have goose bumps. The intensity of his gaze triggered the response. He'd looked at her as if she were dipped in chocolate and he was a starving dessert-aholic.

He was pointing to the parachute, no doubt asking Owen about his experiences on D-Day. His sunglasses glinted in the sunshine. His T-shirt wasn't tight, but the sleeves stretched slightly over his biceps. No doubt finding T-shirts that fit his chest but didn't swallow his narrow waist wasn't easy. Perhaps sensing her stare, he looked her way and smiled. She couldn't see his eyes, but his smile was the one that she knew put a twinkle in them. Had he known she was checking him out and essentially drooling?

"Ready to go inside the church?" She linked her arm with Paul's. She needed to get out of the sun as it was frying her brain. Or maybe it was Caleb frying her brain. Chatting as they went, they slowly made their way to Notre-Dame-de-l'Assomption. Once inside, the beauty of the ornate, but musty-smelling, building struck her. Weathered white stone walls and aged arches surrounded well-worn benches, yet the front of the church was elaborate: a gold arch hanging from the ceiling with a cross mounted to the top and an intricate painting, ornate golden trimming, and a beautiful altar. The contrast seemed at odds and yet somehow perfectly fit the church.

"This place was built to stand forever." Slade joined Ivy and his grandfather. "They don't build them like this anymore, do they, Grandpa?"

"Not that I'm aware of." Paul took in their surroundings.

The church did look as if it had been standing forever and as if it would still be there long after they'd passed.

"These days it seems many are built to be more beautiful on the outside, rather than focused on what's inside. I appreciate this way more," she mused to the veteran, Slade, Mary and Roy who had joined them. "Plain on the outside and stunning once you go through the doors."

"Ivy, will you take mine and Dad's picture with the altar in the background?" Mary handed her phone to Ivy, then posed next to Roy.

Ivy snapped a few shots, then a few of Slade and Paul. Then, they perused and were awed by the church for a few more minutes prior to the board member rounding them up. "Come on, guys. It's time for our tour of the Airborne Museum."

The museum was walking distance across the

courtyard, but they insisted the veterans ride in wheelchairs. None of them were too pleased, but they did so with only Owen grumbling in protest. Once they arrived at the museum, he was immediately up and out of the chair. Ivy smiled at his determination and was proud he was that way. The more he moved in life, the longer he'd be able to.

They toured the museum. She couldn't look at any of the displays without thinking that they reflected a portion of her grandfather's life. He'd been in the Eighty-Second, rather than the 101st, but both units endured great hardships. Ivy snapped several photos of the guys, crew and the many displays, some of which squeezed her heart tightly with awe and renewed appreciation for her great-grandfather and for her freedom. Pausing at a display of a wedding gown, she read the placard.

"Isn't that just the most romantic thing?" Mary came to stand beside Ivy. "That he saved and carried his parachute around until he could ship it home so he could ask his girlfriend to marry him and she could use the silk to have her wedding dress made? Just the thought of some man doing that for me makes me all giddy inside. Can you imagine?"

No, Ivy couldn't. Not really. She'd seen photos of her great-grandparents on their wedding day and best she could recall, the plain silk dress hadn't once been a life-saving parachute. But it wouldn't have surprised her had her great-grandfather done something similar. He'd loved Grammie so much and been so proud of his service that any meshing of the two would have made sense.

"Simple and yet so absolutely perfect," she agreed.

"I doubt many women would go for a dress made from a parachute these days."

"I would." It was true. "I can't imagine anything more special than to give myself to a man I loved while wearing something that had been vital in bringing him home to me."

Mary gave a look of approval. "Me, too, not that I'm in the market for another wedding. I can't imagine my husband having carried around a parachute just so I could wear it, but he's a good guy. We've been together for almost forty years."

"Forty years is a major accomplishment," Ivy praised.

"It's not always been easy, but I can't imagine life without him." Mary shifted her gaze to the men joining them. "What about you, Caleb? You were a paratrooper. Did you save one of your chutes so that you can have your bride make a wedding dress from it?"

Ivy's cheeks burned at Mary's question, which was quite silly as it was an innocent enough question and Caleb didn't seem to mind her having asked.

Chuckling, he shook his head. "I didn't save any of my chutes. Unlike during the Second World War when parachutes were made from silk, the chutes I jumped with were made from nylon, which is what most chutes these days are made from. I doubt any woman would want a nylon wedding dress."

"Oh, I don't know," Mary countered. "As with back then, knowing the material had saved your beloved's life definitely makes a difference to the right woman."

"Saving his chute may have had more to do with rations and the price of silk than romance." Ivy was ready to move on from the conversation. Talking about weddings with Caleb made her palms clammy. Mary had said he was single. Had there been a time when there was someone special in his life? Someone that, had his chute been silk, he'd have saved the precious material in hopes she'd wear it to walk down the aisle to him? Or maybe he had been married and no longer was? *Single* could mean a lot of things.

What do I want it to mean?

Nothing. Her fingers curled into her palms. She was not interested in Caleb's love life, past or present.

"You're probably right," Caleb agreed. "Saving his parachute was likely the only way his bride would have a silk gown unless they were wealthy. Carrying that chute around saved him a lot of money. Smart guy."

"Maybe," Mary conceded. "But I like my way better. Yours isn't nearly as romantic as a besotted beau carrying around his chute so his beloved can become his wife while wearing a dress made from it."

"You a hopeless romantic, Mary?" Caleb teased.

The woman nodded. "Absolutely. It's one of my greatest personality traits. I get it from Dad."

Caleb laughed. "Does Roy know you just called him a hopeless romantic?"

So ready to move on from wedding conversation, Ivy pointed to another display. "Speaking of Roy, I'm going to check on him and the other guys."

Because she wasn't a hopeless romantic or anything close. Yet, she had just told Mary she would have worn a dress made from her beloved's parachute, so that meant her having struck out three times hadn't left her impervious to romance. She would have preferred imperviousness.

That evening, restlessness hit while waiting to leave for Phillipe and Delphine's friend's home.

Perhaps feeling the same, Caleb asked, "I think I'm going to walk around town, maybe check out a local pub and have a drink. Do you want to join me, Doc?"

Ivy didn't want to waste a precious moment of

being in France. She might never be again, and wanted to see and do all she could. That was why she said, "I'd love to."

CHAPTER SIX

WITH IVY AT his side, Caleb wandered along the streets, checking out the touristy shops, going in to several to look for souvenirs.

When he selected several cool key chains, Ivy arched a brow. "You must have a lot of friends."

"They're for my coworkers at TransCare. I plan to pick up a few at different places and bring them back for the crew."

"That's nice of you to bring something back for them."

"You're sounding a little condescending there, Ivy," he teased as they headed to the front of the store.

Still wearing her practical black pants with zipper pockets on the side and bright blue SMVF T-shirt that made the color of her eyes pop, Ivy shrugged. "I'm not a huge fan of tourist trinkets."

"No way." He gave her a dubious look. "Key chains, spoons and snow globes don't excite you?"

She curled her nose.

He laid the assorted key rings on the counter. "Elaborate because I know there's more to that look than just simply not liking travel mementos."

Her brow arched. "You're not buying that I think they're an overpriced waste of money?"

"Perhaps," he agreed. "But then, how do you put a price tag on letting someone know they were special enough for you to have thought of them?"

She gave him an "Are you for real?" look.

"You don't bring back travel goodies? Not even for close friends and family?"

She shook her head. "My parents traveled a lot. Without me." She sighed. "You know my embarrassing reason for not going with them. They'd bring back magnets, postcards, T-shirts, snow globes, that kind of thing. I have quite the collection."

Imagining her with a box full of trinkets, he grinned. "Well, you obviously liked the mementos a little if you saved them."

"Oh, no. It's not really that I saved them, but that my parents did. They're boxed up in my old room's closet at their house, so definitely not prized possessions that I've hauled with me to school or residency moves." She tapped the edge of the cashier counter, then picked up one of his key chains, studying it. "My parents meant well. I just never saw the point of bringing back a gift labeled with a place where the recipient hadn't been, you know?"

That sort of made sense to Caleb, but not so much that he put the key chains back. Instead, he pulled out his credit card. "They probably wanted you to see all the places you were missing out on and hoped you'd push through your fear of flying."

"They didn't stand a chance of that because I got to stay with Gramps when they traveled. In my eyes, it was a win-win. No flying *and* visiting my favorite person in the world for the summer. I'd have found a reason to stay with him if they'd tried to force me to go. I loved being with him on the farm."

He handed the cashier his card, then glanced at Ivy. Her gaze had gone beyond him to stare out the window, her thoughts obviously far away. "You speak of him with such adoration. He must have been a great person."

"He was." She took a deep breath, glanced around the shop, then motioned to the door. "I'll be out there when you finish with your tourist bling."

When Caleb had paid for the key chains, he found Ivy on the sidewalk taking a selfie with a soldier statue in front of another shop. The silliness surprised him. He hadn't taken her for a selfie-taking girl, especially not after how serious her expression had been.

They stopped at a pub. He ordered a beer and Ivy a lemonade. The place was crowded with young soldiers also there for the anniversary events. Watching them, their camaraderie, hit Caleb with such nostalgia that he downed his drink. He hadn't expected to be struck with such longing.

From where she sat next to him at a table across from the bar, Ivy poked his arm. "Thirsty?"

"Not anymore."

She eyed him curiously, letting him know that she was aware that his "thirst" hadn't been normal. She didn't pry, just sat next to him, sipping her lemonade and people watching the noisy crowd.

Caleb took in the wall decor featuring soldiers and past anniversary celebrations. But his focus was torn between where they were and how he felt such a part of the events and yet felt so distanced from them as well, then jumping to where Ivy sat quietly taking it all in, and his being so aware of her that it was as if her light vanilla scent beckoned every cell within him even through the crowded pub.

What a wonderful and complex woman she was with her box of tourist trinkets, idolized grandfather, brilliant mind, skilled hands and generous heart.

"I asked before but didn't get a direct answer.

Is there someone you aren't buying a tourist trinket for, Ivy, but that you should be?"

Her gaze cut to him. "No, Caleb, there's no one in my life in need of a key chain. I've alluded to my poor dating habits of the past and have no desire to add another round." She finished off her lemonade with almost the same gusto he'd shown earlier, then stood. "Come on, Caleb. Let's head to Phillipe and Delphine's so we can get ready to go to dinner at their friends' home."

The next few days passed quickly. Their mornings were filled with scheduled activities for the veterans, each one visiting a school to speak to students and answer their questions, often via an interpreter. Each day, Ivy was more and more impressed and intrigued by the man who made her smile more than she'd dreamed possible. She didn't want to like Caleb so much, but she couldn't help it. He was intelligent, quick-witted and oozed pheromones that had her insides all aflutter.

In Colleville-sur-Mer, they met up with a larger World War II veteran organization who'd brought forty precious veterans and one female nurse veteran for the celebrations. A former NBA player had started the foundation. He and his wife traveled with the group, overseeing every aspect to make sure everyone was taken excellent care of by the many volunteers with their organization.

Ivy was impressed and enjoyed meeting the veterans, the volunteers and the locals who worked so diligently to make sure all the events went smoothly. She was also impressed with how Caleb interacted with each one, shaking their hand and sharing obvious mutual respect from one soldier to another. With the way she'd idolized Gramps, she should have known she'd be attracted to someone with a military background. It made sense, especially when they were in this unique, almost surreal world of Normandy where their veterans were treated with the same recognition as movie stars were back home. They were treated as the heroes they truly were. No wonder her insides were all mushy.

They visited the museum, then the American Cemetery. A small ceremony took place at the memorial where children presented gifts to the veterans. Lots of photos and media interviews were done. Then, they strolled through the cemetery grounds.

The American Cemetery was a humbling place that overlooked Omaha Beach where so many had died on June 6, 1944. The enormity that each of the precisely placed crosses represented a person who had lost their life in the name of freedom wasn't lost on Ivy. She wavered between her own emotional reaction to the nine thousand plus crosses and remaining aware of where each of her veterans were being rolled by their host families on the walkway through the grounds. They'd given up protesting using the wheelchairs as many of the places they visited covered too far of a distance for them to ambulate the entire time. As always, Owen stood each time they came to a stop. The man was as independent as he was a flirt. She imagined he'd been something else during his heyday.

Speaking of men in their heyday, where was Caleb? Glancing around, Ivy spotted him knelt at one of the crosses. The set of his jaw was tense. She was too far away to read his eyes even if his sunglasses hadn't shaded them, but she suspected she knew what they held. She understood. Curious as to whose cross Caleb stared at, she motioned to Lara.

"Keep an eye on the guys. I'll be right back." Not waiting for a response, she took off to where Caleb was and respectfully approached him. The wind caught at his SMVF shirt, plastering the cotton material to his bowed shoulders and chest. Her fingers itched to touch him. In comfort, she assured herself. That was why she wanted to put her hands upon his arm. No other reason.

"Someone you knew?" She took in the name and state engraved upon the marker.

Seeming surprised she was there, Caleb shook his head. "Never heard of him." He took a deep breath. "But I could have had I been around during that time, you know?"

Ivy's stomach squeezed. "Had you been around during that time one of these crosses could have had your name on it."

She quivered, then wondered about the nine thousand plus who were buried there. Most had been so young they'd barely begun their lives. They had left behind mothers and fathers who had mourned them. Left behind girlfriends they might have become engaged to and someday married and had families of their own. The knot in Ivy's stomach tightened further. There was so much she took for granted each day. Her freedom being one of the many.

"Thank you for your service, Caleb." For a moment, she thought her words were lost in the wind coming off the ocean just beyond the cliff overlooking the beach.

Caleb's head bowed. "Don't thank me. Not here. My service was nothing compared to what these guys did."

"You'd have done the same, would have willingly given your life that day had you been here." It was true. She'd only met him a few days ago, but that Caleb was as patriotic as they came oozed from his every pore. The thought of his having done that, of his life having been snuffed out, gripped her insides and twisted, making her nauseous. Her knees wobbled so much that she wouldn't have been surprised if she landed next to his feet.

"Many of these guys weren't necessarily willingly here," he reminded her. "Many of them were drafted and had no choice."

"The paratroopers were all volunteers, though." Gramps had told her that. Thank God he'd survived the war.

"For an extra hundred dollars' pay a month." Sighing, Caleb glanced around the somber graveyard with its white crosses, memorial and chapel. The wind whipped at an American flag that stood near the memorial reflecting pool and held his attention. "After Pearl Harbor, there was a flurry of enlistees, but over the next few years, many more were drafted. War is hell. Then, and now."

The wind lifted his words and carried them through the trees lining the pathway, swaying branches and rustling leaves. Ivy shivered, but not from the crispness of the breeze. "It's difficult for you to be here, isn't it?"

A *humph* sound rose from deep in his throat as he stood. "Being where over nine thousand people are buried shouldn't be easy."

"No." She fought wrapping her arms around him. Putting her arms around Caleb for any reason was a big no-no, but she longed to ease his obvious pain. "I'd say that I understand, because that's the first thing I want to say. But the truth is, as a civilian I'm not sure I can understand how being here feels to someone who served." She eyed his rigid stance and an awful thought swept over her, one that might have her hugging him yet. "Caleb, did you lose friends you served with?"

"Lose them?" He turned toward her, and she wished she could see his eyes from behind the shield of his sunglasses, but only her reflection shined back at her. "You mean, did any of the men and women I served with die in the line of duty?"

She knew the answer before he continued. The clenching of his jaw said it all.

"Yeah, Ivy, some of them died, a close friend of mine, specifically." Glancing back down at the tombstone, his shoulders lifted with the deep breath he sucked in. "I'd have taken Blake's place, any of their places, if that had been an option given to me."

Her heart ached for the things he'd seen and done, for the people he'd lost. Even beyond her grandfather, she'd cared for veterans during her residency, was familiar with the survivor's guilt so many of them felt when they'd survived skirmishes that others hadn't, was familiar with the post-traumatic stress symptoms so many experienced. That he'd lost a close friend—

Oh, Caleb.

"I'm sorry about your friend, and very glad you didn't die."

She may have just met him, but the world was a better place because he existed, a safer place.

She was sure of it. Giving in to whatever that warmth moving through her was, she placed her hand on his arm, hoping he understood what she didn't know how to express given the short time since they'd met.

How had it only been days when she felt as if she'd always known him?

How was it that touching him felt so right and yet as if she should jerk away her hand before it was branded by the feel of his skin beneath her fingertips?

Seeming to pull himself from wherever his thoughts had gone, he shifted his mirrored gaze to where her fingers pressed against his arm, then back up. Ivy dropped her hand to her side. She didn't drag her gaze from where he looked at her from behind those blasted sunglasses, though. She didn't feel as if she could.

After what felt like an eternity but couldn't have been more than a few seconds, he broke the contact. "I'm glad I didn't die, too. Sorry if I sounded as if that's not the case."

Thank God, because she couldn't imagine not having met him.

"Blake was a good guy. The best. Being here, it may sound crazy, but I swear that earlier, I felt his presence."

"It's a powerful place." She itched to touch him, to grasp his hand, but since he'd just pulled his arm free it felt weird to remake the connection.

"That it is."

Throat tight, Ivy stared at him in awe. Not just at who he was, but at how he affected her.

"What?" His brows drew together above his shades.

"You're a really nice guy, aren't you?"

Snorting, he shook his head. "For the record, being described as a really nice guy isn't the way a soldier wants to be known."

"I certainly didn't mean my words as an insult. Quite the opposite. But perhaps I should have said that you're a really good man, instead."

"Not always, but these days, I try to be."

Ivy's ever-present curiosity where he was concerned had her wanting him to elaborate, but his gaze shifted beyond her to where their group had moved far ahead.

"Come on, Doc. We need to catch up with our veterans."

"Smile, Doc." Caleb held up his phone to snap a photo of Ivy talking with two French reenactors at the Brevands memorial ceremony. Both men were in full "Filthy Thirteen" regalia with their hair shaved into mohawks and their faces painted like the First Demolition Section of the Regimental Headquarters Company of the 506th Parachute Infantry Regiment, 101st Airborne Division. The paratroopers had emulated the Native Americans in appearance and reportedly, yelled "Geronimo!" as they jumped. The "Filthy Thirteen" were also credited with liberating the French village and the town honored their legacy with the memorial and annual ceremony. Caleb and Ivy's veterans were part of today's events.

At his request, Ivy smiled. Caleb snapped the picture. Then the two reenactors, both around his and Ivy's ages, moved in for a posed shot with her sandwiched between them. Her smile was real, and Caleb felt a green twinge. He didn't like it but couldn't help but be aware of the sensation. He wasn't the jealous type, not even with Katrina. Other men hadn't been his ex's issue; his lack of interest in worldly goods had been what drove her away. But even if he were the jealous type, he sure didn't have any right to feel that way with Ivy.

"Your turn." She reached for his phone. "Get with them and I'll take one of you. Say, 'Eiffel Tower.'"

Caleb didn't hug up with the guys the way they'd done with her, but he smiled, then thanked them. The reenactors' English was limited, as was his and Ivy's French, but with patience and a little creativity they managed to have a decent conversation. A costumed, beautiful woman and young boy of around four, also in costume, joined them. One of the reenactors' eyes lit and he proudly introduced them as his wife and son.

More photos were taken, including one Ivy

snapped of the cute kid giving him a high five. Pure joy shone on her face. "*Merci.*"

The kid grinned.

When others joined them for photos with the reenactors, he and Ivy stepped back to give them room. They relocated to a monument, where Ivy motioned for him to stand next to the eagle with its wings spread and he did so.

"Oh, let me get one with both of you." Mary took Ivy's phone, then snapped a few shots of them next to the monument. She handed the phone back to Ivy. "Y'all look so good together."

Her cheeks going pink and not from the sunshine, Ivy averted her gaze. "Um, yeah, thanks for taking the photo, Mary."

The woman beamed at them a moment, then went back to where townspeople were swarming her father for autographs of his preprinted postcards.

"You'll have to text me copies of your photos."

"Sure." Ivy looked relieved that he hadn't directly commented on what Mary had said. "You'll have to do the same with the ones you've taken. Although, I've already taken so many that I've no idea when I'll have time to go through them."

"I hear you. I'm not normally one for taking many pictures, but you certainly wouldn't know that based on this trip." He had taken quite a few. More perhaps than he should have that featured Ivy. He assured himself that it was because they were both on the medical team and often paired together. He suspected it had more to do with the fact that he saw her in his mind even when he shut his eyes. As far as Mary's comment, well, he imagined any man would look better when standing next to a stunning woman like Ivy.

Soon it was time for the ceremony to begin. The Brevands mayor and a few other civil servants spoke. As flowers were being laid at the foot of the etched memorial stone, Caleb glanced toward Ivy. She appeared completely enthralled with what was happening. Her gaze was hidden behind her sunglasses, but she'd lifted her hand to her chest, as if powerfully moved by how the soldiers who'd freed the village were being remembered and honored.

Was she thinking about her great-grandfather? How she wished he were there, too? It was obvious she'd been close to him. She'd barely mentioned her parents other than the tourist trinkets, just her great-grandfather several times throughout the week. His gaze went to their veterans, then he leaned close to her ear and whispered, "Paul looks as if he's fallen asleep."

"He's almost a hundred. They'll forgive him." Frowning at his interrupting her viewing of the ceremony, she went back to watching.

Yeah, she was right. He needed to focus on what was being said and not be distracted by the lovely brunette at his side. That was pretty much how his trip was going. Be in awe of how grateful the French people of Normandy were and be in awe of Ivy McEwen. Emotions felt more intense in France.

After the ceremony ended, the crowd swarmed around the veterans for photos and to thank them. The men smiled, gave thumbs-up and handed out photo postcards.

Ivy smiled. "They're rock stars over here. You must be proud to have served."

His chest puffing with that pride, Caleb nodded. "It was my honor."

A soft smile played on her lips, drawing his gaze to her mouth. "Spoken like a true hero."

"That I'm not. Just a kid who grew up wanting to jump out of airplanes and shoot things. Joining the military let me do that without going to jail."

Her eyes widened and she gave a low laugh. "Well, when you put it that way…"

Staring at where the veterans greeted one local after another, Caleb shrugged. "Just telling you the truth."

One small part of it, but still, the truth.

Ivy eyed him. "So, when I can tell how much you loved being in the military, why aren't you still?"

"It's not because I don't want to be," he admitted. "My military career ended when I was medically discharged."

"You were hurt?" Horror darkened the blue

of her eyes as she stared into his, then her gaze skimmed over him, assessing for damage that she must have somehow missed. "Are you okay now? What happened?"

"I'm fine." Mostly. "I landed wrong during a jump." He'd leave off the reasons why he'd landed wrong and that he'd been lucky to land, to live, at all. Had that parachute been silk, it wouldn't have been fit for anything other than tattered rags. Just recalling those harrowing moments had him grimacing, but he forcibly relaxed his face and jaw.

"I'm glad you're okay." Her voice sounded overly emotional, causing him to study her and almost tell her more. That he wanted to tell her stunned him. There were some things he didn't discuss. Some things he hid behind the smile he kept ready on the surface. Life was good. He'd learned long ago he could focus on the good or the bad. He chose the good and did his best to forget the bad. Occasionally the nightmares refused to let him, but for the most part he was proud of how he survived day by day. But he didn't talk about it. Not to the therapist the army had arranged for him. Not with friends or family. Talking about it didn't help a thing. So the strong urge to say more to Ivy threw him off-kilter.

Not once during those long, painful days of recovery had he been tempted to tell Katrina that his internal pain far outweighed the physical. That Blake's death gutted him. Now, knowing that she'd only stepped back into his life because she'd thought he'd join the family business, he was glad he'd not been tempted.

So it made no sense that he'd want to tell Ivy how his best friend had died when their mission had been compromised and their plane had been shot down mere moments after they'd cleared it, that they'd both been hit by shrapnel, Caleb's leg. Blake's chute.

Her gaze bore into him, seeing things he'd always preferred no one see. Some things were better to keep to one's self. Caleb glanced at his watch, then the still-thick crowd near the reenactors they'd photographed with earlier. "What do you think? Should I let my hair grow out down the middle?"

He didn't look toward her. He didn't have to. His quick subject change said what he couldn't, but she let him get away with it.

"They're definitely impressive, aren't they?"

As was Ivy.

"Dr. Ivy!" Mary's voice rang out above the crowd. "Someone get Dr. Ivy."

Without looking his way, Ivy took off toward where Mary's voice had come from. Caleb followed close behind.

A heavy-set male who appeared to be in his late fifties slumped forward, gasping for air and clutching at his chest. *Gray* best described his skin color.

"What's going on?" Ivy asked, slipping her backpack off and swinging it around for easy access. Caleb followed suit.

"I was with dad, when this man said he didn't feel well," Mary began. "Next thing I knew, he sat down on the ground. He doesn't look so good."

"Thanks for your help, Mary. I need someone to call for emergency services and then if I can get you and the others to step back to give him room to breathe and us room to work, that would be great," Caleb assured the distressed woman.

"What's your name?" Ivy touched the man's shoulder, drawing his attention to her. When he continued to stare blankly at her, she tried again. *"Comment t'appelles-tu?"*

"Baptiste," the man said, wincing as he did so.

"Is there someone here who can translate for me?" Ivy asked, glancing around the gathering crowd. One of the reenactors stepped forward. "Ask him if he has a heart problem or is on any medications."

Caleb slipped his pulse oximeter onto the man's fingertip, then reached for his blood pressure cuff to check the man's pressure while Ivy and the interpreter continued to question the man. While talking, Ivy dug through her backpack, pulling out her medication bag.

"Tell Baptiste, this is nitroglycerin." She removed a bottle's lid and shook a tablet into the cap. "It's a tablet to increase the blood supply to the heart and decrease how hard the heart is having to work. I need him to put it in his mouth. He doesn't swallow it, he just needs to let the tablet sit beneath his tongue."

The interpreter told the in-pain man, who nodded and held out his hand. Ivy upturned the tablet into his palm and Baptiste put it in his mouth. Caleb held up the blood pressure cuff, showing Baptiste what he intended to do. The man nodded, then wincing, grabbed at his chest again.

Working fast, Caleb checked Baptiste's blood pressure. Or tried to. The cuff wasn't picking up a pressure. He looked at the pulse oximeter, watching as the number raced. "Pulse is bouncing around from the one-forties to the one-sixties."

Ivy gave a slight nod of acknowledgment.

Caleb had grabbed the defibrillator at the last moment, thinking he probably wouldn't need the equipment that took up a good chunk of his backpack. Unless emergency services arrived soon, he might well be glad he did.

"Baptiste, stay with me," Ivy said, tapping the man's cheek. "Look at me."

Baptiste had been sitting up but slumped over. Ivy and the interpreter laid him back on the grass.

"Pulse is over two hundred." Caleb wished they had oxygen as he opened the defibrillator.

He placed his mouth barrier guard close in case they needed to deliver breaths. "Get his shirt off."

"Here. Give me the razor." Ivy reached for the razor at the side of the defibrillator kit. "Those are never going to stick, otherwise."

With a few quick swipes, she shaved patches where Caleb needed to put the leads. As soon as she finished, he pressed the lead to the man's chest. Then waited as the machine read the man's rhythm.

"He's in ventricular fibrillation." He pulled the pulse oximeter off the man's finger. "All clear," he ordered.

Ivy leaned back, putting her hand out to keep the interpreter away from the man. "Don't touch him. Not anywhere."

The second no one was touching Baptiste, Caleb pressed the button to deliver the shock that would hopefully put Baptiste's heart back in rhythm. The man's body jerked, and Caleb held his breath as he watched the defibrillator's screen.

"It didn't work." Ivy moved over the patient. "I'm starting compressions. Keep a check on his breathing. Give breaths if needed."

Caleb slipped the pulse oximeter back onto Baptiste's finger; oxygenation was in the eighties. "You still have that extra epinephrine from the plane in your backpack?"

She rhythmically compressed his chest. "It's there."

He grabbed her bag, found her liquids bag and pulled out the vial of epinephrine. He gathered a syringe, alcohol swab, and set them aside. He hoped they got a rhythm restored to where they didn't need the medication. If they didn't have Baptiste's heart out of the rapid quivering within a few minutes, he'd inject it.

"Caleb, deliver breaths. He's quit breathing."

He let loose with a low curse, ripping open the cellophane covering on the mouth barrier that would protect him and Baptiste from pathogens. He gave two breaths, then glanced toward the defibrillator, making sure it wasn't recommending another shock yet.

"Not yet," Ivy said, apparently also keeping a check on the screen. They worked together, her compressing, him delivering breaths.

"Swap with me," Caleb suggested, knowing her arms had to be jelly at this point.

She didn't argue, just quickly exchanged positions with him.

"Time to deliver another charge." He moved back, waited until she'd also done so.

"All clear," she said. "If this doesn't restore rhythm, I'm giving the epi."

"Understood. All clear." He pressed the button, causing Baptiste's body to jerk.

"Come on," Ivy told the machine as they waited to see if the electric charge knocked Baptiste's heart out of the dangerous rhythm. "Come on."

"Yes!" He reached out to high-five her when the screen no longer showed ventricular fibrillation.

Baptiste didn't open his eyes. But gasped, then coughed.

They monitored him closely, ready to restart cardiopulmonary resuscitation if needed. Baptiste didn't regain consciousness, but he continued to breathe on his own and, although his rhythm was irregular, it wasn't the dangerous initial one.

"The *Les secours* is here," the interpreter told them as a uniformed duo joined them.

After Baptiste was on his way to the hospital, Caleb grinned at the brunette who was knelt next to Roy, chatting with him.

She glanced up, caught him watching her and grinned. "What?"

"Looks like you saved the day again," he praised.

She stared into his eyes a moment, wild emotion swirling in her blue depths. "Looked more like *we* saved the day again to me. We make a good team."

CHAPTER SEVEN

LATER THAT DAY, a local attorney had everyone from the SMVF to his home for a late lunch. The estate ran as a bed-and-breakfast with a gorgeous event room. Red, white and blue decorations and small flags on the tables gave a festive, patriotic look. Caleb and Ivy ended up at different tables, but she was in his direct line of vision. It might have been better if she hadn't been, though. He was having trouble staying focused on what Roy said. Seemed as if he was having trouble focusing period. While taking care of Baptiste, he and Ivy had worked seamlessly. They made a good team, she'd said. He'd not thought in terms of being a team with a woman since Katrina. The first time, he'd been young, a mere high school kid at an expensive prep school his parents had hoped would steer him in a nonmilitary direction. The second, he'd been hospitalized and she'd been a welcome distraction from his misery. It hadn't taken long for her to leave him again when she realized he'd had no plans to join the rest of his family at the shipping business. A broken man who could have had a great life as part of a power couple with her but chose to wallow in his misery instead, she'd accused. He had grieved Blake's death, grieved his medical discharge from the career he loved, but "wallow" had been harsh. He'd just been driven to get back on his feet, literally.

"She's a looker, isn't she?" Roy interrupted Caleb's meanderings.

"Who?" Caleb shifted his gaze to the grinning older man, took a sip of his water and pretended complete ignorance, as if Roy hadn't just caught him staring at the woman who'd said they made a great team. *As a couple* had been a long way from what she'd meant, but it was no secret he was attracted to her, hence Roy's incoming comments.

"You know who." Roy chuckled. "If I was younger, I'd give you a run for your money."

"You and Owen, but for the record, I'm not sure I'm in the running." He wanted to be, though. He sure hadn't thought about meeting anyone when he'd agreed to go on this trip. He'd have laughed if Stan had suggested anything of the sort. Ivy made him curious to know more and uncover the many layers of who she was. She was different from anyone he'd ever met. Or maybe it was just the way he responded to her that was different from anyone else. Ivy was beautiful, inside and out from the best he could tell, but he'd met good people before and not been drawn to them like the proverbial moth to the flame.

In a different day and time, he'd have made moves on her, charmed her, had his way with her. Since Katrina's last reminder of why relationships were a bad idea following his accident, he rarely dated. But he was interested in Ivy. He sensed her interest, and her hesitation. Wooing her tempted, but there was an inherent fragility beneath her tough exterior that gave him his own hesitations. She'd obviously been hurt in the past. Who hadn't been these days? But he sure didn't want to be the guy who added to someone's pain, and Katrina had nailed home that was all he was good for since his heart belonged to the military and everything, everyone, would always take a distant second place.

"Sure, you aren't." Roy's wrinkled face brightened with merriment as he cackled. "Good thing you've got a week left to admit the truth to yourself and to her. Youth is wasted on the young."

"Yes, sir," Caleb agreed. He'd sure taken jumping for granted right up until his ankle shattered. Maybe Katrina had been right in that he was a broken man. He'd not viewed himself as whole since waking up in a military hospital and realizing the extent of his injuries, that he'd likely never qualify as a paratrooper again. Sometimes he dreamed, though.

"When you get to my age you've learned a

thing or two. One of those things is not wasting time on silly games," Roy continued. "Time is short. Don't be a dunce."

"You think I'm playing a silly game with Dr. McEwen?" Maybe he should take better advantage of the time they'd been given together. He'd not even thought of dating since Katrina. Now, with Ivy, his body reminded him he was a healthy male. He'd thought himself through with relationships. Did meeting Ivy change that or was it just that they were two healthy adults who found each other attractive and were in forced proximity?

"Game that's older than time." Roy grinned. "I've watched it a hundred times during my life. I always wonder why people do that and waste so much precious time. I've seen how you watch her. So has she, for that matter. You make her nervous, but in a good kind of way. Back in my day, we'd have at least asked to hold her hand by this point."

Mary, who was sitting opposite her father and had been in deep conversation with a French couple, was now curiously listening in to what her father said and nodding in agreement. Caleb was beginning to feel cornered and natural instinct had his fight or flight kicking in big-time.

"By this point? You realize I just met her a week ago, right?" Caleb reminded. But perhaps Roy was on to something. Maybe Caleb was overthinking everything where Ivy was concerned.

Maybe he needed to just put everything that had happened with Katrina in the past where it belonged. Ivy was nothing like worldly Katrina, who had cared more about his parents' wealth than she had about Caleb. Even if he was on board, Ivy might not be. He could see her response going either way and that might be part of his hesitation. Which was interesting as he'd never let the risk of failure stop him in the past. How often had he jumped that the odds weren't in his favor and yet he'd never paused? What held him back? Would Ivy even care that being a soldier mattered more to him than anything? And that now, peace mattered more than his bank account?

"A week? That long ago already? You're slacking, kid." Roy reached out and patted his hand. "Take it from an old coot, that girl is something special."

Hadn't Caleb thought the same thing? That he'd never met anyone like her? His gaze went back to where Ivy was laughing at something Owen was telling her. Her long hair was pulled back into a ponytail and pink tinged her high cheekbones. There was no telling what Owen had said. The man might be close to a hundred, but he was an incurable flirt.

And Ivy was something special.

After they'd eaten their delicious lunch, including more fresh baked bread that he was quickly becoming accustomed to having at each meal, they moved outdoors to enjoy the beautiful weather. Along with a few others, Caleb helped carry out chairs.

When they'd finished, he looked around for Ivy, spotting her heading down a gravel road.

"She asked Lara to keep an eye on the guys, saying she needed to walk off some of her lunch. If you hurry, you can catch her." Had Mary overheard all of what her father had been saying earlier?

Since stretching his legs would feel good, Caleb jogged to catch up with Ivy. It didn't take long. She'd paused to snap photos of an old outbuilding that had gorgeous roses growing near it.

"Want one with you in it?" he offered, wanting to be helpful and give himself a reason for joining her walk.

"I'm good." She slid her phone into her pocket. "Thanks, though."

"What if I'd like one?"

Seeming surprised, she shrugged. "Okay, pose and I'd be happy to take one."

Not what he'd meant, but Caleb went with it, handing his phone to Ivy, then giving her a cheesy smile.

"Here." She handed back his phone. "Check to make sure you like it."

Rather than check the photo, Caleb hit his camera icon, then leaned in next to Ivy for a selfie. "Say cheese."

Rather than look at the camera she stared at him in surprise. He snapped a photo. Shrugging, she glanced up, smiled and said, "Eiffel Tower."

Caleb took a few shots. "So much better than saying cheese. Have you been?"

She shook her head. "Not yet. I'm hoping there's time on the day we travel back to Paris."

Caleb hoped so, too. Seeing the iconic tower hadn't been on his radar but now, seeing it with Ivy ranked up there. Her eyes would sparkle more magnificently than the tower ever could.

There really must be something about France. He wasn't the kind of guy who went around thinking about how a woman's eyes would sparkle. The French must put something in their water. Or maybe it was all the delicious bread that made a person view things differently. Apparently, life just got all rose-colored glasses when you were drinking fine wine and eating fresh-baked bread.

Gravel crunched beneath their feet as they resumed their walk toward the pastures. There was a slight breeze that rustled the lush green trees lining the country road. A cow bellowed in the distance. If Caleb had been searching for peace, this moment was it: a full belly, beautiful surroundings and with a great person.

"Hope you don't mind me joining you," he told her, then patted his stomach. "With all the bread I'm eating, I needed to move. I may be bigger than a house by the time we go home."

"Yeah, I don't think you have anything to worry about with how fit you are." Her gaze dropped to his midsection, then, realizing what she'd done, she looked away. "I mean, um, oh, never mind."

Pleased with her compliment, Caleb couldn't resist teasing. "You think I'm fit?"

"You have to remember that I've been hanging out with men who are knocking a hundred. It's all in one's perspective."

He laughed at her quick-witted comment. "And here I thought you were giving me a compliment."

"I was, not that you need compliments to know that you take care of your body. It's obvious that you do. You go for a run in the mornings before I've awakened."

He wouldn't be winning any marathons with his jogs, but he strove to keep his legs strong by his exercise and stretching regime. "Then, thank you for the compliment. I'm glad you noticed."

Ignoring his comment, she pointed down the gravel road that ran deeper into the farm "Let's walk to where those horses are near that fence. My great-grandfather's farm has a section with fences like those made from cut trees and I want to see them up close."

"Did he have horses?"

"Not for years. Actually, he hasn't had any animals in years other than ones that belong to others. In his late eighties, he sold his cattle and most of his farm equipment and started leasing the land out to one of his neighbors." Ivy glanced his way. "He left me his farm."

"You going to take up farming?"

"For now, I'm hoping his neighbor will continue to lease the land. There are a lot of things I have to figure out after I get settled in Knoxville. I'd barely finished residency prior to our leaving on this trip."

"Are you planning to live at the farm?"

She nodded. "It's what I'd always planned to do. I'd just planned on Gramps being there with me."

"He will be. In your heart and your mind."

Ivy's gaze cut to him and she smiled. "He's always there. Always."

Caleb loved his family, but he was the black sheep by not following in his parents' corporate footsteps. What would it have been like to have someone who he felt such a connection with? "Tell me about him."

Ivy looked shocked at his request. "You want to hear about my great-grandfather? Luke couldn't stand me to talk about him."

"I'm not Luke."

"Thank God. I stayed with that man longer than I should have."

"I'd like to hear about why you did that, too, but that's a conversation for a different day. It's much too beautiful a day to ruin it by talking about someone who makes your nose curl that way."

Relaxing her face, she nodded. "You're right. It is. I'd much rather talk about Gramps."

"What's your favorite memory of him?"

"I have lots of great memories so it's difficult to pick just one. He'd take me out on his tractor with him, we'd fish in his pond, but maybe my favorite was watching him with my great-grandmother before she died. They made being in love look like so much fun. I wanted that so badly that I settled for less. That's why I've put conditions on any future relationship."

"Conditions?"

"Things that I hope will increase odds of any future relationship's success."

Curious, he wanted to know more, but she was so relaxed talking about her great-grandfather that he didn't want to risk her clamming up on him.

"So Gramps was your great-grandfather? What happened to your grandparents?"

"My grandmother died giving birth to my mother. My grandmother was Gramps and Grammie's only child. They were devastated. Mom says they never forgave her for being born. I'm not sure I believe that, but she and Gramps never jibed, not the way we did."

"I'm sorry. Is that why he left the farm to you?"

"Mom would have sold it. He knew that."

"And that you wouldn't?"

"I loved the farm."

"Then he left it to the right person."

As they meandered toward the fence, Ivy told him stories of her great-grandfather's farm. Of how the ninety-eight-year-old man had rarely sat down at any point in his life, having come back from the war, married her grandmother and lived life to the fullest.

"Like the guys here, Gramps never sat down. I think that's why he did so well, why Owen and these guys do so well. They've stayed active."

Caleb was all for following in their footsteps. He hoped he never had a reason to sit down and stay down.

Not ever again.

The months following his accident had been the roughest point in his life. Maybe that's why he'd allowed Katrina back into his life. He'd been desperate for any connection outside the rehabilitation facility. She'd accused him of being like a trapped animal. That's how he'd felt. Trapped. By his own body's limitations.

Staying committed to taking care of his body wasn't difficult when he recalled how miserable he'd been laid up and dependent upon others for the simplest things.

A waste of air. That was what Katrina had said.

*You should have done your family a favor and
died when that plane went down.*

He might not have the relationship with them
that Ivy had had with her great-grandfather, but
they hadn't wanted him to die. They'd just been
too busy working to come around much while he
was healing. Not that he'd wanted them or anyone
to see him that way. Maybe that was why he'd
let Katrina come back, because ultimately, he'd
known she'd leave because she'd never settle for
his footloose and fancy-free lifestyle.

Glancing at the woman leaning against the
fence, petting a mare who'd come over to check
them out probably hoping for a treat, Caleb wondered at Ivy. He was a minimalist with no real
roots. Her roots ran deep on a Tennessee farm.

He was attracted to her, wanted to date her, but
she was looking for what her great-grandparents
had had. She deserved that. Until his accident,
Caleb had never stayed in one place long during his adult life. He likely wouldn't have stayed
in Knoxville if not for Blake's widow needing
his help with TransCare. Now he didn't know
what his future held. He was content, and yet,
he wasn't. He blamed his inability to jump, but
perhaps it was more than that.

"You're very quiet." Still stroking her hands
over the horse's neck, Ivy glanced toward him.
"Have I bored you with all my talk about Gramps
and the farm?"

He shook his head. "You could read an old phone book and I don't think I'd be bored, not with how expressive your face gets."

"Yeah, well, if I was reading an old phone book, the expression on my face would be boredom, so nothing exciting about that."

It really didn't matter what she was saying. It was Ivy herself that was exciting, being near her, reveling in the electric vibes she sent through him, wondering what she'd say or do next.

"This may sound cheesy, but I don't think I could ever be bored when looking at your face no matter your expression."

She eyed him suspiciously, then laughing nervously, turned back to love on the horse. He suspected she didn't know what to say. He understood. He didn't, either, because what he said was true and he'd only known her less than a week.

"I think you were supposed to turn back there," Ivy pointed out when Caleb drove past a road on the turnabout. Turnabouts were apparently a big thing in this area, because they'd come upon several of them during the trip. Ivy found them confusing as did her phone's GPS system, obviously.

These days, she found a lot of things confusing, especially in regard to Caleb. Since the prior day when he'd made his cheesy remark about her face, she'd been able to think of little else.

"You're sure?" He glanced toward her. "I

looked at the directions earlier, and I think we're on the correct road."

She studied her phone map, then looked back at where they were. "According to my phone's GPS, that was our turn."

"No problem. The directions I'd looked at earlier had routed us a different way, but I imagine that there's more than one way to get there. We'll take your phone's directions." Caleb circled the car around the turnabout, then exited at where she indicated.

"We can always backtrack if my GPS leads us astray." Hopefully, it wouldn't. They weren't in a time crunch, but she didn't want to take away from their seeing as many iconic places as possible during their free afternoon. Pointe du Hoc wasn't on the veterans' itinerary, so needed to be visited during downtime. When Phillipe had offered his car, they'd jumped at the opportunity to explore some of the iconic spots along the coastline.

Caleb strummed his fingers against the steering wheel. "Do you know the history behind Pointe du Hoc?"

"It's where army rangers scaled hundred-foot cliffs to take out artillery that could fire upon Omaha and Utah Beaches on D-Day."

Caleb looked impressed. "I've met well-seasoned soldiers who don't know about Point du

Hoc or what happened there. Did you study up for this trip?"

"I've been studying for this trip my whole life." She laughed. "I was forever asking my Gramps questions. As a child, I didn't realize I was asking about things he didn't talk about, but for whatever reason, with me, he did and I soaked up every word."

"That was probably cathartic for him. At least, that's what the therapist I was forced to see told me. That talking about the things that I'd seen and done was good for me. I'd say talking to you helped him heal."

Ivy's heart warmed at Caleb's comment while simultaneously clenching that he'd seen and done things requiring him to see a therapist. No doubt the military had required it after his friend had died. She couldn't imagine the heartbreak that he must have felt to have been there and survived when his friend hadn't. "That's a wonderful thought and I hope I helped him find peace. That's what this trip is supposed to do for the veterans, to help them find peace. Regardless, Gramps never seemed to mind my questions and I asked him lots because I was fascinated by his military history. His WWII service was a bond we shared."

"My love of the military was an oddity in my family, so your relationship with him sounds idyllic to me. So you shared WWII history and the Tennessee Volunteers?"

"We kept up with the team together, just as we kept up with anything and everything that would come out about World War II. When a new movie or documentary would air, we planned ahead for me to visit so we could watch it together if it was at all possible. I grew up in Nashville, so just a few hours from Gramps. He'd drill me on the accuracy, so I had to know my stuff." She smiled at the memories running through her head. "As I advanced in school, watching together became more difficult with life commitments, so we'd watch, then discuss over the phone."

"You're lucky to have had such a close relationship with your great-grandfather. My family had no military interest. My brother attended my basic training graduation, but none of my family understood my passion for my career. Does it sound terrible if I admit I'm jealous of your great-grandfather?"

Ivy hated his lack of support and wondered why his family hadn't been there for him. She'd been lucky to be so loved.

"It doesn't sound terrible. Everyone should be envious of Gramps. He was the best, so I totally understand why someone would want our relationship. It was enviable," she admitted. "I was blessed to have him for so many years in my life and should have found a way to see him more, you know? Med school and residency could have waited." Grief and guilt hitting, she closed her eyes. "They would have waited if I'd known I was going to lose him."

"Everyone dies eventually and he lived a good, long life. It sounds as if you had a great relationship, and he knew you loved him. That's what is important."

"Gramps knew I loved him." She repeated his claim, her words choking her. She cleared her throat. "What about you? Are you close with your family?" She really wanted to know more, to know why only his brother had been at Caleb's graduation from Basic. "Was there someone in the service who influenced your desire to be in the military?"

"No one in the military that they're aware of, although I think most Americans had at least one extended family member drafted for one of the World Wars."

"No direct military family members, but one day you decided you wanted to join the army?" she pressed. "How did that happen?"

"I always wanted to be in the army. I liked playing with those little green plastic men and watching war movies. Maybe that was what influenced me."

"Did the toy company make those army men with parachutes?" Ivy teased, trying to picture him as a child playing with the toys. It was difficult to imagine Caleb as anything other than the virile man sitting in the driver's seat.

"Those only came in the fancier sets." He grinned. "What about you? With your obvious love and appreciation for the military, what kept you from enlisting? You could have pursued medicine in the military."

"At one point in time, I considered," she admitted. "But that would have meant having to fly and we know how I feel about that." She wrinkled her nose with displeasure. "Even Gramps agreed that I shouldn't enlist."

"What did he want you to do?"

Ivy's heart swelled as she recalled the conversation with her great-grandfather. "To be happy."

Caleb cut his gaze toward her. "That's it? He didn't have a preconceived idea that he tried to force upon you of what would make you happy? Didn't try to push you to go into the family business?"

"Our family business would be farming, I guess, and he never tried to push me to do that. I enjoyed being with him on the farm, but it wasn't my calling. He was pleased when I told him I planned to follow in my great-grandmother's footsteps and become a doctor. I'm named after her and he thought it perfect that I carry on her love of helping others. He said he always thought that's what I should do but hadn't wanted to influence my decision."

"I'm sure he was proud of you. Going to medical school is hard work."

"Tell me about it. Oh, turn left up here." She pointed at an upcoming road. "There were days when I wondered if I'd get through med school."

"I can't see you quitting something you started. You seem like a very determined person who keeps pushing forward."

Even when she should just admit she was wrong. She should have called it quits with Luke eons before she did.

"You're right. I'd never have dropped out of school and let him, or myself, see me as a failure. I wouldn't have dishonored my great-grandmother's legacy that way." Her relationship with Luke had been a dishonor. How many of her "friends" had known he was cheating, but had failed to tell her? Had they all been laughing behind her back?

"Her name was Ivy, too?"

"No, but my middle name is Rose. My great-grandfather always said she was the prettiest flower in the garden and that's why he picked her."

Slowing the car to make the turn, Caleb glanced her way. "Then, you carry on her legacy in more ways than one."

Caleb's compliment had Ivy's heart thudding hard against her rib cage. Ha! Everything about Caleb made her pulse pound. Including the fact that he'd taken the route she'd recommended even though it was different from the one he'd intended. It had already taken them ten minutes longer than the time frame he'd given when they'd left the bed-and-breakfast at Sainte-Mère-église, but he'd not said one negative word or pointed out that his way was better. The contrast to Luke couldn't be more stark. Why had she stayed in that relationship so long when there were men like Caleb out in the world?

Not that she was in a relationship with Caleb, just…just, maybe she wanted to be. Yes, they were in a magical bubble of spending two weeks away from their "real" lives, but there was something about him that was different from any man she'd ever known. Not true. He reminded her of her favorite qualities in Gramps. The qualities she'd thought the current generation lacked, but that she found so attractive and had hoped to someday find. Face heating, she knew she needed to get her thoughts under control and refocused on the matter at hand, which was getting them to their destination.

But the past had taught her that dating a man who wasn't her economic equal would eventually lead to problems. Problems she could avoid by only becoming involved with men who wouldn't be threatened by her independence.

"Pointe du Hoc is only about four miles from Utah Beach, right?" She needed a subject change because she wasn't ready to delve into what Caleb had meant by his sweet comment. Had he been implying that he found her the prettiest flower in the garden and planned to pick her? And, if that's what he meant, what was she going to do about it? Go with it to see what happened or set him straight that she wasn't in the market for another heartbreak? That they were in an environment that forced togetherness, but back in the real world, he'd see her in a different, less flattering, light. "We're getting close."

Not taking his gaze from the road, he nodded. "This was one of my top places to visit."

"It was great of Phillipe and Delphine to let us use their car." See, she could make normal conversation even when he'd made cheesy compliments two days in a row.

"The people of Normandy are impressive in their hospitality." He tapped his thumbs against the steering wheel, matching beat with the crazy pounding in her chest.

"With your history as a paratrooper and all the airborne history in the area, I'm surprised that Pointe du Hoc made your top list."

He shrugged. "Just because I was a paratrooper doesn't mean that I can't appreciate what the rangers accomplished here. Those brave men deserve to be remembered. All the soldiers from D-Day do."

"Agreed." She pointed to a sign. "There's our turn."

They parked and walked the short distance to the entrance. The cliffs were hauntingly beautiful as they jutted above the coastline. The wind whipped at Ivy, loosening hair strands from her ponytail and dancing them about her head in defiance of her repeated attempts to recapture them. Despite the summer heat, the breeze carried a chill, perhaps as a reminder of the past. Ivy rubbed her arms.

"The wind cuts right into you, doesn't it?" Caleb asked as they made their way toward steps that led into an old bunker.

She crammed her hands into her pockets. "Yes, but I'm not going to complain. Not here about something as insignificant as the wind being cold."

His gaze met hers. "Perhaps here is the best place to say how you're feeling. The freedom to speak your mind is one of the things those men were fighting for."

Again, awed by his insight, Ivy studied him. "True, but you aren't going to hear me complain."

The corner of his mouth lifted. "I wouldn't expect to. You're much more a grit-your-teeth-and-bear-it kind of person."

Ivy couldn't argue. She would much rather just suck it up and deal than to verbalize negativity. Complaining sure didn't change anything. Gramps had always told her that if she didn't like something, to do something to make it better. For the most part, she felt that was what she did in life. Where she'd failed was when it came to relationships. For whatever reasons, she'd turned a blind eye to things she didn't want to acknowledge. Delaying the inevitable rarely proved beneficial. Today's nippy wind was nothing in the grand scheme of life.

They went through an old bunker, peering out the slit windows that looked out to the sea, then moved back to the path where they marveled at the many craterous land indentions made by bombings that had occurred so long ago. They took in the sights, the smells of the ocean, the continued whipping of the wind, the heaviness of the knowledge of what had taken place as the rangers took out enemy forces to protect their comrades landing at Utah and Omaha Beaches. While all that had been going on, Gramps had been jumping near Sainte-Mère-église with his company in the Eighty-Second.

Ivy stumbled on her way down a set of steps. "Oops."

Caleb grasped hold of her hand, making sure she stayed upright. Electricity shot over her skin, prickling her flesh, and almost made her lose balance again. His fingers were warm and strong as they clasped with hers and didn't let go.

"You okay?" Concern shone on his face.

"Fine." Why hadn't she pulled her hand free? Why, instead, were their fingers still clasped as they made their way through the bunker? Why was she still holding his hand fifteen minutes later as they made their way through the memorial area with its placards denoting different brave men who'd taken Pointe du Hoc? Why did the heat of his skin eradicate the wind's chill? Whatever it was, having her fingers laced with his made her feel better, as if he could protect her from even the elements. How silly was she that she was marveling at their held hands rather than putting a quick end to his presumptuousness?

Was it presumptuous when she liked his hand holding hers and she hadn't pulled away? She obviously didn't mind too much, or she wouldn't allow him to do so as they continued to make their way along the pathway overlooking the sea far below and back toward the park's exit.

After they'd left and were heading to find somewhere to eat, they passed a beautiful building with ivy growing up the side, she pulled out her phone to take photos along their drive back.

A thought hit and disappointment gripped her belly. "Oh, no! We forgot to take any pictures."

Caleb's amber eyes shifted toward her, connecting and mesmerizing with their intensity. "We've not gone that far and we can go back if you want to take a few, but I don't need pictures to remember today. Visiting Pointe du Hoc was unforgettable, don't you think?"

Ivy's breath caught. He was right. Their visit had been unforgettable.

Just as she suspected the man sitting next to her was going to prove unforgettable.

CHAPTER EIGHT

IVY PAUSED TO peer into a shop window along the cobbled street running between the colorful buildings in Le Vieux Bassin at the Honfleur harbor. "Stopping for an early dinner in this gorgeous town was a wonderful idea."

"I wasn't necessarily thinking about buying our meal from a street vendor, but I enjoyed the sunshine and watching the boats."

"I can't imagine it being more delicious if we'd sat down at a five-star restaurant. My mackerel was yummy."

"Mine, too." A couple walked past them, eating ice cream cones. Caleb glanced her way and waggled his brows. "What do you think? There's always room for ice cream."

Glancing his way, she shook her head. "You think I'm going to trust you when it comes to dessert? I think not after you convinced me to try *crottes de mouettes*."

His eyes twinkled with mischief. "You looked as if you were enjoying them."

"Right up until you told me they were seagull droppings," she muttered.

Caleb chuckled. "I'm not sure why they're called that, since they're just a candy made of caramel and chocolate, but your face was priceless when I told you."

"Priceless?" She rolled her eyes. "Ha ha. I mean, I thought you were just teasing, but we are in a foreign country. Dietary habits are different, so I did wonder for a second."

"They were just candy." His lips twitched. "At least, as far as I know, they were. My French leaves a lot to be desired, so anything's possible."

She poked him in the ribs. "Stop. You're ruining how good those tasted."

He grinned. "We should talk about what they make their ice cream from."

She put her hands over her ears. "La-la-la… I can't hear you."

He laughed. "Milk."

"You're bad," The smile on her face undermined her comment. "Come on. Let's go in this shop. Maybe you can find more key chains, because I'm sure the hundreds you've already bought aren't nearly enough."

"I may have to buy an extra suitcase to carry them home," he teased as they went into the shop.

"Are you a habitual key chain giver?" she accused when he made a beeline for the shop's souvenir trinkets.

"Not really. Most of my past travels had to do with deployment or military assignments." Picking up a key chain, then putting it back, he turned to her. "I hadn't really thought about it, but this is my first time traveling since returning to civilian life."

The emotion in his voice had her heart squeezing. "Why key chains?"

He shrugged. "Why not key chains?"

"Just trying to understand if there's any symbolism to the key chains. I mean, are you trying to give your friends and family the key to the world or is there some deeper meaning?"

Rather than laugh, his forehead scrunched. "It's just a key chain, Ivy. Nothing more."

But something about his tone made her wonder if she hadn't hit a sensitive spot, perhaps one he hadn't even realized he had.

"Well, if they have one with a photo of these gorgeous buildings along the inner harbor, I may have to get one."

He arched a brow. "You? Buy a souvenir?"

"Shocking, I know." She followed him out of the shop, taking in the beauty of where they were with the gorgeous boats in the harbor, red-canopied vendors along the cobblestoned streets and the multicolored buildings. "Maybe I should just take some pictures. I still can't believe I forgot to take any while we were at Pointe du Hoc."

"I offered to return." Side by side, they walked down the street.

"I know and I appreciate that, but I didn't want you to have to turn around just to take pictures. You were right when you said it was an unforgettable day."

"Not just at Pointe du Hoc."

She glanced his way, met his gaze, and her breath caught. He meant now because they'd spent the day together. She couldn't disagree. Their afternoon strolling along the inner harbor, looking at the boats, watching the waves come in along the beach, popping in and out of shops, then eating at the delicious street vendor, had been relaxing. A perfect date.

Only it wasn't a date.

"Ivy, I…" He hesitated, then seemed to change his mind on whatever he was going to say. "Hand me your phone and I'll take your photo with the harbor in the background."

Wondering what he'd started to say, she passed him her phone and smiled as he snapped pictures.

"Would you like me to take a photo of you together?" a woman with an American accent asked just as Caleb handed her phone back.

"That would be great." Ivy grabbed Caleb's hand and pulled him to where they could take a photo with the picturesque harbor in the background.

She didn't look at him, just held on to his hand as she smiled while the woman took a few shots.

"Get closer together," the woman encouraged, snapping another photo. "Now do something funny."

Ivy contorted her face, then realizing Caleb had given her bunny ears, frowned. "Hey!"

She grabbed at his fingers to pull them down, but, laughing, he held them higher than she could reach.

"Oh, these are great," their photographer praised, laughing at their antics, then handing Ivy's phone back. "How fun. You guys have a great rest of your trip. How much longer are you guys here?"

"About a week."

They said goodbye, then continued through the town, stopping to window-shop from time to time, and just soaking in the relaxed atmosphere of the quaint town.

"Let's ride the Ferris wheel."

Her spur-of-the-moment suggestion surprised her almost as much as it did Caleb.

"What about your fear of heights?"

"I don't have a fear of heights. I have a fear of flying," she clarified. "There's a difference."

"Okay. If you want to ride the Ferris wheel, we'll ride the Ferris wheel."

"You don't think I'm silly for wanting to ride it?"

He studied her a moment, then shook his head. "I think you're perfect because you want to ride it."

His praise did funny things to her insides, like make her breathy and feel as if she might float away. "And if I said I want to ride the carousel, too?"

"I'd say, you're in luck. I like carousels."

They rode the carousel first, choosing galloping horses next to each other. Feeling giddy, childlike even, she glanced Caleb's way, met his gaze, and he winked. Okay, there went feeling childish, because his wink made her feel very much womanly.

When the ride finished, he dismounted, then mock bowed and held out his hand. "My lady."

His lady. Ivy's breath caught. She could get off the horse just fine, but she placed her hand in his, let him assist her. She slid a leg around to where she could step down, but Caleb's hands went to her waist, lifting her. Rather than putting her on the ground, he held her, his hands burning through the cotton of her T-shirt. Ivy swallowed, keeping her eyes locked with his as he slowly lowered her, their bodies brushing as he did so. Fire shot through her at the contact. *Fire* because there was no other way to describe his touch.

Desire flickered in his eyes and Ivy sucked in a breath, reminding herself they were in a very public place, even though the emotions hitting her were all of the private variety. "Caleb?"

"Hmm?" His hand grasped hers, giving a gentle squeeze.

"I like carousels, too."

His amber eyes burning into her, he grinned. "Ready for the Ferris wheel, Doc?"

The following day, the town of Carentan hosted a ceremony at Cabbage Square attended by government and military officials from numerous countries. A massive canopy tent had been set up to keep the veterans out of the sunshine as the "distinguished" speakers reminded of why everyone was gathered there, celebrating France's liberation and continued freedom. A community center was set up for lunch and to rest prior to a parade. That evening, there was another meal and ceremony followed by a dance.

Throughout the day, Ivy stayed close to her veterans. All the WWII veterans from SMVF and the other veteran group were honored again during the meal that represented French, British, American and German cuisines. The sport's complex had been decorated with red, white and blue streamers draped from the ceiling, giving it a festive look. Veterans, the veteran association groups, dignitaries and current military there for various events were all present.

Caleb set his plate down on the table next to hers.

"Hungry?" she teased. Ivy had limited her choices to small helpings of two items representing each country. Caleb's plate appeared to have healthy samplings of every item offered.

"Starved."

Had she not met his gaze, she might not have thought anything about the exchange, but his look had her gulping. Did he feel as confused by their hand-holding as she did?

She was confused, all right. Confused over her own thoughts, emotions, and her own silly fantasies of meeting a man like Gramps.

Today, they'd been friendly, but he hadn't reached for her hand or given any indication that he'd held her hand the evening before.

Because his holding your hand was innocent and you're being silly, reading too much into an innocent gesture. Just stop.

Only, Ivy didn't buy it. There had been nothing innocent about his touch. Not on either of their parts. Holding hands might be a common gesture, but for them, it had been a big deal.

She ate most of her food. Caleb cleaned his plate. Where did he put all he ate?

Ivy's veterans claimed they were tired, so their host families left with them, rather than stay for the dance. Ivy would have been great with leaving, as well, but Phillipe and Delphine had commented on how much they looked forward to the dance each year. As Ivy and Caleb had ridden with them, they were left at the table watching the others. People of all ages, including a few of the hundred-plus-year-old veterans from the other group, danced and laughed.

"That's how I want to be," Caleb mused from beside her. He'd donned khaki slacks and a navy button-down that he'd rolled the sleeves up enough to reveal his smartwatch and tan forearms sprinkled with dark hair. In all her life Ivy couldn't recall finding a man's hands and wrists sexy, but Caleb Rivers's had her wishing she could fan herself. Okay, lots about him had her insides warm. Like the way he almost always had a smile and treated everyone in their group with genuine kindness and respect. Her gaze lingered on his hand. The one that had held hers. Something so simple and yet, his having held her hand had freed some complex reactions. She couldn't deny her interest. He appealed to everything inside her except for her logic. That part of her advised her to run as quickly as she could.

Wearing the one dress she'd brought with her, a simple red number that fell to just above her knees and that she'd even matched with red lipstick to pull the look together, Ivy gazed into his sunshine-hitting honey eyes. "How is it that you want to be?"

"Laughing and dancing until my dying day," he clarified. "They're having the time of their lives right here where so many of them could have lost their lives. They're enjoying the moment without worrying about the past or their limited future. They're truly living in the present. That's a marvelous place to be."

Looking toward the dance floor, her gaze landed upon a veteran who seemed to be especially enjoying himself as he held on to a younger woman's hands. Ivy couldn't help but smile at how happy he looked. A memory from her early childhood hit of Gramps grabbing her great-grandmother at the waist and spinning her around the kitchen, causing her to giggle. They'd pulled her in to join their happy carousing. Their love and joy for each other had been so obvious even through her childish eyes.

She'd thought she'd eventually marry Luke and raise their children at the farm she loved while practicing medicine in Knoxville. She never settled in her professional life. Why had she been willing to settle in her personal one? Luke hadn't deserved her. She should have sent him packing long before she had. Being alone was better than being with someone who made himself feel better by belittling you.

"Laughing and dancing until the end sounds like a good plan for everyone to have," she agreed. "Few seem to achieve it, though."

Despite having gone through a few rough patches, her parents loved each other, but they weren't laughing and dancing kind of people. Maybe because of her mother's traumatic birth and having been raised by a grieving father. Ivy couldn't say she'd been a laughing, dancing kind of person with Luke, either. She'd enjoyed the good parts of their relationship, especially in the early days, but she'd never looked at him the way her grandmother had looked at Gramps. Nor had he ever looked at her the way Gramps had Grammie.

"We aren't laughing and dancing at this moment of our relatively young lives." Eyes twinkling, Caleb nudged her with his elbow. "We need to do something about that. Dance with me?"

Excitement bubbling through her, Ivy eyed him. "Did you set me up to feel as if I couldn't say no to dancing with you without contradicting what I just agreed to?"

His grin was lethal. "Whatever makes you think that I'd do something like that? I'm just trying to make sure you're laughing and dancing and enjoying your present."

Oh, yeah, he'd set that one up perfectly. The way her heart raced said she didn't mind one bit, either. Ugh. What was wrong with her? She knew better than to get caught up with Caleb. As wonderful as he was in this controlled environment, eventually he'd be no different than Luke or the others back home.

Standing, he held out his hand. "Come on, Doc. Let's dance."

Why did taking his hand seem like such a big deal? As if, if she put her hand in his she'd never be quite the same? It wasn't as if she hadn't held his hand yesterday. But this felt more meaningful. More revealing.

She gulped back her own imaginings, because that was all this was. She wasn't the prettiest flower, and he wasn't picking her. He just wanted to dance and enjoy life.

"Just remember you asked for this, because I never said I could dance." She placed her hand in his, marveling at the instant electricity of the skin-to-skin contact.

"The same could be said about me."

"If not, asking me to dance doesn't seem a wise decision."

His eyes twinkled. "Let's just say that I wanted to dance with the most beautiful woman here enough to risk exposing my dancing skills, whatever they may be. Especially since she'd been eyeing the dance floor with longing to join the others."

Had she? Maybe. Everyone seemed to be having so much fun. She had a good life and had enjoyed time with her fellow residents, but how long had it been since she'd done something just for the fun of it? Since before her breakup with Luke, before Gramps had died, since... It had been much too long. She'd not gone in to this trip thinking it would be fun, but it was, a lot of which she attributed to the man holding her hand as he led her toward the dance floor.

Holding Caleb's hand for the second day in a row was so not why she felt giddy. Or, maybe, it was.

"You may regret this. I wasn't kidding about not being much of a dancer. I mean, I know the moves to several dances, but can never relax enough to be any good." She gave a nervous laugh. "Does that make sense?"

"Tonight's about having fun, Doc, not perfection. Don't sweat whether or not you know the steps. Just move however, and wherever, the music leads you."

"What if it leads me off a cliff?" she teased, marveling at him.

"Then we'll hope there's water beneath so we can go for a swim." He began to move in a similar fashion to the other dancers to the upbeat song. "Don't let what anyone else thinks keep you from enjoying yourself." His eyes sparkled as he pulled her to him and leaned near her ear. "How likely is it that you will ever see any of these people again?"

"Well, that's just sad." She felt so close to the veterans and their families, not to mention the crew and wonderful French people they'd met. And then there was Caleb. She'd been with him almost nonstop. She would see Caleb again. He'd said he made calls to the hospital. Thank goodness as the thought of not seeing him again put her stomach in a vise.

"But realistic, unfortunately." He gave her hand a gentle squeeze and slowly turned her on the dance floor. "Do you think you'll come back next year?"

"Maybe." She could smell his spicy scent and fought leaning just a little closer to brush her cheek against his to feel the very slight stubble she'd find there. "They may not ask me."

He pulled back, arching his brow. "After the incident on the plane and how you handled it so smoothly, they'll ask. You're a shoo-in for life."

"Right place at the right time with the right medicines," she said, her senses full of how close he was. How his palm rested on her low back and his other was pressed against hers. How if she took a step forward her body would similarly be pressed against his. The song wasn't slow but wasn't fast, either, to where there was a huge variety of movements happening on the dance floor. It would be easy to close that distance, lean against Caleb and forget anyone else was even there.

"It was more than that, but it's too gorgeous of a night to argue over the specifics. You rocked the plane. You've rocked this trip." Eyes twinkling, he lifted their hands in an exaggerated movement, swaying his hips to the side as he did so, then grinning when she laughed. "I'm glad I get to be a small part of your greatness."

His compliment spread heat through her. Luke

would never have acknowledged her role in what had happened on the plane and that Caleb appreciated her efforts made her feel good, and a little embarrassed. Then again, Luke hadn't been all negative. In the beginning, he'd been nice, complimentary and somewhat supportive.

"I could say the same about you." She attempted to ground herself with recalling that all attractions were exciting in the beginning. Whatever was between her and Caleb was new and that's why it felt so good, so right.

From the dance floor, Delphine spotted them. The French woman waved, then laughed as her husband spun her around, dipping her back.

"Yeah, I don't do that." Ivy suspected that Caleb was a much better dancer than the simple moves they were doing. His body held a grace that said he could move any way he liked and with finesse. His dance moves were fluid, graceful, tantalizing, even. Would his lovemaking be the same? Not rushed or selfish, but a pleasurable dance of his body meshing with hers? Gulping back at the heat seizing her, Ivy squeezed her eyes closed, trying to clear her mind. She didn't need to be thinking of Caleb that way. Only, closing her eyes made her more aware of his hands touching her, of his spicy scent, of the energy of his body near hers.

"No need to close your eyes, Doc. I won't dip

you back if you don't want dipped," he promised, chuckling. "However, for the record, I'd never let you fall."

Please be telling the truth. Please don't let me fall for you.

Knowing that wasn't what he'd meant but desperately wishing it was, Ivy opened her eyes, replacing her mental image of Caleb with an up close one of him staring into her eyes. Although his tone had been light and he'd had that husky chuckle, there was a seriousness in those amber eyes that made breathing difficult.

"There's no worry that you might cause me to fall so long as you don't dip me back."

Oh, Caleb. What's happening here?

"How about we just go with the music and have fun?"

It's what she needed to do rather than overanalyzing the moment.

"Is that not what we're doing?" His gaze searched hers. "Dancing and laughing until our dying day, remember?"

The light in his eyes hinted that he'd read her thoughts. Read them, knew she'd been thinking of things much more serious than dancing. Although that light twinkled brightly, it didn't hide that she wasn't the only one concerned over what could happen between them if they let it.

"Quit."

She swallowed. "What?"

"Thinking about whatever caused that look on your face."

"I was thinking about you." So much for not telling him her thoughts. No matter. He knew. He knew so much more than what she wished he knew, and yet, he didn't really know her, did he? They were in a romantic bubble in France that would burst the moment they returned to reality. Men like him would eventually resent her success, would eventually feel the need to pull her down. Luke had taught her that lesson well. She didn't need a repeat course.

"Thinking of me made you grimace? I'm going to have to do something about that. Or at least earn the reaction." With that, he playfully spun her as Phillipe had done with Delphine. Ivy kept up with the beat he set as best she could, grateful for the distraction, laughing and shaking off her missteps.

"Much better," he assured. "This is how I want to see your face. Smiling with joy." With a mischievousness in his eyes, he dipped her back, keeping her secure within his hands as the song came to an end.

"Caleb!" she screeched, clasping onto his arm. Not that it was necessary. The movement was fast, sure, and at no point did he not have a secure hold.

When she rose, he pulled her to him, her body close, and looked directly into her eyes. What she

saw there stole her breath much more so than the
dip had. She was imagining things. Had to be.
In her happy fairy-tale bubble, he was looking at
her like Gramps had looked at Grammie when
they'd been dancing around the kitchen. Obviously, Ivy was hallucinating, just seeing what she
wanted to see.

"See." Did he sound a little breathless, too? "I
told you I wouldn't let you fall."

"What happened to you saying you wouldn't
dip me if I didn't want dipped?"

He pretended confusion. "Did you say that you
didn't want me to dip you back? Or just that if I
didn't, then I wouldn't have to worry about letting you fall?" His gaze held hers. "I was never
worried that you'd fall, Doc. Trust me."

Trust him? What if it was herself that she didn't
trust? What if her track record was so bad that
she'd already struck out of the relationship game?
What if every cell in her body wanted to clamor
closer and that terrified her? Even if she wanted
to trust him, she doubted she'd ever trust any
man again. Luke and the others had permanently
ruined that for her. Caleb was wonderful, but this
wasn't real life. She needed to remember that.

They danced the slow dance, Ivy painfully
cognizant of everything about him. When the
music changed to a faster number, they continued to dance. Caleb seemed determined that she
have a good time. Appreciating his efforts, she

did her best to do just that. It was so easy to have fun with Caleb, but the physical tension she felt when near him never let go. Her awareness of him, his broad shoulders that her hands rested upon, the strong lines of his nape where her fingers brushed over his hair, the thick strength of his chest and the narrowness of his waist, the warmness of his smile and eyes as they looked into hers, had her insides winding tighter and tighter. She'd never been one to be overcome with physical desire, but Caleb made her want to forego logic and just feel everything that he elicited within her body.

She wouldn't. To do that would be much too complicated. But that didn't mean she was oblivious to how sexually aware he made her feel. The way he looked at her, touched her arms, her waist, held her hands…he made her feel desirable, as if she was the most beautiful woman in the room and he only had eyes for her.

Like the prettiest flower in the garden and he'd picked her.

Caleb didn't feel that way about her, so the comparison was ridiculous. Still, as another slow song came on and they moved together, his heartbeat beneath her cheek where it was pressed against his chest, lulled her so that, temporarily, it was okay to just pretend.

For the moment, resting against a man like

Caleb was quite nice because she knew he really was strong enough to catch her, not that he'd have to because his hands were secure at her waist, warming her low back as their bodies swayed to the beat. It was probably her imagination, but she'd swear his lips brushed her hair, pressing a soft kiss there. If he had, he didn't comment and neither did she because the sensation was so brief, so light, she truly couldn't decide if it had really happened.

Delphine and Phillipe were chatty during the drive back to their home. Caleb chatted back. Ivy made noises every so often and was proud she managed that with Caleb's hand clasping hers in the car's dimly lit back seat.

When they got back to the house, Phillipe asked Caleb to help him with moving something. Ivy went on upstairs, got ready for bed, listened for him to come up the stairs. When he did, she yanked the door open, but filled with disappointment that he'd gone into his room and closed the door.

She stood there a moment, wondering what she was doing, what she'd have done had he been in the hallway.

Not anything good.

The veterans had the morning off to rest prior to the following day when they'd have a big ceremony in Colleville recognizing the date. Ivy smiled at Caleb when she came downstairs, not surprised to find him already there. He sat at the table with Phillipe, Fred and Trista, drinking coffee and eating slices of Delphine's delicious bread.

"Good morning, Ivy. I was just asking Caleb if you had been to the church at Angoville yet." Trista took a sip from her coffee bowl. "It's one of my favorite places to visit. With your medical backgrounds, I imagine you two will feel the same."

"We'd love to visit the church."

"Take my car. I will be working here this morning," Phillipe told them.

Ivy had first heard of the church, which had been set up as a medical station to treat the wounded, from her grandfather. Two American medics had worked through the night, caring for all wounded regardless of which side they fought for. It had been one of Gramps's favorite stories to tell.

Within the hour they were at the church, with its weathered tombstones marking family gravesites. No one else was at the out-of-the-ordinary tourist stop site.

"One of the medics requested to be buried here. His ashes were brought here at a later time. There's a marker in his honor to the front of the church," she told Caleb, opening the heavy wooden side door and entering the church. As with many of the places they'd visited, evidence of the past had left its mark on the building and its contents.

"The medics used the pews as beds for the wounded. The stains are from that night. They saved a lot of lives." Ivy ran her hand over a pew's worn smooth armrest. A wounded soldier had bled there. Had he been saved? "During the bombings, the church windows were shattered," she continued, moving away to stare up at one of the windows. "The French replaced some with stained glass honoring the paratroopers. Those are the two medics." She pointed to the names beneath an image of the Statue of Liberty.

"It blows my mind at how they honored the paratroopers." Caleb stared up at the stained glass.

"I wish Gramps could have seen this, everything we're seeing during this trip, so he'd know what a difference he and his fellow soldiers made."

This trip had meant so much to him. He should have been there. Should have been at her side, teasing her and showing her places he'd seen, things he'd done, finding the healing these trips were meant to bring. Ivy turned, her gaze going back to a pew stain. Emotion flooded through her. Grief, sadness, anger that he was gone and maybe even fear over how entangled she'd become with Caleb. No wonder, with how her heart had been so raw from missing Gramps. Sitting, she stared toward the altar and let her tears flow. "Why did he have to die? He should have been here with me."

Her question was a rhetorical one, so she was surprised when Caleb sat down next to her and answered.

"Everyone dies, Ivy. Everyone."

"I know that. It's just…" She swiped at her eyes. "I miss him. I had to finish residency and then there was this trip, and I've held it together, but I ache that he isn't here, that he's never going to be here again."

Caleb wrapped his arm around her and pulled her close, letting her bury her face against the strength of his shoulder. "I'm truly sorry for your loss, Ivy."

Leaning against him, Ivy quit fighting her tears and let the sobs rack her body. "He was almost a hundred, but he was vibrant, Caleb. I wasn't expecting him to die. Maybe I should have been, but I wasn't. Not yet."

"You loved him."

She nodded. "More than anything or anyone. He was my hero."

"How wonderful to have someone like that in your life to look up to."

Sniffling, she raised up to look at him. "You're right. I know you're right, but it doesn't make the pain any less. Sorry I let loose with the tears that way."

"Don't be sorry for grieving your grandfather."

"It's more that I cried in front of you. I don't want you to think I'm weak."

He snorted softly. "No worries there. I'd pit your strength and determination against anyone's."

"Really?"

Wiping his thumb across her wet cheek, he nodded. "You're an amazingly strong person, Ivy. I imagine you get that trait from your grandfather. Because of that and many other reasons, he'll never really be far away, because he'll live on through you."

Ivy blinked at him in awe. "Were you also a psychologist in the service?"

"The forced recipient of one's services a few times."

Flinching at the things he must have seen and done, Ivy stared into his eyes. Last night she'd been so caught up in the physical. This morning the attraction was still there, but it was something more she felt as she looked into his beautiful eyes. Something that spread through her, threatening to consume her, and leaving her both afraid and grateful to have met him. "Well, you must have learned a few things. I've kept all that bottled up inside me since Gramps's death. I think part of me has been in denial right up until the night before we left to come here and my grief has been waiting to burst free ever since we arrived."

"It's okay to grieve, Ivy, to cry for the loss of someone you love. That's straight from me, not the psychiatrist. Although they probably all said the same to me several times."

He'd been through so much, seen so much, and yet was full of strength and goodness. "Do you ever cry, Caleb?" she wondered out loud.

His gaze shifted to the paratrooper on the stained glass window. "Not in a long time."

He took her hand into his, lifted it to his lips and pressed a kiss there. "This church is still a place of healing, isn't it?"

"It must be." She took a deep breath. "I feel more at peace than I've felt in months."

Maybe the two paratroopers' spirits lived on, healing those who ventured inside their church's walls. Or maybe it was the man sitting beside her.

CHAPTER NINE

AFTER IVY AND CALEB returned to Phillipe and Delphine's, Ivy went through the motions, was fairly certain she said the right things at the right times as no one called her out for verbal bumblings, but she couldn't stop thinking about Caleb. Sweet, wonderful Caleb who had held her while she cried, and made it easy to lean on him, to be comforted by him, to not feel as if she had to keep up her defenses even when she knew she should.

Hadn't she promised herself that she was not going to become involved? Caleb hadn't done anything to make her think he was like her exes. Quite the opposite, and that scared her more than anything Luke and the others ever had the power to do.

Caleb was different.

Late that night, she sat on her bed, toying with a frayed quilt edge while waiting for Caleb to finish in their shared bathroom. He'd offered to let her get ready for bed first, but she'd insisted he go ahead. As tired as she was, her mind raced with trying to figure out things she wasn't going to solve in a single night. She flopped back on the time-softened quilt and stared up at the old wooden beam supports that made up the room's ceiling.

How could she sleep when her mind was filled with what-ifs, maybes and reminders of all the reasons why she shouldn't be interested in Caleb beyond friendship. None of which convinced her body that Caleb as anything more than a friend was off-limits. This wasn't some have-a-quick-fling getaway. She didn't have flings. She didn't. Never had. Never would.

So why did her pulse kick up at the thought of marching into the bathroom, taking his tooth-brush out of his hand and tasting the minty flavor on his breath as she kissed him so thoroughly that it left him breathless?

Kissing Caleb would be a mistake. Pleasurable, but still a mistake.

A rustling sounded in the hallway, then there was a light knock on her door. Ivy held her breath as if he was somehow going to hear the air moving in and out of her lungs. She worried she wasn't strong enough to see him and not give in to throwing her arms around him and kissing him until the world, and logic, subsided.

"I'm finished," he called through the solid wood. "The bathroom is yours."

Thinking it better if he thought she'd gone to sleep rather than her seeing him again when her tired mind was playing with her common sense, Ivy waited more than half an hour after she'd heard his bedroom door close prior to getting off her bed.

Still thinking on Caleb and how she needed to keep reality in focus, she quietly gathered her toiletries and pajamas. Being in France, in Normandy where she'd planned to go with Gramps, she was projecting things onto Caleb that just wouldn't hold the test of time. Admitting that to herself was vital. Everything felt magical and more intense because of where they were, because of her emotional state prior to even meeting Caleb. Once they were back to their ordinary lives, the sparks between them wouldn't feel so electric or shine so brightly.

What if it didn't end, though? What if Caleb wouldn't be threatened by her independence? By the fact that she made more money than him? What if he'd never feel the need to insult her intelligence or tear down her confidence?

Who was she kidding? Caleb was a gorgeous alpha male. She was an average female with a terrible track record with men. Of course, they'd end. To think otherwise would be nothing short of foolishness.

She opened the bedroom door. A barefoot Caleb wearing a T-shirt and loose shorts stood in the hallway. He looked almost as startled as she was. "Caleb!"

That her opening the door had caught him off guard said a lot regarding his state of mind as she doubted much took the former paratrooper by surprise. Why was he outside her door? She'd heard him go into his room, but not when he'd returned. She was obviously a mess.

Why did he come back?

Why talking to Ivy felt so imperative that Caleb had gotten out of bed made no sense. Which was why he'd hesitated outside her door for longer than he cared to admit. He would see her the following day and night as they went through the D-Day ceremonies, and the following day they'd tour the Collins Museum, then head to Paris overnight prior to catching their flight. They'd have plenty of time to talk. Yet, he hadn't been able to stay in bed. Not when he'd known she'd been awake and was ignoring his knock rather than face him. Had she thought he'd knocked on her door with hopes of an invite into her room? That hadn't been his intent. But if it had, why would she pretend to be asleep? He'd swear she was interested in him, too. Him the person and not his parents' bank account the way Katrina had mainly been. Ivy didn't even know about his parents' shipping business.

"You don't have to pretend to be asleep or

avoid me, Ivy," he assured. "Surely, you know that I'd never pressure you for something you didn't want."

Not that he didn't want her. He did. He wanted to kiss her. To lift her loosened hair and press his lips to the curve of her neck and work his way around to nuzzle her ear where he would whisper all the things he wanted to do to her, with her. He wanted—

"I thought it best if we didn't see each other again tonight."

"Because?"

"I don't want to do something I'll regret."

"You're positive you'd regret something happening between us?"

"I—I'm not sure. The past two weeks have been wonderful, but they're not the real world." Her tone doused him with cold rejection. "I've just finished residency and have a lot of life changes. I'm starting a new job, moving to my grandfather's farm, and then, there's the whole breakup with Luke. He cheated on me, had been cheating for months, and he's not the first man in my life to do so."

"I'm not a cheater, Ivy. If we were in a relationship, I'd be faithful and expect the same from you." Was that what he wanted? To be in a relationship with Ivy? Was that why he'd come to her door?

"I-it's not that I don't believe you, it's just that

the past few months have been so full of changes that I need to find balance and peace in my life." Her gaze connected with his, and were big, blue and full of doubt. "Spending time with you once we're back in Knoxville doesn't feel conducive to those things."

Katrina's barbs echoed through his mind, her accusations that he wasn't good enough, wasn't worth her time if he didn't come attached to his parents' bank account. Broken. That's what she'd called him. Mentally, emotionally and physically broken. Did Ivy see him in the same light? He hadn't thought so, but maybe she was right. Maybe the attraction between them only existed because of their enforced confinement.

"Going to dinner with a friend isn't conducive to your finding balance and peace?" He kept his voice neutral as best as he could considering his level of frustration.

Ivy's tongue darted out, moistening the corner of her mouth. Had he moved closer or had she? He could feel her body heat, could feel the magnetic pull of her body to his.

"Is that why you're outside my bedroom door, Caleb? To ask me to go to dinner with you as a friend once we're back in Knoxville? Because I'm not buying that." Her gaze dropped to his lips. "You kissed me in Carentan. On the dance floor, I felt your lips against my hair. I wasn't sure at first, but you did, didn't you?"

"I did." Just a gentle touching of his lips before he'd caught himself and pulled back. He'd had no right to kiss her and certainly shouldn't have in such a public place. All the quick kiss had done was leave him hungry for more.

"That kiss didn't feel friendly." Her hands went to his chest, perhaps to put a barrier between them as their bodies were almost touching, but the movement had the opposite effect. Her warm fingers burned through the thin cotton of his T-shirt.

"No? Then I did it all wrong."

She stared at him in confusion. "What do you mean? Wrong?"

What did he mean? Great question. He wasn't sure he knew. What he did know was that he wanted Ivy more than he'd wanted anything in a long time. He understood her concerns. He had ones of his own, but that didn't stop him from wanting her.

"I've never been that great with words, Doc. I'm more a man of action."

"I—" Her throat worked. The blue of her eyes darkened in the hallway's shadows. Her pulse throbbed at her throat. Her chin lifted. Challenge, and something more, shone on her face. "Okay, then no words. Show me."

Caleb's heart pounded at the brevity of what she was saying. He lost himself in her gaze long enough to be sure he'd not misinterpreted, then captured her lower lip between his, and eyes locked with hers, he gave a slow, gentle tug on the plump flesh.

"That doesn't feel friendly, either," she whispered against his mouth, her voice hoarse. Her hands splayed against his pecs, but rather than push him away, they slid over his chest, settling on his shoulders.

"No? I'll have to do better." With that he gave in to the hunger burning inside him and kissed Ivy. He kissed her so thoroughly, so hungrily, so completely that he struggled to know where he ended and she began. Her fingers were at his nape, pulling him closer as she kissed him back. Never had he experienced anything like kissing Ivy McEwen. Never. The closest thing he could liken the giddy sensations assailing him was to those first moments of jumping prior to opening his chute when he was free-falling. Until her, nothing had compared to the rush, to the peace of shutting out the whole world to focus on the moment, to the inherent danger that came with what he was doing.

Kissing Ivy was free-falling.

He was falling.

For Ivy.

They kissed for what felt a lifetime and yet ended much too soon. When their lips parted, he saw the invitation in her eyes. All he had to do was march her two steps back into her room, close the door, and he could spend the night exploring every tantalizing inch of her. He was tempted to do just that, to make love to her so thoroughly that she couldn't deny what was happening between them.

But lurking hesitation also darkened her eyes. It was that hesitation, knowing she'd regret anything they did come morning, that gave him the willpower to step back rather than into her room. Even if he never got another chance to make love to Ivy, he couldn't in good conscience do so tonight when he knew she wasn't fully on board. She wanted to, but she'd blame it on the late hour and being caught up in the moment. If they made love, he didn't want her looking for excuses on why it had happened.

He cupped her face, stared down into her beautiful face. Unable to resist one last taste, he kissed her again then pulled away before he reached the point to where he lost the will to do so.

"I'm going to go to my room now, Ivy, but not because I don't want to carry you into your room."

Her eyes widened, obviously surprised. "I, um, okay. If that's what you want."

Caleb wanted a lot of things, but for tonight, her answer was all that he'd get. When he did make love to Ivy, she'd have no regrets. Not regrets like the ones his body already had that he'd be spending the night alone in his room down the hallway rather than with the woman who was backing away from him physically and emotionally, because uncertainty now far outweighed the eagerness he'd witnessed only moments before. What was it about her that made him want her to trust him enough to come to him with no hesitations, and for him to be enough just as he was?

If not spending the night alone had been his end game, then he'd have never walked away. Which begged the question: What was his end game where Ivy was concerned? Did he have one, or was she right that they were just caught up in their close proximity?

Their midmorning Collins Museum tour was their last scheduled event of the trip. The Château de Franquetot had been purchased several years prior with the new owners turning the rundown castle into a museum. Now the home was much as it had been when used as the army headquarters. The owner himself greeted them, giving their veterans a private tour, and even allowing Owen to sit in a chair at a desk General Eisenhower had once used. Although she still battled with the sting of his rejection, Ivy laughed when Caleb picked out more key chains from the gift shop.

He scooped up a few more. "What?"

"I'm wondering if you truly have that many

friends or if you've got a problem and secretly hoard key chains."

"You've figured me out." His grin had her heart flopping around as if it had forgotten how to properly beat.

"Not even close," she said before she could think better of it.

He didn't seem fazed, just continued smiling as he put the key chains on the counter, then paid for them. Ordering her pulse to calm down, Ivy thumbed through some postcards. She paused at one that was of the church in Angoville-au-Plain.

"You should get that one."

Recalling how she'd sobbed into his shoulder there, Ivy frowned and put the card back. "You forget my aversion to touristy trinkets."

"Here." He removed the card she'd just replaced. "I'm buying this for you."

Heat flooded through her body. "I don't need a postcard, Caleb."

"Sure, you do. If nothing else, you can add it to your trunk."

"That trunk is at my parents' house." She watched as he selected a few more postcards. "What are you doing?"

"Buying postcards. You should pick something to give to your parents. You mentioned doing so to be funny."

"I'm not that funny."

"You make me smile."

Ivy's cheeks heated further. Yeah, she imagined she had. He'd probably been laughing his butt off at her expense two nights ago. The day before he'd acted as if nothing had happened, smiling frequently, but she'd felt awkward. Fortunately, with it being June 6, their schedule had been packed, starting with the ceremony in Colleville at the American Cemetery and ending with a farewell dinner hosted by a local veterans' organization. Not once had he acted as if anything unusual had happened the night before and by the time Ivy had gone to bed, she'd almost questioned if she'd dreamed his kiss and what followed.

"My parents haven't visited Normandy but have been to Paris several times. That's much more their style of traveling." As they'd loved history, she might have questioned that except her mother had an aversion to most things that had to do with Gramps.

"It's not on a lot of folks' top vacation spots."

"If they'd ever been here, seen the way it is now, it would be." It truly was one of the most gorgeous places she'd ever been. "The wide-open green fields, the gorgeous coastline and beaches, and the people who are so wonderful."

"We'll have to come back."

Her gaze cut to his, but he'd turned toward the cashier and was paying for the postcard.

She studied his profile, wondering why her

heart flew at such an innocent comment. He hadn't meant they come back as in they come back *together* but rather as part of SMVF. Of course, that was what he'd meant. It was all she'd wanted him to mean. Anything more would just complicate an already complicated situation.

Frustrated with herself, she left the gift shop and headed toward the small restaurant at the other end of the main floor. Groups of soldiers and reenactors laughed and shared stories. It was a merry scene and somehow grated on Ivy, to where she opted to wait outdoors instead of inside with the others.

Mary followed her. "I can't believe it's over and that we're about to head back to Paris."

Ivy couldn't, either. This time the following day they'd be on their flight home. Then what? Other than the panic attacks she was sure to have while on the plane, that is.

"Hopefully, we'll make it there in time to see some of the sites," Mary continued, sounding wistful. "I've never seen the Eiffel Tower."

"This was my first time to Europe, so I've never seen it, either," Ivy admitted. "Once we get settled into the hotel, we'll hire a car. We can't be in Paris and not see the Eiffel Tower."

Several of the others wanted to go, too, as most hadn't seen the iconic tower. Slade and Suzie were quite enthusiastic about going, just as they'd become quite enthusiastic about each other. They didn't mind who knew as they held hands and looked at each other with googly eyes. Oh, to be so young and naive that it always started that way but ended with one party's heart broken. In Ivy's case, it was always her.

Mary nudged her. "You look at Caleb the same way as those two lovebirds."

"Stop it," she told Mary, shaking her head. "You're mistaken."

Mary obviously didn't believe her as she grinned and asked, "Are you going to see him when we get back to Knoxville?"

"I imagine we'll see each other at the hospital from time to time." Would it be torture to see him, or a reminder of a close call she'd narrowly escaped?

Mary's gaze met Ivy's. "Not what I meant, but also not my business. Sorry."

Ivy sighed. "It's okay. I just don't know how else to answer. Caleb is a great guy, but we're just friends." Were they even that? Recalling his "friendly" kiss, Ivy swallowed. What had his kisses meant? His walking away? How could he act so normal, as if nothing had happened, when she wanted to demand answers from him? Had he lain in bed the night before thinking about their hallway encounter? Had he closed his eyes and relived the feel of his lips against hers the way that she'd done? Probably not. Otherwise, how could he be so casually relaxed around her when she was wound tighter than the Gordian knot.

Mary gave her a disappointed look, then her eyes brightened. "There's still time. We should invite Caleb to go with us tonight."

"Go with you where?" Caleb joined where they stood on the lawn. Had Mary seen him walking toward them and that's why she'd said what she'd said, knowing he'd hear? Not that Ivy wouldn't have invited him to go. Anyone from their group was welcome. Caleb had done nothing wrong other than witness her embarrassing surrender to their chemistry. Thank goodness he'd not done the same or their last two days would have been tough.

"To the Eiffel Tower," Mary supplied before Ivy could. "We're hoping to arrive in Paris in time to see the tower for ourselves."

Caleb turned toward Ivy. "You realize the Eiffel Tower is about an hour's drive from the airport hotel where we'll be staying?"

Ivy winced. No, she hadn't realized. She should have looked at a map. Paris was a big city. Disappointment showed on Mary's face and Ivy made a quick decision. "How far away it is doesn't matter. We're going to the Eiffel Tower even if it means we don't sleep until we're on the plane. We can't come all this way and not see France's most iconic structure." When else was she going to be in Paris? Probably never. "Getting our veterans on and off the train wouldn't be easy, so we'll splurge and hire a driver. More than one, if needed. We'll figure it out after we get to the hotel and know our time frame and who wants to go."

Mary clasped her hands together. "This is exciting. I've always dreamed of seeing the Eiffel Tower. I'm so glad we're going for it."

Not looking directly toward Caleb, Ivy nodded. "Sometimes life only gives us one opportunity to do certain things. If we choose to let them pass us by, we'll regret it forever."

Caleb's brow lifted. She hadn't consciously aimed the comment at him, but if the shoe fit… unfortunately, she suspected that she was going to be the one living with regrets.

CHAPTER TEN

BY THE TIME they'd ridden the four hours from Normandy to the airport, the veterans were too tired to want to travel into central Paris. Doing so would put them arriving back at the hotel after midnight. Knowing it was his last night in France with Ivy, Caleb could push through any fatigue. At some point before they arrived back in Knoxville, they needed to talk. He'd upset her with leaving her room and he wanted to set the record straight to make sure she understood why he'd done what he had. They'd had their busiest schedule the day prior and hadn't had a chance to talk. At some point prior to arriving in Knoxville, he'd make sure they found time.

"We can't leave the veterans here without medical." Disappointment shone on Ivy's face. "I'll make arrangements for cars to pick up those going, and I'll stay to keep watch on those staying here."

"I'll stay," Caleb offered. He couldn't imagine anyone he'd rather see the Eiffel Tower with than

Ivy, but if they couldn't both leave the hotel, he wasn't going at the expense of Ivy being able to.

"No, I will," she immediately countered, not surprising Caleb. To the end, she viewed taking care of the veterans as mainly her responsibility and she put that first.

He started to insist he be the one to stay, but Lara shook her head. "Both of you go. I was on the fence anyway. I'm worn out and saw the tower when my husband and I visited Paris last fall." When Ivy started to protest, the nurse shook her head. "No, really, go. I'm looking forward to changing into something comfy and relaxing." When Ivy started to protest more, Lara gave her a pointed look. "Go. I'll make sure all the guys are safely in their rooms and be here if they need anything. Y'all have taken care of most everything on this trip. Let me do this. Have fun and take lots of photos."

Caleb shot the nurse a grateful smile. He owed her big for the extra time with Ivy, especially with it being a whirlwind night viewing of Paris's most iconic tourist spot. "Thanks, Lara."

Once at the hotel, a local helped arrange for a hired van to drive them for short stops at a couple of central Paris sites with a longer stop planned at the tower. Seven of their group ended up in the van. The thirtyish-years-old French driver took them to the Arc de Triomphe first. The talkative man pulled the van to the side of the road.

Laughing, they jumped out, snapped photos, including a group shot taken by their driver, then hopped back into the van. Their next stop was the Louvre. Slade and Suzie were all giggly as they posed for pictures with their fingers touching the top of the glass pyramid. Everyone took similar staged photos, making silly poses, then marveling at the architecture.

"How gorgeous this must be in the daylight where you can make out the intricate details," Ivy mused, staring in awe at the museum.

"It's amazing," Caleb agreed, enthralled with her expression as much as he was with the magnificent building. "Just as you are. Thanks for making this happen. The others are having a great time."

Her gaze cut to his, challenge sparkling there that he knew was rooted in his having gone back to his room. "But you're not?"

"I thought that was a given." But maybe not. They needed to talk. In private.

Ivy eyed him a moment, then went back to taking in the museum. "I'd love to come back and just wander around. I bet you could spend an entire day and not get close to seeing everything."

"Probably not. The *Mona Lisa* is here," he said. "If we saw her, do you think we could figure out what she was smiling at?"

Ivy's brow lifted. "Opposed to the millions of others who've seen her and speculated?"

Caleb laughed. "I have my theories."

"Okay, now you have me curious. What are your theories on why da Vinci painted her smiling?"

"It's obvious." Pausing for effect, he kept a straight face. "To make us wonder."

Ivy rolled her eyes. "Brilliant. The mystery is solved."

He chuckled. "Seriously, it's the smile that gets folks to talking. Who was there with them? Or was anyone? Who was she thinking about? A lover, perhaps?"

"Of course, you'd wonder that."

His gaze cut to hers. "Why 'of course'?"

"Because you're a man." Even as she said it, she averted her eyes and he'd swear she was blushing.

Knowing she was thinking about the other night and not wanting her to throw additional walls up, he puffed out his chest. "Glad you've noticed."

"Difficult not to."

"Good. I want you to notice."

Her gaze narrowed. "Really? Because that's not the impression you gave the other night."

He held up his hand. "We need to talk, but now's not the time. Mary's on her way over here. So, we'll just enjoy Paris with our friends and each other. Deal?"

Looking torn, she sighed. "You're right. It's

our last night in France. Who wants to dwell on past mistakes?"

He'd like to question her on just what past mistakes she meant, but Mary was walking toward them. He had a pretty good idea, anyway. He hadn't been wrong to go to his room, but he had dwelt on doing so. Mostly because he kept questioning why he had felt he needed to. Why hadn't he just taken what Ivy offered? Why had it mattered so much to him that she freely give herself to him rather than just be caught up in a passionate moment?

Wouldn't that only make sense if he wanted something more from Ivy than just a night or two? He'd not wanted that since Katrina. Since the first round of their relationship, because he realized he'd never wanted more from Katrina the second time, when he'd been laid up in a hospital bed, mourning his best friend's death and the loss of his career. She'd swooped in, beautiful and breaking up the boredom of his hospital stay, and he'd let her because he had nothing else to do beyond rehabilitating his busted body. When she'd given him the ultimatum of "making something of his life" or losing her, saying goodbye was easy. Much easier than saying goodbye to Ivy would be after only knowing her two weeks.

"Come on, guys. Our driver is ready to roll," Mary called, gesturing to the parked van.

They got back in, oohing and ahhing as they

crossed the Pont de Bir-Hakeim. The Frenchman drove them the short distance to the Eiffel Tower, then pulled over for them to jump out, telling them he'd arrive in an hour to the exact spot so they could return to their hotel.

Street vendors were along the sidewalk leading to the tower. They sold everything from balloons to sparkling replicas of the majestic structure towering above them.

"I read that the tower twinkles like a Christmas tree for five minutes on the hour each night," Mary enthused. "Look at how magnificent it is lit. I think seeing the tower at night is better than if we'd come during the daylight."

"That's awesome that we'll get to witness the twinkling lights," Ivy agreed as they continued to walk toward the tower's base. "It's surreal that we're in Paris, looking up at the Eiffel Tower. It really is magnificent."

"Let's take photos here," Linda suggested. "If we get too close it'll be more difficult to get all of the tower in the shot."

"Good point."

They paused and took group shots with Caleb holding his cell phone as far out in front of him as his arm would reach. He angled his hand to where he could get as much of their entourage and the tower as possible.

Slade and Suzie took multiple selfies, then had Linda take a picture of them. When done, they took off, saying they were going to watch the tower from the bridge.

"Here, let me take a picture of you and Ivy with the tower in the background." Mary reached for his phone and Caleb handed it over.

Ivy's eyes narrowed for the briefest second, but she smiled as Mary took several photos.

Mary handed back his phone, then looked ahead as a couple vacated a bench where they'd been sitting. "I'm going to snag that bench and watch the lights from there."

"Me, too," Linda said, joining her, and patting the bench. "Jimmy," she said to the son of one of the veterans. "There's room if you want to keep two ladies company."

Everyone other than Ivy and Caleb opted to view the tower without walking to the park.

She turned to him as soon as they were outside hearing range. "Did you pay them to do that?"

He feigned innocence. "To do what?"

"Ditch us for a bench so we'd be alone." She eyed him suspiciously.

"Not me, but I wouldn't put it past Mary." He glanced toward her, making eye contact. "I can't say I'm sorry, though."

"That we got ditched?"

He nodded. "I like them, but I'd rather see the Eiffel Tower with you without an audience."

She didn't say anything in response to his comment, just looked away to stare up at the tower.

"It's such an iconic place that I've seen photos of so many times that actually being here doesn't feel real."

Being at the Eiffel Tower with Ivy, strolling toward the base, just the two of them, was surreal. The moon was bright above them, casting an almost magical blue hue to the night sky. With the tower magnificently jutting upward, they could be walking into a movie scene. A romantic one. One where he got to be the hero, without flaws or a past.

He reached for Ivy's hand and was grateful she didn't pull away. Maybe she was caught up in the magic of where they were, too, because she clasped his hand, giving it a slight squeeze.

"This trip was everything it should have been, except that Gramps wasn't here."

His heart ached at how much grief he heard in her voice for her grandfather. Holding her while she'd cried at the Angoville church had about gutted him. He understood grief. Not a day went by that he didn't miss Blake. "He'd be so proud of you, Ivy."

Just as Blake would be proud of him for what he'd accomplished in Knoxville, for being there to help his wife, Jordan make the ambulance service a success.

Pausing, Ivy turned toward him, her big blue eyes pinning him with the yearning in them. "How can you know that?"

Brushing a hair back from her face, he nodded. "Because any grandfather or parent would be proud to be related to you."

Swallowing, she gave a nervous laugh. "Maybe. I'm not always easy to live with."

"I'll make a note of it."

Her eyes widened.

"Sorry. I didn't mean—"

"I know," she interrupted. "I just, oh, never mind. We had a deal not to discuss anything too serious. How much longer until the sparkles?"

Not exactly how he recalled their "deal" conversation, but Caleb glanced at his watch. "About twenty minutes. Let's find a place to sit at Champ de Mars."

Maybe they could talk once there.

The park was decently lit. Mostly couples with a few families scattered over the grassy lawn. A few vendors went from group to group. They came to an area that wasn't too close to the others dreamily watching the tower.

"This looks like a good spot." Ivy moved her foot around over the grass.

"If I'd known we were going to do this, I would have brought a blanket." Or at least the lightweight jacket in his suitcase so that he could spread it for her to sit on.

"If I'd known we were going to do this, you wouldn't have had to," she countered, still riffling through the grass with her foot.

"Because you would have brought a blanket to sit on?" He hoped that's what she'd meant and that she wasn't implying that she'd have insisted upon being the one to stay at the hotel.

Nodding, then, facing the tower, she sat down. "I'm not worried about getting dirty, Caleb. This is a park. I just didn't want to have a smelly surprise if someone didn't clean up after their pet."

"Good thinking." He sat down next to her and might have gone for her hand, but she wrapped her arms around her knees and gazed up at the tower. The reflection lit her face, giving her an ethereal look. Beautiful.

Caleb grabbed his phone and snapped a shot.

Turning toward him, she arched a brow. "You missed. The tower is that way."

He shook his head. "I got what I wanted."

She breathed in sharply. "I think this place is getting to me."

"In what way?" Although, he knew. They were surrounded by amorous couples, and he longed for that blanket so they could lie back and stare up at the tower while cuddled together. *Cuddled?* Had he seriously just thought cuddled? He was not a cuddler. Not ever. Not even with Katrina when he'd been little more than a schoolkid.

"Being here makes me wonder at my life priorities," she answered after a few moments.

"Such as?"

"Actually, it's not really my life priorities that

are in question. At one time, I wanted a relationship, marriage, all those things, you know?"

"But you don't now?" he asked, glad she was foregoing their not discussing anything serious. They needed to discuss serious things. They'd be on the flight home in the morning.

"I've been telling myself I don't ever since Luke and I broke up."

Luke. The boyfriend who'd done her wrong. The guy must have been an idiot to mess things up with Ivy. "You said he cheated on you. What happened?"

She hesitated, then blurted out, "He went astray and blamed me."

"That's ballsy."

"I thought so at the time."

"You don't now?"

She propped her elbows against her knees and stared at the tower. "Now I can't believe I'm wasting my breath talking about him, especially while at one of the most romantic places in the world."

"With me."

"With you." Emotion gave her words a raspy sound, hinting that being with him was as pertinent as where they were, perhaps more so.

"Can I hold your hand, Ivy?"

"You didn't ask a few minutes ago when we were walking here," she reminded, eyeing him curiously.

"True, but I feel as if I should ask now." Because his question was about much more than holding her hand and they both knew it. "Can I hold your hand, Ivy?"

She swallowed and for a moment, he wondered if she was going to reject him as she seemed to believe he'd done to her outside her room. But after a few moments, she shrugged.

"If you want to."

"I wouldn't have asked if I didn't want to, Ivy. The question is, do you want to hold my hand?"

Ivy wanted to. No doubt about that. Should she? was the real question. They would be heading home tomorrow, and everything would change. They'd no longer be caught up in the magic of France, but back in the real world. Nothing would be the same. Not between them and not in her life. She'd be sorting things at the farm, starting her job, and…missing moments like the one she was living.

"Yes, I'd like that."

"Me, too." Caleb took her hand, laced their fingers, and hand in hand, they tower-and-people-watched in silence. Again, it struck her how, despite everything, comfortable silence with Caleb was. She felt no need to say anything or to try to entertain him.

He glanced at his watch. "Less than a minute to go until the light show."

Never in a million years would Ivy have believed it if someone had told her two weeks ago she'd be sitting in a Parisian park with the most wonderful man she'd ever met, holding his hand even though he'd rejected her, and waiting for the Eiffel Tower to begin its show. Life sure could be strange.

The tower began to twinkle, sparkling in the sky.

"Oh! That's beautiful," Ivy breathed.

"Yes."

She glanced toward him. Around them couples were kissing and snapping photos. Ivy couldn't pull her gaze from his as the sparkling tower reflected in his amber eyes. "Caleb."

She didn't say anything more. Nothing more was needed. He knew everything she was thinking, feeling. He must have because he leaned toward her and, gaze locked with hers, pressed his lips to hers.

Ivy's stomach did flip-flops and somersaults and gymnastic moves worthy of a gold medal. Part of her longed to deepen the kiss, to throw her arms around him and push him back on the lawn and kiss him until neither of them could breathe. Another wanted to demand why he was kissing her when he'd walked away from her kisses just two nights ago. But there was something so magical about his gentle caressing of her mouth that she could only stare into his eyes and feel, completely mesmerized by what he was doing. By what was happening inside her chest. She was sparkling every bit as brightly as the tower. More so. Surely, she shined as bright a beacon over the city?

"Ville de l'Amour," a man said in a strong French accent from nearby, causing Ivy to jerk back from Caleb. How could she have forgotten that they were in a public park? Yes, there were lots of other couples, some of whom were still kissing, but Ivy had never been big on public displays of affection. Or maybe the men she'd dated had never been into PDA. She honestly wasn't sure.

"We should meet up with the others." She covered her mouth with her hand, as if that would somehow protect her from whatever it was Caleb's kiss had done to her. She certainly felt as if he'd cast a spell. Or maybe it was Paris. But whatever it was, it wasn't love. That's not what she was feeling. Friendship. Attraction. Euphoria from being in the most romantic city in the world. No wonder crazy things were happening inside her. That was the real allure of Paris. It made people long to believe in something that didn't seem to exist in her generation.

Ville de l'Amour, indeed. More like City of Make-Believe.

Their seating assignments were more scattered on the flight back to the States than they had been on their trip to France. Caleb had been assigned the aisle seat next to Owen and Suzie, but Slade asked to swap seats so he could sit beside Suzie. Caleb hadn't needed convincing. Slade's seat had been next to the woman whose kiss had added fireworks to the Eiffel Tower's light show the night before. No one might have seen the display, but Caleb had felt the explosions rock through him. Mini ones were going off while he currently held her hand.

No one could readily see their hands with how they were tucked low between them, but Ivy had held on tight when he'd taken her hand as the plane taxied down the runway for liftoff.

Glancing toward where Ivy hunkered into her seat, eyes closed, focusing on her breathing, he wished he could ease her fear of flying. "You okay, Doc?"

She lifted one lid enough to peek out at him. "I'm zooming through the air at five hundred miles an hour. What do you think?"

That she was beautiful, smart, funny and that he wished the plane would slow down so they'd have more time together. Two weeks with Ivy hadn't been nearly enough. Surely, she felt the same. How could she not after the kiss they'd shared the night before? He didn't consider himself a romantic man, but he couldn't imagine a more perfect kiss than sitting on the grassy lawn with the twinkling Eiffel Tower providing the mood lighting. Good grief, with thoughts like that, maybe he was a romantic man. Ivy made him feel romantic, made him want to be so he could shower her with affection and erase all traces of her exes' wrongs.

"I think you're doing great. Just keep focusing on your breathing. Deep breath in. Slow exhale out."

Her nostrils flared with another big breath in that she slowly blew out through pursed lips. "Yeah, it's not working. Distract me, Caleb," she ordered. "Tell me about you, something that I don't already know."

"Something you don't know?" He felt so connected to her it was difficult to imagine that there were still many things she didn't know about him. Yet, when those big blue eyes connected with his, he'd swear she knew him better than anyone in the ways that mattered most. "I grew up in Atlanta. My family still lives there."

"Atlanta's not too far from Knoxville. Just a few hours." They hit a bump of turbulence and she sucked in a few rapid deep breaths. "Keep talking."

Caleb gave her hand a reassuring squeeze. "I'm a middle child. My brother is older, and my sister is younger."

"You're lucky. I always wanted siblings. Tell me about them."

"They're both seemingly happily married and

have a couple of kids a piece, which is just another way I'm different."

Her gaze cut to him, and curiosity shone in her eyes.

"Not happily married and as far as I know, no kids," he continued, thinking her grasp had relaxed a little where she gripped his hand.

"How else are you different?"

"By worldly standards, they're very successful."

"And you're not?"

He'd never questioned his success while serving in the military, but what about since? He'd gone to school while rehabbing, was working to help Jordan, but did he see himself as successful when he no longer did what he longed to be doing?

"My life isn't what my parents would have chosen, but I'm content." He paused, then started over. "Actually, to say I've accepted my life would be more accurate than saying I'm content."

Had he really accepted that he would never jump again? His orthopedic surgeon assured him that jumping wasn't worth the risk and advised him not to do so. That Caleb had recovered too well to blow it on a moment's pleasure. Some days, he considered taking the chance just to feel the wind whipping around him again. Not as a paratrooper. He knew the army wouldn't take him back as a jumper with the hardware that remained in his leg, but just to jump for the exhilaration doing so gave him.

"I always knew I'd eventually have to do something after my paratrooper days, but I saw myself continuing in the army. I can reapply for enlistment, but my right tibia and fibula have plates and pins holding them together. They'd have to be removed first." Which his surgeon also did not recommend. "Even if I have surgery to remove my hardware, I'm in my thirties. That's older for a paratrooper, so if I opted to enlist, it would be to pursue a different military occupational specialty. I'd be starting from the ground up and have to requalify on all points."

Her eyes widened. "Are you considering enlisting again?"

"The army is never far from my thoughts. Going out on medical doesn't prevent me from reenlisting once healed. That doesn't mean they'd approve me again, though."

The plane shook with more turbulence and a noise sounded from deep in Ivy's throat.

"I've healed better than the orthopedic surgeon expected due to the amount of damage in my leg. I'm always aware of the injury, but it doesn't stop me from most aspects of my life."

"Did you land wrong? Is that how you fractured your leg?"

He hesitated long enough that she likely knew it had been more than a simple landing mishap.

He considered not telling her, but he wanted Ivy to know him the way he felt she already did. Things like how he'd gotten hurt were just life details to fill in the blanks of who he was.

"We jumped behind enemy lines, not knowing our mission had been compromised. Our plane was hit not long after we'd jumped. Shrapnel was all around us." The noise, smell and fear he'd felt in those moments flashed though his mind. "I was lucky that I was close to the ground when a piece of metal hit my leg."

Ivy's jaw dropped. "You could have been killed."

Blake had been. She'd wanted distraction. He'd achieved that because she looked at him with such intensity that, at least momentarily, she'd forgotten all about the plane.

"But I wasn't," he reminded. "My injured leg gave way upon impact with the ground, fracturing my leg bones in multiple areas." Was that pity in her eyes? He didn't need pity. Not from her or anyone. "I can do whatever I want except for high impact activities."

"Such as jumping out of an airplane?"

He snorted. "It's not the jumping that's the issue. It's the landing."

This time it was her giving his hand a squeeze. "Sorry, not sorry."

His brow arched.

"The thought of you jumping out of an airplane terrifies me," she admitted.

Yet he longed to experience that rush. "It's the greatest, most peaceful feeling in the world when you're up there."

"We'll just have to disagree, because I can assure you 'a peaceful feeling' is not what I'd be experiencing if I was free-falling through the sky."

He half smiled. "Maybe not, but for me, there's nothing better than when I'm up there."

He attempted to explain the beauty of the earth below, the intense colors of the atmosphere, the way he connected with every breath and beat of his body and how everything came into focus. Ivy listened to his words, hearing the passion in his voice, hearing the grief in how much he obviously missed something he'd loved so much. But no amount of words was going to convince her to jump out of a plane.

"How did you end up a paramedic?" she asked. "Did it have something to do with your care after your leg injury?"

"That would make sense under normal circumstances, but I was in the Middle East. The only help coming for me was my brothers-and-sisters-in-arms. So my accident wasn't how it happened. Not really, although it indirectly played a role," he admitted. "I was in a bad mental place after my injury. I was pushing my body as far as I could with my physical therapy, but my mind had too much free time to dwell on the things that had happened. It wasn't good. I wasn't good. An army buddy convinced me to go back to school so I could work at TransCare. It was a turning point for me. I owe Jordan a lot."

"I've seen TransCare advertisements."

"Probably the billboard on I-40."

"That's right. I have seen that. If your friend was smart, he'd put your photo on that ad. You'd be getting all kinds of calls."

Caleb chuckled. "Jordan's a she and I'll be sure to tell her."

Surprise shone in Ivy's eyes. "Your army buddy is a woman?"

"Yep. There are women paratroopers. We met in airborne school. I had planned to be a lifer, but that was never her intention. She always talked about how much she loved Knoxville and, as much as she loved jumping, she didn't reenlist, but went to paramedic school instead."

"And convinced you to do the same."

"As I said, I was in a bad mental place when she convinced me that she needed my help. I'm not sure she really did. She's tough and would have made it without me, but as my buddy Blake's widow, I'd do anything for her, and she knew it."

Ivy had a million questions, but hadn't she already decided that she and Caleb were just a fairy tale of their circumstances? They'd been thrown together for two weeks in the most romantic country in the world. No wonder they'd gotten caught up in the fairy tale. Who wouldn't have?

Soon they'd be home and back to the real world. Caleb Rivers wouldn't look so wonderfully perfect then. Besides, did she really think he was any different from every other man who'd interested her? That her making more than him wouldn't eventually get to him and undermine how he viewed and treated her? But what if she was wrong?

"Do you see yourself working for TransCare long term, then?"

He considered a moment, then shrugged. "I'm not sure. I'd reenlist if I could jump, but that isn't in my future. I enjoy working at TransCare, plus I owe it to Blake to help Jordan for however long she needs me, so who knows? I might stay there."

"What about money?" What an awkward conversation? "Do you make enough to get by okay on your paramedic pay?"

"I get by. My wants are pretty basic." He eyed her curiously. "What about you? Are you going to get by okay or are you bogged down with student loans from med school?"

She was botching this but didn't know better words to use than just asking him forthright. "Does it bother you that I make more money than you?"

His forehead scrunched. "Should it?"

"I…" She thought over Luke's cruel words, his accusation that she'd made him feel inferior. She couldn't imagine Caleb ever feeling inferior. But in the beginning, would she have thought Luke would? He'd had a good job, was successful at what he did and had seemed secure in who he was. That he'd eventually felt the need to berate her at every opportunity, had her saying, "Yeah, I think it should."

What was she doing? He'd not said he wanted a relationship with her. Not really. Yes, she saw it in his eyes, but the past haunted her. She just didn't think she could take Caleb breaking her heart. Much better to be up-front and give voice to her concerns.

He let go of her hand, twisted in his seat to more fully face her. "It doesn't, but that you think it should, does bother me. Care to explain?"

"It's not that it bothers me. It's that it's going to bother you that you aren't more…" That didn't come out right, because, really, could she imagine him being more than what he was when he seemed close to perfect? But she couldn't take back her poor word choice, couldn't erase how his face splotched red.

"That I'm not more than who I am?" His jaw tightened. "You mean financially?"

Ivy inwardly cringed. This conversation felt so wrong. It was wrong. They were sitting on a plane over the Atlantic Ocean and she was grilling Caleb over the mistakes she'd made in choosing past relationships.

"After my breakup with Luke, I promised myself that I wasn't going to become involved with anyone who didn't make more money than me. Then, I met you and you seem so wonderful, but be honest, the past two weeks have been anything but reality. Relationships are difficult enough without disproportionate incomes creating feelings of insecurity. I've been through that three times, and each time it's ended with my heart getting trampled on."

"I'm not your ex."

"I know that, but what about down the road? Relationships always seem shiny in the beginning, but eventually a person needs to learn to keep her eyes open to what's coming." Was she trying to convince him or herself?

He eyed her a minute then shook his head. "So, basically you don't want a relationship with me because I don't make more money than you?" Disappointment shone on his handsome face. "There are things far more important about a person than what's written on their bank statement. I didn't think that was who you were, Ivy, that a job title or bank account mattered so much to you."

How did she explain that she knew it would matter to *him* at some future point? That the past had taught her that eventually his masculinity would feel threatened, and he'd take it out on her? Caleb feeling threatened by anything seemed impossible, but she refused to be made a fool of again.

"The past two weeks have been wonderful, Caleb." Taking a deep breath, she said what she believed needed to be said. For both of them. Better to end things now than to feel the complete devastation that would come if she and Caleb embarked on a relationship, and he betrayed her. How would she ever recover from *him*? "A trip I've dreamed of in so many ways, but I never intended to meet someone. I have a lot going on in my life and you don't fit in with those plans."

Was that disgust in his eyes? Or just a reflection of what she was feeling bouncing back at her? Her words made her stomach roil. No matter. If she didn't completely end things with Caleb, he might convince her to give their relationship a go and then when things fell apart, she'd be utterly devastated. She might not have known him long, but she recognized that Caleb was different, that her reactions to him were more potent, that he had more power over her than any man ever had and that scared her. Much better to remember France as the magical experience it was than to sully the memory with a tragic ending to the fairy tale.

CHAPTER ELEVEN

"You're invited to join Roy at his A Century of Life celebration." Ivy read out the card and smiled. She'd gone to the last Smoky Mountain Veteran Foundation monthly meeting. Being with the group had filled her with such mixed emotions. Happiness at seeing the people she felt so close with. Glad that Caleb wasn't there. Glad? That wasn't the only emotion she'd felt. Not by far. She missed him.

Had she secretly been hoping he would be? Apparently, he and Stan had volunteered with a fundraiser a few weeks prior. Ivy had been scheduled in the emergency department that Saturday and hadn't been able to attend. When she'd heard that he'd been there, she'd felt…longing. How could she miss someone she'd only spent two weeks with?

Other than the fact that she couldn't seem to keep him from her mind, she'd fallen into a good routine over the past two months, working at the farm to sort through her grandfather's paperwork and business affairs. Fortunately, Mr. Griggs wanted to continue leasing the land for his cattle and crops, lifting a huge burden off Ivy for at least the next few years. Her hospital work crew was awesome and she'd already made several friends whom she adored. Life was good.

Only, it wasn't.

There was a huge hole in her chest the size of which she'd never known. Yes, she grieved Gramps and always would, but she'd come to terms with his death, knowing he'd lived a good life, and that he'd known how much she adored him. She'd miss him always. But it was Caleb she missed in ways that made no sense. Then again, how many dates did one have to go on to equal being together almost nonstop for two weeks?

He'd never been to the farm, so why could she look around the kitchen and see him standing at the sink? Or walk to the pond and see him sitting on the bank, fishing pole in hand, trying to catch one of the many fish her grandfather had stocked it with years before? Why, when she closed her eyes, did she transport from a grassy park at the base of the Eiffel Tower to lying on a blanket in a field with him with the Smoky Mountains as their backdrop?

Would he be at Roy's party? Outside of her imaginings, she'd not seen him. Not that he hadn't been at the hospital. He had. There was always an excited buzz from the single female hospital staff anytime he was in the building. One bolder nurse said she'd given him her phone number.

Oh, how that would hurt, to see or hear of Caleb with another woman. She'd experienced it before. Kenny had almost immediately started dating other girls when Ivy had left for college. Beau had gotten his ex-girlfriend pregnant while he and Ivy were still dating. Luke had cheated on her with the college student and looking back, that probably wasn't his first time cheating, just the first she'd caught him. And, although Ivy had been heartbroken, she wasn't so sure it had been over the man so much as the betrayal. Three times and she was out. It was what she'd told herself prior to her trip to France.

One of the cardiologists had asked her out a few times, but Ivy hadn't gone, telling him she had no interest in dating. He met the dating conditions she'd set, was a nice guy, but it was the truth. She didn't want to date. How could she when she missed a man whom she'd spent two fantastic weeks with more than she'd thought possible.

Going to her bedroom, she opened her nightstand drawer and pulled out the postcard of the church he'd given her. Nostalgia hit, as did tears, and soon she was sobbing as intensely as she had while sitting on the bloodstained pew. Only, this time, Caleb wasn't there to hold her while she cried. No one was.

Reaching for her cellphone, she dialed a number. "Mom, is my trunk still in my old room's closet? Yes? Awesome. Is it okay if I come to Nashville? I'd like to have it and spend some time with you and Dad."

"Happy birthday to you. Happy birthday, dear Roy. Happy birthday to you! And many more!" Cheers erupted in the Strawberry Plains church community room where Roy's birthday party was being held. Roy had lived in the east Tennessee town most of his life and there was a large crowd of friends and family, including many from the SMVF.

"Can you believe our whole group from Normandy made it today for Dad's party?" Mary enthused, handing Ivy a cup of punch. "I can't begin to convey how happy that makes me. Dad and I talk about how close we felt to everyone there and how much we've missed seeing everyone together the past three months."

Ivy knew exactly how Mary felt. She experienced it herself.

"Would you look at Slade and Suzie?" Mary beamed at the young couple. "They're as cute as can be and still making googly eyes at each other."

Ivy glanced toward them, and they did look very much in love as they chatted with Linda and her husband. Owen was with them, as was Paul.

"But I will admit that I'm disappointed about one thing," Mary continued, causing Ivy's gaze to shift back to her. "I am stunned that you and Caleb dropped the ball on what was happening between you in France."

Ivy inwardly cringed. She had enough second guesses without Mary adding to them. So she took a sip of punch then smiled at the lady she'd come to adore. "France was a magical place and made things seem shinier than what they were, Mary. That's all."

Mary's red-brown brow arched. "Do you believe that?"

Ivy sought out where Caleb stood, fruit punch in hand, talking with Jimmy. As if sensing she was looking his way, his amber eyes shifted to where they stared directly into hers. Then, just as quickly, he looked away, dousing her with ice water.

Ivy swallowed the lump that formed in her throat, but still could barely breathe. She'd not been able to stop thinking about him. The shine hadn't worn off. Not for her. For Caleb, he couldn't even stand to look at her. Nausea tightened her throat.

What had she done?

"France wasn't what made certain things appear shiny," Mary unnecessarily pointed out. "A person only had to look at you two together to see the sparks."

"It doesn't matter now, Mary." She'd been too scared of failure, of getting hurt, to even try with Caleb. What was it about relationships that always had her making the wrong decisions? "It's too late to go back to the way things were."

"What do you mean, go back to the way things were? You don't need to go back. You need to go forward, working through whatever it is that kept you two from the kind of happiness that Slade and Suzie have found in each other."

Ivy's knees wobbled, and she moved to a nearby chair. "I'm not sure going forward is a possibility."

Mary sat down in the chair next to her. "You disappoint me. I didn't think of you as someone who was afraid to love."

"I'm not." She'd loved Gramps with all her heart. She loved her parents, even if they were very different from herself. She'd seen them twice over the past month, once when she'd gone to Nashville, and again when they'd visited the farm. Her mother had admitted that she'd felt Gramps and Grammie had resented her for being born because their only child had died giving birth to her. Ivy wasn't so sure they hadn't. But whatever the disconnect between her mother and great-grandparents, they'd all loved her. And she'd loved them. She wasn't afraid to love.

She'd loved Kenny in the way one loves their high school sweetheart. She'd loved Beau in the way that one loves the guy they date through their undergrad. And she'd loved Luke in that way one loved someone they date through residency. But she'd not been in love with any of them. Not a one.

Her gaze shifted to Caleb and she bit into her lower lip. She didn't love him. She couldn't.

"Maybe I *am* afraid to love." Her eyes stung. Her lungs ached. Maybe she'd been afraid all along and that was why she'd clung to her stupid "condition" to not date anyone who didn't earn more than her. It had never been about the condition, but about how she feared making herself vulnerable to someone. Because that's what she hadn't done before, what had made the real disparity in those relationships. She'd never let anyone in, never put them on equal ground to guard her heart and best interests.

Mary stared at her a moment, then shook her head. "Then you don't deserve him."

"You're right. I didn't." Question was, could she change that? Could she prove to him that she could love, and could he ever love her in return?

With a busy crowd of birthday guests, Caleb hadn't had too much difficulty in avoiding Ivy. At least not until she had specifically sought him out. Which he found surprising after the way she'd decimated him on the plane.

"I wanted to thank you for my postcard." Looking at him a bit nervously, she smiled. "I brought my souvenir trunk home." She half smiled. "My parents were shocked that I wanted my trunk."

"What made you after all this time?"

"You."

"Glad I could be of assistance on something." Ivy was full of surprises. Surprises he didn't need to hear. The past three months hadn't been great for him. He could have easily slipped into places he never wanted to return to. "If you'll excuse me, I'm going to go tell Roy happy birthday one last time, then head home."

He turned to walk away but her words stayed him.

"I miss you."

He sucked in a deep breath. "I can't do this, Ivy."

She glanced around the crowded room. "You're right. This isn't the time or place to talk about us."

He shook his head. "There is no us."

She'd ended any possibility of that on the plane.

She winced. "I… Will you come to the farm, Caleb?"

He stared at her, wondering what it was about her that got to him so much. He'd been wondering for three months and come up with a thousand answers. Her eyes. Her smile. Her laugh. Her intelligence. Her passion. The way she'd loved her great-grandfather. The list went on. There were just as many reasons for him not to go to her farm. Reasons that included two weeks in France that had forever changed him.

Perhaps she sensed that he was about to refuse, because she touched his arm, shooting awareness through him just the same as her touch had from the beginning. "Please. There are things I need to say. If you don't want to hear them, then I understand, but if I ever meant anything to you, then please do this for me."

If she'd ever meant anything to him? That was almost comical. Just two weeks ago, he'd had lunch with Josh, and stunned himself and his brother by asking about the company. He'd quickly relented, knowing he didn't want to work for the shipping company. But for a moment, he'd considered. Because he'd wanted to do something to impress Ivy, to prove to her that he was worthy. He was worthy. He didn't need a title or to work for a big company to prove that. That he'd even for a second considered it because of the woman standing before him was enough that he should run. She made him want to do whatever it took to win her heart.

But if she couldn't love him for who he was, then she didn't really love him.

"What did you have in mind?" Because he always had lived on the edge. Why stop now?

Her gaze searched his and she gave him a hopeful look. "What are you doing right now?"

"I have plans." When he'd told Jordan about his

mental lapse with his brother, she'd made him an offer that he might not be able to refuse. And that might, eventually, impress the woman standing before him. Not that Ivy was why he was meeting with Jordan or likely to take up her offer.

"Oh." Ivy's face fell. "I…okay. I understand. When are you available?"

Caleb ran his fingers through his hair, then glanced around the room. Roy and Owen were watching them and simultaneously gave a thumbs-up. Mary, too. Caleb sighed. "Text me your address. I'll message you when I'm free."

Ivy glanced around her home, wondering how it would look through Caleb's eyes. She'd not made any major changes to the decor, but had hired a contractor to have walls painted, the kitchen modernized, a few other odds and ends around the place that needed done. She'd been slowly going through things, deciding what she wanted to keep, and what she wanted to replace with items that were more her style as she made the farmhouse truly into her home.

She worried that having Caleb inside the house meant she'd never be able to erase the images of him having been there. Already he haunted everywhere she looked. Because no matter where she went, what she did, he was there. In her heart. Which she was about to completely expose to Caleb. She didn't expect him to easily forgive her, but she prayed he'd at least hear her out and give her a second chance to prove to him that, through her eyes, he was perfect just as he was. Perfect for her.

If he didn't give her that chance, well, she'd wish him well and die a little inside. A lot inside.

A knock sounded at the front door. Ivy sucked in a deep breath. Too late for doubts. He was here. Thank God, because part of her had wondered if he'd text that he had changed his mind.

Oh, God. He'd liked her. Although he'd gone back to his room that night at Phillipe and Delphine's, he had liked her. On that plane, he'd not looked at her with "like." Far from it. What had she done, pushing him away because of her own silly insecurities? Had she really let Luke's digs punch such holes in her belief in her worthiness to be loved that she'd pushed away a man who'd stolen her heart and might have grown to love her someday?

She opened the door, damping down the butterflies in her stomach that Caleb was at the farm and about to enter her home. He still wore his jeans and TransCare T-shirt and looked so gorgeous she could barely breathe. "You came."

He took his sunglasses off and slipped an earpiece over his T-shirt collar. "I told you I would."

He was a man of his word. She knew that about him. Caleb was honorable and lived by a code she'd admired for so long. It was a remnant from a dying generation. He was whom she'd been waiting to meet her entire life, whom every day of her life had been preparing her for, and she'd been too blind to realize it.

She gulped back the ball of emotions clogging her throat.

Get it together, Ivy. He's here. That has to mean something. Maybe not as much as you want it to mean, but it's a start.

"I thought we could sit on the back porch. I have lemonade made."

"Lemonade?" He raked his hand over his jaw. "This isn't really a social call, Ivy. Tell me what you wanted me to come out here for and let's get this over with."

He didn't want to be here. That code of honor she'd just acknowledged demanded that he give her the opportunity to say her piece, but he didn't want her under the false impression that he wanted to be there. He obviously didn't.

"I— Okay, then, I'll get right to it." Part of her just wanted to forget all the things she'd been mulling over, trying to figure out how to say how wrong she'd been. But Mary's words haunted her. If she wasn't strong enough to risk her heart, she didn't deserve Caleb. Mary was right. Baring one's heart wasn't easy after a lifetime of never sharing it. "I have missed you more than I would have believed possible of someone I spent two weeks with."

Caleb's jaw tightened. Ivy rushed on because she wasn't weak. She wasn't content with being the product of Luke's derogatory remarks. She was the granddaughter of a brave WWII paratrooper and she wanted this man standing before her. More than wanted him.

"I told myself that what I felt for you was because of where we were, because we were away from reality in this idyllic place that was in many ways a fantasy for me. I even tried to tell myself that my grief over Gramps played a role in my emotions latching on to you. And maybe all of those things did set the background for what was happening, but the reality is, no matter where I met you, no matter what the circumstances, no matter how long we had together, my heart still would have chosen you."

Caleb couldn't believe what Ivy was saying. The entire drive to her place he'd run a dozen scenarios through his mind of what she wanted to say. He'd settled on her wanting to apologize, maybe be friends.

"What happened to you not dating anyone who wasn't your financial equal?" Technically, she hadn't said she wanted to date him. But surely saying her heart would have chosen him implied that she wanted to date him?

Looking repentant, she took a deep breath. "That stipulation was my safeguard after Luke's betrayal. I told myself that if I eliminated that issue then I didn't have to worry about a repeat happening. But deep down I knew Luke's cheating wasn't because of the disparity in our incomes, but because I never trusted him with my heart. He cheated because he wasn't the man he should have been. He didn't have the honor he should have had. Gramps was never crazy about him, you know?"

Feeling as if he needed to do something with his hands, Caleb hooked his thumbs into his jeans' belt loopholes. "I can't imagine he'd like someone who cheated on you."

"Gramps never knew. Thank God or there's no telling what he would have done. I might have had to bail him out of jail. He'd have seen it as his duty to defend my honor."

Caleb imagined if he ever had a daughter or granddaughter that he'd feel the same.

"He'd have liked you."

His gaze met hers. "You think?"

"I know. You're all the things he found important in a person."

"You spent two weeks with me, Ivy," he reminded. "You barely know me."

What she had known hadn't been enough. She'd wanted him to be more, to have more. She'd said that had just been an excuse, but she'd echoed Katrina's words and that couldn't be a coincidence.

"Do you really believe that?" Ivy shook her head, then reached out, taking her hands into his. "Because I don't. Oh, I may not know all the details of your life, but I know you, Caleb. The man you are inside, the things that make you tick. I know you're honorable, kind, generous, loyal, determined, strong and exactly the man I need in my life just as you are."

He was stunned. Completely and totally stunned by what Ivy was saying. He sucked air in, then slowly blew it out. "Well, that may be a problem because I just committed to a major change in my life."

Her head spun. She'd laid out her heart, and deep down, she believed Caleb cared about her. He wouldn't be here if he didn't. But his tone was foreboding. What kind of commitment had he made prior to arriving at her house?

"What kind of commitment?"

"A couple of weeks ago, Jordan asked me to be her partner at TransCare."

"That's great." Then worrying that he'd think she would think that because of the things she'd said on the plane, she started over. "I mean, if that's what you want. Is it?"

He nodded. "I think so. When TransCare was first getting started, she offered to make me a partner if I'd help her with the business. I thought she was just trying to pull me out of where I was and there's likely some truth to that, but she was serious."

"That's wonderful, Caleb. I'm happy for you."

"I'm going to be busy over the next few months as I transition into taking on more responsibilities." Was he trying to tell her that he wouldn't have time for whatever she had in mind? Or was he spitting her own words back at her that she'd used on him on the plane?

"Too busy to share dinner with me from time to time?"

He hesitated, seeming to consider. "As your friend?"

"My friend. My lover. My everything." There. She'd dropped all barriers and exposed her poor heart.

He stared at her, not saying anything.

"Caleb?" Her heart thundered in her chest. "I... I basically just told you that I love you. Please say something."

"You love me?"

She gulped back the fears assailing her that she couldn't read his face. "With all my heart. I'm so sorry for the things I said on the plane, Caleb. I didn't want to make another relationship mistake. It took being away from you for me to realize that, no matter what happens in the future, not giving us a chance is the biggest mistake I could ever make." She gave his hands a gentle squeeze. "There's nothing you need to prove. There never was. I was just too blinded by fear of exposing my heart." She stared straight into his eyes, emphasizing each word of her next sentence. "You are worth everything."

Slowly a smile spread across his face. "Everything?"

"Everything that matters." Her hands shook. "Honestly, nothing seems to matter much without you, Caleb. I've missed you so much."

"The feeling is mutual, Ivy."

"Then you forgive me?"

He lifted her hands to his lips and pressed a kiss there. "Always."

"Always should work out just about perfect. Because that's how long I'm going to want you in my life, Caleb. Always."

His gaze locked with hers and she'd swear they were watery with emotion as he said, "Show me."

Ivy did, giving him her heart and having his. Then and for always.

EPILOGUE

"You doing okay over there?"

Eyes tightly closed, Ivy squeezed the edges of her plane seat. "You're distracting me, Caleb. Don't talk."

From where he sat beside her in the aisle seat, Caleb chuckled. "I distinctly recall you asking me to distract you the last time we were in a plane together."

"That was my way of getting you to tell me all your secrets," she admitted, still not opening her eyes.

"And now that you know everything there is to know about me, you want me to keep quiet?" He sounded amused.

"Do I know all of your secrets?" She opened her eyes long enough to glance his way.

"All that matter."

"I guess you're going to have to come up with a new way of distracting me during flights, then." Not that she'd learned everything there was to know about him over the past nine months. She was sure she hadn't, but he had proven her right to give him her heart. Caleb made her feel treasured, and just as he'd done while in France, when he spoke to her, of her, it was with praise and admiration. With love. She glanced at him, filled with how much she adored him. "I can't believe I let you talk me into this."

"If I recall correctly, you were the one who said we couldn't tell the foundation no when they asked us to head up the medical team again this year."

"We couldn't," she admitted, glancing around to visually check on their veterans who were within her line of vision. "I was just in denial about how we'd have to get to France. Too bad we can't drive."

"Across the Atlantic?" He arched his brow at her. "No thanks."

"Okay, you're right." She took a deep breath, then admitted, "It will be nice to see Phillipe and Delphine. It was so nice of them to agree to host us again. You think they'll give us our old rooms?"

A noise crackled over the PA system, then a stewardess announced, "Are there any medical personnel on the plane? Would any medical personnel on the plane please come to the back galley."

Ivy gasped, her gaze going to Caleb's. "I can't believe this is happening again."

"What is it with you and planes?" he said, undoing his seat belt. He was already halfway to the back of the plane by the time Ivy had her seat belt unfastened and her backpack slid out from beneath the seat. This time she was bringing her bag with her from the get-go, so they'd hopefully have whatever they needed close.

Only, when she rounded the corner of the galley Mary and several of the stewardess huddled around Caleb, but Ivy didn't see a distressed passenger.

Confused, Ivy glanced around, looking for whoever needed medical help. "What's going on? Is there an emergency?"

Suddenly she registered that Mary and one of the stewardesses held phones, recording what was happening. Her eyes widened. Her heart pounded. She could barely breathe. Her fingers flew to her mouth, covering the cry she emitted. Over the past several months they'd shared so many dreams, including hopes for their future, but she hadn't been expecting this, not yet. Not *here*.

"Ivy McEwen, one year ago, we were on a flight to Paris, and you saved a woman's life. Everyone knew that. What most didn't realize was that you also saved mine. After my injury, I thought the best parts of my life were over, but I was wrong." He took her hand into his and kissed her fingertips. "The best parts were just beginning with meeting you."

Ivy's hand shook. Her entire body shook. Was this really happening or had she fallen asleep over the Atlantic? Or maybe the plane had gone down and she was in heaven?

Caleb knelt on one knee and Ivy's legs wobbled.

"Ivy, I've been thinking about how I wanted to do this for a long time. On a plane seemed the obvious choice."

"Obviously," she mumbled, still stunned by what he was doing and by the sparkly diamond and ruby ring he'd pulled from his pocket.

"I've never known anyone like you, Ivy. I know that's because you are one of a kind. Your uniqueness just adds to your charm, and you've certainly charmed me from the moment we met. Will you marry me, Ivy?"

Placing her hands upon his cheeks, she lowered to her knees because she didn't feel capable of standing a moment longer. "Yes, Caleb. Even on a plane, which you know I hate, my answer is yes!"

His amber eyes looking glassy, he smiled, slid the ring onto her finger, then laced their hands. "I love you, Ivy. With everything I am I will love you forever and protect you and any children we may have."

Happiness bursting from her, she nodded. "I love you right back, Caleb. Now and forever and any future babies we have." She thought a moment, then told him, "I'm going to want a boy to name after Gramps."

"I'd be proud for our son to have your great-grandfather's name. And if we have a girl, we'll just keep trying until we have a boy." Caleb kissed her. A deep kiss that had her thinking the plane was plummeting as she held on to him.

Clapping and cheers sounded around them from those in the galley.

Caleb stood, then helped her to her feet only to lift her and spin her around. "You make me feel like the luckiest man alive."

"Good, because you just made me the luckiest woman alive."

Ivy hugged Mary, showed her ring off proudly, then eventually, hand clasped with Caleb's, made her way back to their seats. They'd made it about halfway there when the PA system came back on. "Ladies and gentlemen, the stewardess informs me that congratulations are in order. She said yes."

The passengers erupted into clapping. Ivy's face went hot, but she smiled and thanked everyone before sliding into her seat.

When they were settled and their seat belts refastened, she shook her head at Caleb. "You've done it now."

He grinned. "What?"

"Completely set the bar high for distracting me while flying. How will you ever top this?"

Laughing, he leaned forward and kissed the corner of her mouth. "I have the rest of our lives. I'll think of something."

And he did.

* * * * *

Pregnancy Surprise With The Greek Surgeon

Luana DaRosa

MILLS & BOON

Once at home in sunny Brazil, **Luana DaRosa** has since lived on three different continents, though her favorite romantic location remains the tropical places of Latin America. When she's not typing away at her latest romance novel or reading about love, Luana is either crocheting, buying yarn she doesn't need or chasing her bunnies around her house. She lives with her partner in a cozy town in the south of England. Find her on Twitter under the handle @ludarosabooks.

Visit the Author Profile page
at millsandboon.com.au.

Dear Reader,

Pregnancy Surprise with the Greek Surgeon was a true labour of love and I'm so happy that you picked up the book. The story follows Camila and Niko, who think they're only meeting once, but of course circumstances arise where they have a reunion with rather unexpected news.

I love the Greek backdrop of the story. Because I met my very own Niko in Greece, I often revisit the country for special occasions. So being able to transport you into this place where great love stories come to life has been really fun.

The journey of Camila and Niko is not just about unexpected surprises, but also about navigating the complexities of life, love and career. I wanted to explore how two individuals, each with their own set of challenges and aspirations, come together to create a new, shared path. This story is as much about embracing change as it is about finding love in the most unexpected places.

Thank you for joining me on this journey. Your support means the world to me, and I hope you enjoy reading *Pregnancy Surprise with the Greek Surgeon* as much as I enjoyed writing it.

Luana <3

CHAPTER ONE

THE LOW AND steady drone of conversation filled the lecture hall. Nikolas Vassilis squinted as he scanned the rows of seats, looking for his own—if there even was enough space for him to sit. He knew the lecture would be popular, though looking at the people lining up along the walls on the left and right had him reconsidering just how impressive Dr Camila Pereira Frey's lecture on the advancement of personalised cardiology would be. He'd heard a lot about her reputation as not only a talented cardiologist but also a dedicated researcher, who was always looking for the next big thing in the field. In this case, combining genetic research to help tailor cardiovascular procedures to patients right down to their DNA.

Though she wasn't the reason he had attended the medical conferences, a part of him was curious to see what all the talk was about. Because the name Camila Pereira Frey was on everyone's lips in the world of cardiology, and as the new medical director of the Athena Cardiac Institute in Athens, Niko needed to know about the major players in his field—even if people chasing fame through medicine weren't the kinds of physicians he wanted to associate with. Not that he knew much about Camila. But someone who spent so much time speaking to the press could only be interested in one thing. He'd seen it with his father, chasing clout rather than helping people. It had been the reason Niko had chosen not to join the Athena Institute after his surgical training was done.

Then his father passed away, and Niko had found himself inheriting the keys of the hospital—and far more problems than he had ever imagined.

Instead of using the good reputation of the Athena Institute to help people, his father had used people's trust to bring them into his hospital to get treatments that cost far more than they should—all in the name of enriching himself.

Medicine should never be about making an exorbitant amount of money. Given how often Niko read Dr Pereira Frey's name in the headlines of medical news sites, he wondered if Camila, too, received a pretty sum for all of her appearances. Was she of a similar make as his father, seeking fame so she could enrich herself by selling people DNA tests they didn't need? His father would have done that without batting an eye.

Niko was about to settle in at the back of the

room when a waving hand caught his attention, the pearly blue-white bracelet a familiar sight. Pushing off from the wall, Niko stuck his hands in his pockets as he weaved through the crowd until he reached the row where his sister sat. She looked up at him with a smile, her hand patting the empty chair next to her.

'I saved you a seat,' she said with a bright smile as he slid onto the chair.

'You're finally useful on this trip,' he replied, earning himself a swat on the arm.

'How dare you. I've provided you with company throughout the week, as well as being an excellent conversationalist and icebreaker.' Eleni Vassilis levelled a glare at him that he'd seen throughout the years growing up with her.

'I don't need help with conversations. You're an engineer, not a doctor, so I don't know why you invited yourself.' The smile he gave her stood in direct contrast to his words.

He'd come to the conference for one main reason—to scope out new talent for the Athena Cardiac Institute. With his father's unexpected passing earlier in the year, Niko found himself at the top of the institute—a position he hadn't thought about since rejecting his father's offer of joining it after his surgical training. Tension between father and son had already been high when Niko finished his training, choosing to go into surgery rather than staying on the cardiology path like his father. He'd never realised how controlling Stavros Vassilis had been until he finally got out from underneath him.

It was up to Niko to change things now, and he still felt unprepared. His father's heart attack had caught him by surprise and had left him with little time to contemplate the change he'd agreed to as he'd taken on the mantle of medical director. Within the first month of starting, Niko had uncovered things he wouldn't have thought even Stavros was capable of. Because of his father's pristine reputation, people had believed him when he sold them expensive treatments that were at best unnecessary, at worst invasive. Some of the more junior doctors had approached him about the situation, wanting to clear their minds of this burden. Niko had spent days going through medical charts and invoices, piecing together a picture that robbed him of his sleep at night.

Each day came with a new challenge, and even though he'd already changed a lot of the policies and put in stricter reviews for procedures, there were still a lot of bad apples to weed out. His father's cronies were all over the hospital, and once they'd realised that Niko was the polar opposite of his father, they began to interfere with his changes.

He couldn't fire them all at once, or the hospital would collapse without the staff to support it. In the quiet of the night, he sometimes wondered if that would be the worst thing. Maybe the Athena Institute was beyond saving, the influence of his father too strong even in death. 'I'm *basically* a doctor—with you and Mum talking shop at home all the time. I bet you that whenever we speak to someone, they don't even know I'm not a doctor myself.' Her grin grew wider when Niko rolled his eyes.

Eleni had decided early in her life that the traditional job for a member of the Vassilis family didn't appeal to her—to the tremendous wrath of their father. Stavros couldn't have a child not dedicated to the pursuit of medical legacy. He'd put so much pressure on Eleni that she had moved out of their family home at eighteen, never looking back. That had been a defining moment for the entire Vassilis clan. Their mother had realised that she was powerless against her husband as long as she stood by him. The choice between staying in her marriage and being in the lives of her children had been a simple one—hard to pull through but easy to pick.

Despite everything, they'd managed to stay close, finding strength in each other when things got tough. Niko remembered helping his mother as she found her way back into her career by opening her own clinic. She'd put her professional ambitions on hold, hoping to continue when her kids had grown.

'So, are you hoping to hire this Dr Pereira for

your new team?' Eleni asked, nodding towards the stage.

Niko scoffed. 'Absolutely not. The Athena Institute is at a pivotal moment. She's as fame hungry as all the ghouls our father hired that I'm now slowly getting rid of.'

Eleni tilted her head. 'Why would you think she's fame hungry?'

Niko didn't *know*—he only had his suspicion to go on. 'For the last year, she's been all over the media, talking to anyone who will listen about her research.'

'That doesn't seem too bad. You don't like her research? I thought using genetic markers to customise treatment plans would be right up your alley.' Eleni laughed when he narrowed his eyes at her. 'As I said, I'm basically a doctor myself at this point.'

Niko said nothing to that and gave her another eye roll.

The room went quiet as Dr Pereira Frey stepped onto the stage, her high heels clicking with every step she took towards the podium. Her gait was calm and measured, her hands casually at her side and a small smile on her lips. She was in her element and appeared to be someone who thrived under this sort of attention.

Niko's hand slipped into his pocket to dig out his phone when Eleni gasped. His gaze shot back up, and he, too, immediately felt the intensity of the woman as she faced the crowd that had come to listen to her speech today. She was much younger than he would have guessed from the amount of research she was engaged with, probably closer to his age when he had thought her to be his senior by a few years. Light brown hair framed her face in gentle waves, complementing her piercing amber eyes. The suit she'd chosen to wear looked tailored to her figure, like a second skin.

Everyone around them had turned quiet as Dr Pereira Frey stood behind the podium and looked out into the crowd. She hadn't even said anything, yet her command of the room was undeniable— Niko included.

'Good afternoon, I'm Dr Camila Pereira Frey, and welcome to my overview on how genetic mapping will transform the future of cardiology.' She took a small step back from the podium and pointed at the projection on the screen, and Niko—along with everyone else in the room— followed her every move as she launched into her presentation with no hesitation.

He'd come into this event wanting to hate her lecture, knowing that she was one of those doctors his father would have loved to hire just because they brought press and prestige with them. But the longer Camila spoke, the more engrossed he became in her presentation and the more fascinating the science behind it seemed. Genetic mapping hadn't really played a role in his cardio-vascular work outside of hereditary heart conditions, but in her research, Camila had gone far beyond diseases.

'With widespread genomic screening, we could predict the likelihood of a disease occurring…'

Niko nodded along as she switched to the next slide, showing the results of a case study she had spent the last year building, and he flinched when Eleni jabbed her elbow into his side.

'Did you change your mind about hiring her?' she whispered, raising her eyebrows in a suggestive gesture.

Niko didn't deign to acknowledge his sister's comment and instead shifted his eyes forward again, more taken by the woman on the stage than he would admit to Eleni. Something in his blood heated as he watched her talk, following every slight move as she spoke about her research. Hiring her wasn't something he considered, but the longer he looked at her, the stronger his intrigue around her grew.

He fished his phone out of his pocket and checked the schedule of the conference. There were a few meetings on his calendar with people he wanted to convince to join his team.

But there was a reception hosted by the organiser, which only a few people attending the conference had been invited to. As the new medical director of the Athena Cardiac Institute, Niko had received one of the coveted invitations, but he hadn't planned on going.

Though he might change his mind. The reception would be an opportunity for high-profile hospital leaders to speak to all of the presenters at the conference, which meant Camila would be there as well.

'I'll have to skip out on our dinner tonight,' Niko said with a sidelong glance at his sister before his eyes slipped back to Camila, as if he couldn't resist her magnetic aura.

He didn't know what it meant or where this decision had come from. Something about her grabbed his attention, despite his best effort to not let her affect him. It was enough to awaken his curiosity—and make him act on it.

By the time Camila arrived at the reception, all she could think about was the bathtub waiting in her hotel room. Exhaustion swept over her with every step she took, and she forced herself to put a smile on her face as one of the waitstaff approached her with a variety of drinks to choose from. She opted for water, taking a big gulp of it to soothe her already sore throat. After a day of talking to a variety of people, she didn't want to be here. She had used up all her extrovert energy and now longed for the tranquillity of her room.

But she wasn't in a position to relax. Not when her research was getting so much attention. After so many years of working on her genetic mapping methods while also keeping up with her regular work, she had finally found something that could change the face of her field. Not only that, but her peers were actually listening to her. Half of the struggle to get here was due to how young she had been when she started with her research—people perceived her youth as inexperience. There had even been some comments about that today as she spoke to different people, but thankfully there had been few. Sure, she might only be in her mid-thirties, but she'd began laying the ground work of her research during her medical training. After defending herself time and time again, Camila finally reached a point where she stopped trying to justify her actions. The large audience in front of her, eager to hear her speak, was a testament that her peers were focused on her work and not her age.

Taking another sip of water, Camila took a deep breath and steeled herself for the last part of the conference. After this, she was free for a few weeks to unwind from it all and pick out her next project. Though the attention was exhausting, at least it brought her closer to her goal. Leaving an impact with her work had been all she ever wanted, and now she was one step closer to making that happen. If she became part of the history of eradicating heart disease, no one could ever measure up to her. It was the one thing she had absolute control over in life.

The warning words of her mother echoed in her head wherever she went, even now, so many years later. Mariana Pereira Frey had been a staunch advocate of traditional gender roles, and seeing her daughter veer from that path at an early age had caused tension in their relationship. Even though they would see each other frequently, Camila had kept everything between them surface level, for she knew if she talked about her 'untraditional life' her mother would have negative comments. She would ask when she was going to forget about medicine and when she would be ready to settle down and bless her with grandkids.

Camila had known back then that her life was more than just finding a husband and having children. She'd *needed* it to be more than that. In a way, her mother's rigid insistence on leading a traditional life had fuelled her own desire to be more than what some ancient picture of society expected her to be.

Sometimes she wondered if Mariana had always been this way or if her husband—Camila's father—leaving the family for another woman, before Camila could form any real memories, had shaped her views on traditional gender roles. Because even though Mariana had wanted her to settle down, she'd also been the one to warn her that men left the second they got bored, so she'd have to work for their affection every day of her life. Or end up lonely.

When her mother had passed away three years ago after a short battle with cancer, it had left Camila in a strange place of subdued sadness—and an overwhelming amount of guilt at how little she felt. Guilt that had driven her to focus even more on her work just so she could forget about things for a few hours.

'Impressive lecture you gave earlier,' a voice behind her said, and Camila's spine stiffened as she realised someone had approached her.

With practiced ease, she plastered on her most convincing smile and turned around. Her eyes widened in surprise as they fell upon the man standing in front of her. His thick black hair was pulled back into a low ponytail, showcasing a close-shaven undercut that would go unnoticed if his hair was let down. A sudden spark of attraction coursed through her body at the sight of him, amplified by the piercing brown-green gaze he fixed upon her. His eyes lingered over every inch of her figure before coming back to rest on her face, sending shivers down her spine.

Was he…checking her out? Of all the interactions she had had with colleagues today, this was rapidly becoming the most unusual one—and he had only said five words to her.

'Thank you,' she said in an automatic response, and the tingle of awareness flooded through her as he stepped closer. This was not her usual admirer coming to talk about her work. No, Camila got the sense he was here for something else. That thought sent another hot spark travelling down her spine.

The man accepted a glass from a passing waiter, and she watched with a near hypnotic focus as he wrapped his long and slender fingers around the stem, holding the glass with a tenderness that was trained. As if he were used to handling delicate things with his fingers...

'I've heard a lot about your research already. Wherever any cardiologist looks, your name appears. But hearing you speak in person is a lot different from simply reading your words. What looks like bravado from afar becomes more... nuanced,' he said, and the smirk on his lips landed a blow somewhere lower in her body—along with a fiery temper flaring in her chest.

Bravado? Her research was the work of her lifetime, and he had read her papers and found them...arrogant?

'But you're not a cardiologist, are you?' she said in return. Why was he even bothering to read her papers? One look at him was enough to tell her he was a surgeon. A cardiologist would have never accused *her* of bravado. No, that type of projection only ever happened when surgeons with a God complex came across her research.

His eyes rounded, and he had the decency to

look somewhat surprised. But then his expression melted back into an easy smile as his eyes dipped below her face once more before coming up.

'Seems I continue not to give you enough credit, Dr Pereira Frey. I'm a cardiovascular surgeon. Niko—'

'Sorry to interrupt. They asked me to fetch Dr Pereira Frey for a few questions with a member of the press.' A young woman wedged herself into their conversation, and Camila forced her eyes shut for two deep breaths to suppress the annoyance bubbling up in her chest.

Despite the man, Niko, questioning her intentions around her research, this had still been the most interesting conversation she'd had in a good while. Probably because he was looking at the subject more critically than any other peers she had encountered. And he wasn't even a fellow cardiologist, but one of the scalpel wielders…

'Tell them I'll be there in a second,' she said, not entirely sure why. Talking to reporters was much simpler—and more beneficial to her. She was here to represent her work, to show the medical world how she intended to revolutionise the cardiology field. A cardiovascular surgeon wouldn't be much use in that. They didn't diagnose, they just cut when they were told to cut. She had need for the people who instructed the surgeons—cardiologists.

'Don't let me hold you back,' he said, no doubt noticing her thought process.

'They're not even supposed to be at this event, so they can wait for a few more moments.' She turned, saying those words to the woman who had interrupted them. 'Please let them know I'll make myself available when I'm ready.'

She blinked at Camila but then nodded. 'You know she's going straight to her supervisor, who will drag you back to that reporter eventually,' Niko said, wrenching a laugh from her lips.

'Oh, no doubt about that. The event organisation was probably the one to let the press in here. They won't stop at anything to gain some traction from my presence here.' The words came out far more unfiltered than they usually would, and Camila blinked. It wasn't that easy to let her guard down, but something about Niko was disarming. Like he didn't care about the stuffy ceremonies of the conference, either.

'Well, in this case, would you join me for a drink?' he asked, his hand outstretched towards her. Camila blinked again, staring at his slightly curled fingers. This was *definitely* not how any of the previous conferences had gone. Niko was giving the impression that he wasn't all that interested in the medicine—but rather her. Where was this feeling coming from?

And why was she reaching out and grabbing his hand, like that was the normal thing to do in this situation? The day must have wiped her out more than she'd realised, but the moment her hand slid into his and she let this man guide her towards the bar, everything inside her stopped. Her senses honed in on that small patch of their palms touching, noticing how his fingers pressed against hers and how the gentlest tug of his had her feet moving in his direction.

Absolutely mesmerising.

'So, what brings you here?' she asked once they reached the bar and after the bartender took their order, turning to face him. Was he standing particularly close to her? She wasn't sure.

Niko rested his arm on the wooden bar, the deep mahogany accentuating the tailored dark grey suit he wore. Whoever he worked for, he must be one of the more prestigious cardiovascular surgeons. Few could afford to look like this *and* make it seem effortless. One look at Camila told everyone all about her upbringing—and her lack of refinement. She'd come into cardiology without any connections or relationships. Everything she was now had been fought for, and she was certain her discomfort in these situations showed. Camila had to focus on medicine and medicine alone to get ahead of her peers.

That included men and might as well be the reason Camila was so flustered in this moment with the attention of this one man. Was he actually flirting with her or just interested in her work? She couldn't tell.

He hesitated before he spoke, his eyes drifting downward to where the top button of her blouse remained open. She balled her hand into a fist so as not to touch her collar as his eyes sparked a small fire under her skin.

'I'm here for work, like anyone else. Here to… hear you speak,' he finally said, and Camila could hear the deflection.

She laughed. 'Oh, please, not even ten minutes ago, you told me you were more impressed with my speech than you thought you would be. You did not come here for me.'

A smile tugged at his lips, and watching them curve upwards set something tumbling inside her stomach. 'Would it help to know that I came to this reception just for you?'

Their drinks arrived, giving Camila a moment to fight the heat rising to her cheeks. There *was* a flirty edge to his words. She was almost sure of it. A subtle…invitation? To what exactly, she wasn't sure, but more worryingly—she really wanted to accept that mystery invitation.

'It might help smooth over the deep insult of thinking my research was more bravado than substance,' she replied, matching his tone and energy.

Niko took a sip from his drink, his eyes never leaving hers, and a shiver clawed down her spine when his throat moved with a swallow. How was this even something she noticed about him? He must have caught her eyes wandering down to his throat, as his smile turned into a smirk.

'My apologies. I've certainly come across as brash. My sister says I have the tendency to go straight to the point, where others like to express themselves with more finesse.' The look in his eyes sent a similar jolt through her as his touch had.

Tucking away that bit of personal information, she went on, 'Okay, say I forgive you and you profess great admiration for my work now. How can I trust you won't change your mind again?'

His low laugh skittered across her skin, and it was infectious enough that she joined in. 'Now you're getting ahead of yourself. I said I was impressed. It's a bit of a leap to go from that to great admiration. Maybe if we got to work together, I could verify some things for myself.'

His eyes dipped to her collar again as he said that—and then dipped even lower. Sparks travelled along the path his gaze took, and her breath caught when he lingered on her mouth before coming back up. What he wanted to verify had nothing to do with medicine. When had been the last time anyone had flirted with her this brazenly? Camila couldn't even remember. Not since she'd devoted herself wholly to her research. Men were a distraction—and a challenge she wasn't comfortable with. Over the years, her lovers had been few and far between, as she never wanted to get entangled, knowing casual was all she had to give. Camila had given up many things in her devotion for her research. All her friends were people working with her, same with her flings.

With the demanding schedule she put on herself, there wasn't time for anything else. She didn't *want* to take any time away from it. People had to fit around her life and oftentimes didn't understand why she was so uncompromising.

That was until a handsome stranger flirted with her at a bar, and even the simplest of suggestions had her blushing. Maybe more exposure would have meant she wasn't so susceptible to his flirtation. She still couldn't imagine herself in a domestic setting the way her mother had wanted her to live her life. But something about Niko told her he wasn't searching for that, either.

'What would you like to verify?' Camila asked, pushing away the voice in her head, telling her to leave.

'Hmm...' Niko hummed, his hand slowly extending across the bar—towards her. 'You need a delicate hand for this sort of work, so that would be important to know. From your conversation, I can tell your bedside manner is excellent. Now... if you're interested in surgery, even as an observer, we would need to test your stamina. Surgeries can run long.'

Her mouth went dry as his voice dropped even lower. Around them, people were chattering, glasses clinking and feet shuffling—but Camila could only hear him. 'You'd like to test my stamina?' she asked, and the darkening of his eyes told her that her own thoughts around how he'd like to do that matched hers.

It wasn't panic making her heart beat faster, but…excitement? The men she usually met were directly connected to her work because those were the only people she ever met. Medical conventions had her far too busy to even contemplate making a connection that wouldn't serve her research. But Niko… Something about him was magnetic.

Niko's eyes shifted away from her for a second, but it was enough for her to catch it—and let out a deep sigh when the familiar face of the press manager of this event came towards them.

'It was only a matter of time,' Niko said, and she was certain a hint of regret wove itself through his voice.

Regret she sensed unfurling in her own stomach. Camila wasn't ready to slip back into her duties as a researcher and doctor. Not when Niko had made it too easy to just…be. Not worry about how she was portraying herself or who she was trying to impress.

'Seems like our time is up.' Camila paused, deciding whether she should ask him to wait. But that thought went as quick as it came to her. Of course not. He would find another person at this party, one that was far easier to get into bed—probably better at it, too. Why would he wait for her when they'd only known each other for thirty minutes?

'It was nice meeting you,' she said to Niko, and turned around with her best press smile as she intercepted the man sent here to lead her to the journalists eager to talk about her work.

One question from the journalist who had somehow scored an invitation to a party she had been promised would be 'doctors only' had turned into an entire question-and-answer session.

The notoriety was the aspect of her research she enjoyed the least, but she had to admit that it opened a lot of doors that had remained shut before people began paying attention to her. But even throughout the interviews, her mind kept wandering back to the man she had met—and the effect he was having on her. Camila wondered who he'd chosen to go home with, because there was no way he was going home alone. Lucky lady...

Exhausted from far too much talking, she now sat on a couch tucked away in a corridor that led to the washrooms, hiding from whoever else wanted to speak to her. Her social battery was all but dead.

Footsteps sounded in the corridor, and Camila quickly dug her phone out of her purse, pretending to be engrossed in whatever was on it so that this intruder wouldn't think about talking to her. Her stomach flipped when the steps slowed and then fully stopped—right on the side of the couch she was occupying.

'I thought you had left,' a familiar voice said, and her eyes shot up to collide with the brown-green eyes she had been peering into earlier in the evening.

'Dr... Niko,' she said, her shoulders relaxing at the small smile on his lips. Heat almost instantly rose in her, leaving her in this space of strange desire for him she'd slipped into throughout their chat. Of all the conversations she had forced herself through, the short one with him had been the only one that didn't require any effort.

'Just Niko is fine—if I can call you Camila.'

She huffed a laugh, then nodded and indicated the space next to her on the couch. She'd been ready to jump on him at the end of their conversation. Calling her by her first name seemed rather tame. 'You would be doing me a favour. These conferences and discussions are always so formal. We're all doctors here. Can we acknowledge that and drop all the honorifics?'

'If I didn't know any better, Camila, I would think you're hiding.' Hearing her name from his lips sent a shiver through her body, and she took in a sharp breath to keep it at bay. This was not a reaction she was used to, even with a man as objectively attractive as Niko was.

There was one thing her mother had taught her—that men got bored rather quickly and would chase after the next skirt, regardless of what commitment they had made. The remarks of her mother had travelled with her, making sure every fling never ended up being more. She'd told herself she didn't mind. That work came first anyway. That she wasn't interested in just being someone's wife. But even such a simple flirtatious exchange like this left her feeling out of her depth, because all she could hear was her mother's voice warning her of the same heartbreak she had experienced.

They all got bored, eventually. She knew this had to be true for Niko as well, even though he didn't make it seem that way. But how reliable was a man picking up women at the after-party of a medical conference? Why did she even care? It wasn't like she was looking for a boyfriend. Her life was fine as it was.

'And I guess you couldn't help but intrude on this poor soul's only respite?' She put a playful lilt into her voice, and Niko laughed.

'If you put it like that, I definitely want to linger around a bit more.' A spark entered his eyes, and his hand slipped below his jacket. When it came back up, he held a slender flask between his fingers. 'Let me provide you with some liquid encouragement for your troubles.'

Camila hesitated when he unscrewed the flask and held it towards her. Their fingers touched as she took it, and the electricity zinged through her, as if amplified by that small touch. She raised the flask to her nose, taking a whiff. Sweet notes of spices and oak drifted up her nostrils. A fruity wine?

She watched him as she brought the flask to her mouth, tipping it over until the sweet liquid hit her tongue. The taste was nothing like she expected from alcohol coming out of a flask, and when she lowered it and looked at Niko, she caught a spark of *something* in his eyes. Though she didn't know what to call this silent intention, it was enough to send another shiver crawling down her spine.

'You keep wine in a flask?' she asked, smiling.

'Not quite wine. Metaxa is a brandy that is flavoured with wine. The perfect after-dinner drink.'

'Metaxa…' Camila repeated the word, unfamiliar with it. Then again, the only time she ever had something to drink was if she was on a date—which didn't happen often, especially not these days. 'Are you in the habit of bringing flasks to medical conferences?'

'Oh, yes, absolutely. How else would I get through talking to so many boring people if I didn't make a game out of it?' He took the flask from her, and Camila watched with the focus of a predator as he raised it to his mouth. His throat bobbed as he took a sip, savouring the flavour with a soft hum that shot to a place somewhere deep inside of her. 'Plus, I delight in the thought of what my father would have said if he knew his son was getting drunk while talking to important people in the cardio field. A bit of an extra kick I get at his expense.'

Her eyes rounded at his words, their meaning ambiguous. 'Is your father a cardio surgeon as well?'

The spark in his gaze banked when she said those words, as if she had stepped over an invisible line. 'He was, yes.' Niko's voice turned icy when he said that, and Camila resisted the urge to pry. He'd used the past tense, which could mean many things. But there was a conflict in his eyes as he said that, and some instinct inside her told her he'd not get the chance to resolve that conflict—and that she shouldn't ask any more questions. Which was just as well, because if there was one thing she understood, it was issues with a parent that remained unresolved.

Screwing the flask shut, he slipped it back into his pocket, and when he turned back, whatever had been bothering him had vanished from his features, and in its stead was that intention again that Camila couldn't quite get. Or rather, what she wanted it to mean was so far out there that she couldn't quite believe it. The fires underneath her skin kept on increasing with every glance of his.

'I'd rather hear more about you,' he said as he leaned in, his breath skittering over her cheeks.

Her? Camila hesitated, the mix of his proximity and his scent in her nose making it harder to think. 'What is there to tell? My lab is in Switzerland, where I was born. They printed my biography in the accompanying material of the conference,' she said, not really knowing what else to say.

Niko seemed to pick up on that as well, for he barked a laugh. 'Yes, yes. You are a Brazilian-Swiss cardiologist who has spent some time studying in the UK before opening her own lab.' He waved a hand in front of his face. 'I'm not looking for the information that can be learned from someone's *biografia*.'

His accent changed at the last word, catching Camila's attention, and bringing the question to her mind where he might be from. The name Niko wasn't giving her enough indications. Maybe that was for the best. They could leave whatever was between them here in Vancouver.

'Then ask me a question. What do you want to know?'

The smile on his lips sent sparks flying across her skin. It was filled with the same intention she could see written in his eyes. She realised she had just given him permission to ask *any* question that might be rolling around in his brain.

'What do you like to do for fun?' he asked, and Camila blinked at that. Not the question she had expected.

'What do I…?' Her voice trailed off as she contemplated the question. 'I've not had much of a life outside of my research for the last few years.'

Was that sad? Camila wasn't sure. Her dedication to her research had begun the moment she went into medical school—wanting to prove to her mother that being a wife wasn't all that she could be. She wanted to show her what she could do, however futile that might have been. But Mariana had been less than impressed, to the point where Camila didn't know why she kept trying. She eventually accepted that their relationship would never be more than a polite conversation about the weather and dodging questions about her personal life. Because those always ended in a lecture about her father leaving them for another woman—and that Camila should make peace with that fate as well.

Was that why she'd never bothered to let her relationships go beyond the surface level? She didn't know, had never felt secure enough to examine these feelings. Work was all she needed, even if that meant she now didn't know how to answer the question from this handsome man.

And good God, he was *very* handsome, and

now close enough that his gentle scent of sea and earth drifted towards her. An intoxicating smell that made her feel light-headed.

'Maybe if you tell me what you like to do for fun, I can learn from you,' she said, grasping at the first thing entering her mind.

His smile broadened and the spark entering his eyes had her thinking he had somehow wanted this to be her answer. Did he already have something in mind to teach her?

With his arm draped over the back of the couch, Niko unfurled his fingers until they were right by her shoulder. He said nothing for a few seconds, then he wound his index fingers through a strand of her hair, gently caressing the curl with his thumb. His eyes were fixed on his hand, as if he had to watch what his fingers were doing, and when he finally looked up at her, Camila gasped at the intensity of his gaze.

'I'm not sure it's polite to say what I would like to do when we have just met,' he said, his voice low and filled with gravel.

The answering squeeze of her core was enough to let her know how she felt about this proposition. Somehow, Niko possessed a quality that didn't require any effort from her part to hold the conversation. After the week she'd had at the conference, she hadn't thought she would be up for a casual night of sex. It might not be a traditional social encounter, but it still required effort and communications—things that were severely hampered when her social battery was on zero like it was right now.

But with Niko… The conversation hadn't felt stilted or like a chore at any point. No, somehow the rising heat between them had infused her with such fierceness that Camila didn't even feel tired any more. The slight buzz probably helped as well.

She bit her lower lip when his fingers grazed her shoulder as he gathered more of her hair, and from his sharp inhale, she knew that her small gesture had the desired effect.

'I would be down for some of that fun,' Camila said, tilting her head to the side so that his fingers connected with her cheek.

Niko released a slow breath, his fingers moving against her cheek until his hand cupped her face, strands of her hair still weaving in and out between his fingers. Camila's breath stuttered when he leaned close enough that she could see where the green of his eyes faded into brown.

'My suite is upstairs,' he said, his face so close now their noses almost touched.

A suite in *this* hotel? That was far more than she had been willing to pay for accommodations. Her hotel wasn't far from the venue of the conference, but even her double room struck her as lavish. How was he able to afford that? Where had he said he worked?

The thoughts left her head as an electrified wave washed over her when Niko closed the remaining space between them and brushed his lips over hers. Questions she didn't remember to ask the next morning when she snuck out of the suite before sunrise.

CHAPTER TWO

CAMILA'S HEAD POUNDED, the letters on the paper in front of her going in and out of focus. Giving her eyes a break, she leaned against the window of the car, the coolness of the glass a contrast to the heat of nausea and pain flaring through her. The streets of Athens passed her by in a slow blur, the buildings getting higher and higher as they entered the city centre. Their destination was the Athena Cardiac Institute, where she would be consulting on a case until it was done. Looking at the complexities of the gene mapping, she expected to be here at least a month, probably two.

Each turn of the streets brought her closer to the building that held so much knowledge and expertise in her field—and the man at the top.

Nikolas Vassilis.

Camila had known of his father, Stavros Vassilis, whose passing had garnered some attention in the cardiology field. He'd been the one to establish the institute and had turned it into a premier destination for both surgical cases and research. When Camila had set out to become an expert in the field, she'd hoped to one day get a chance to collaborate with the institute and add her name to its history.

Now she wasn't so certain of that desire, and it all hinged on who was now in charge. How they would interact with each other since that night in Vancouver.

He hadn't been the one who'd invited her, and Camila hadn't realised who he was until after she'd agreed to consult on the case. His assistant had sent her an email with an invitation to meet the medical director of the institute. One look at the website of the hospital had her eyes wide in shock—and the memories from their night in Vancouver coming back.

Those memories didn't help with the nausea roiling in her stomach, and she couldn't quite pinpoint the source. Camila wasn't someone to be nervous. She'd spoken in front of massive crowds and been interviewed for prestigious publications. With the mounting success of her research, she'd got used to the limelight. Meeting someone as important as Nikolas Vassilis shouldn't rattle her.

No, the discomfort had been a constant companion for the last few weeks, and a part of her wondered if she was working too much. With her unpredictable schedule, chances were she was suffering the consequences of poor nutrition and dehydration.

The car came to a jolting halt, and Camila looked up. The Athena Cardiac Institute rose from the ground in gleaming white stone. With its front almost entirely of glass, the marbled stone married the classic Greek style with the modern look of glass and steel. Greenery lined the steps to the doors, giving the outside the feel of a comfortable courtyard. People in scrubs and those wearing street clothes stood and sat with each other, enjoying the afternoon sun of Athens.

A renewed wave of nausea crashed through her, and Camila closed her eyes for a second, taking a deep breath. This didn't have to be awkward. She would simply follow Niko's lead. If he wanted to pretend like they were meeting for the first time, then she was okay with that. And if not… Well, either way she'd find out soon enough.

She thanked the driver as he opened the door for her, and then she ascended the steps to the front door, willing her heart to stop beating in her throat.

'Welcome to our hospital, Dr Pereira Frey. I can't tell you how excited we are to have you here. What an honour, truly.' Dr Emilia Seo greeted Camila as she stepped off the elevator. 'I thought I'd come and escort you to Niko's office personally.'

Camila smiled as she shook the hand of the other woman. Emilia, as the head of Cardiology at the institute, had been the one to approach her about a collaboration. 'The pleasure is all mine. Sounds like an interesting case you have on your hands.' She'd yet to get familiar enough with it to voice any recommendations, but what she'd seen was certainly intriguing. High-performance athletes could, at times and under the right conditions, be susceptible to heart failure. But in this case, all of those factors weren't applicable—making this a medical mystery they were hoping to unravel with the use of her research.

'Yes, and we're keen on getting your input on it all tomorrow. Niko was excited to hear we had secured your expertise. I think he's keen on the Athena Institute to be a part of your research,' Dr Seo continued, and Camila nodded along, not letting her thoughts show on her face.

The Niko she'd met in Vancouver had shown a great interest in her—but it had nothing to do with her research. That had been the reason she'd reciprocated his interest. Why they had spent the night together. She couldn't imagine him suddenly turning enthusiastic because of her research.

But at least Camila now knew that Niko was expecting her, and apparently with enthusiasm. 'I had the pleasure of meeting him six weeks ago at a conference in Vancouver,' she said, noting again how casually Dr Seo used his first name.

Was he informal with all his staff? That, at least, would match the image she had of him.

They stopped in front of a reception desk, and behind it, Camila glimpsed a first look at Niko's office through the open door. Her heart tumbled against her chest in an unbidden reaction. This was not what was supposed to happen after she'd told herself to remain calm in front of him. She was here because of work and not for anything lingering between them after the night they had shared.

'This is where I'll leave you. I can't wait to get started tomorrow,' Dr Seo said, pointing at the open door. Camila looked at the woman sitting behind the reception desk, who got to her feet with a smile as she greeted her.

'Nikolas is already expecting you,' the woman said, and that small and insignificant piece of information sent her pulse ticking higher. No time to catch her breath and steel her nerves. She'd have to go straight in there.

She followed the woman the few steps between them and the open office doors and watched as the assistant knocked before announcing her arrival. The rustling of papers filled the air, and then the all too familiar voice said, 'Please come in.'

Camila put on her best smile as she took a breath, knowing who she would meet in that room again—and it still wasn't enough to prepare her for the impact Nikolas Vassilis had on her.

He was dressed similarly to what he'd worn that night, a crisp white dress shirt tucked neatly into tailored black pants. But this time, the sleeves were rolled up, revealing the toned and defined muscles of his forearms. The same arms she had felt wrapped around her six weeks ago, holding her close as they found release in each other. The sight of them sent a shiver down her spine. She tried to swallow back the sudden rush of desire that flooded through her, but it was useless.

Because as her brain processed the awareness of *him* flooding through her, Nikolas did the unthinkable—he smiled. His lips parted, revealing a sliver of his straight white teeth as he got off his chair and strode towards her. Camila's brain short-circuited. Even though she'd gone over several scenarios on how this first meeting after their night together could go, the warmth was still unexpected. At most, she'd anticipated professional friendliness, but definitely not this…joy?

It stole what little air was left in her lungs.

'Camila, it's so good to see you again. Welcome to my hospital.' Niko stood in front of her now, the familiar scent of earth and rain enveloping her, and she smiled back as he put his hand on her bare arm, leaning in to brush a kiss against her cheek.

Then his eyes went to the assistant. 'Please

close the door,' he said, his voice as low as Camila remembered, bringing up memories she had meant to keep under wraps. They might have a connection, but she was still here for business.

She sat down on the seat he indicated just as the doors clicked shut and she finally dared to look at him. His brown-green eyes were sparkling with the warmth of his greeting, a small smile still playing on his lips.

Only when the quiet grew did she realise she had said nothing since his greeting—had only stared at him, really.

'It's good to see you, too. And so soon again,' she said, saying the first thing that came to her mind. How was he so calm about this? He either had an incredible poker face or…maybe he was just used to sleeping with women in the medical field. Enough so that meeting someone again wasn't that big of a deal to him.

He chuckled, the sound skittering over her skin. 'I know, I definitely wasn't expecting that, but it came as a delightful surprise when Emilia suggested she'd like to bring you on board to consult on a high-profile case.'

Camila nodded, some semblance of calm coming back to her. Work, yes. That was the topic she wanted to discuss. 'Alexis Theodorou. I haven't read much of his file, but it seems like an intriguing case. I haven't worked on an Olympic swimmer yet.'

'Was there any data from other professional athletes in your research?' he asked, nothing but calmness on his face. Emilia had clearly asked for his input before bringing her on board, so maybe that was the source of his steadiness. He'd chosen to extend her this invitation long before she'd known about it.

'Some, yes. Athletes like to do genetic mapping for their training, so some of that data was available to me through collaboration with other labs,' she said. 'It paints quite an interesting picture. I also received some data from a veterinarian studying cloned dogs, and despite the owner getting a second chance to raise the dog, major health issues matched the original dog almost one to one.'

Niko leaned forward, bracing his arms on his thighs, and Camila couldn't stop her eyes from dipping down just for a second. 'Even though some health issues can be prevented with a different diet or exercise routine?' he asked, his excitement for the research showing.

'You would be surprised how much of our life is already written in our DNA.'

'I can't wait to learn.' He smiled again, just as devastating as it had been a few minutes ago, and Camila was grateful to be sitting down. The nausea still danced on the edge of her senses. Paired with the tension Niko's proximity brought her, her focus was hanging by a thread.

'Alexis only arrived in our care a few days ago, and we've already experienced some roadblocks. The Swimming Federation is asking for hourly updates, and I spend too much of my time talking to them when I should be talking to the patient.' A slight edge appeared in his voice, one she couldn't quite understand.

'You're actively working on this case?' That was far more surprising to her than hearing about the Swimming Federation's involvement.

Niko shrugged his shoulders. 'I try to stay involved. My leadership at the Athena Institute is a new development. I was a senior surgeon at a different hospital before I took on the role of medical director. Even though I spend most of my time here, I believe there's a benefit to continuing to practice.'

'It must have been a hard transition, having to mourn your father while also taking on the legacy of the Athena Institute. I was sad to hear of Dr Vassilis's passing.' She'd never met him but heard enough of the institute to gain an appreciation for him as a leader in the field. This building had produced many of the doctors she now worked with closely, and that spoke of his leadership quality.

Something in Niko's eyes shuttered, his mouth disappearing into a thin line. 'This is a new era for the Athena Institute' was all he said to that, and Camila wasn't sure if the distance appearing between them was real or imagined.

Niko couldn't get caught up in his animosity towards his father. Stavros was gone now, and Niko would change the direction of the Athena Institute. After their night together, he hadn't thought he would see her so soon. His thoughts had often strayed, thinking of their night together. Camila's research was brilliant, her determination admirable, and her body had been his favourite thing to explore in a long time.

His first instinct when Emilia approached her about a potential collaboration was to refuse her. Mixing business and pleasure wasn't something he was in the habit of doing. But Emilia's arguments had been solid, the references to the research interesting enough for both parties. So he ended up saying yes, promising himself that he wouldn't start something with her again. They'd spent one night in Vancouver as consenting adults. Surely they could work together without it being awkward.

Except his desire had already pulled on its leash the second she'd walked through his door. His professional courtesy had melted away in her proximity until he couldn't help himself and wanted to touch her. Brush a kiss onto her soft cheek and inhale her scent once more.

Maybe that could be an added benefit to their

collaboration. Nothing wrong with having a bit of fun on the side as long as the stakes remained clear. But that was a proposal for later, if he even wanted to go down that path with her again. Or rather, if he could convince himself that it was wise to do so—because he *definitely* wanted to.

'I'll be there tomorrow morning for the first meeting with Emilia and Alexis,' he continued, steering the discussion back in the direction he wanted.

The less they spoke about Stavros, the better. His father had brought enough misery to far too many people who had come to the hospital seeking the support of the best people in the cardiology field. It had appalled Niko to learn how many unnecessary procedures Stavros and his cronies had performed just because vulnerable families were in a panic about a loved one. Getting rid of anyone who had been a part of this scheme had been his first act as medical director, and it grated on him how much time it had taken. But he couldn't risk the hospital becoming non-functional, either.

'Are you on a first-name basis with all of your staff members?' Camila asked, taking him out of his thoughts.

'I try to be, but I respect everyone's preference. Informal communication is important, especially in high-pressure situations. As a smart woman once said to me, "We all know we're doctors, so we might as well drop all the honorifics."' Warmth radiated through his body when she chuckled, giving him exactly the reaction he'd wanted to avoid.

'After this, you'll remember me for a lot more things,' she replied, her voice bordering on the flirty tone that had brought him to his knees that night in Vancouver—many times in a row.

'That sounds like an interesting promise.' His voice dropped low, and he leaned in farther, encouraged by how she looked at him through lowered lids. That spark between them had clearly not been a one-off thing. But he couldn't let himself get carried away by the high of chasing after her. Not when he had a hospital to focus on.

But…maybe he should see if they could find their connection again. She was here now, after all, and he hadn't been able to get her out of his head. Maybe another night with her would cure him of this particular hangover. 'Would you join me for dinner tonight?'

The blush dusting her cheeks was exquisite and told him she knew what he meant. How dinner was just a set-up. Her lower lip vanished between her teeth, and when she gave it a good squeeze, Niko's skin tightened and sparked with a low fire.

Then she said, 'If you have the time. I wouldn't want to trouble you.' A smile tugged at his lips. His evening had suddenly become a lot more interesting.

He got up from his chair and walked to his desk, taking one of his business cards out of the drawer. Camila stood when he got back to her, handing it over. 'I'll pick you up at the hotel tonight. But here is my card in case you need anything from me.' He paused when their fingers brushed against each other, the paper between them almost forgotten. 'You're my guest, so if there is anything, let me know.'

'Thank you.' She nodded, the smile she showed him was almost shy, but it still hit him somewhere low in his gut. This woman was absolutely stunning. He just couldn't take his eyes off her, couldn't help but reach out and wrap a strand of her hair around his finger. Just as he had on that couch at the conference reception.

One step and he was close enough to touch her. His free hand came down on her waist, and she turned her face towards his, looking up at him through thick lashes. He angled his head and—

A knock on the door interrupted them. Camila gasped, eyes wide, and took a step back. The strand of her hair fell out of his hand and left only the ghost of a silky wisp on his skin.

'Yes?' he called out, and his assistant opened the door, poking her head in.

'They're waiting for you down in the surgical wing,' she said, then looked over at Camila. 'Should I let the car know they can pick you up?'

'Yes,' Niko said, just as Camila shook her head with a soft, 'No.'

He looked at her and she went on, 'I'd like to stretch my legs for a bit. The hotel isn't far, and I have my phone, so I'll find my way around. Thank you, though.'

Her voice wavered just a bit as she said that, prompting Niko to raise his eyebrow. But then his phone buzzing in his pocket caught his attention. The OR was paging him.

'I have to go, but—' Niko looked at her, smiling again '—I'll see you tonight.'

CHAPTER THREE

CAMILA'S HEAD WAS splitting from a headache by the time she arrived at the small walk-in clinic she'd found near the Athena Institute. Everything inside of her had gone upside down when Niko had looked at her, and his attention had been enough to cast away any lingering nausea. Only for it to return with a vengeance when they'd been about to wrap things up.

Was it really a lack of nutrition, or had she just put her body through too much with all her travelling and the late nights? The nausea and headaches were constant enough for her to seek out help.

The nurse triaging her sat in front of her with a clipboard and went down a list of questions Camila was very much expecting. Her name, age, asking her to stand on the scale to get an accurate weight—Camila frowned at the number being higher than when she'd last checked—and if there were any changes in her environment recently. She was about ready to wrap it up when the nurse asked, 'And when was your last period?'

Camila glanced at her smartwatch, looking at the date.

Her last period had been two weeks ago—or rather she'd expected it to have been two weeks ago. She'd travelled to another conference in South America, had wondered if cramps would interrupt her work, but…it hadn't happened.

'Um…' Camila stared at the nurse, who still kept a kind smile on her face, giving her the time she needed to recall. To…

Her voice shook as she said, 'I think it's been eight weeks.'

The nurse nodded, writing her answer down on the clipboard. 'Is there a chance you could be pregnant?'

The question sank into her consciousness like a stone, the memories of the night in Vancouver coming back. It wasn't possible, was it? They'd discussed this before they did anything. She was on the pill and Niko…he had used a condom. She wanted to say, *No, it isn't possible. How could it be?* But the symptoms painted a different picture.

Camila swallowed the lump in her throat as she said, 'Yes.'

After completing the form, the nurse took her vitals and samples for standard testing. Now Camila sat in the small exam room, staring at the name plaque sitting on the desk that read Dr Thea Kostas.

The door opened, and a short woman with a pixie cut walked in holding a folder in her hand. 'Hi there, sorry for the wait. I was just looking at the results from the test,' she said, sitting down in her chair and then meeting Camila's eyes with a smile. 'The nurse said you've complained of nausea and headaches for a sustained period?'

Camila nodded. 'Yes, that's right. I've been travelling a lot in the last eight weeks, so I wanted to rule out anything related to that. It might just be fatigue, but I've never experienced it so persistently.'

The friendly smile of the doctor only set her at ease for a second as she nodded along with her and then looked back at her notes. She flipped one paper over, reading what was on it. Unfamiliar with both the language and the Greek alphabet, Camila couldn't glean anything that would help her anticipate the results. What if it really was...?

'Okay.' Dr Kostas looked up, weaving her fingers together under her chin. 'We can confirm that the pregnancy test has come back positive. Given that your last period was eight weeks ago, that would put your pregnancy at the eight-week mark.'

The doctor's words rippled through the air,

crashing through Camila at a high speed that had her catching her breath.

Pregnant.

She was pregnant.

'Eight weeks?'

Two months? The news was so shocking, she couldn't even wrap her head around that number.

Had she forgotten to take the pill?

'I understand this might be unexpected news for you,' Dr Kostas went on. She must be familiar with the stunned silence of women who were confronted with an unexpected pregnancy. 'Do you have any immediate thoughts or concerns you'd like to discuss?'

Camila looked up from where her hands were knotted together on her lap. 'Are there any recommendations on prenatal care for the eight-week mark?'

Her mind sorted through the last eight weeks, analysing her own behaviour. She didn't know what to think of the news, but there was one topic that had never failed her in life—medicine. If she could understand the next steps on a medical level, she could deal with her emotions in time.

Dr Kostas stood and opened the cabinet behind her, retrieving some blister packs from a drawer. She set them on the table, then opened another door and retrieved what looked like a business card that she put on top of the blister packs.

'Here are some samples for prenatal vitamins.

These are all over-the-counter, so you can also go to any pharmacy and buy them. Looking after your and the baby's health by cutting down on stress and harmful substances is important. And then you should think about making an appointment with an obstetrician for your prenatal care.' She tapped the business card with her finger. 'This is a friend of mine who has her own clinic nearby. If you call her and tell her that I referred you, she will make sure to see you.'

Camila gathered the things on the table, slipping it all into her bag before looking back up at the doctor's sympathetic eyes. She didn't know what else to ask—or what else Dr Kostas could even tell her. Though this wasn't her specialty, she knew enough about pregnancy to understand the mechanics behind it. Her lack of understanding was not medical but emotional.

She forced herself to nod, her mind still racing. With the news so fresh, she couldn't even contemplate what that would do to her—to her career. Her role demanded so much travel. How would that even work? How would she tell the father?

Niko.

A night that should have meant nothing had now changed her life forever.

Camila's hand came down on her still flat stomach, cradling the life that had sparked into existence just like that. The responsibility lay heavy on her shoulders, and the walls of the small exam room suddenly pressed in on her. She needed some air, some space to breathe.

Jumping to her feet, Camila grabbed her bag. 'Thank you for the clarity, Dr Kostas, and for the referral. I'll be sure to be in contact with your colleague. If you'll excuse me...'

As Camila rushed out of the clinic, her mother's voice became louder in her head, warning her of the tremendous blunder this was. The moment he finds out, he will leave—just like her father had—making her a single mother raising her child while working. They all eventually left, Mariana had said, and Camila had never stuck around long enough for her to find out. With her work demanding so much of her time, she'd never even looked for a person who could be worth the risk of heartbreak. Of eventually being left, like her mother had suggested.

Camila tried to slow down her breathing as she walked, her hand coming to rest on her stomach. Things would be different. Whether Niko would be around to help or not, she would remember how her mother's words had moulded her into someone unable to trust. Camila would be different. She just needed to figure out how.

Lying on the bed of her hotel room, Camila stared up at the ceiling. Minutes ticked by, and she knew Niko would be here soon to take her to dinner. She had already decided that she would invite him in—to talk. Because there was no way she could focus on anything tomorrow without having *that* conversation out of the way.

Her brain was busy contemplating all the scenarios of how this pregnancy could play out. Camila had thought about her future child before and how she wanted their life to be easier than hers had been. Usually so confident in her own abilities, she was at a loss at how to go about this new situation. Her mother, her own home life, left her nothing to go by. Even though she lost her husband to someone else, Mariana hadn't believed women should be career-oriented. Had never wanted to talk to Camila about her work—only ever about when she would have grandchildren.

But more than doing better by her child, what Camila wanted was a father for her child. A real father, one that would be there every step of the way during the pregnancy and as the child grew up. Having not had that herself, she often wondered what life would have been like if her father had been around.

All she had to show for it now was an unhealthy dose of trust issues.

Would Niko stand by her once he heard the news of their accidental pregnancy? She thinks he's a decent man, and the warmth with which he'd greeted her today made her hopeful. But these feelings could change at the drop of a hat at such life-changing news. Wasn't that what her mother had always warned her about? Men will tell you anything you want to hear—until you no longer suit their needs.

Camila didn't *want* to believe that Niko was like that, but she didn't know him at all. All she knew was the explosive electricity jumping between them. It had snapped back into place the second they'd been close to each other in his office.

Now she was forced to figure out whether or not Nikolas Vassilis would be the person to stick around in her life—in a strict co-parenting sense. Because there was no way a man who slept with her after knowing her for all but one hour was someone who wanted to settle down. And even though Camila wanted to have an intact family unit, she was not willing to sacrifice her child's happiness for the sake of having a father figure in their lives.

Her mother had walked through life unhappy, blaming all of her misfortunes on her no-good ex and, by extension, Camila. There was absolutely no way she would settle her own child with the same burden.

Niko stood in front of the hotel room door, staring at it with mixed feelings. Heat coursed through his veins as he remembered the last time he'd stood in front of Camila's door and that night.

She now waited beyond that door—only now she would be here until they solved this medical mystery.

The women in his life came and went. Almost all of them were career-minded people like himself, looking for a similar arrangement, where emotions wouldn't impede a night of hot release. They didn't think about him the next morning, and Niko preferred it that way. He didn't have the time or energy for personal attachments now that he was the medical director of the Athena Institute.

And before that... With his father's obsession of creating a legacy in the wealthy circles of Greek society, he'd been urged to go on far too many dates with prospective matches that would combine two families into one powerful one. Not wanting to play any of his father's games, Niko hadn't agreed to any of these dates and resisted any attachment. Now the resistance was more of an instinct than an active choice, but one that he thought still served him well.

Until Camila somehow slipped under his skin during their night in Vancouver. Because since then, Niko could not get her out of his mind. On the flight back, he'd pored over her research, including her published papers and interviews, to learn more about her.

Why? he'd asked himself many times, especially since she wasn't someone he wanted to join the Athena Institute. Their research leaned more towards surgical applications, while hers was all about the applications of gene mapping to help with long-term cardiological diseases.

But then their conversation had turned flirty in his office, the memories of their night coming alive with the heat in his blood—and he wanted more. Wanted to see her come undone underneath him again and again. That was a fresh development for him, who never saw the same person again.

Willing the fire inside him to cool, he knocked on the door. Maybe this would be just one more night, or maybe they could figure out how to keep things going. Just as long as they both agreed on where this thing between them ended.

As the door swung open, Niko's eyes widened at the sight before him. The once perfectly styled locks of Camila's hair were now thrown haphazardly into a messy bun, with stray strands cascading down her neck and framing her face. Gone was the professional attire she'd worn earlier, replaced by an oversized T-shirt and baggy sweatpants. Despite the stark contrast to his custom-tailored suit, he couldn't help but admire her radiance. Her natural beauty shone through, making his breath catch in a momentary stutter as he took her in.

She was absolutely stunning.

'Hey,' he said, unable—unwilling—to keep the smile off his face.

'Hey... I think I would like to change our plans to something more casual,' she said, looking down as her hand dug into her sweatpants. 'I thought we could settle in here and just order some room service. It...it has been a long day.'

He raised his brows at that last part, looking her over from head to toe. Smart business suit or casual homebody style didn't matter to him or his libido apparently, because she was so stunning in both that he didn't know how to express himself. Except Camila had just given him an obvious hint.

It has been a long day.

He nodded with a smile and then stepped in as she invited him in with a wave of her hand. Camila wasn't looking to rekindle their passionate connection tonight. No, for whatever reason, she needed comfort.

'Did the flight wear you out?' he asked as he approached the living area, choosing to sit in the armchair while Camila took a seat on the couch. She folded her legs beneath her, leaning back in a gesture that was strangely casual, but he could see tension rippling underneath the surface.

'Yes, and the last few weeks have been rather busy. I've left my time zone more times than I can count, and it's messing up my inner clock,' she said with a smile that wasn't as convincing as her tone. She wanted to *appear* fine, but Niko saw the subtle signs.

'I can leave you to rest for today. We have plenty of time to catch up in the weeks you're here.' The only reason he'd wanted to talk to her this evening was because of their night in Vancouver. Bringing her into his hospital had been a purely professional opinion—or so he'd thought until he saw her earlier. Now he wasn't so sure about it any more. Had a part of him wanted to see her again, even if he had to invite her to his hospital?

Camila shook her head, but when she looked at him, there was nothing of that burning fire left. No, what he saw there was something just as raw but so different. Panic? He sat up straight, his brow bunching. Something in his gut tightened at that spark in her eyes, the low dread creeping across the space between them and spearing through him.

'What's wrong?' he asked, and he could see Camila searching for the words.

'I need to talk to you about Vancouver,' she said, holding his stare with a fluttering breath. Nothing of the earlier passion was left, and for a moment he wondered if he had made it up. Was she dreading telling him she didn't want to rekindle their affair?

'You can tell me anything.' A strange thing to say to someone who was hardly more than a stranger, but Niko meant it. With how fragile Camila looked right now, he didn't think he could turn anything down.

'Okay, well… I've not been feeling great for the last four weeks. I blamed the constant flying and long hours on the fatigue, but even with a few days of rest, it persisted.' She paused, her fingers knotted into a tight ball. 'With the importance of this case, I didn't want to be distracted, so when I excused myself after our meeting, I went to a walk-in clinic in the area.'

Niko leaned forward, bracing his arms on his thighs. 'You're unwell?'

'Not exactly. I'm well enough, but I am…pregnant.'

Pregnant.

The word clanged through him, sinking down like it was tied down with a stone until it found the depths of his being. Camila was pregnant. Coldness trickled through him as his thoughts caught up with the information, because…there was only one reason she would tell him like this. In private. With her hands wound into the fabric of her baggy sweatpants. Looking at him with such nerves and anguish that he wanted to reach across to her and offer comfort.

Except Niko found himself frozen in place. He couldn't offer anything because his own brain was processing the words she'd left unsaid. Words he really needed to hear now.

'And you're telling me this because you think I'm…' His voice grew thick, and he cleared his throat to force the words out. 'I'm the father?'

She took another shuttering breath and then nodded into the quiet spreading between them.

It was his child.

The words didn't sound real in his mind. His child? When children were the furthest thing from his mind? Not only that, he'd long ago made the decision that children probably didn't fit into his vision of the future. Not when his father had been so obsessed with the idea of a legacy that it had destroyed their relationship. Lacking a role model to learn from, Niko had just resigned himself to a childless existence. That was better than the risk of passing on his own dysfunctional family dynamics onto the next generation.

But now that was no longer a choice. He was going to be a father.

The armchair suddenly shrunk around his body, creating a sense of claustrophobia, and he surged to his feet. Bursts of energy cascaded through him as he processed the information. Of all the things to come from the cooperation with Camila, this had not even registered on his radar.

He took a few steps towards the window, looking down at Athens' busy streets. 'How is that possible?' he asked without turning around and heard Camila shift in her seat.

'It's my fault… Travelling through time zones

messed up the rhythm of my medication, and I must have forgotten to take the pill one day,' she said, and her hurt tone prompted Niko to turn towards her.

She was blaming herself? The memories of that night were fuzzy, but one thing was certain—he'd been a willing participant in full awareness of the consequences. 'This isn't on you. It takes two people to make a child, and sometimes it happens even when those two people are trying to avoid making one.'

Camila sighed, hiding her face behind her hands. 'I know, but I still feel awful. I know neither of us had planned on walking away from our one-night stand with a child, and I don't want you to think any of this is designed to…trap you.'

Niko blinked at her choice of words. 'Trap me? You think that's what I'm worried about?'

He walked over to the couch, kneeling down in front of her and prying her fingers away from her face. His skin sizzled where he touched her, but he ignored the feeling and focused on the woman in front of him.

'That's what *I'm* worried about when it comes to you. Despite everything, I care what you think of me, and this situation…it's difficult,' she said.

His grip on her hand slackened at her words, too stunned by them to say anything else for a few breaths—because they mirrored so keenly what had been going on in his mind since he knew she would come back into her life. He, too, cared what she thought about him. That was the only reason he had asked her out to dinner. For weeks she'd been on his mind, despite his best attempts to forget about her. His mind never lingered on the women he slept with, knowing there was nothing to linger on. Somehow the night with Camila had been different from the very start— enough for him to agree for her to come here as a doctor. To work with her.

But that had now changed, too. They were having a child.

Niko sighed, slumping back against the coffee table, his hand still wrapped around hers. 'I don't know what to say except that I know you didn't plan this. I know this because you didn't have any intentions to speak to me further after our initial meeting at the party. You have a lot of things to worry about, but this doesn't need to be one of them.'

Tension left her body as her fingers relaxed against his. 'I don't know what to do about this or what my thoughts are right now. The only thing I knew was that I needed to tell you because I wouldn't have been able to work tomorrow otherwise.'

Right, because even after this bombshell announcement, their lives had to go on as usual. She had a case to solve, and he had an entire hospital to run. He let his head droop forward, leaning his forehead against her hand wrapped around his. Her fingers twitched against his skin and that small touch rushed through him in a confusing heat.

'Okay, good. I… I'll need some time to think about this,' he said as he willed his body to move and get onto his feet. 'Maybe we can talk more tomorrow? After work?'

She nodded. This matter was far from resolved, and he could tell this was as surprising and complicated to her as it was to him. Even though he said he needed to think about it, he knew there was only one choice—whatever Camila wanted. If she wanted to go through with this pregnancy, he would give her whatever support she wanted. It was the right thing to do.

'I'm sorry about dinner,' Camila said as he straightened his jacket, taking his phone out to call the valet to bring his car round.

'Don't worry about it.' He paused as he looked around. 'Is there anything you need?'

She shook her head, and a part of him wanted to walk back to her, wrap his arms around her and hold her tight. Something about this woman had him completely enchanted, calling on deep-seated instincts within him to protect her. Care for her.

Dangerous feelings. Ones he couldn't afford. His hospital was the focus of his life, and if they were going to have this baby together, there would be even less space for romance. Niko hardly remembered his father's involvement in his early years, only becoming more interested in his son once he started med school. His mother, Daphne, had put her own career on hold to take care of him and Eleni. She hadn't once complained about it, but ever since she'd returned to work, he'd seen a difference in the happiness of his mother.

Camila would never want that for her life, and he would make sure this wasn't the fate his own child would suffer. But that meant focusing on his work and his offspring.

'Call me if you need anything, even in the middle of the night. Okay? We…' He hesitated, not sure what or how much of himself he wanted to share. 'We'll figure it out.'

When Camila nodded, he mustered a small smile before turning away and leaving the hotel, his car already waiting when he reached the exit.

CHAPTER FOUR

'GOOD MORNING, DR PEREIRA FREY. It's so good to finally get started on this.' Just like yesterday, Emilia Seo's enthusiasm for Camila's arrival took her by surprise.

After her conversation with Niko, she'd tried to read the patient file and figure out what her next steps would be in the diagnostic process, but her mind hadn't stopped spinning. Parts of the conversation replayed in her head, and even though she didn't know what to do, somehow she'd hoped that Niko would. That he had some magic solution to figure out their situation amicably. That thought was, of course, laughable, and when none of that had come to pass, Camila hadn't been able to do more than to lie in bed and try to rest.

'Yes, I can't wait to get started. I've seen the patient notes, but can you walk me through everything you've done? It helps to hear it in your unfiltered words.' Camila sat down in the chair Emilia indicated, and just as the other woman took her own seat, a knock sounded on the door as it swung open.

Niko stepped in, his white lab coat a stark contrast to the black chinos and grey shirt he wore underneath. Just like the first day they'd met, he commanded most of the oxygen in the room. All she could do was look up to him and imagine what her life with him would be like from now on. Because they were now linked forever. Would her reaction to him be as intense every time she saw him? Or would the sensation eventually dull, making way for more practical emotions with the person she would co-parent her child with?

If anything good could be had from last night, it was the firming up of her decision about the baby. From the second she had heard the news, something had sparked alive inside her, a gentle warmth that hadn't been there before. The shock and worry about delivering the news to Niko had taken over her entire system, shutting down anything pleasant before she could contemplate it for too long. But as the night went on, she realised what that spark was growing inside of her—a tiny thread binding her to the life growing there.

Camila would keep it, no matter what.

'Sorry for the delay,' Niko said, and Camila fought the shiver clawing down her spine when he sat down next to her—thankfully with more than enough distance between them.

'Your timing couldn't be better. I was about to

start,' Emilia replied with a smile and then continued addressing Camila, as she handed her a tablet loaded with the patient's file. 'Our patient's name is Alexis Theodorou, and he's an Olympic level swimmer. We admitted him last week after he suffered a cardiac arrest shortly after his training session.'

Camila scrolled through the file, her eyes skimming over the notes taken. Some of her usual calm returned to her as she slipped into the familiar pattern of diagnostics. That was the thing she was good at—much better than interpersonal relationships. 'Although an Olympic athlete suffering cardiac arrest is unusual, it has happened in the past. Especially if we are now thinking about hereditary diseases. Did you run a toxicology report when he arrived? I didn't see it in the information pack you provided me.'

Emilia nodded, pointing at the tablet just as Niko said, 'We sent you over the patient history with some files missing. A safety precaution his team asked us to take. They didn't want any sensitive information to leave the hospital grounds.'

His deep voice slithered down her spine, threatening to undo the composure she'd put together so painstakingly. What was it about him that let him break through to her with such ease? Maybe they needed to step away from the tension building between them if they wanted their co-parenting relationship to work… Though that thought hit her deep in her gut.

'I understand, of course. Did you find anything? Anabolic steroids? Amphetamines? Diuretics?'

Emilia started, 'Nothing out of the ordinary—'

'Diuretics? How are those a concern?' Niko interrupted, shooting her a glance.

'Athletes will sometimes abuse diuretics to lose weight before an important competition, or to mask other substances. They can cause arrhythmias when misused.' Camila brought up his latest echocardiogram results, her eyes flying over the peaks and valleys of the grid. 'The echocardiogram and electrocardiogram look as I'd expect them to look on a healthy twenty-year-old man. Did you do an MRI as well?'

She looked up to see Emilia nod.

'So, you're probably thinking hypertrophic cardiomyopathy?'

Emilia's eyes rounded as she nodded. 'We are testing out our assumption of early stage hypertrophic cardiomyopathy. With no family history of any heart disease and the clean toxicology report, HCM is the most likely diagnosis.'

Camila nodded, forming a supplementary diagnostic plan in her head. 'Most likely, yes. But in this case, not. With a murmur at the left sternal border, we could interpret the echocardiogram results as HCM. But the septal measurement looks normal to me.' She flipped the tablet around, pointing at the specific part of the report.

'That's why we're thinking of early stages,' Emilia said, getting a nod from Niko. 'We are doing some further imaging today to see if there were any changes. Maybe this afternoon we can sit together with the radiologist to look at it? You probably also want to meet the patient.'

'Yes, a short meeting with him would be great. We'll discuss what we hope to achieve with mapping his genes and go into more details about his family history.'

Camila followed the other woman's example when she got up, and behind her she sensed Niko move as well. She turned around to catch his eyes and immediately regretted doing so. Intention darkened his eyes, mixed with a conflict she could feel on her skin—without him having to voice anything. She knew what his look meant because she sensed it, too. The simmering attraction that wouldn't let up, not even after their discussion yesterday.

The discussion that had led her to the conclusion that co-parents were all they ever could be. She wouldn't risk a relationship with him, not after they had met under such fleeting circumstances. What if he got bored with her the way her father had grown tired of her mother?

'Are you going to join us for the entire day?'

Emilia asked Niko, giving voice to the question in Camila's mind.

He shook his head—and disappointment wound itself through her unbidden. 'No, I have some meetings to attend. Camila, will you come by and give me an update on your thoughts about the case? The Swimming Federation will want an update from me today.'

Her name slipped from his lips as if it were the most natural thing in the world. The sounds of his voice skittered over her skin, raising the fine hair along her arms and nape, and leaving her fighting another shiver.

'Of course. Now, let's meet the patient.'

Though he'd asked Camila to come to him when she was done, Niko had begun to feel more and more restless as the day went on without seeing her. He knew that his thinking around this was absurd. Of course, he wouldn't spend a lot of time with her. In actuality, he wasn't supposed to spend any time with her. There was a reason he had Emilia as his head of Cardiology. His job was to focus on the day-to-day of the hospital and bring more opportunities to the institute. More diverse opportunities for people from all walks of life—unlike the way his father had run this place.

But despite knowing all of that, he headed out of his office during a break in his schedule to seek her out. To check up on his guest doctor, he said to himself, not to follow her around like she'd cast some spell on him. Or was it that connection now standing between them that would always be there—their child?

Niko still couldn't quite wrap his head around that revelation. Of all the things he'd been prepared to hear, this hadn't been anywhere near the list. Now they went from a one-night stand to needing to discuss what their future together would look like. Not that he expected her to have an answer already. But after going over their conversation from yesterday again, he realised he hadn't given her his support—hadn't expressed that he would be there for her no matter what.

They had made this child together, and he wouldn't shrink away from that responsibility. Even if being a father terrified him more than anything. Was choosing to be the opposite of his own father enough to make a decent parent to his child?

The nurse near the patient's room told him Camila had already taken Alexis Theodorou for some testing. He thanked her when she told him what exam room they had checked into and Niko finally found her. Her voice filtered through the door as he knocked, and her eyes widened when she saw him step into the room. A quick glance around told him they were alone.

'Did you get rid of Emilia already?' he asked

with a smile, and the delightful sound of her laugh rolled over him.

'No, but as you well know, she has to look after all of your cardiology needs and not just one patient,' she replied, her eyes flicking between him and Alexis, who was walking on a treadmill at a leisurely pace, and the way he held himself upright, no one could ever guess that his heart had stopped just a few days ago.

They set up the room to stress-test people as a method of diagnosis, connecting each treadmill to several monitors that displayed their signals inside the room itself—or in the room next door, which connected the exercise room with a two-way mirror. Camila had left Alexis to his own devices in the room, monitoring him next door.

'How are things? I can see you're not wasting any time getting started,' Niko said, looking at the patient as he increased the tempo of the treadmill.

'I was planning on waiting until tomorrow, but when I spoke to Alexis about my immediate thoughts, he begged me to do the stress test with him right now. It seems he's bored with lying in bed,' Camila replied with a smile, then turned slightly to look at him. 'It's astonishing how easily he bounced back from a cardiac arrest.'

Niko nodded as he pulled up a chair to sit next to her—with an appropriate measure of distance between them. 'It makes little sense. None of our scans revealed any physical abnormalities on his heart, either.'

Camila's lips curved in a smile. 'Look at the scalpel wielder wanting to cut as a first option.'

The comment was so unexpected, he couldn't help but laugh. 'I didn't peg you as someone who perpetuated the rivalry between medical and surgical.'

She shrugged. 'I'm highly competitive. I'd probably play up any kind of rivalry I'm involved in.'

'I see.' Niko hummed his agreement. Anyone working at the level they did was hyper-competitive. It was the only way of getting anywhere. Long hours and endless sacrifices were needed to maintain this kind of lifestyle. Their one-night fling in Vancouver was proof of that. Neither of them was in any position in life to make room for a partner—and now they would have to find the space for a child.

'Can I go faster?' Alexis's voice came through the speaker, steady and clear with no signs of exertion.

'We agreed on the pace, Alexis. You can set the speed higher every five minutes. We need to raise your pulse gradually, okay?' Her eyes went to the monitor displaying the speed of the treadmill before checking over his heart rate monitor again.

'I don't see anything suspicious here, either. Not yet at least,' Camila said, releasing the button of the microphone so Alexis couldn't hear her any more.

Niko watched the monitor as well, his gaze flittering between it and Camila. There was a deep-seated care even in the way she watched the vital signs in front of her. He hadn't expected her to be this way. Through all the press coverage and interviews he'd read, a different picture of Camila had formed in his head. One that cast her in a similar light as his father, where she was only looking for the highest bidder to sponsor her research.

But then she wouldn't be here with such a hands-on approach to the patient's care. Surely, if she wasn't in medicine for the joy of helping people, she would let Emilia deal with all these tests and focus solely on interpreting his gene mapping. Would she not?

Guilt needled at him as he considered her— how easily he had judged her on nothing more than his own preconceived notions to go on. It was instinct more than choice, expecting the worst because of what he'd experienced in life. Would his father's shadow haunt all of Niko's future relationships? Had he missed out already because of his inability to trust?

His mind drifted towards the child they'd created, some of his doubts easing. Though he knew a lot of the credit for his achievements went to his mother, Niko didn't have an exemplary father figure to look to for inspiration and support, but maybe Camila did. Maybe whoever had raised her had instilled this high level of care and compassion he was seeing in her diagnostic approach.

'Did you ever want kids?' he asked, suppressing a laugh at Camila's shocked expression. There was no gentle way of initiating the conversation they needed to have.

'Yes, I did. And… I still do. But the concept has always been nebulous because I've never had the right person at my side.' She turned her chair towards him. 'What about you?'

Niko froze. His first instinct was to tell the truth with a simple no. But that wasn't really what he thought. Children had never been a part of his plan because he'd never thought he would have the freedom to have them. Doubted his own ability as a parent enough not to try…

'Same answer, to be honest. I set out to find my own path in medicine, independent of the Athena Institute. Being so focused on my career, I didn't give children a proper thought.' He stopped, chuckling at his own words. 'It's a bit ironic that we're sitting here now.'

'You didn't want to work at the Athena Institute?' Concern creased her brow, and Niko blinked.

People knew that he hadn't joined the hospital after finishing his training, and Stavros had spun it in a way that made it look like his heir was gathering more experience elsewhere before joining up to continue the Vassilis legacy of the Athena Institute. Only he had never joined, even after spending years away and holding high positions at other hospitals.

This wasn't the first time Camila had slipped past his defences just to walk into his sanctuary. Was that because of their physical connection that burned so much hotter than he'd ever imagined? Or did this go far deeper?

That was a worrying thought and one Niko didn't dare to follow further. There couldn't be more than that. Not when they would have to figure out things with the child. Bringing even the hint of a romantic connection into this complicated things far more than they needed to be.

Niko stayed quiet at her question, so when he finally did answer, Camila turned back to look at him.

'After medical school, I left to do my training and then work for a different hospital. I didn't want to…rely on my father's reputation but rather my own skill to get me ahead in my career. I knew I wouldn't be able to do that in my father's shadow. Now, with his passing, I find myself in charge of the place I turned my back to—and I'm still figuring out the state of the Athena Institute.'

The state of the Athena Institute? Was something wrong with it? This conversation was far more personal than she'd prepared herself for, and she didn't know what to think of that. This connection between them wasn't supposed to be this…intense. Then again, she hadn't thought she would ever see him again—or carry his child. Maybe this wasn't actually about the attraction she sensed simmering between them, but a result of having a baby together.

'A few years back, when my research was still fresh, I got in touch with your father. I thought he would be interested in my work. With the reputation the Athena Institute enjoyed, I knew it was a long shot, but I also really believed in the work I wanted to do,' she began, recalling a time with far fewer opportunities than she had now. 'I received a fairly generic answer back that I'm sure his assistant wrote for him.'

Nikolas chuckled, tilting his head to the side. 'I sometimes forget his contributions to medicine. For me, he was always just…' He paused, then shook his head. 'I'm sure you would have made an excellent addition to the team.'

'Maybe…' Camila looked up when a soft beep echoed through the room, and on the treadmill, Alexis Theodorou was picking up speed. 'So even though neither of us had seriously thought about children, we now find ourselves in a situation where we're having one.'

'Does that mean you want us to…do this together?' For the first time since they met Camila saw hesitation in his eyes, as if he didn't dare to say the words out loud. Was it because he didn't want them to be true? Or because he wasn't sure that she meant it?

Nervous energy bubbled up inside her as she thought about the conversation she'd had in her head in the middle of the night, explaining how she planned on keeping the child—and how he felt about being a part of their lives, too. On a strict co-parenting basis, of course. Their unexpected pregnancy was already messy enough as it was without adding any unnecessary stress to it.

Swallowing the lump in her throat, she nodded. 'Yes, I would like to figure out how we can do this. Together. I know this wasn't what either of us had expected to come out of our one-night stand, but…' She paused, and then decided to give him a piece of her—since he had just volunteered a piece of himself not a minute ago. 'I grew up without a father, and I remember the struggles of single motherhood. That's not a life I'd want for my child.'

Niko's chair creaked as he leaned forward, closing the gap between them. 'Okay, then we'll make a plan. We both have things we want to avoid in this arrangement, so let's make sure we are both in agreement on what this should look like.'

Camila paused at that. Though he was still occupying his own chair, she felt his proximity through her entire body—rushing in a wave of delicate heat. 'What are the things you want to avoid?' she asked, her voice far raspier than she'd anticipated.

He noticed that little detail, too, for his eyes narrowed on her in a way that was all too reminiscent of their night together in Vancouver. *This* was one thing they wanted to avoid. Right?

'I don't want to overcomplicate things between us. We'll have to come to some sort of arrangement where we can be in the child's life in equal parts. Giving in to the tension between us seems like an ill-advised choice.' Niko's hand grabbed hers, lacing their fingers together in a stark contrast to his words.

'I couldn't agree more,' Camila breathed out, though instead of taking her hand back, she gave his a squeeze, leaning in until their foreheads touched. Where had this heat suddenly come from?

During their entire exchange, they had moved closer to each other, their magnetism something outside of their control. All they could do was obey to the call urging them together. Even if they had just said that they *shouldn't* give in.

'So that means we have about seven months to figure out our plans and how we want to…interact with each other.' His tone stood in direct opposition to his words. One drew her into his orbit while the other told her not to come too close.

And she wanted nothing more than to be close, to feel him on her skin once more.

'Seven months is a long time. Plenty to reset our relationship and start from the beginning—as strict co-parents.' She forced the words out even if they burned in her throat, set alight by the desire coursing through her.

Niko said nothing. He hummed as he nodded his agreement, putting his other hand on her cheek and swiping over it with his thumb. Each sweep was like kindling to the low-burning fire.

'It'll probably involve a lot of trial and error to figure out what our relationship should look like,' he said, and Camila took a sharp inhale when the tip of his nose grazed hers.

She couldn't find the words to put a stop to this. Couldn't find the will to push him away. The want sat too deep, was much too overpowering— even though they had just decided to cool things. Time slowed down as Niko got closer, angling his mouth over hers and—

The blaring alarm of the heart rate monitor tore through the room, and Camila jerked back. Her eyes went wide as she turned in the chair and read the information on the monitors. 'Oh, no, his heart rate is suddenly all over the place. He might be at risk of—'

A thud interrupted her as Alexis collapsed on the treadmill, crumpling to the floor behind it as the force of the spinning band propelled him backwards. Both Camila and Niko jumped to their feet and into the room towards the patient. She hissed when Niko turned him over. Blood from a small but deep cut on his forehead leaked over his face and onto the floor.

'Do you have a—' Before Camila could finish her sentence, Niko was already back on his feet, pulling a crash cart towards them and pressing the alarm button on the wall to alert the nurses' station. He handed her a pair of gloves before putting on his own. Then he grabbed some gauze and began pressing against the wound while looking at her. Waiting for instructions, she realised with a start. Even though he was the medical director, he was looking to her for the principal care of the patient she was in charge of.

Even after she had completely messed it up by getting distracted and not watching the monitor during an active treatment... When they had just said the attraction between them shouldn't interfere with their work not even two minutes ago.

'This other arrhythmia is brought on by physical stress,' she said as she looked at the monitors she'd put on him for the test. 'Pulse is still spiking and dropping. Let's get him unhooked of everything so we can transport him. It's not ventricular fibrillation, but it has the potential to escalate into a similar condition as his emergency room admission.'

Niko nodded, reaching towards the crash cart

for the medical tape. With two quick moves, he affixed the swath of gauze to the wound, putting enough pressure on it to begin the clotting process. When he got to his feet, a nurse opened the door. Her eyes darted to the patient, and when she saw him unconscious on the floor, she turned around and wheeled a stretcher in.

'Will we be able to move him?' she asked as she lowered the flat bed of the stretcher so they could shift him over.

Camila got to her feet, squatting down on one side, and Niko mirrored her action on the other side. They looked at each other, and when he nodded, they lifted Alexis off the floor and onto the stretcher. 'Lead the way,' she huffed at Niko, clenching her jaw as she caught her breath.

One of their emergency treatment rooms was right around the corner, and Camila nodded when she saw everything she needed in the room. Not hesitating another second, she got started on the ECG machine as she pulled it closer to the unconscious Alexis.

'Can you please hook him back up onto the monitor again?' Even before she'd finished the sentence, Niko was already moving. He wiped down the area of Alexis's chest before helping her place the electrodes onto the skin. His fingers brushed against hers at one point, and she pushed away the shiver clawing down her spine. She couldn't afford any of these distractions.

'Let's prepare IV access. He will need some intravenous liquids and potentially beta-blockers,' she said, and Niko nodded.

He looked at the nurse and said, 'Prepare an infusion for esmolol while I set up the IV access.'

She nodded and walked over to unlock a cabinet housing the required medicine. The echocardiogram came alive as the electrodes picked up the signals, and Camila's eyes darted between the monitor and the place in the patient's arm where Niko was now inserting the cannula.

Tension built in her chest as she watched the spikes on the monitor pass by, looking at the distance between them, and she pressed her lips together when the picture became clear. 'He's having arrhythmias, but it's not a ventricular fibrillation. It's…something else.'

Camila shook her head and turned back to the patient, nodding at the nurse. 'We can hang the esmolol to stop the arrhythmia before it can become a VF.'

The nurse handed Niko the IV bag, who then placed it on a hook next to the stretcher before inserting it into the cannula and giving it a squeeze to get the liquid flowing. Knowing esmolol to be fast-acting, they didn't need to wait long until they saw an improvement on the echocardiogram. The tension drained out of the room when Alexis's heart rate finally came back into an acceptable range.

Camila breathed out, turning to Niko with a smile that faltered when she encountered a quiet intensity in his gaze. She knew she had messed up by taking her eyes off Alexis. But he'd been right there with her, encouraging the distraction. What right did he have to be angry with her?

She swallowed as the guilt of her lapse mixed with the anger simmering underneath her skin. She was happy to take on the bigger share of the blame, but only if Niko could acknowledge he'd done his part, too. Instead of saying anything, she turned to the ECG, hitting the button to print out the readings from the moment they had attached the machine to Alexis.

'This should give us some indication of his condition. I'll go have a look at it.' The sharpness in his eyes lingered, so Camila chose not to spend any time looking at him. Instead, she turned to the nurse. 'Could you organise transport back to the patient's room? And please inform me when he wakes up so we can have a conversation.'

Without another look at Niko, she left the room, too preoccupied with her own anger to see confusion ripple over his face.

Camila was halfway down the corridor when Niko caught up to her. He wrapped his hand around her wrist, tugging her to a halt.

'What was that about?' he asked, his voice echoing loudly in the empty corridor. He flinched at the sound of his own voice, much more brash than he intended. Looking around, he checked the sign next to the door to his left before pushing it open and pulling them into an empty exam room.

Camila shook off his hand as the door closed behind him, staring at him with an angry glint in her eyes. 'You can't even give me a minute to myself before you chew me out?' she said, crossing her arms in front of her.

Niko blinked. 'Chew you out? That wasn't my intention.' He wasn't oblivious to the points of failure that had led to Alexis falling from the treadmill, but he blamed mostly himself. He'd been the one to distract her from work by going down a path he knew he shouldn't. There was nothing down there for them, yet trying to resist her had been close to impossible. Niko needed to get a better grip on himself.

'Then what's with that look on your face when Alexis stabilised? You were this close to reprimanding me.' Her brows narrowed, a stark line appearing between them.

'I...really wasn't.' He took a second to take a breath. 'I'm not about to say we didn't mess up in there. What we were about to do was a bad idea on many levels—with patient safety taking the top spot. But *I* was the one to follow you into the room. If anyone is to blame, it's me, so that's probably what you saw in my face. I wasn't annoyed with you.'

Camila kept staring at him, searching his face and words for the truth, and then her arms relaxed to the side of her body. She heaved out a deep sigh, shaking her head. 'This is so…complicated. Something like this has never happened to me before. I never get distracted, but within only ten minutes, I was in a completely different space. This could have been so much worse.'

When she took a shaky breath, Niko stepped closer, but when his hand touched her arm, she shook her head and took a step backwards. 'Camila… I'm sorry.' He wasn't sure what he was apologising for, only that something had upset her, and he wanted to fix whatever it was.

'I just…' She swallowed and his chest tightened when he saw tears form in the corners of her eyes. It took all the strength in him not to wrap her in his arms. Camila wanted her distance, and he would give it to her. Taking a shaky breath, she continued, 'I don't normally cry, so I can only imagine this is part of the whole hormones thing of pregnancy. I saw your annoyance and thought it had to be because of my mistake there. To learn now that you did not direct this at me at all makes me question my judgement, which is clearly off when it comes to you.'

Camila took a shaky breath, dabbing at her eyes with the sleeve of her blouse before looking back at him. 'What I'm trying to say is that with being pregnant and us figuring out how to be in this child's life together, I can't be around you getting distracted by all of this…this…'

She didn't finish her sentence. Niko didn't need her to. It was the nebulous *this*, the heat of attraction simmering between them since their night in Vancouver that was the root of the problems they were having. They didn't know each other very well, and misunderstandings like this one would continue to happen until they had a better read of each other's emotions. But how could they do that when the moment they were alone, searing need overrode any other thought?

'I get it. You don't know me very well and now we're having a child together. You don't know how to read the emotions on my face or interpret my glances, my gestures, my mood. Those are things we need to learn about each other.' He paused, unsure if he should say the next thing, but then decided to do so anyway. 'As friends.'

Her eyes widened, and the redness dusting her cheeks was so exquisite, he wanted to take the words back. Wanted to keep touching her until she came undone in his arms. But she was right. There were too many things between them now, too many complications that meant they couldn't just pick up where they had left things in Vancouver. Even though it had only been six weeks ago, they were now completely different people.

Expecting parents.

He let out the breath he'd been holding when

Camila nodded, a tentative smile showing on her lips. 'Okay... I agree. You don't really know me, either. So that's the first thing we should change.'

'How about I take you for a tour of Athens next weekend? This is your first time here, right?' Niko hadn't needed to become friends with anyone for a long time. Some people wanted to get close to him, but he rarely trusted their intentions and stuck to the people he knew—or the people on his payroll. What was he supposed to do with someone if he wanted to get to know them on a platonic level? A tour of the city was the first thing to pop into his mind.

'It is my first time, yes,' Camila said, and when her smile grew brighter, his stomach flooded with regret that he couldn't touch her any more. Because even though he knew it was the right thing to do, he knew it would be hard to keep to himself when the magnetism between them demanded he touch her. Cherish her. Worship every centimetre of her body.

God, he needed to get away before he ruined what little understanding he'd just established between them. 'Okay, then I'll pick you up next weekend and show you around,' he said, daring a smile himself before he left with a short wave.

A few days outside of Camila's orbit would do him good, so he could steel himself for the weekend to come. This would be *really* difficult.

CHAPTER FIVE

WHAT LOOKED LIKE a manageable hill turned out to be a lot higher and much steeper than Camila had thought. They stood at the foot of the stairs that led up to the Acropolis towering over Athens on its rocky outcrop. Niko had guided her here through the Plaka District, taking several detours to show her different stores tucked away in small side alleys—all the while narrating interesting tidbits from his youth. Each step showed her a different side of the Greek capital, and when they approached the Acropolis, Camila was all but green with envy at the opportunity of growing up here.

'Why?' Niko asked as he nudged her along, taking the first step up the hill. 'Where did you grow up?'

'In rural Switzerland—which is basically all of Switzerland. My mother moved from Brazil to Switzerland before I was born. She met my father when he was on vacation in Brazil, and he apparently whisked her to his homeland. I only spent a few years abroad before opening my lab back in Switzerland.'

Niko held out his arm as the steps got steeper, and Camila did her best to ignore the zing of electricity travelling down her arm as she held on to him. They had agreed that they wouldn't be more than friendly to each other. They had agreed to that. Her lapse of judgement with the stress test almost two weeks ago still weighed on her mind, and even though she could admit that they had both played a part in it, she was determined not to be distracted again.

Especially with the pregnancy taking its toll. Even at almost ten weeks, the nausea came and went at odd hours of the day, but what she had first noticed with Niko and then several times more since then was that she couldn't quite trust her own feelings any more. Everything seemed more amplified—be it good or bad. Good turned into amazing and bad became horrendous, to the point where she was the one turning up the severity of situations. Like she had with Niko. Convinced that he'd been furious with her, she'd fled rather than talk it out with him.

Camila knew she shied away from confrontation, had done so since she was little. Her mother had never entertained any arguments when it came to anything, really. From the moment she could remember, Mariana had foisted her choices onto her daughter—along with the warnings born out of bitterness over her own fate. It had taken a few years after her passing for Camila to unravel all of the feelings around her mother's anger at how her own life had turned out. And how she had let it influence her daughter's life.

Maybe with the help of her own child, she could now be different. Her child would be free to do and be whoever they wanted to be, without bitterness or pain. Because she wouldn't go down that path with Niko. No, they would figure out how to co-parent together.

'Aren't most people jealous of the beautiful landscapes in Switzerland? I feel people are often far more impressed with that than with Greece. There are enough documentaries and books about our history that they don't need to come and visit,' he said as they continued up the stairs, one step at a time.

'I think what people come to Switzerland for, they can easily replicate with a postcard of the Matterhorn. Sure, it's impressive, but it doesn't quite hit the way this does.' She looked around again, pointing at the Temple of Athena Nike. 'I mean, Greek mythology must have played an important role in your household if you named your entire hospital after the goddess of wisdom.'

Niko shook his head with a chuckle. 'I think my father was just overplaying the whole Greek thing. Athena Institute has a much grander ring to it than the Vassilis Hospital.'

'Do you really think he would have named the hospital after himself?'

'Seeing how much that man loved himself, I think the chances were high. I'm glad he didn't because I don't know if I could work in a building with my name on it.'

Camila nodded. Though her research had brought her into a lot of conversations, she still found the fame that came with it odd—if she could even call it fame. Outside of the tiny circle that made up the cardiology elite, people had not a single inkling of who she was. But there were some advantages to being who she was, like coming to the Athena Institute and sharing knowledge. Even though Niko didn't believe in it, for her, the name of the hospital was a lot more accurate.

By the time they reached the top of the steps, Camila's calves were burning, and she held on to Niko's arm a lot tighter. But the moment she looked at the Parthenon, the pain faded into the back of her mind.

The stone columns rose to the sky, far higher than she could ever reach. Despite standing here for hundreds of years, the stones hadn't given way to the forces of nature, remaining steadfast in their place—as the testament to the beliefs of the people back then. The sight was extraordinary and reminded her of the mark she wanted to leave in the world.

'I can't believe humans built this,' he said, mirroring her awe. 'I grew up here, and yet the sight of the Parthenon never gets less impressive. A true mark of human ingenuity.'

Camila turned to him, smiling. 'You took the words right out of my mouth. I thought, 'That's the reason I'm putting so much effort into my research.' Back then, they built these impressive structures with their bare hands to honour an ideal. Now we get to do the same on a much different scale.'

They walked around the plaza, looking up at the Parthenon as they went. 'Is that your intrinsic motivation? You want to save lives?' Niko eventually asked when they stopped underneath one column, craning their necks to look up at it.

'Yes, of course.' She tilted her head at the question. 'Don't you?'

'I do… I just like to know that the people I'm working with feel the same way,' he said, and Camila couldn't grasp the expression that fluttered over his face.

'If I had said I was in it for the money, would you not have agreed to bring me here?' Her motivation hadn't even come up in any conversation. How could this be important to him if he'd never even asked?

Niko shook his head as he ruffled his hair. Was he regretting this conversation? Before her brain could go haywire, Camila took a deep breath to ground herself. The last thing she needed was a repeat from earlier in the week, because Niko was right. She didn't know him or how to read his feelings. Understanding why he liked to work with people of a certain motivation would get her closer to unlocking more about him.

'No, I can empathise with that. We all need to make a living, and as long as health care doesn't become a privilege only the wealthy enjoy, I don't mind if you treat it like a job,' he said, giving her another glimpse of the conflict in his eyes.

'But there is an aspect that you mind, then?' she dug deeper.

They completed the circle around the Parthenon, and when they stood on top of the stairs, Niko waved his hand at them. 'You want to have a seat before we make our way back down?'

'You saw me hobbling, didn't you?' Camila asked, because she had tried her best not to make it too obvious, but the blister on her toe was pressing against her shoe, making each step a challenge.

'Of course not. I'm feeling fatigued. I rarely get to climb these stairs.' Camila levelled a stare at him, scanning the perfectly chiselled face of this Greek god. There wasn't even a bead of sweat in sight for him. Just glowing brown skin that looked as soft as it tasted.

To distract herself from the thoughts, she walked down a couple of steps before sitting down on the cool stone. Niko took a seat right next to her, his thigh brushing against hers and leaving tiny sparks underneath her skin. They sat in silence for a while, listening to the mumbling of the people around them conversing in more languages than Camila could name.

'I want to know that my values align with the people in my life. Both professionally and on a personal level,' he finally said, coming back to her question.

Camila looked at him, seeing the same conflict from earlier rise in his eyes. Like he was still making his mind up about something. About… her? Even though she knew that was fair, given how little time they knew each other, the thought still hurt.

'That's why we're here, right? So we can figure each other out. Otherwise, this one will have a grand time playing us against each other.' She patted her still flat stomach, taking comfort in the warmth of their bond.

His hand reached for hers, but he stopped just before he could grab it—balling into a fist instead. They had agreed not to be too close to each other, on her insistence no less. But she still felt the absence of his touch.

They weren't together, so the pain stabbing at her was unexpected. Unwelcome. But knowing he questioned their compatibility set something loose inside her that she didn't want to consider further. It shouldn't matter. The only important thing was how they would raise this child together.

'Is this what it's like to grow up in Athens?' she asked to change the subject and gestured around her.

Niko followed the motion of her hand, looking down the steps and onto the Temple of Athena stretching out below them. 'You get used to seeing so much ancient history all around you and end up with a bit of a…lack of appreciation,' he said, his shoulders relaxing a bit. Whatever conversation he had started, he was just as glad to move on from it.

The young couple sitting on the steps in front of them got up. The man groaned as the woman pulled him to his feet, then placed her hand under his arm as she helped him down the steps. They descended the stairs one at a time until they vanished out of view, the man's loud complaints fading with each step.

'He probably ran the marathon,' Niko said when she followed the couple with her gaze.

'There's a marathon happening?' Looking around, she spotted another couple in a similar state as they helped each other climb up the stairs this time.

Niko laughed, sending an involuntary shiver down her spine. 'Not just a marathon. The marathon that inspired all others. It starts in a town called Marathon, which is—'

'Forty-two kilometres from here?' The smile he gave her pushed her heart rate up and Camila did her best to ignore it.

'The finish line is at the Kallimarmaro, and the route passes along many landmarks in Athens. Both locals and tourists alike come here to face the challenge of the original marathon.' He pointed at several structures they could see from their vantage point, naming each one and explaining its significance.

'See, that's what I mean when I say I'm envious of the history that surrounds you,' she said, referring to the beginning of their conversation. Before his comment about values had hit something soft inside her. Were they really so different that he questioned that?

'Switzerland has been around for just as long. You know that, right?' His tone was friendly, bordering on teasing, and Camila wanted nothing more than to get lost in his voice. Not care about the thing looming between them.

Maybe the problem was that he didn't know enough about her. That was the whole reason they were here, was it not? She had misread his emotions, his intentions, to the point that she had thought something to be true that wasn't. What if that comment about values came from the same place?

That meant she needed to share something of hers, however daunting it seemed. He already knew she grew up without a father. But she could tell him why. Tell him what scared her when she thought of their child.

'Switzerland may be just as old, but I think there is something to be said about growing up with so much history around you and having someone who can teach you about it,' Camila said, her mind already tripping over all the words she wanted to say but was too afraid to do so freely. 'I…didn't get to enjoy much of it. My mother was a single mom most of the time, struggling in a country unfamiliar to her while trying to raise me.'

Keeping his hands to himself was a test of strength that Niko was about to lose. Something about Camila reached him in the furthest corners of his heart, and he didn't know what to do with that sensation. Because Niko had always believed that he wasn't built to care—at least not about any romantic interests. With his father's constant shadow looming over him and pressing him to continue the legacy of the Vassilis family, he'd decided early on that fatherhood wasn't for him.

While trying to figure out what this reality meant to him, he had neglected to see it from Camila's perspective, despite being the one to urge them to get to know each other. He hadn't

expected the vulnerability he was now seeing—
or how drawn to it he would be.

'What happened to your father?' he asked
when she didn't continue, the urge to know this
woman inside out too powerful for him to resist.

'He wasn't up to parenthood, I guess? That's
what my mother told me—that he left to get a
better family. He left a few months after I was
born and I haven't seen him since. It changed my
mother. She became so focused on his absence
and couldn't talk about anything else.' Camila's
hand came to rest on her stomach, her fingers
digging into the fabric of her blouse.

Camila paused, looking at him, and the caution in her gaze dropped a boulder in his stomach. Even though he knew their feelings were a
tangled mess, he never wanted her to feel cautious around him.

'Where is your mother now?' he asked, sensing a familiar distance in her words.

'She passed away a few years back. Pancre-
atic cancer,' she said, and he gave her a subdued
smile. Another thing to connect them—a complicated relationship with a parent who was no
longer here.

'I'm sorry to hear.' Camila shook her head as
he said that, returning his tight-lipped smile.

'That's why I want us to…find some common
ground on which we can be the co-parents our
child deserves. I never want them to feel any re-

jection from either of us. We both have to be on the same page.' Slowly, he could see her coming out of her shell. Finding some tentative trust between them that would let them talk about the important things. But he wasn't done building her trust. Not yet.

'Nothing you can say or do will scare me away. I promise you that much, Cami. This may be a surprise for both of us, but I will not shy away from the responsibilities that come with this.' It was a safe version of the truth. He couldn't deny that the prospect of fatherhood struck fear through his entire being. With how lousy his own father had been, how could he take care of a child with confidence? Would whatever instincts his mother had passed on to him be enough to guide him?

Niko itched to ask her for advice, but he hadn't found a moment in the last two weeks since Camila had arrived with the news to sit his mom and sister down to tell them. Their reactions would no doubt be of pure joy, which wasn't something he could currently deal with. Not with all the confusion swimming around in his brain.

Camila's face remained impassive, not letting him glimpse even a hint of any thoughts going on behind those dark eyes. Eyes that he shouldn't enjoy peering into so much. They had agreed that their relationship needed to be based on one of mutual understanding—where they both could have some distance. Because they both knew where things led when they let themselves get overwhelmed by the magnetism between them.

'Good…' she said, a sigh escaping her lips. 'I'd rather do this on my own to begin with than have you disappear halfway through.'

Niko blinked at her words as an unfamiliar pain flared through his chest. None of her words sounded like an accusation, but they still landed like one. Like she thought him so unreliable and fickle that she needed to hear his intentions out loud, or she wouldn't believe them.

Was that the impression he'd left with her? That she couldn't rely on him? From the moment he'd learned of her pregnancy, he'd done nothing but treat it with the seriousness the topic deserved.

'Did I leave the impression I would disappear on you and our child?' Niko couldn't stop the words from leaving his mouth. Wasn't the reason they were spending this day together because she had assumed the worst of him at the hospital? Now they were here again, in the exact same situation.

At least she had the decency to blush. Camila stared down at her feet, rocking them back and forth as if she were testing the feel of her shoe on the rock. 'We don't know each other very well. Forgive me if some of my questions seem too harsh. They come from a place of concern. I want to know that my child won't ever wonder what made them so reprehensible that their parent abandoned them.'

The indignation billowing in his chest drained out of him with a long exhale, leaving a sour taste in his mouth as her words sunk in. The glimpse of vulnerability was back, that thing that pulled him towards Camila with a gravity he couldn't explain—or resist.

Everything she had done and said in the brief span of their reunion had been because of a hurt still growing inside her. That was something Niko understood far too well. Something told him they would have many such conversations soon, as they figured out how to navigate the situation they found themselves in.

'There's a lot we still have to learn about each other,' he said and then got to his feet and extended his hand towards her. She took it with a tentative smile and held on to it as they walked down the stairs.

'Wow, this is beautiful!' Camila looked around with wide eyes, turning on her heels to take it all in.

A spark of male satisfaction ignited in the pit of his stomach as Niko watched her do another turn. They'd walked through a district littered with small shops and cafes until they had arrived in this neighbourhood, just as he'd planned.

Rolling hills of small white houses surrounded them, each one looking both similar and completely different from one another. The laughter of children filled the air as they walked the streets of the neighbourhood. Some people sitting outside their houses in plastic garden furniture waved at Niko as he passed by, and he returned the greetings.

'These are my humble beginnings,' he said as they continued to walk, hooking into a small alley that led them downhill.

Camila paused when three cats darted towards them. The felines came to a stop a metre in front and looked up at them wide-eyed. Her gaze flickered to Niko with a questioning look. Reading the question in her eyes, he raised his hands.

'I don't know them,' he said, just as one cat closed the gap between them and wound itself around his feet.

'Do they belong to someone here?' Camila studied them. 'They're not wearing a collar or anything to identify them.'

'The cats here belong to the neighbourhood. My sister used to feed them whenever we could afford to do so. Growing up, she was convinced she would one day be the queen of all cats.' Niko laughed at that memory of his sister. 'She had a chair set up in front of the house, and if she sat in it long enough, her court of cats would assemble and meow at her.'

Camila smiled at him, a small one but free of any strain. They'd stayed quiet as they'd left the

Acropolis, but the tension between them had been palpable—their conversation a bit more stilted. It was becoming apparent that they had a lot of ground to cover and far too little time to do so. Once Camila was done with this case, she would return to Switzerland, and Niko would…

He didn't know how to end that sentence. They would have to make a plan to see each other somehow. For the sake of their child. Neither had brought up the logistics of it all, not with so many other things floating between them.

Niko had focused on showing her more of Athens and steering clear of any personal discussions, believing they'd had enough of those for one day. Slowly, the tension had drained out of the space between them, and the stretches of silence had become companionable. Enjoyable even.

'What's your sister's name?' Camila asked, steering the conversation towards his personal life. At least it was only about his sister.

'Her name is Eleni. She ended up becoming an engineer rather than feline royalty,' he said, the fondness for his sister softening his voice.

'An engineer? I see all the Vassilis children are high achievers. Seeing what your father achieved with the Athena Institute, it's unsurprising that you both also aimed for higher goals,' Camila said.

His stomach turned inside out at the mention of his father, and Niko willed his expression to remain impassive. All Camila knew was that they'd had their disagreements and what little he had shared earlier in the day. Despite growing closer and needing to know about her, speaking about his father was still an insurmountable hurdle inside him. How could he trust anyone with that secret when it could have such a far-reaching impact on his family? The institute? Especially with Camila, who still saw him in such a positive light.

He needed to deflect. Talking about Stavros Vassilis would only bring them back to the same tension-filled space they had left behind at the Acropolis.

'I'd love for you two to meet. She will take her role as aunt very seriously,' he said, grasping for the first thing that came to his mind.

Camila's step faltered, and she stopped, forcing him to turn around to look at her. Her eyes rounded, and something rippled over her face. Shock? Concern?

'Only if you want, of course,' he added. 'She can be a bit…much, so don't feel obligated.'

Camila shook her head. 'No, that's not it. I would love to meet her. It's just that…' Her voice trailed off and she gave another shake of her head with a chuckle. 'I didn't think that…our child would have more family. It just hit me in this moment when you said it.'

The icy boulder in the pit of his stomach melted at the genuine smile parting her lips, turning into a warm puddle. Even though he didn't know how to explain their relationship to Eleni, he was excited for them to meet. There was no doubt in his mind that they would get along well—probably far too well.

'I always wondered what it would be like to have siblings,' Camila said as she resumed walking beside him and down the hill back towards the city centre. 'Maybe a sibling would have made the pressure from my mother more…bearable.'

He shot her a sidelong glance. 'Did you have to face down the expectations of your mother?'

Her shoulders stiffened, and as she stared straight ahead, Niko could see the cogs turning in her mind. She hadn't intended to reveal anything this personal, and a part of him felt let down. Because even though he understood her caution, he *wanted* to know these things about her. Wanted to understand what made Camila Pereira Frey the person she was today.

Despite the mounting affection for her inside him, he still did not know what kind of person she really was. What drove her to work so hard? What values did she stand for? Niko had alluded as much at the Acropolis but had dropped it to keep the conversation light—only for it to turn tense, anyway.

'She was, yes. Her expectations didn't always make sense. In her mind, I should have lived a traditional life, seek out a less demanding career so I could focus on children. That was what had been important to her—when she would have a grandchild. So when I went into such a demanding career, my mother was not supportive,' Camila said after a brief stretch of silence, and he sensed the deliberation of each word.

She was still working her way around to fully trust him with herself. But the glimmer of fragility in her voice was enough to clamp down around his chest, tightening it with sympathy. Regardless of her motivation, he knew what it was like to struggle with a difficult parent. Knew that he, too, wanted to avoid being like that at any cost.

'Our child will have many reasons to be proud of you,' Niko said, meaning every word. He might not be sure of the reasons she had achieved greatness—whether it was for the fame and glory or because of the genuine need to help people. But regardless of that, her achievements in medicine remained all the same.

'You think so?' Camila tilted her head to the side to look at him, and the flicker of pain in her eyes had him closing the gap between their bodies. He wrapped his hand around hers, their fingers threading together, and they held onto each other as they walked in silence.

The streetlights turned brighter as the sun sunk beyond the horizon, bathing the white houses around them in an eerie glow. The cars that he had ordered to pick them up and bring them to their respective homes parked at the end of the street. They were approaching the border of the neighbourhood, where buildings rose taller until they swallowed any view of the sky.

Warmth prickled at his fingertips where they brushed over Camila's soft skin. He wasn't sure that they had actually achieved what they set out to do. Camila was still an enigma, her true nature floating just at the edge of his senses. Had they just skipped too many steps in their relationship, and now there was no way to find the mutual ground they desired? Would they be parents that hardly spoke to each other, and only when it was relevant to their child?

He squeezed her hand as these thoughts trickled through him and warmth pooled in the pit of his stomach when she returned the squeeze, along with a smile that took his breath away.

God, she was the most beautiful woman he'd ever met. There was no use in fighting her allure—his attraction to her—because it came swinging back at him like a pendulum. He couldn't resist her, just like he couldn't resist gravity keeping his feet planted on the ground. Without even trying, she had found her way under his skin, and Niko was powerless.

Camila stopped when she noticed his lingering stare, raising a delicate eyebrow. 'What is it?'

He glanced at the cars waiting for them, then

back at her. 'I enjoyed my time with you today, Camila,' he said, his thumb drawing circles over the back of her hand.

'You did?' There was a brittle quality to her voice, like somehow his words were surprising—which couldn't be the case. Sure, they had their tense moments, but there was no way she didn't see how hard it was for him to keep his distance. Especially now, as they stood so close that he could make out each individual eyelash.

'We're trying to figure some things out between us. There's bound to be more disagreements, but I'd rather do that than not be involved at all,' he said, and as she looked up at him, Niko couldn't help it. He reached out to her face, brushing his fingers over her cheek.

Her skin was soft against his, warm to his touch, and his mind filled with the promises of pleasure and release as he touched her. The intensity was the same from when they'd first met, but the feeling itself was different. Softer, gentler and so much more fragile than the instant passion that had engulfed them in Vancouver. Desire was something he could keep in check, but this—whatever this was—it had full control over Niko, leaving him unable to resist.

He wound his finger through a strand of her hair, and his muscles tightened at her small inhale. Camila looked up at him, and he saw the heat burning in him reflected in her eyes. Letting his body take control, moving on instinct rather than intentional thought, he bent down and brushed their noses against each other.

This was the opposite of what they had wanted to achieve, yet in this moment, he didn't care. It was the one thing he'd wanted all day, been fighting it so much because that's what they had agreed on. Being too close to each other had landed them in this situation, yet Niko couldn't help it. He wanted this, wanted *her*.

'We really shouldn't do this,' he whispered to regain his composure. If Camila gave him enough of a reason, he could pull away and save them both.

One hand came to rest on his chest, the other one wandered up until her fingers were brushing over the skin of his neck. The heat pooling in the pit of his stomach exploded through his body, infusing his blood until the fire her touch caused had spread through him. All his focus narrowed on Camila as she drew closer, diminishing the space between their mouths to almost nothing.

'Yes, we better not...' she said, her voice sounding out of breath and her lips so close that their touch ghosted over his skin.

The last link on his restraint broke when she lowered her lashes with a flutter, and even that wasn't enough to dampen the heat in her gaze. Niko closed the gap between them with a strangled groan as he buried the warnings and caution going through his head, leaving him with nothing but the fire coursing through his veins to fuel him.

The world underneath Camila's feet shifted, tilting and twisting until she thought she would lose her grip. That was the potency of Niko's lips on hers. And she gave in, letting her body sink into his as she kissed him back, her arms coming around his neck to pull him closer.

This wasn't even near what they had agreed on, and it was exactly the thing they had both said they needed to avoid. How were they supposed to handle the difficult task of co-parenting when they couldn't keep their hands from each other? Those thoughts drifted at the edge of Camila's mind, and the longer the kiss lasted, the further away they floated. Because something that shouldn't be…couldn't feel this *right*. As a woman of science, she didn't believe things could be predestined, but that was the word that kept on bubbling up.

Her lips vibrated with a moan—either his or hers, or maybe even a combination of both—and a delicious shiver ran down her spine when his arms came around her waist, hugging her closer. The noises around her dimmed, her focus solely on Niko and the exquisite tendrils of warmth his kiss shot through her. Nothing else had space in her mind except his touch and what it did to her.

And when his hand slipped over her cheek, angling her head back so he could deepen the kiss, Camila almost wanted to believe that they could make it. That all of this had been some strange way of bringing two people together and have them work things out. Though she still knew little about Niko or any of his plans for the future, she knew how she felt—how he made her feel. There was nothing fleeting about it. Nothing temporary. It hadn't been since the moment they had entered his suite in Vancouver.

Camila let her hands wander up, relishing the feel of the short hair of his undercut between her fingers before the strands grew longer. She needed him closer, needed more of him, more of this moment that was reaching such an unimaginable fever pitch and—

Something fuzzy scraped against Camila's ankle, and her eyes flew open. She reeled back with a yelp, looking down at her feet, and watched as a black cat head-butted her ankle.

'Oh my God...' she huffed out, her heart rate elevated for a very different reason than a few moments ago, and when she looked back up, Niko's eyes had a hungry, glazed look. It almost made her forget about the furry intruder at her feet.

'That's what we get for not picking a more appropriate place,' Niko said with a chuckle, and she joined in, not letting any of the awkwardness pushing up her throat set in again.

Because maybe...maybe the distance wasn't necessary. What if they could figure something out that acknowledged what was clearly brewing between them? Her first instinct had been to push him away, to focus on their child and everything that came with that. But even with their best efforts, they didn't seem to be able to let go.

What if her mother's warnings were wrong, and Niko wanted to stay with her, too? Wanted to give it a shot?

Her breath left her in a stutter when he slid his finger under her chin, his forehead coming to rest on hers. He stared at her with stormy eyes, a myriad of emotions whirling through them. 'What do you want to do now?' he asked, and the gravel in his voice melted her insides.

She wanted to go wherever he was going and repeat what they'd done so many weeks ago in Vancouver. But skipping steps was why they were in this situation now, where they didn't even know each other well enough to understand their moods—their way of communicating. What they needed was to start from the beginning.

'I think this is a wonderful note to end the night on. You showed me not only Athens' most important landmarks but also where you grew up.' She paused with a smile as she looked around the neighbourhood, casting one last glance at the white houses. 'To think that someone like Stavros Vassilis came from such humble beginnings to found the foremost cardiology institute in all of Europe. You must be proud to continue the path he's set for you.'

Camila turned back to smile at him but paused when her eyes scanned his face. The warmth had drained away, along with the passion-glazed eyes, leaving a veiled expression that she couldn't decipher. Traces of their kiss were still lingering, along with a laboured breath he was trying to even out.

'What the matter?' She reached out to brush her fingers over his cheek, and Niko let her, but his expression remained muted.

'Nothing,' he replied with a smile that didn't quite reach his eyes, but before she could say anything else, he took her by the hand and tugged her along to where two cars were waiting. 'Thank you for spending the day with me. I'll see you at work.'

'I...' The sudden change in his demeanour threw her off, but before Camila had a chance to recover, Niko reached for the door handle of the car and opened it for her. She looked up at him and froze when he bent over to brush a gentle kiss onto her cheek.

Warmth spread through her, colliding with the chill his sudden change had set loose in her and leaving her feeling adrift as Niko pulled back, his expression not letting her glimpse his thoughts.

'We'll speak soon?' she asked, to understand his intentions but also to reassure herself. Had something bothered him?

A smile appeared on his lips again, a similarly shallow one that she didn't buy for even a second. But then he nodded and left Camila with no alternative but to set these thoughts aside as he closed the door, and the car began moving.

CHAPTER SIX

FOR THE FIRST time in what felt like an eternity, Camila's nerves were calming as she looked over the data she'd received from her lab in Switzerland. They'd sent all the samples over to her staff, they had done the gene mapping over the last four weeks, and the results had only just arrived. Even though Camila could have done it with the equipment here, she'd ultimately sent it to her own lab. That way, they could immediately catalogue their findings and add them to their database for further reference.

She sat behind her laptop in the staff room closest to Alexis Theodorou's room, staring at the screen. All the colourful graphs and lines in spreadsheets were blurring together as a headache bloomed just behind her eyes. It had been a strange two weeks, and she still wasn't sure she'd shaken it all off.

For one, she had hardly seen Niko the last two weeks. Every now and then, she'd glimpsed him as he stalked down a corridor or requested Emilia for a status update. She noticed that it was *always* Emilia now—never her.

That, along with his general elusiveness, cemented the thought in her head that something had gone wrong during their tour of Athens. That *something* wasn't hard to guess. Niko regretted kissing her. The kiss hadn't been one of an unwilling participant. He couldn't fake chemistry like that, and she certainly wouldn't have dreamt it up. And Camila knew he hadn't regretted it immediately.

No, he'd even asked her what she wanted to do next, and if she'd said she wanted to see his place, she knew Niko would have taken her there. To his bed, where they would have repeated what they'd done in Vancouver all night.

The thought sent a trail of sparks racing down her spine before settling in her core with an uncomfortable pinch. It was pathetic how much she wanted to feel him on top of her again. Could that be why he was angry? Had he perceived her declining his invitation as a slight?

Two weeks had come and gone, and the father of her child hadn't deigned to speak to her because she wouldn't jump into bed with him again straight away?

Her mother was right, after all. Men really couldn't live up to the responsibilities they themselves brought into their lives. Not without being prompted and hounded for a contribution that should be freely given. They were all the same. To think she'd genuinely believed that she and Niko could become something real, a loving family for the child they'd created… Only for him to burst that bubble in less than five minutes.

The realisation tasted bitter in Camila's mouth, and she shoved it away, looking back at the screen of her laptop, but the throbbing behind her eyes intensified as she squinted at the data. With a frustrated sigh, she closed the laptop, slamming her notebook on top of it.

'No luck with the gene mapping?' Emilia stepped into the staff room just as Camila shoved her laptop away and came to sit next to her.

'We got the sequencing today, so now it's a matter of combing through it all and making sense of it,' Camila said, rubbing her temples with her fingers to get rid of some of the tension. 'I just need some peace to do it.'

Camila looked at the cup with a deep longing. She'd stopped drinking caffeine a few weeks back when the nausea had begun. Initially, she'd thought nothing of it, though thinking back now, maybe some subconscious level of her mind had already known what was happening to her.

'Oh, I couldn't possibly…' Her voice trailed off when Emilia shook her head with a smile.

'Don't worry, it's decaf. You can drink it,' she said, giving the cup another push until Camila wrapped her hands around it.

Her brows rose as she looked at the other woman before looking down at the cup in her hand. How could she have known about...? Standing naked in front of a mirror, Camila could see the rounding of her stomach as a first visible sign of pregnancy. But she was only approaching the twelve-week mark.

Emilia chuckled, reading the silent question in her eyes. 'Call it a sixth sense.' She slipped her hand into the pocket of her lab coat and retrieved her phone. Unlocking it with a swipe of her thumb, she tapped on it several times before showing it to Camila.

The picture was of two small children wearing the same clothes and identical hair styles, though one of them was slightly taller than the other. They were standing in a miniature kitchen and handling what looked like wooden vegetables.

Camila looked back up at Emilia. 'These are your daughters?'

The other woman nodded. 'They are. I was struggling with fertility issues, so my husband and I were speaking to many adoption agencies. Not even a week after we brought June home, my pregnancy test came back positive, and that's how we got Min.'

She tapped her finger on the face of the smaller child, smiling, and the joy radiating from both Emilia and the photo infused Camila. *This* was what she had let herself believe she could have two weeks ago when they had kissed. Before Niko had decided to ignore her.

'This is my first,' she said when Emilia took her phone back and took a sip of the coffee she offered her. There might be no caffeine in it, but maybe the flavour was enough to trick her brain into a more focused state.

Emilia nodded, then her gaze drifted towards the screen. 'What are your thoughts on what you were able to look at so far?'

Camila scrolled through the document in front of them, not looking for any particular points. She'd have to spend a good amount of time cleaning up all the information to narrow it down to specific genetic markers. For that she needed to come prepared with a few potential diagnoses already. She looked down at the notepad, skimming over the long list.

'I'm confident it's not hypertrophic cardiomyopathy. Myocarditis seems unlikely with the presentation of his ECG. The lab findings also didn't indicate any viral infection of the tissue. So—' she paused, looking at Emilia with a frown '—right now, I think it's between Wolff-Parkinson-White syndrome and catecholaminergic polymorphic ventricular tachycardia. CPVT makes sense because only physical activity would trigger it. The two times Alexis had an episode was during his regular training and our stress testing.

But again, the ECG we took right after the episode doesn't look quite right.'

'What about Brugada syndrome? I've been looking into that, but the ECG presentation is throwing that diagnosis off as well,' Emilia said, tapping her finger against her chin.

Camila picked up her pen and added it to the list of diseases to check. The genetic markings would at least make it easier to confirm a diagnosis, even if they still had too much to choose from at this moment. With all the weirdness floating around between her and Niko, she was yearning for some distance. Maybe they would have an easier time speaking about any arrangements once she was back in Switzerland.

'It could be a drug-induced QT prolongation,' a deep voice said behind them, the familiar timbre sending an involuntary shudder down her spine. Even with all the confusion hanging over them, her body reacted to his proximity. That needed to stop right now.

Even though Camila didn't even want to acknowledge Niko talking, the ECG diagram she'd been looking at moments ago appeared in front of her mental eye as she considered his suggestion. 'Was there an unusually prolonged QT interval? I thought the T-wave morphology was inconsistent with typical drug-induced changes,' she said as she turned to him, and the shrug he gave her in response sent her pulse beating for all the wrong reasons.

First, he ignored her for a solid two weeks, and when he did finally come around to talk to her, he spat out an unsubstantiated diagnosis and *shrugged* when she challenged him? Her jaw tensed as she swallowed her replies. She still had to be a professional, and he was still the medical director of the Athena Institute. This wouldn't be her only collaboration with the staff on his team. That was one of many reasons she had to play nice with Niko. Even if that thought grated on her right now.

'Dr Pereira Frey, would you mind joining me in my office? I have a meeting with the Hellenic Swimming Association later in the afternoon, and I'd like to ask some questions to understand the current diagnostic trajectory better,' he said, not bothering to answer her objections to his diagnosis. So Camila decided he wasn't worth any of her words, either.

She just nodded, grabbing the laptop, notepad and coffee before saying goodbye to Emilia with a grateful smile as she took a sip of the coffee. Camila didn't miss Emilia's pointed stare between her and Niko, and she suppressed a sigh. With her keen eye, the other woman had already discovered her pregnancy. The last thing she needed were rumours flying around that the medical director of the Athena Institute had a child on the way with a visiting researcher.

'Is this decaf?' Niko said into the silence as they walked down the corridor towards the administration wing, her heels clicking on the white marbled floor.

She stopped dead in her tracks, looking up at Niko through narrowed eyes. 'That's what you want to know? I've not seen or heard from you for two weeks, and your first concern is about *coffee*?'

Niko's spine stiffened, and he had the decency to look somewhat surprised. His throat moved as he swallowed before he said, 'Caffeine can have a negative impact on the birth weight of the child.'

'I know that, seeing that *I'm* growing this baby from scratch, Niko. Despite having many delicious options here, I've also cut out seafood and many other things that are just rife in the Mediterranean cuisine. You would know that if you had bothered to check in with me in the last fourteen days.' Squaring her shoulders, she took a sip of her coffee. She knew it was over the top, maybe even a bit petulant, but in this instance, she didn't care. Their kiss had changed something inside her, infused her with a sense of want that wasn't just about their physical connection. For a moment, she had been certain that they could find some way to each other—and then it went away as if it had never existed. Here one moment and then gone the next. And to add to her already mounting confusion, Niko had then chosen to ignore her existence for the last two weeks.

Niko crossed his arms in front of his chest and Camila forced her eyes to stay on his face. There was a time and a place to admire this man's ridiculously built forearms, and that moment wasn't now. It would only distract her from her righteous fury.

'I told you from the beginning that I wouldn't be overly involved in Alexis's treatment outside of any special requests you might have,' he said, and the low hum in his voice only incensed her further.

'Don't give me that. You know this isn't about work. This has *never* been about work. No, this is about us.' She levelled a finger at him before pointing it at herself. 'About how you were thrilled with kissing me one minute and then sending me on my way the next.'

A muscle in his jaw feathered, and his chest expanded as he took a deep inhale. 'That's not... I didn't mean to come across as if I'm ignoring you. It's just that—'

A shrill beeping interrupted him mid-sentence, and Camila dug out the pager Emilia had given her on the first day. She'd said not to expect any pages as she was only looking after one patient but that it would be good for her to have one just in case. That case was apparently now.

'I have to go, something's wrong with Alexis,' Camila said, but when she turned to leave, Niko was already by her side, moving in the same direction as her.

Three people were in Alexis Theodorou's room when Camila and Niko arrived to respond to the emergency call. He recognised the person standing at the cardiac monitor as a junior cardiologist on staff, Ilias Georgiou. He looked up as they arrived, giving the small IV bag hanging from one of the wire frames a quick squeeze.

'Unexplained arrhythmia started about forty-five minutes ago. We have administered intravenous beta blockers. There was an initial dip in severity, but then another arrhythmia happened,' he explained, and Camila shot him a sidelong glance.

There was a lot floating in the space between them, many things he needed to tell her. Like how the mention of his father had freaked him out enough to back away from her. The reason he'd gone to Vancouver was to recruit new people for the institute—to replace his father's people as he pushed them out. Most of his effort since becoming the medical director at the Athena Institute had gone into repairing the place from the ground up and changing its focus. A big part of that was to disassociate with anyone who spoke too favourably of Stavros Vassilis or his days as the director.

Niko knew Camila lacked some important context around his father, knew that his reaction to hearing his name wasn't rational. But that didn't change his instinctive reaction. Before he'd known what he was doing, he'd pulled away—and had struggled to get his thoughts straight ever since.

'The beta blockers aren't working?' Camila asked, her lower lip vanishing between her teeth. The sight sent a longing through him, but Niko pushed it back. Ignored it like he had ignored everything else these last two weeks.

'We just administered another dose to see if it improves the arrhythmia,' Ilias replied, looking from Camila to Niko.

'Did we do any testing or procedures on him today?' Niko asked, to keep his attention focused on the patient. He'd looked over Alexis's chart today to prepare for his meeting. The stress test had triggered an arrhythmia, but the tilt test had come back with no adverse effects—effectively setting the diagnosis back a few steps.

Camila nodded along with his questions, clearly following a similar path with her thoughts.

'Nothing out of the ordinary. The patient had some supervised time outside the bed and felt reinvigorated afterwards. There was only minimal stress on his walk around the gardens, and we kept an eye on his cardiac monitor throughout it all.' Ilias paused, looking at Alexis. 'By his own admission, he was feeling fine.'

Niko followed Camila's glance towards the cardiac monitor, looking over the vital signs for any clue what was ailing Alexis. They had done exactly that so many times since his admission already, and though they had ruled out some diseases, many of them remained—and Alexis seemed to get worse for no particular reason.

'You received the gene mapping data this morning. Is there anything we can use to kick-start the process of diagnosis?' Niko asked, his first words directed at her since their conversation in the corridor. One he wasn't keen on resuming but knew he had to—for the sake of their baby.

He frowned when she shook her head. 'Not in a short time frame like this one. We need to stabilise Alexis first before we can think further on the diagnosis. Even if we knew what it was, we'd need him stable to confirm our suspicions.'

She turned around to face Niko. 'You're here to help?' she asked, and he nodded, not trying to read too much into her question. He was the medical director, and he couldn't fault her for believing he might have other things going on.

'What are you thinking?' Niko asked as she moved over to Alexis, whose breaths were leaving him in short bursts, each one fogging up the oxygen mask. His eyes were squeezed shut, his brow dotted with sweat.

'The arrhythmias are refractory. Our best bet here is electrical cardioversion,' she said, looking around the room and pointing towards the crash cart.

'Get the defibrillator ready. I'll take care of the sedation.' Shocking a patient's heart while he was still conscious was never pleasant, and the least they could do was to sedate him so he wouldn't remember the pain.

Camila pulled the cart closer to the bed, then turned a dial on the machine. When Niko stepped back with a syringe in his hand, she nodded as she turned to Alexis. 'Your arrhythmias are showing resistant to the beta blockers. We'll have to try to stabilise your heart with an electrical shock, okay? We are about to give you a sedative for the procedure, so you'll feel the pain stop soon.'

She stepped away, knowing Alexis was in no state to muster an answer, and Niko inserted the syringe into the cannula of the IV, pressing down until it was empty. It only took a few moments for the fast-acting sedative to wind itself through the patient's system. When his face slackened and his hands relaxed, they both moved in tandem.

Camila picked up the paddles on the machine while he moved the gown away from the patient's upper body, giving her the access she needed. When she placed the pads on the right upper sternum and the left side of his chest, she looked first at him and then at Ilias standing off to the side.

'All clear,' she said, then the machine whirred to life, delivering an electrical shock timed to the beat of Alexis's heart.

Her eyes darted to the monitor, checking both cardiac signs and other vital signs. The pattern remained the same as the seconds ticked by, and he could hear her muttering under her breath.

'Again?' he asked, looking towards Camila for guidance, but she raised her hand to stop him, staring at the screen—until it evened out.

The entire room relaxed, letting out a collective exhale. They exchanged glances, concern for their patient written on their faces, and the tension broke when Camila put the pads to the defibrillator down with a clatter.

'Was this his third arrhythmia?' she asked, and when Ilias nodded, she turned to face Niko. 'Do you have an intensive care unit?'

'Not an isolated space where we put all our critical patients. We have an ICU protocol. Alexis will stay here, but there will be around-the-clock monitoring and vital checks.' He paused, thinking about the current roster of available cardiologists. Since the Athena Institute had become a very specialised hospital, they functioned differently from any traditional hospitals and didn't have the same structures in place. On any given day, he'd only ever assign one or two people to a night shift, never needing more.

Camila must have read his thoughts on his face, for she said, 'I'll stay the night to observe him.'

'That's not necessary. I'll talk to Emilia and have her assign someone.' He was about to turn around when he noticed the flicker of annoyance in Camila's eyes and he paused. Looking over to Ilias, he said, 'Please go brief Emilia on what happened here and tell her that Alexis Theodorou needs to be put under observation until we can confirm the arrhythmias have stopped.'

Ilias nodded, pulling the door closed behind him and leaving them alone. When Niko turned back towards her, Camila was standing at the cardiac monitor, looking at the printout of the echocardiogram.

'This is ventricular tachycardia. If we catch one of these too late, we might lose him. It's better if I stay.' Camila held the piece of paper out to him, and Niko took it even though he knew he didn't have to check it. The last time he'd handled any sort of arrhythmias outside of the OR had been many years ago at this point.

'I'm not saying we shouldn't observe him. Just that someone else in Emilia's team can do it. You don't have to stay here.' Niko wasn't sure why he was pushing back on it. The protectiveness surging within him was misguided. Camila knew how to take care of herself, and he'd been the one to cool things between them—for reasons he wasn't ready to examine further.

When they had kissed, things within him had shifted, and he knew he'd come out of it a different person. He'd even gone as far as to invite her to his place. A part of him was glad she hadn't accepted, because if she had, he wouldn't have been able to let her go again.

A part of Niko wanted to keep her. Be *with* her. That was the thought that sent thrills of fear through him. A relationship had never been part of the bargain they'd struck. He didn't do relationships, didn't have the space in his life to let someone in like that. Not when he still had so much of his father's work left to undo. He wasn't in a position to give so much of himself.

And Camila… Would her ambitions get in the way of things? She saw his father as this important pioneer in the cardiology field, as did many others. None of them saw what went on behind the curtains.

'You can't stop me from staying here overnight if I want to, Niko.' Camila crossed her arms in front of her chest in a combative gesture. His first instinct was to rise to the challenge, meet her blow for blow. He was the medical director of the institute. He could bar whoever he liked from entering *his* hospital.

But he forced a breath from his throat, calming the tempest brewing in his chest. With Camila, nothing was ever easy or straightforward. That was what drew him to her. No one had ever challenged him like that in his entire life.

'Do you genuinely want to take the overnight shift or are you digging your teeth into this because you know I don't like the thought of it?' he said with a bone-deep sigh.

Camila scoffed, and that small exhale hit him right in the pit of his stomach. 'Believe it or not, I'm not basing any of my decisions on how you might feel about it. Otherwise, I'll get nowhere if you decide to ignore me for another week.'

Niko's eyes widened as her verbal blow struck true, burying deep into his flesh. He knew he deserved the barb despite having needed some space from her. To think, to…get over this *thing* stirring inside his chest whenever he saw her. Because whatever this nameless thing was, he needed it to stop. Before it got too big for him to contain.

Maybe having her be angry at him was easier than letting her get closer to him. Once that tension between them had cooled, they could figure out what to do with their child.

'Fine, suit yourself. Emilia can walk you through our night-shift protocols and I'll see you for the meeting with the Hellenic Swimming Association,' he said, turning on his heel and leaving before Camila could add anything else.

CHAPTER SEVEN

THE RUSTLING OF paper woke Camila up from her unsteady sleep. She blinked several times before the world came into focus, and when it did, her eyes met Niko's. He sat on a chair at the foot of the bed, leafing through a stack of papers and stopping every now and again to make a note.

'What are you doing here?' Camila asked, groping for her phone and looking at the time. It was almost eight in the morning.

Emilia had come in early to relieve her of duty. Camila had contemplated going back to the hotel, but her tiredness had overwhelmed her. So she'd gone back to the empty patient room she'd used all night and had promised to only close her eyes for twenty minutes. That had been two hours ago.

'I could ask you the same question. Last time I checked, you weren't a patient in this hospital,' he said, and Camila sat up at his tone. The words echoed the way they had left things yesterday, but she could hear something else beneath—concern.

'How did you even know I was still here?' She

sat up gingerly, the stiffness in her muscles protesting as she moved. Camila leaned against the plastic headboard of the hospital bed, a dull pain throbbed from her leg to her abdomen.

Niko didn't look up from his paperwork as he said, 'Emilia sent me an update when she took over and my driver reported he hadn't taken you back to the hotel. There aren't a lot of empty rooms, so it was just a matter of checking each one.'

Camila furrowed her brow. 'You came here to check up on me?'

Niko's hand paused mid-sentence, and when he finally flicked his gaze up to hers, her breath caught in her throat. After the way they had left things yesterday, she'd expected tension or even annoyance, but what she saw in his eyes was raw. Vulnerable. But why would her staying overnight in his hospital have him in such a state of concern?

'Of course I came to check on you.' He closed the folder with a sigh, setting it down on the chair as he got up and came to stand at the foot of the bed. 'Camila, I care for you, for our child. Your surprise shows me I haven't been clear enough about that.'

Her eyes flared wide at the admission, her mind going blank. After Niko had left last night, Alexis had suffered a few more arrhythmias that they had to get under control. In between attending to him, Camila had pored over the data on her laptop and managed to exclude a few more potential diagnoses. Now she had narrowed it down to three.

'Alexis experienced an electrical storm last night. We had to call several code blue emergencies on him, and he will need constant cardiac monitoring until we figure out his diagnosis and next steps,' Camila said, though she wasn't sure why. He'd just told her he cared about her, after she'd spent two weeks wondering why he didn't—why he would ignore her after sharing such a passionate kiss with her.

Somehow, this was the first thing that popped into her mind. To Niko's credit, he didn't show any surprise at the change of topic. He rested his hands at the bottom of the bed, looking at her. 'Emilia told me. I've already assigned extra staff, so we have pairs looking after Alexis,' he said, his tone much milder than it had been last night—when she insisted she wanted to do this.

'What happened over the last two weeks?' Camila asked, her voice far calmer than she felt on the inside. Throughout the night, she had had no space to think about them; about the tension building. But now, as she woke up with him observing her, it all came rushing back.

Niko sighed, his gaze dropping to his hands, which turned white at the knuckles. 'I was confused, and I didn't handle it well. There are a lot of factors to consider when it comes to…us, and I'm not sure how to navigate any of this.'

There was a hesitation in his words, like he needed to deliberate on everything he said. Camila knew it well, because she was the same way, needing to think her words over before she could commit to them. Her mother had chided her often for speaking before thinking, cultivating that habit in her early on. Speaking from the heart became so much more complicated with that trait, since she'd been taught that she couldn't trust people with her feelings. Did Niko feel the same way?

Was that why they couldn't find a path forward that didn't hinge on their physical attraction to one another?

'We have to figure these things out, eventually. For the sake of our child, if nothing else,' she said, though the words didn't seem quite right. She meant them and believed that they had to reach an agreement. But, for once, her pregnancy didn't factor into this. Her attraction—her desire—for Niko didn't involve the life they had created.

Niko took a deep breath, letting it out slowly and deliberately. 'There is still a lot you don't know about me and my circumstances. Two weeks ago, I froze because… I experienced a very different side to Stavros Vassilis than the one the rest of the world saw.'

Camila's spine stiffened. Of all the ways this

sentence might have ended, this wasn't what she had expected. She knew something was going on behind those gorgeous eyes, but she'd never thought… 'What happened?'

Niko stepped closer, then settled down at the end of the bed when Camila withdrew her legs to give him some space. 'The image of the pioneer and entrepreneur in the cardiology field was a carefully curated one. At home, he was nothing like that. My sister and I barely saw him, and when we did, he was pushing both of us into places we didn't really want to go. All in the name of this image he'd created.'

The bed creaked when Niko shifted more of his weight onto it, leaning back so he was supporting himself on his arms. Camila kept her distance, looking at him with what she hoped to be a veiled expression. The explanation for his behaviour was looming just within reach, and she didn't dare say anything.

'Though I don't regret it, he's the reason I went into medicine. From a very young age, I was told that taking over the Athena Institute was my birthright. That the continuation of his aspiration to make our name one of great importance in the medical field lay on my shoulders.' His gaze shifted upwards, scanning the ceiling for something only he could perceive. 'The day I decided to turn my back on his demands—on this hospital—was a defining day for me. Working with other doctors and seeing how other medical directors ran things, it showed me a perspective I'd never had before. All I knew was whatever my father told me and the things I read in the press about the Athena Institute. But rejecting his tempting offer gave me agency over my own fate and afforded me some clarity I didn't have while close to Stavros.

'Then he died, and I found myself taking over the hospital. Digging into all the things he's done just to garner both fame and money—for his own vanity.'

Niko paused, shifting forward again so that he was bracing his arms on his thighs. He shot her a sidelong glance, and the chaos of emotions in his eyes sent a stab through her chest. The surrounding air became charged as she waited for him to continue his confession.

'Once the institute became more famous, he began charging people a premium for minor procedures that would be just as suited for a public hospital. He convinced people that he and his team were the best shot at people's survival and added a premium on top of the already expensive cost of health care.' Niko's breath left him in a stutter. 'He used his good name to profit off people who didn't know any better. If I had done my training here, would he have dragged me down this path as well? Or did my desire to avoid my father make me complicit? If I had come here, I might have picked up on it. Might have been able to…stop it sooner.'

By the time Niko was done speaking, Camila's eyes were round. Stavros Vassilis had done these things to innocent people? The thought was unimaginable to her. How could someone who had inspired so much change in the cardiology field turn out to be so soulless? She opened her mouth, but the right words for comfort wouldn't come. So instead, she pushed her legs over the bed and hopped off. Her muscles protested, the dull pain in her abdomen increasing with the pressure of standing, but she pushed the sensation aside to focus on Niko.

He lifted his head when her legs brushed against his. She put her hands on either side of his face as she stood between his legs. 'And you have been dealing with the aftermath of this all on your own?' she said, brushing her thumbs over his cheeks. He turned his face so that his mouth was now pressed against her palm. She shuddered when he pressed a gentle kiss to it.

'When I took over the Athena Institute and found out how deep this all went, I swore I would undo everything he'd done. It's harder than I thought it would be, and rooting out everyone he hired into his devious scheme is an arduous task. I have to make sure that I still have enough doctors to take care of our patient load. But that's why I reacted poorly the other night.'

He swallowed hard enough that she could hear it in the room's silence. 'You mean something to me now. You're the mother of my child. So when you spoke so highly of my father, it brought up some unpleasant emotions. And I panicked—*because* I enjoyed kissing you.'

The truth floated around them, and Camila breathed out the air she'd been holding as he spoke. Her heart fluttered inside her chest, reaching out to his words and wanting to say them back. Wanting to let him know that she, too, cared for him. That she was willing to try, despite all the warnings of her mother in her head. Niko wasn't like her father or the other fickle men she had encountered in her life. From the second he'd learned about their child, he'd stepped up to take responsibility.

Would he have even shared any of this stuff about his father with her if he wasn't serious?

Camila bent down, ready to cut the tension by brushing a kiss onto his lips. But a soft cry escaped her lips as she lowered her face and the dull pain shooting through her legs and stomach sharpened—leaving her doubled over and clutching her stomach.

Niko jumped to his feet, switching positions with her so she was now sitting on the bed. He appeared in her field of vision as he crouched down, concern etched into every feature on his face. 'What's wrong?' His hand wrapped around hers, shielding her stomach. 'Is it…?'

Camila forced her breathing to remain even as more pain shot through her—right through her abdomen. Panic threatened to take over all her senses. She thought her muscles had been sore from lying on the bed in her clothes all night, but… Was this normal? She tried to recall symptoms and discomforts during pregnancy she had researched. The OBGYN clinic she had visited had given her a pamphlet on what to expect.

The clinic. 'We need to go see my doctor,' she said, each word punctuated with a sharp exhale.

'You already have a doctor?' he asked, taking his phone out of his pocket. 'What's the name of the clinic? I'll call them right now.'

What was wrong with her baby? The increasing panic wrapped her in a confusing fog and thoughts became harder to articulate. They needed to see her doctor now. 'Her name is Dr Karalis. Her clinic is right around—' The last word turned into another cry as Camila doubled over again.

'Your doctor is *Daphne* Karalis? *Skata*.' The last word came out rough, and Niko scrolled through his contact list, stopping halfway down and pressing one of them. 'I know where her clinic is. She'll see us right away.'

Camila didn't question how he knew that. All that mattered was that they got there before anything could happen to their baby. She was only a few days away from her twelve-week milestone. If anything happened, she would…

She didn't let herself dwell on that thought as she tried to stand on her own, but couldn't with the pain shooting through her. Seeing her struggle, Niko put his arm behind her before sliding the other arm under her legs, lifting her into his arms. With his phone pressed between his shoulder and ear, he began rapidly speaking in Greek as he carried her through the hospital.

As a cardiovascular surgeon, Niko had lived through many tense moments in his career. All of them put together didn't even compare to the sheer, undiluted terror that had swept through him when Camila had first cried out, clutching her stomach. That fear sat deep in his bones, far enough that he couldn't shake it even now as she lay on the exam table, her face more relaxed than it had been before.

Dr Daphne Karalis stood next to the ultrasound monitor and lifted Camila's gown over her stomach. 'Like last time, this will be cold, and it might trigger some pain again,' she said as she spread the lubricant on Camila's stomach.

She hissed, and Niko immediately stopped his pacing to hold her hand. Her tight squeeze showed how much of her own fear she was still wrestling with, and he willed himself to be calm.

She needed him right now. Their child needed him. He could fall apart later.

'Okay, let's see what's happening here. You were about to come in next week for your dating scan.' Daphne paused, smiling at her. 'The nurse said you had a stabbing pain in your abdominal area?'

Camila swallowed as she nodded, quickly glancing at Niko. He wrapped his hand around hers, squeezing it with a calm he didn't feel on the inside.

'Yes, that's right. I just finished a night shift, and when I got up, the dull pain I was having increased drastically,' she explained, and he knew she was trying to sound as clinical as possible while panic still nipped at her heels. He squeezed her hand again, and he didn't miss Daphne's glance towards where their fingers connected.

'Was that accompanied by any bleeding or spotting?' she asked, and when Camila shook her head, she took the transducer of the ultrasound into her hand and lay it on her stomach.

There was no doubt in his mind that the monitor was intentionally turned away from them. To keep people calm under normal circumstances, but they were special. Daphne knew that both he and Camila would know how to read an ultrasound, potentially getting ahead of any news she wanted to share. The thought tightened his throat, making his next breaths harder to swallow.

'Ah, yes, here we go,' Daphne said, and Niko's heart fell out of his chest when she pressed a button on the machine and the strong and fast heartbeat of his baby echoed through the room.

Camila had a similar reaction, freeing her hand from his to press it over her heart, each breath leaving her lungs one of relief.

Daphne flipped the monitor around. 'Your baby is fine, and you have nothing to worry about. What you're experiencing is round ligament pain. It happens when the uterus expands, and it often manifests as a jabbing sensation in the lower abdomen. It can be quite a shock for first-time mothers.' She paused, looking between Niko and Camila. 'I know it is your first, Niko, but I assume it is your first child as well?'

Niko clenched his jaw to suppress the annoyed sigh building in his throat. With the terror leaving his body the moment he heard his baby's heartbeat, he had room to focus on other things now—like Daphne Karalis-Vassilis finding out he was having a child in the worst possible way.

Camila caught on to Daphne's phrasing, to how intimately her doctor had addressed him. Her eyes darted between them with a puzzled look that ever so slowly turned to shock.

'Camila, this is my mother, Daphne,' he said, voice tight as he made the introduction.

'It's a pleasure, Camila. I fear my son hasn't

told me much about you,' Daphne said, the smile on her face a genuine one.

Camila's lips parted, and he could see her searching for the right words. Hell, he didn't even know what to say. He hadn't told his mother or sister that he was expecting a child. He'd planned on having the conversation many times, but with the tension between him and Camila, the right moment had never presented itself, so he'd kept quiet during their weekly family dinners.

'Mother, let's not make a thing out of this. She just had a stressful moment. If you want to be annoyed, you can be annoyed with me later,' he said to Daphne in Greek.

'Fine, but you and I will have a chat about what other things you might be keeping from me,' she said, giving him a pointed look before wiping the excess lubricant from Camila's stomach and putting her blouse back into place. 'The best you can do when you experience pain like that is take it easy, okay? Rest up, only do gentle exercise and have a warm bath if the pain spikes.'

Camila nodded, her eyes still darting between them with an unsure expression. He couldn't blame her. This was definitely not how he'd planned on delivering his message—or how she was supposed to meet the grandmother of their child.

'Why don't you take Camila home, son? We'll keep the appointment for next week and set your due date. If you have questions, just call and we can talk it through.' She paused, looking at him again with an expression he'd known all his life. Even now, in his mid-thirties, he knew he was in trouble and that he would hear of it later.

CHAPTER EIGHT

CAMILA DIDN'T PROTEST when Niko opened the door to his car for her before getting in on the other side and giving the driver quick instructions in Greek. Still too wired, she didn't care when the car drove right past her hotel and only stopped in front of a large house behind a white marble fence. The gate swung open on its own, and the car pulled in. When it stopped, Niko exited the car and circled around again, opening the door and helping her to her feet.

Saying nothing else, he led her into his house and down a corridor that opened into a bright living area. Everything in sight was a cool white and grey marble. From the decorations along the wall to the coffee table sitting in front of a lavish dark grey couch, every single thing was high end and selected by a meticulous interior designer.

It was also sharp. That was the first thought that popped into Camila's head. There wasn't a single rounded corner in sight. Glassware and bottles of alcohol stood in the centre of the coffee table, just waiting to be tossed over by a rambunctious toddler that was only just learning how to walk.

She pressed her hand against her stomach as the vision of their child in this space came upon her unbidden. Round ligament pain. Of course it had been something completely harmless, and if her own panic hadn't swept her up, she might have remembered that discomfort during pregnancy was quite normal—even to be expected, really.

'Let's get you in that bath,' Niko said, tugging her along.

The bathroom was just as bright and modern as the living area, with a white-grey marbled floor and large windows facing the fenced-in backyard. Camila marvelled at the large rain shower she spotted at the far end of the bathroom and could almost feel the warm water washing over her body. That was until Niko pressed a button on the wall and the burbling of water filled the air.

The luxurious bathtub was seamlessly incorporated into the floor, inviting her to soak in its depths. Its gleaming white porcelain surface reflected the muted light of the bathroom, drawing her eye to it again and again. The sun's rays filtered through the windows and danced across the silver adornments lining the walls.

'Oh, my God...' she breathed out as water

poured into the tub, her muscles yearning for the warm relief.

'It takes quite some time to fill up. I can show you around the house while we wait,' he said, and for the first time since they left Dr Karalis's office, they looked at each other. His eyes still had a haunted quality, and Camila was certain that she and he both had the same drain reflected in their faces.

They stared at each other for a few breaths, silent words passing through them as they processed the shock and subsequent relief that had been their morning. When Niko's hand came up to her face to stroke her cheek, she leaned into the touch.

'I was scared out of my mind,' he said, and the quiet admission of this usually stoic man broke the grip she had on her own feelings.

They surged to the surface with unbridled ferocity. Camila flung her arms around Niko, pressing herself against him as the dam inside her broke and tears finally spilled out of her eyes. His arms came around her and his chin came to rest on her head as he tugged her closer to him, rubbing her back and whispering calming words Camila couldn't understand. It didn't matter. They reached her anyway, his voice wrapping around her like a warm blanket.

'Me too,' she whispered into his chest, her grip tightening around him. 'This wasn't even planned, but when I thought something was wrong, my mind went blank. I've never been so scared in my life. Niko, I…'

He pushed her away enough so he could look at her. His hands framed her face, brushing at the tears sliding down her cheeks. 'I know. I felt the same way.' He leaned closer until their foreheads touched. 'This is what I meant when I said you've become important to me, Cami.'

Her heart stuttered against her chest, her pulse tripping and continuing at double the speed. This was the conversation they'd been about to have when she'd had her scare. Niko had confided in her, shared some of his pain surrounding his father. How his mission since becoming the medical director had been to reverse the damage caused by his father.

But the exhaustion from the night sat deep in her bones and her emotional battery was all but empty. Niko must have seen her thoughts reflected in her face. He tilted her head towards him, angling his mouth over hers and brushed a gentle kiss onto her lips. A quiet moan left her throat at his touch and she stood on her toes as he broke contact.

'We can talk about it tomorrow. My first priority is to get you nice and relaxed for your bath.' He took a step backwards, his hands falling to her shoulders and turning her around. After peeling off her jacket, Niko pulled her closer again until her back was flush with his front. He buried his face in her neck, his warm breath grazing her skin as his hands came around her and began unbuttoning her blouse.

Camila let out a stuttering breath as he opened her blouse and peeled it over her shoulders until it slid down her arms and onto the floor. A sudden heat exploded through her, banishing the exhaustion into a far corner of her mind. All she could focus on now was where Niko's fingers touched her skin, gently brushing over the slope of her stomach.

His lips connected with her neck, breathing kisses onto her as his hands skated up either side of her torso. Then one hand slid between them and, with a skilled flick of his finger, Niko unhooked her bra. His moan echoed through the bathroom as his fingers brushed over the sides of her breasts, gently cupping both of them.

A delicious shiver shook her body, even his gentle touch enough to ignite the long slumbering fire she'd been tending for him since their night in Vancouver. She moaned when his thumbs brushed over her taut nipples as she arched back into Niko. His excitement was apparent, his considerable length pushing against her back.

Niko grunted a word she could only assume was an expletive as she ground against him. With all they had gone through today, this form of primal connection was exactly what she needed to soothe herself. To help both of them forget about their fear and just…be with each other.

'I'm supposed to get you into this bath,' he whispered into her ear as one of his hands slid over the plane of her stomach and down to her jeans. His fingers danced over her waistband, with his thumb close enough to slip under.

The anticipation was enough to get her to the edge. Her head lulled back onto his shoulder, her lips parted to let out another moan. 'Dr Karalis said to relax. A hot bath can be relaxing. But you know what else relaxes me? Orgasms.'

Niko muttered a word she didn't understand, his fingers playing with the button of her jeans before finally, agonisingly slowly, unbuttoning it. His fingers grazed the top of her mound as he pulled down the zipper.

'Believe me, she would have probably suggested that right after the warm bath idea. I'm just glad I got you out of there before she could say anything else,' he said against her skin, pushing down her jeans until they hung around her mid-thigh. Camila shuddered when he brushed over her underwear, and a part of her mind that wasn't completely wrapped up in the desire thundering through her clung to his words—remembering what she'd learned at the doctor's office.

'About Daphne…' She tried turning around, but Niko kept a tight grip around her waist, keeping him pinned to her.

He pressed his nose against a sensitive spot behind her ear, nuzzling into her skin as he breathed her in deeply.

'Let's talk about that later,' he said, and as if to underline his words, he slipped his fingers under the waistband of her underwear, pushing it down until she was exposed. 'I need to take your clothes off for that bath.'

'Right, the bath…' Camila had no intention of slipping into the beckoning water. Not when her entire body was on fire with a mixture of arousal and the leftover adrenaline rushing back at her. She was fine, their baby was healthy and Niko…he cared about her. That confession had struck her deep, opening up a path in her heart that she wanted to run down. She needed to feel Niko's weight on her, have his scent all around her, to feel him stretching her out…because last time she hadn't known how much this encounter would change her life.

She broke out in gooseflesh when Niko's hand glided down her thigh, pushing the rest of her clothes down until she could step out of them. As his grip loosened, she tried to turn around again, needing to feel his mouth on hers, but Niko had other plans.

His hand came back up her thigh, twisting enough so he was grazing over the sensitive flesh there. The strokes of his thumb were slow and deliberate, but by the heaviness of his breath, she could tell that he, too, was holding back.

When he reached the spot aching for his touch, and his fingers connected with the bundle of nerves there, Camila let her head drop back as a low moan burst from her throat. Molten lava broke free from her core, spreading through her body until every far-flung corner was alight with a blazing fire. Niko kept working his magic with his fingers, brushing over her in delicate strokes.

Her mind went blank except for one thought— she needed him now. Her hands slipped between their bodies, palming his length through the fabric of his trousers. Niko hissed at the touch, the sound loud and arousing in her ear.

'Please, Niko… I need you,' she panted as the first waves of a climax began building inside her. Her thighs tensed as she sensed the approach, and Niko did, too. For he changed his tempo, his fingers wandering lower until they were nudging at her entrance. And then they were inside of her, and all of Camila's senses could only focus on his hand and what it was doing.

Her hand fell away from him, unable to focus on anything but the pleasure building at the base of her spine. Niko's other hand stroked over her bare stomach, his fingertips reaching the underside of her breasts.

'How is it that the smartest woman I know is also the most beautiful thing I've ever seen?' he whispered in her ear, his voice thick with his desire for her. His words clanged through her, the sound of his voice wrapping around her. She had put him in this state, had him whispering all these sweet things into her ear.

Pressure built inside her, approaching its crest as Niko continued to slip his fingers into her wet heat. Camila let herself go limp, knowing he was right behind her to support her when she couldn't. She was too far gone in the luscious fog of desire. Her eyes fluttered closed and her lips parted, letting out a long and drawn-out moan as her muscles clenched around his fingers in a wave of searing release.

Niko's arm around her waist tightened, pushing her closer to him. His breath was a ragged growl in her ear, his fingers still stroking her through her climax.

'How is that for relaxed?' he asked, and Camila gave a soft chuckle.

Her limbs felt like rubber as she attempted to stand on her own, and when Niko's hand finally slipped out from between her legs, she shuddered at the emptiness—at how right it was to have him there. To…share his pleasure.

'Definitely more effective than a hot bath,' she replied, turning around in his arms. This time he let her, and when she faced him, she leaned her head beckoning him towards her mouth. Niko obliged with a throaty groan, sliding his lips over hers in a kiss that renewed the heat that had just ebbed in her.

Her fingers dug into the fabric of his shirt as he angled his head, deepening their kiss until there was nothing but tongues and teeth and heaving breaths. Feeling around his broad chest, Camila found the row of buttons and slowly started removing his shirt, slipping her hand inside to caress his skin when she got halfway down his torso. Niko's groan was deep, vibrating through her skin and bones even though it was muffled by their kiss. She traced her fingers down his abdomen as she unbuttoned the shirt the rest of the way, and when she reached the top of his waistband, she paused.

His manhood twitched against her, making her smile into his kiss. 'Did you change your mind about showing me your bedroom?' she asked in between kisses, slipping one finger underneath his waistband.

Niko hissed, but he shook his head, leaning his forehead against hers. 'I don't want to hurt you,' he said, his hand caressing her back in slow circles.

'You're not going to hurt me. This pain was never anything serious,' she replied, knowing his sense of honour would prevent him from taking her right here, right now. Except that's what she wanted, what she *needed* from him. To set the connection they had established throughout her time here in Athens.

He brushed his lips over hers in a gentle kiss, one hand slipping down to her backside to press her closer. 'You've been through something today. I can't…take advantage of that. You should really…get in that bath.' His last words came out strained when she popped the button of his trousers open, her fingers brushing over the tip of his erection.

Camila huffed out a laugh, having expected this exact answer. 'Fine, but then you're joining me in the bath if you're so adamant about it,' she said as she pulled both his trousers and underwear down his legs.

Niko didn't know when control had fully left his grasp, but as he watched Camila take the two steps down into the bathtub, he knew it was over for him. Every muscle in his body wound tight, seeking the release of pleasure that only Camila could give him. Any other experience paled against the connection they had with each other, one that had only deepened after today.

He followed her into the bathtub, and when he settled down onto one of the inset benches, Camila was already standing in front of him. The ends of her long hair were dripping wet, draping over her shoulders and obscuring her breasts. He reached out to push her hair away, and he saw her shudder when his fingers brushed over each nipple.

His self-restraint crumbled into dust when a small moan escaped her lips, filling him with the instant need to hear it again. And again, until they were both hoarse and spent.

Grabbing her hand, Niko pulled her closer. His other hand slipped around her back and guided her down onto the bench—where she straddled him. He hissed when his erection strained against her as she moved her hips. Acting on instinct rather than on rational thought, Niko pushed her chest closer to him and took her breast into his mouth, swirling his tongue around her nipple.

The taste of her skin exploded through him, making him groan against her, and need erupted through him. Camila gasped above him, her hands burying into the long strands of his hair and tugging him at the roots, pulling him even closer. Her hips jerked against him and he released a shuddering breath.

'I will never get enough of your taste, Cami,' he whispered against her skin, delighting at the shudder his words sent through her.

'I'm yours to taste,' she replied, her voice stuttering when he licked at her other breast.

Her head fell back, exposing the long column of her neck, the view so enticing he couldn't resist. He wound his way up between her breasts, leaving trails of kisses on her skin as he moved.

Her fingers tightened in his hair, tugging at him hard enough to hurt, but Niko didn't care. He rode the line between pleasure and pain, burying his face in her neck and giving her all the attention she deserved. Worshipping her like the goddess she was. That's what he planned on doing from this moment onwards.

The thought emptied out of his mind when Camila slipped her hands between their bodies. Niko groaned when she wrapped her fingers around him and gave him a long and lascivious stroke. Her touch was everything. Losing control of his body, his head fell forward, resting on her shoulder.

'You can probably use some relaxation yourself,' she said, her lips brushing against the shell of his ear and sending shivers down his spine. 'You've been through the same thing. What applies to me should apply to you, too.'

'Cami…' Her name was a plea on his lips as she aligned her hips, his tip nudging her entrance.

Camila looked at him through half-closed lids, her breath coming out in soft pants and her cheeks dusted with the redness of her pleasure. How could he ever let her go again? The thought swirled in his mind as she bore down, taking all of him in. They both gasped, their breath mingling as their mouths crashed into each other. His fingers came down on either side of her hips, guiding her path as she began moving back and forth, up and down.

'You are…so perfect,' he whispered into her neck as he nuzzled her, coaxing another high-pitched moan from her.

This somehow felt like a continuation of their connection in Vancouver and a whole new thing at the same time. Her body was familiar, her noises and expressions at the height of pleasure a vision of pure beauty. He got lost in his own passion as he looked at her, wishing this moment would never end.

'Niko, please, I… Niko…' She breathed out his name, her voice light and airy, and from the pressure around him, he knew she was close. He was, too, yet he slowed down, not wanting this to end. He would never tire of hearing his name from her lips as she looked down at him with pleading eyes.

His hand dipped below the surface of the water, slipping between their writhing bodies and finding the spot where she needed him the most. 'Is that what you want, sweetheart?' he said, gliding his finger over her. Camila rewarded him with a jolt that crashed through him.

'Yes, yes, please. *Never* stop.' Her voice was a low whine, one that thundered through him and fuelled the ecstasy her touch brought him.

They moved as one, giving and taking as the strand already connecting them solidified into something real. Something heartbreakingly beautiful, and as he sensed her muscles flutter around him, Niko let go of the last vestiges of control. He thrust into her one, two, three times as stars began to shine in front of his eyelids. Every muscle in his body went taut before going loose, and they swallowed their shared moan in a kiss filled with passion and affection for one another.

This bed was so much more comfortable than the one at her hotel. Camila wanted to drift back to sleep, but a gentle touch willed her mind into consciousness. Warm hands drifted up and down her back, drawing large circles onto her flesh and leaving goose bumps in their wake. She let out a soft moan, sinking down into the pleasure of Niko's touch. Beside her, the linens rustled and a second later she sensed his lips on the back of her neck, placing gentle kisses onto her skin.

This moment was perfect in so many more ways than Camila could count. After the weeks she'd had and the health scare earlier today, she almost couldn't believe that she was now lying in Niko's bed, curled up in his embrace and moaning softly as his lips explored her neck.

'I didn't mean to wake you. I just wanted a little taste,' he whispered onto her skin, his tongue darting out to lap at the sensitive spot just behind her ear. She shivered and forced her eyes open.

'I don't want to sleep the day away,' she mumbled as she reached her arms above her, her toes flaring out in a full body stretch. Then she rolled onto her back so she could see Niko.

He was lying on his side, his head propped up on one arm as he looked at her, and the spark of affection in his eyes had her melting all over again. His gaze lingered on her face, then dipped lower down over her breasts and stopping at her stomach. His free hand moved slowly as he extended it, and a soft current of electricity ran through her when his hand connected with her stomach. He brushed over the gentle slope now visible, almost too small to detect if one didn't know.

'What are you thinking?' she asked when his eyes glazed over, his thoughts clearly wandering.

'How beautiful you are.'

Heat flashed through her face as a smile pulled at her lips. Had she ever heard a man say that to her? Definitely not with such earnestness as Niko was showing right now. His words sent her stomach swooping through her body in free fall. Was it silly that she wanted to throw her arms around him and never let him go? Wasn't that what her mother had warned her about? They would lure her in with words of passion and grand promises that were easily abandoned when things got hard.

She pushed those thoughts away. This wasn't like her mother's relationship with her father. Niko was nothing like him, either. There was no way he could have slipped past her guard the way he had if he wasn't a good person—a kind man who would be a wonderful father to his child. Their child.

Could she really hope that this one accident had led her to the person she was supposed to be with? Before Vancouver—before her pregnancy—she hadn't believed that person even existed, but this... This was now more than merely a physical connection.

He splayed his hand across her stomach, caressing the gentle slope, and Camila was so overwhelmed by the warmth in that gesture that she reached out, placing her hand on top of his. He raised his eyes towards her and the rawness in them stole her breath. 'It's strange... Before you arrived, I didn't even know this tiny human existed, but the second I learned about them, my life changed. Something inside me opened up, made space for all of this,' he said, his tone low and the thickness of emotion in his voice had her shivering. 'I felt it building inside me, but I didn't know what it was. Not until I thought I would lose it. The sheer panic...'

His swallow was audible, and Camila tightened her grip around his hand. 'I know what you mean. It was the same for me,' she said, almost not daring to think back to that moment a few hours ago. Though it had turned out to be fine and nothing serious, the fear it had triggered still sat in the back of her mind. 'I don't know what I would have done without you.'

He bent down, brushing a kiss onto her temple. 'For starters, you would have never known that your obstetrician is my mother,' he said with a chuckle.

The memory of that interaction came rushing back at her. Between the exhaustion of the night shift and the adrenaline the scare had released into her system, she hadn't even thought of that. A different heat rose to her cheeks, and she slapped her hand over her eyes. 'Oh, my God, your mother is going to see so much of me,' she said, looking at Niko when he chuckled. 'How can I get naked in front of the mother of my...'

Her voice trailed off as she realised where her words were taking her and that she didn't know how to finish the sentence. What was Niko to her now? They were co-parents, but that wasn't what the sentence had been leading her to. Her eyes flared wide as she looked up at him, thinking he must have caught on to it, too. Wasn't that what her mother had warned her about? That men were only out for themselves and to not let herself get in a situation where things were unclear? Where he had sway over her because of her emotional attachment?

But the eyes staring back at her were warm. Calm. He moved his arm away from his face, sinking back into the pillow so they were facing each other eye to eye. Then he took her hand, pulling her onto her side, placing his hand on her cheek. 'What is it you want to call me, sweetheart? Co-parent? Guy you're seeing casually? Boyfriend?'

He brushed a kiss onto her lips between each suggestion, his mouth lingering on hers after the third, their tongues briefly mingling before he pulled away again. It was enough to set her on fire all over again, need pooling between her legs.

'I don't know… Shouldn't that be something we figure out together?' she asked, blinking up at him. A part of her stomach was still in knots, but his reassuring smile drove away most of her anxiety.

He nodded. 'Whatever you call me, I don't care. As long as you're mine.'

His? The word sent a spray of heat coursing through her. There was a primal part of her buried deep down below the surface that surged at the word he'd chosen for her. Like there was no one who could be his equal—only her. And she wanted him to be hers, too.

Camila pulled herself closer to him, their naked bodies pressing against each other. His erection pushed against her as she angled her hips towards him, and she smiled into the kiss he pressed onto her lips. 'I think I'm feeling tense again,' she said, sinking her teeth into his lower lip as their kiss deepened. 'Maybe you could—'

Their shared moan swallowed the rest of the words as Niko thrust into her, the rawness of their passion wiping away any other thoughts.

CHAPTER NINE

NIKO OPENED THE car door for Camila, helping her out by grabbing her hand. She smiled at him as she emerged, and his heart almost gave out at her luminescence. Two weeks had passed since the health scare, and Camila had practically moved into his place at this point—a fact that he cherished far more than he thought he would. Living the endless bachelor life, he'd thought having someone in his space would be exhausting.

The dating scan last week had come in inconclusive. Their child had been positioned in a way that had made it hard to get an accurate measurement. They would have to go back soon for another try. But Niko didn't care. Not when they had heard the heartbeat of their child again. The genuine joy on Camila's face had sent his heart soaring, his insides buzzing with the same excitement—and that he got to share it with her.

Was two weeks enough to figure out what the rest of their lives would look like? Niko's rational side was telling him no, that wasn't possible, and he was letting himself be carried away by whatever was between them. The high the feeling gave him. But there was this other part, one he had never known existed within him. The part that had just been waiting for Camila to walk into his life. The part of him that was falling in love with her.

That was the only explanation he had for bringing her with him all the way to Nea Makri to spend the weekend with his mother and sister.

Camila looked up at the Vassilis family estate, her eyes wide as he guided her up the sloped driveway and into the main courtyard. The main house stood to the left, all imposing white stone, like many other houses around them.

'If that little house on the outskirts of Athens is where you grew up, what is this?' she asked as they walked the steps up to the house.

'I guess you could call this our beach house?' He pointed at something beyond their view. The beach was only a short walk away, the sea so close they could see it spreading over the horizon.

'You come here often?'

'Not as often as my mother would like,' he replied with a low chuckle. 'If it were up to her, Eleni and I would be here every weekend for some family time.'

Camila's eyes darted up to the house, her hands clutching around the handle of her handbag. He reached out to her, the back of his hand gliding over her cheek in a tender caress. God, how he loved touching her. Everything inside him went taut at the feel of her skin against his, and he had to remind himself that they weren't alone. His mother was probably standing behind the door staring at them.

'Everything will be fine,' he said, wishing to soothe her nerves. 'And remember that we can leave at any point. No explanation necessary. You just say the word and we go.'

Though Camila had wanted to meet his family, he could see her nerves fraying, but he wasn't sure why. He knew she'd grown up with a single mother but was that the reason she was uncomfortable in family situations? Or was something else behind her discomfort?

'Okay,' Camila breathed out, taking him out of his thoughts before he could dwell on them any more, and he reached for the door handle, pushing the doors open.

They walked in to a large reception area with a few chairs strewn around in pairs—one of which was occupied by his mother. She looked up from her book—undoubtedly a prop—and smiled as they entered.

'Son, it's good to see you,' she said, coming over to wrap him in a hug before turning to Camila. 'And Camila is here, too. How is the baby? Any more pain?'

She pulled Camila into her arms as well, and

by the flare in her eyes, he could see Camila hadn't expected that. Had she never had a partner's parent show interest in her? He filed that stray piece of information away to examine later.

'No, it's all good. No changes since you saw us for the dating scan,' she said, a lot shier than he was used to from her. Whether she was on a stage or standing among her colleagues, Niko had never once seen her hesitate or struggle to find her confidence.

'I trust my son is keeping you well fed. It's the highlight of my week when he comes over to cook,' his mother continued brightly, either not noticing Camila's hesitation or barrelling over it with the determination of someone who would get to know the first person her son had ever brought to family dinner.

And what surprised Niko the most was that it wasn't even about the baby. If their relationship had progressed the way it had here, he would have brought her over as well. This wasn't because he needed the mother of his child to know his family—though that certainly was another reason. But he just wanted them to know Camila because… That was the point where his thoughts stuttered. Never having been the person to do relationships, too wrapped up in spiting his father with his eternal bachelor life, he didn't know what life with Camila would look like.

Camila looked at him wide-eyed. 'He has kept

me fed, yes. But not with home cooking. I thought the kitchen at your place is just decorative.'

He shrugged, catching her by the wrist when she playfully swatted at him and pulling her close to his chest. Her head fell back, looking up at him, and he brushed his lips over hers in a hint of a kiss. 'You'll get to enjoy my skills tonight,' he said and enjoyed the blush warming her cheeks when she picked up on the double meaning of his words.

How they had landed in a situation where he was so open with his affection towards Camila, he didn't know. All he knew was that he wanted her to stay, and that he would do anything to have her here. Niko intended to talk to the real estate team of the Athena Institute to figure out how to relocate Camila's labs from Switzerland to here. He didn't care how many rooms he needed to move or if they had to build onto the hospital to accommodate her.

But he would have to talk to Camila, too. Their lives had almost blended into one these last two weeks and something inside him hesitated. Things between them were so new—so fragile—and he didn't know how much pressure he could put on it. If talking about it would somehow make it all go up in smoke.

Soon, he told himself. He would talk to her about their living arrangements soon. Right now, he just wanted to enjoy what they had and ignore the need to define it—to plan.

'I hear your next visit to the obstetrician is going to be extra awkward.' Eleni stepped to where Camila was leaning against the kitchen island, dipping a slice of pita into a small bowl of tzatziki Niko had put there just a few moments ago. The taste of cool cream spread through her mouth and was chased by the refreshing tang of lemon and garlic. Why had he been feeding her takeaway food and bringing her to restaurants when he knew how to make this?

Watching him cook brought a fresh wave of arousal crashing through her, one that she desperately needed to tuck away somewhere with both his mother and sister around them.

Camila laughed as she turned to the other woman. 'It turned awkward the second she learned about her grandchild when he burst through the door with me.'

She nodded towards Niko, who stood at the induction stove stirring something in a pan while talking to Daphne in a slow and steady rhythm of Greek. Though she still didn't understand a single word of his native language, the cadence of the language was becoming more familiar to her ear.

'Ah, yes, I heard that story already,' Eleni said with a smirk, and Camila laughed. She'd taken an instant liking to Niko's sister, just as he had predicted a few weeks ago—a moment that felt like a previous lifetime. One where they hadn't been together and didn't have any plans to cross that line, either.

She was so different from her older brother, far bubblier and outgoing. With Niko, she had to work to peel back the layers that kept the real man hidden behind his professional veneer. His sister was the exact opposite. From the second they had met in the foyer, Eleni had let her see her thoughts and who she really was. There was something oddly free about her, and it hit Camila with a twinge of jealousy.

She'd never been able to let loose like that without a care in the world. Not when her mother had always loomed behind her, pushing her spirit down whenever she got too independent. Blaming her when things didn't go her way…

'Don't stress too much about it, though. Mum will be happy to fuss over the baby once it's here, and by then, she will have worked through her feelings with Niko. He had plenty of chances to tell her he was expecting a child. Or that he even had a girlfriend.'

Eleni gave her a pointed glance at that last part, and Camila almost choked on the mouthful of pita at the last word. The other woman handed her a glass of water, a melodic laugh dropping from her lips. 'Don't tell me you two didn't have *that* conversation yet.'

'No, we did. We just…didn't really finish it.' Camila wasn't sure why she was being honest with Eleni, but the words left her mouth before she could contemplate any other answer. Something about the warmth in the other woman's eyes, ones that were a slightly different shade from Niko's, sparked a sense of safety inside her. So she continued, 'We didn't exactly plan this, so now we are just taking it one day at a time.'

She put her hand on her stomach for emphasis. Niko had told her she could call him whatever she wanted, that it wouldn't matter to him, and she was both relieved and confused by that. Everything in her life had a label and fit into a predetermined space. Camila's entire career—her research—was about knowing someone to their very DNA. Her work here with Alexis was proof of that. Attaching descriptions and labels to the things she found was how she made sense of the world. That was how she would help the swimmer find an answer to his question—and maybe even get him competing again.

Niko's indifference was a good sign in the way that if she wanted to, he'd be okay with being her boyfriend. She could solidify their relationship like that. But…how could she know he really wanted it when his strongest opinion was 'I don't care what you call me'?

And how were they imagining their life together? The last two weeks had been a glimpse into what they could expect. But if she wanted Daphne and Eleni to have the opportunity to fuss over her child, she would need to be here, wouldn't she? A move was something she hadn't contemplated, and her first instinct was to reject the idea out of hand. Her life, her work, it was all in Switzerland.

Niko hadn't brought anything up, either. In fact, outside of enjoying their time together, neither had really brought up the topic of the logistical steps around their co-parenting arrangements. Not a small part of her was scared to do that, too content with enjoying the quiet and calm between them. But Eleni was right. They needed to have a conversation—even if not knowing was easier.

Eleni reached for a slice of pita and dipped it into the bowl of hummus before popping it into her mouth. 'He's never brought someone over for us to meet. Granted, that was most likely to spite our father.'

Camila raised her eyebrows, but Eleni didn't clarify any further. Niko had never brought anyone he'd been involved with home in order to infuriate his father? She knew what it was like to have a difficult parent, but how they had dealt with it was so different. While she'd always tried to fit her mother's expectations into her own wishes and desires, it seemed like Niko had withdrawn from their relationship, only doing what was necessary to get to where he wanted.

Maybe if Camila hadn't buried herself in her work the moment she entered med school, she wouldn't feel so ill-prepared right now. So much of her mother's voice still threaded through her own, making it so much harder to distinguish what was her own voice and what were the toxic musings of her mother. If Camila had gathered more of her own experiences, would she know what to do now? Would she know how to handle the hesitation giving her pause when she thought about discussing their future together?

'Well…it's nice to be open about it,' she said when she swallowed a sip of water to soothe the dryness in her mouth.

Eleni nodded, but there was a curious glint in her eye that made Camila want to squirm. She felt like she was being studied, like she was under the microscope. 'Do you think he's happy?' Eleni asked, some of her playfulness fading.

Camila didn't know how to answer that question, not when she wasn't completely sure of Niko's feelings herself. Happy? They had spoken about a lot of things, but happiness was such an intangible concept. 'I hope so,' she said finally, voice soft.

Eleni stared at her as if she were weighing up her words. That her suitability for Niko would be under scrutiny was something Camila had expected. But seeing it happen was another thing altogether. How would her standing change in the

Vassilis family once the dinner was done? Would Niko even care?

After a beat of silence, Eleni took another slice of pita and said, 'He seems different with you.'

'What do you mean?' That was a sentence that could be a great compliment or point out a worrying trend. Like their connection was somehow changing something fundamental about Niko.

'I see him at least once a week, and ever since you arrived here, he has been…softer. He's always been so guarded, even with the people closest to him.' Eleni's eyes slipped away from her and onto the back of her brother, who was now juggling three different pots and pans while laughing with his mother. 'It's nice to see him let go of control a bit.'

Camila wished she'd known the Niko from before, even if it was just for a bit. But the version his sister described now, the more laid-back person, that was the Niko she knew. The one who had approached her twice at the cocktail hour in Vancouver. Control hadn't ever been a thing between them, and she was glad for it. Her mother had exerted enough control over her, even now, without being in her life any more, that she needed the person in her life to just let her handle things.

As she watched Niko from across the room, Camila felt a warmth in her chest that had nothing to do with the spicy hummus. She was glad that she'd met him and even more glad that they were having a child together. Watching him with his family, seeing how he interacted with them and how they loved him… She wanted her child to have that, too.

Doubt's icy fingers crept through her, threatening to snatch the perfect picture building in her mind. Despite the tension between him and his father, Niko had grown up knowing the support of his mother and sister. They had pulled each other through the difficulties in their lives and stuck to each other. What did Camila have to look back to? Nothing but resentment that still bubbled to the surface from time to time. A conversation she'd wanted to have with her mother floated through her mind, and the feeling of leaving things unfinished still stung so many years later.

Camila knew that she was a different person, that she had taken the lesson and learned from them. There was no way she would repeat any of it. Her child would be free to be whoever they wanted to be, and she would do everything to support them. But even that knowledge couldn't chase away the pangs of doubt needling at her.

As if sensing her stare, Niko shot a look over his shoulder and caught her gaze. The smile spreading over his lips was slow and lazy, one she had seen so many times this week—and it never failed to stoke the low-burning fire inside her. She wanted to get used to that feeling, wanted to lose herself in it as she pleased. But was such a thing even possible for someone like her? Or did her mother's bitterness leave too much damage for her to ever recover?

'I definitely hope he's happy,' she said, letting some of her insecurities bubble to the surface.

They all get bored eventually. Once they do, they move on to other things. Her mother's words surfaced in her mind unbidden, stealing away the heat and replacing it with a creeping darkness.

Niko was different, though. From the moment he'd learned about their situation, about their child, he had done nothing but step up. There was no way he would just get bored and leave, was there?

As long as you're mine. That was what he had said. A phrase that had previously sent chills down her spine and set her blood on fire now gave her pause. What if that wasn't the romantic gesture she thought it was? What if it was the warning her mother had taught her to watch out for? That there were conditions to his presence in her life? Like her being near him, moving her life here.

Why hadn't they talked about this? Camila had wanted to so many times, yet never found the right moment. The right time. Enough courage to do it—because what if she didn't like the answer?

Niko's brow creased as he kept looking at

her, and then he turned, saying something to his mother before coming up to them. 'Eleni, Mum needs help setting the table,' he said to his sister, who gave him a mock salute before scurrying away with a knowing glance towards them.

When he turned his attention to Camila, his gaze was heavy on her. 'You okay? Need a break from all the conversation?' He raised his hand to her face, brushing his knuckles along the line of her jaw.

I need to know what this is to you. Camila shook her head, swallowing the words forming in her head. They would have enough time to discuss this in the coming days. Even as doubt crept into her chest, she pushed it away, rooting herself in the present moment as much as she could. His family surrounded them—her child's family. Those were connections worth building, even if the relationship between her and Niko might eventually break down.

They all get bored eventually.

Dinner turned out to be far less disruptive and embarrassing than Niko had expected. For the first time, both his mother and sister had been on their best behaviour and kept their anecdotes appropriate. Not that he had anything to compare it against. Camila was the first—the only—person he'd taken to see them.

Her hand lay against his, their fingers threaded

together as they walked across the lush grass to the tiny guest house at the other side of the estate. The air was still warm despite the late hour, the stone flooring around the pool releasing all the stored up heat and keeping the surroundings from cooling down.

'You really can cook exceptionally well,' Camila said into the quiet, giving his hand a squeeze. 'It seems even now I'm only scratching at your surface.'

Niko smiled. 'During my surgical training, one of the senior surgeons would urge us all to train our stitches on chicken breasts. I didn't like the thought of wasting so much food just for training, so I began cooking it—and bringing it to the hospital.'

'You must have been popular with your peers then.'

'Not at first—because I was terrible at it. But as with anything, I stuck with it long enough. It became a calming ritual in my life. A moment to slow down when everything around me was just so hectic.' He paused in his step, wrapping his arms around Camila when she bumped into him. His heart flipped over when she rested her head on his chest, as if they had been doing so for years.

'Maybe you can teach me some things. My mother wasn't very…maternal. She was too busy working two jobs to keep us going,' Camila replied, and the edge of her voice had him tighten his grip around her. 'Which was hard for her because she was of the opinion that women shouldn't have ambitious careers.'

He picked up on the usual hesitation in her voice whenever she spoke about her mother. That she'd grown up only with her, he already knew. The absence of her father had made her suspicious of his own motivation—something he was glad they had talked over. But whenever it came to her mother, she had remained fairly tight-lipped.

Having his own fair share of family problems, Niko had never wanted to dig deeper. He didn't react well to people pushing him on Stavros, and so he wouldn't do that to someone else. Even though he was dying to know more.

'For what it's worth, I know my mother and Eleni really enjoyed getting to know you today. They already asked you to become a regular guest at the weekly family dinner,' he said, smoothing his hands over her back.

He ignored the kernel of doubt blooming at his own words. How would she be able to come to dinner with him if she returned to Switzerland? Would she even want to live here? Niko would do whatever it took to give her everything she needed, was already reaching out to people to make it happen. But a block formed inside him when he formed the questions inside his mind.

Soon, he promised himself again.

She exhaled, and he could feel her smiling as some of the tension left her shoulders. It was that smile that halted the burning questions in his mind. The balance between them was already so delicate. 'I'm glad. I've never met someone's extended family, and after dropping the news on Daphne the way we have, I wasn't sure how she'd feel about me.'

'My mother adores you. I can see it from the way she didn't want us to leave the house.' He put his hands on her shoulders, pushing her away to look her in the eye. This far away from the city, the sky was bright with the light of stars and the moon hanging far above them.

'I'm glad to hear that. I already liked her as my doctor, and so it'll be nice to have her as a…' Her voice trailed off and her eyes left his face, looking towards the guest house. Niko picked up on her silent request, letting her out of his arms and leading her towards their place for the night.

The inside of the guest house was much cooler than the outside, the windows shut tight to keep the heat from seeping in over the day. He turned the lights on, dimming them down until they were only a low glow bouncing off the white walls. A large bookshelf lined one wall, filled with various novels and medical textbooks, and the couch at the centre of the living space inviting the guests of the Vassilis family to unwind and relax.

His eyes roamed over her as Camila stepped in, taking in the casual decor and cosiness of the guest house. Was she picturing how much time they would spend here in the future? Would she want that? Niko couldn't imagine why she wouldn't. He had a state-of-the-art hospital, a support system and more space in his house than he knew what to do with. She would say yes to moving here. She had to. He couldn't be so far away from her—from his child.

The slight slump in her shoulder had him draw closer to her, putting an arm around her waist. 'Did you not enjoy yourself?' he asked.

Camila leaned into his touch and shook her head. 'No, that's not it. I love that our child will have a grandmother and an aunt. It's something I wish I could give as well...'

Wrapping his hand around her wrist, he pulled her to the couch and into his lap. Camila shifted, wiggling against him enough that blood rushed to the lower half of his body. He tamped down on the surge of need rising in him.

'What happened between you two?' Something he had wanted to know for a while but never felt confident to ask. Clearly seeing his family had unearthed some of the more painful memories.

'I don't necessarily know, but my father leaving must have changed something fundamental inside my mother. She was so bitter and sad for basically my entire life, never letting go of the hurt my father's abandonment inflicted on her. I couldn't remember it myself, so to me it was as if he had never existed. But she made sure I remembered him the way she had.'

Niko remained quiet, stroking her back in long and lazy motions. He could do it all night if she wanted to.

'My mother cared little about my career choices—or anything about me, really. Despite her experience, she thought that being a doctor wasn't a suitable career for a woman, and had such strong opinions around what I *should* do. She tried her best to imprint the bitterness in her heart on me. Reminding me that these men had their uses but not get too attached to them. And if they bothered to stay, they would soon leave anyway because that was what all men did. They left.' Her chest rubbed against his as she swallowed a deep breath. 'A part of me thinks even though it was my father who left her, she resented me for it, too. Like if I hadn't happened, she might have lived happily ever after with that man.'

Her fingers began their dance across his scalp again, tangling her hand through his hair and closing what little gap was left between them. The heat rising in his chest met the ice in his veins and summoned a storm that raged through him. Even if he had any words for her, he knew they wouldn't ever be enough to erase the indignity of how she was treated.

Now it all made sense, and the final piece of the puzzle fell into place. The reason she had reacted so strongly when they had first discussed things. Why she'd wanted to hear from him that he wouldn't leave when things got hard. But they were way beyond that point now. He'd never entertained the thought of leaving his child behind, but now they were so much more than that.

A real family. And once Camila agreed to come live with him, she would see that commitment reaffirmed every day. He would make sure of that.

Camila shook her head, as if she had just finished a silent conversation with herself. 'What is it?' he asked, and she again shook her head.

'It's nothing…' she said, her voice trailing off. 'Once I left for university, we spoke less and less. And then she died, and I never got to resolve any of the tension between us.'

Niko hummed his agreement, her words finding a vulnerable spot inside him. Though his struggles with his father had been different, he knew that concept all too well. Stavros had wielded it against him with an expertise of a man used to cowing people.

'My father only ever saw me as a means to an end for his legacy. He treated me less like his son and more like an instrument through which he could reach immortality.' The concept sounded ridiculous, but there were no other words to describe it more accurately. The continuation of his name and the Athena Institute were the only thing he ever cared about.

And even though Niko had worked hard to redeem the hospital, to make it a place of good where they actually helped people, a part of him remained hollow to the achievement. Him being the medical director was still more his father's dream than his own.

Camila let out a wobbly laugh, and even though he winced at the strain in her voice, the sound still opened his chest wide. 'So we were both raised by narcissists, and we just need to make sure our child grows up level-headed.'

Her tone had him smiling, pushing his nose into her hair to breathe her scent in. 'I'm sure we will manage just fine,' he said, each word a small kiss on the top of her head.

Despite the gravity of their conversation, a sense of lightness settled within Niko. They both had things they were dealing with, but now he was more certain than ever that they would see it through together. Tomorrow he would call the real estate team at the Institute and put things into place so Camila could move her lab here.

Camila shifted, looking up at him with large eyes. Her lush lips were slightly parted, and when Niko cupped her face with one hand and brushed his thumb over her bottom lip, she let out a shuddering breath. That tiny exhale was enough to kindle the fire of passion within him, and he brought his mouth down onto hers.

The kiss turned from tentative to longing with one stroke of her tongue against his, and Niko buried his hands in her hair, pulling her up to his face. 'I've been thinking about doing that all night,' he ground out between kisses.

This time he didn't leash the passion ravaging through him, demanding her touch on his skin, her breath to mingle with his. The night had brought him so much closer to her, so much more than he even thought possible, and the desire to be with her was all-consuming. He couldn't stop his feelings any more than he could stop the rotation of the earth.

'Niko... I shared these things with you because...' A low moan interrupted her words as his lips trailed down her neck, finding that sensitive spot behind her ear. 'I need...to plan so I can... Oh!'

While she spoke, Niko undid the buttons of her blouse and pushed her bra aside. His tongue flicked over her already taut nipple, and the rest of her sentence vanished in a throaty moan. He kissed the slope of her breast and then down her stomach, marvelling at the slight curve of it.

'I'm taking care of it, Cami,' he whispered against her skin, breathing in her alluring scent. 'I'm not like the men you have encountered in

your life. I'm here to stay, to make this work—
no matter what.'

Camila's sigh was shaky as his face dipped
lower, his hands pushing underneath the waistband of her trousers and pulling them down.
'Okay, so you…'

Niko pushed himself up and pulled her into
a kiss. Camila's moan vibrated through his lips
when he slipped his hand underneath the lace of
her underwear, finding her wet with need.

'You're mine, Cami. And I'm yours. Trust me
on that,' he whispered against her mouth, and
smiled when she lifted her hips in response, eager
to meet his.

CHAPTER TEN

AFTER SIX WEEKS, they finally had a diagnosis. Niko had been in the middle of a call when Camila's message arrived, and he'd asked her to come by his office so they could tell the Hellenic Swimming Association together—after he'd received the entire debrief himself. When she'd offered to have him join as they told the patient, he glanced at his overloaded schedule and decided to take that chance anyway.

It had been far too long since he'd been involved in any kind of treatment for a patient. Alexis Theodorou's case came the closest to him being involved, so being there just felt right.

Camila and Emilia were standing outside the patient's room when he arrived, both of them had a smile on their lips. They turned as they heard his footsteps echo in the corridor, announcing his arrival, and the small smile on Camila's lips turned into a brilliant one as she laid eyes on him. Niko's heart stuttered inside of his chest and he had to remind himself that they were at work and that he couldn't sweep her into his arms just because he wanted to.

'I found some interesting genetic markers that indicate a particular family history,' Camila said when he was close enough to hear her. 'So I went to interview some of his family members, and eventually a pattern of a heart disease popped up.'

Niko looked at Emilia with a brow drawn high. 'Aren't family interviews the first thing we do?'

'They sure are, but we have to repeat them with shocking frequency. People don't always remember things the first time around. Only when prompted with very specific questions do they suddenly remember their great-grandfather who died of a heart attack.' Emilia shook her head in exasperation and Camila laughed, the sound ringing through him like the chime of a bell. Even in this professional environment, he wanted to surround himself with her. Would that feeling ever dull?

He hoped not.

'Shall we?' Camila glanced between them and when everyone nodded, she knocked and pushed the door open.

Alexis Theodorou sat up, leaning against the back of his bed with a laptop on his thighs. He looked up from the screen as they entered, and even though Niko had been involved in some emergency situations, he realised how young he looked.

A quiet resignation surrounded Alexis, like they weren't the first doctors to visit him today and they definitely wouldn't be the last. But when both Camila and Emilia said nothing straight away, his spine stiffened and his eyes rounded.

'You know something?' he asked, his voice laced with a hopefulness he was trying his best to clamp down on.

Camila nodded, then pointed towards Niko. 'I believe you've seen Dr Vassilis in passing. He's the medical director here at the Athena Institute and he's been communicating back and forth with the Hellenic Swimming Association. He's also the person who ultimately helped me figure out your diagnosis with a suggestion he had.'

Niko's head snapped towards Camila just as Alexis gasped, 'You know what's wrong with me?'

'You have long QT syndrome—or LQTS for short. It's a heart rhythm disorder that, in your case, leads to a fast and chaotic heartbeat. It can lead to seizures and fainting, as well as sudden cardiac arrest. The telltale sign of LQTS is a prolonged QT interval. Something Dr Vassilis suggested when we were trying to narrow down the potential diagnosis,' Camila explained, stepping closer to the patient's bed. 'Cardiac arrest is the most severe of symptoms one can have with this.'

Niko frowned at her last words and saw the moment Alexis's stomach sank on the patient's face. Camila was threading a careful needle in giving him the diagnosis and the next steps without instantly crushing him.

'Okay, so now that we know what it is, how do we cure it? You have a cure, right?'

Camila took a deep breath. 'We cannot cure LQTS. It's a genetic disease that you were born with and that manifested at this time in your life. I brought Dr Seo with me here because we have to talk about how to manage the disease.'

'Okay, but if I can manage it, that means we just have to figure some things out and then I can swim again, yes?' There was a desperate edge to his voice, one Niko understood well enough. His eyes flickered towards Camila, who looked at the patient with sympathy.

'The answer is unfortunately a very vague maybe. I don't want to rule it out completely, but at the same time, you have reacted adversely to the exercise stress tests we performed,' she explained, laying out all the information Alexis needed to come to terms with his new reality. 'We've had some success controlling your arrhythmias with beta blockers, and that is something we will prescribe you. But the most effective way of dealing with long QT syndrome is to make lifestyle modifications and avoid triggers like stress or intense exercise.'

Alexis stared at all three of them, his eyes bouncing around as the truth sank in. When it did, his face contorted into an expression of pain that wrenched at Niko's heart. This wasn't the good news any of them were hoping for, but eventually he would come to appreciate that an answer—even one that was as troubling as this one—was better than no answer.

Emilia stepped up to Alexis. 'I'm willing to try for you, Alexis. We will have to do some very careful testing with medical staff at hand to jump in as necessary. But I know how much swimming means to you, so we will work on a plan to test if you can still compete with LQTS.' She paused, giving him a smile. 'I can't promise it will work, but we shall try.'

From the defeated nod, it was apparent Alexis didn't share the quiet hope present in Emilia's word, and Niko couldn't blame him. There was a lot to process before they could make any decisions.

Clearing his throat, Niko said, 'With your consent, I will speak to the Hellenic Swimming Association and inform them about your diagnosis. I'm sure they will want to offer you whatever support they can to figure out the next steps.'

Alexis nodded again, his gaze dropping down to his closed laptop, knuckles turning white where he gripped them. Even though having a confirmed diagnosis was a milestone for everyone at the hospital, it was much harder to celebrate the success of their collaboration with

Camila when it changed the life of their patient adversely.

'We have counselling services available as well, which I urge you to use, Alexis. Life-altering information comes with its own trauma, and we can help you cope with it,' Emilia added, then looked towards him and Camila. 'We will give you some space to absorb the information. If you have questions, we're here to help you sort through everything.'

They both nodded, saying their goodbyes, and Niko cast a last glance at Alexis before following the other two out the door. When he approached them, they were already putting their heads together, talking animatedly.

'...but anyway. A profile on this case will really help to get more press on my research,' Camila said to the other woman, and a boulder dropped inside Niko's stomach. *That* was the first thing she was concerned about after changing their patient's life forever. That she might get a few more mentions in the press?

They had spoken about this, had they not? Her motivations had been clear—she had said so. Had that really been the truth, or had they been in a situation where she'd told him what he wanted to hear? To keep the peace between two people struggling with a new reality? Their conversation seemed so long ago now...

Niko pushed down the rising doubts spreading

ice through his veins. But one stubborn thought remained—that even though they were having a child together, they still had so much left to discover about each other. So many unknowns around what made them tick as people.

Emilia nodded. 'I'm glad we both got out of this collaboration what we wanted. I hope we will get to do this again and soon. What you're working on will no doubt become commonplace soon.'

'That's the goal. My diagnostic team is already working on the textbook. This will be such an excellent case study to add.' Camila's smile was bright as she turned toward Niko, and the rock in his stomach grew heavier, bringing up an unpleasant taste.

'My office now, if you please,' he said to Camila and Emilia, walking past them at a brisk pace. He sensed their stares on his back, but he kept on walking without looking back.

Confusion uncoiled in his chest, sending cold shivers raking down his spine. Wasn't this kind of motivation exactly the one he didn't want to have around in his hospital? Niko didn't object to people making a living. They all needed to survive so they could keep helping, and he'd be the first one to admit that he was in a much more fortunate position than others.

But Alexis had just received the news not even a minute ago, and those were the concerns in her head? Not how he was doing? How they could help him further? The thoughts surfaced in his mind unbidden, no matter how hard he tried to clamp down on them until icy water pooled in the pit of his stomach.

Had they maybe moved too fast? They may be having a child together, but their involvement with each other… Was now the right time for that when he still had so much work left to do in the hospital? When he barely knew her? Were they doing right by their child by jumping into this relationship headfirst?

He didn't have time to think about any of this right now. The Hellenic Swimming Association was waiting for his call, and it would be up to them and a team of doctors here to see if they could get Alexis Theodorou swimming again.

The air between her and Niko was strange ever since their conversation with Alexis, and she wasn't sure why. All throughout the call, she'd been trying to catch his eyes, read his intentions in his gaze. But whether or not on purpose, Niko had avoided looking at her, his eyes catching onto anything in his office except her.

'I know this isn't what we wanted to hear, but that's how things are. It would be good to bring some people in here soon—both to talk to Alexis and to figure out our next steps,' Niko said, and the person on the other side of the line gave a deep sigh.

'Let me discuss this news with the medical and coaching team. I'll have my assistant call yours to figure out a date that works for us,' he said, then hung up after a brief goodbye.

The tension in the room was palpable, and Camila gave Emilia a sympathetic nod. Things might have turned out great for her own research efforts, but they would struggle with a patient that was hoping for better news.

'I'll let you know the date when it comes through,' Niko said to Emilia, and some of the frost she'd detected in his voice still remained. 'Now, would you please excuse us? Dr Pereira Frey and I have some matters to discuss now that we rendered the diagnosis.'

Emilia nodded, sending a muted smile Camila's way before closing the door behind her.

Something wasn't right. There was a shift in the air between them, and Camila didn't know what it was about. What had happened between this morning, when he had pulled her back into the car to smother her in a passionate kiss, to now? She didn't know, but her veins were filling with ice, her gut warning her about something intangible. Despite her efforts to banish her mother's toxic words from her brain, they thundered through her in this moment, reminding her the truth she didn't want to believe.

Was this the moment where Niko would let her down? The moment she'd been waiting for with bated breath ever since their night together at his place?

She swallowed the lump in her throat and asked, 'What's wrong?'

'It's a tough diagnosis for Alexis,' Niko said, his hands steepled in front of him and his chin leaning on top of them. His lips were pulled into a frown, which only increased the bad feeling sloshing around in her gut.

'Yes, but if anyone can figure it out, it'll be Emilia and her team. And even if worse comes to worst, I'm sure they will have a plan in place to keep him taking part in one form or another.' This wasn't about Alexis. Niko had hardly been involved in his treatment, and even though she wouldn't dispute how much he cared about the patient, the reaction was disproportionate. No, somehow this was about her. About them.

The blood in her veins froze. He really was going to leave, wasn't he? And she didn't even know what had happened.

'Is that what this is about? You had some strange epiphany while we spoke to the patient, and you realised that fatherhood isn't for you after all? That I don't mean enough to you to change anything?' She let the insecurities out, too tired and wrung out to pretend to keep her composure. If they were going to have an argument, then she might as well let him see all of it.

Her words were enough to grab his full attention. Flared eyes locked onto hers, a deep line appearing between his brows. It was the first time since they left Alexis's room that he had directly looked at her.

'What? Why would you…?' His voice trailed off, and he stood, circling around his desk until he was on the other side. Leaning against it, he crossed his arms in front of his chest and looked down at where she sat. 'I'm annoyed because the second you were out of the patient's room, all you could talk about was how much more famous this case was going to make you.'

Camila looked up at him and blinked, his words only slowly making sense in her mind. 'Famous… I never said famous. I said it will bring more press to my and my team's work. Niko, I'm doing this to help people, but I need to pay my staff. I need to pay rent,' she said, the ice in her veins slowly melting as her indignation flared up.

It wasn't about his commitment to her, but somehow it was far worse. Niko was accusing her of something unsavoury, yet she couldn't quite pinpoint what it was. How did he expect her to operate without funding? Of course she had to court investors and medical journals to do so; otherwise, no one would even know what she was doing.

'We're talking about a man who has lost everything in the span of two months. One morning, he woke up and went to train, and then the next thing he knows, he's living in a hospital. His life is changed forever now, and the first thing you thought after delivering this news was how it would fit into your textbook.' His tone was flat and robust and unlike any voice Camila had heard from him ever since their first meeting. She searched for the usual warmth, the strands of affection hidden in his lilting accent that she could listen to for hours on end.

She clenched her jaw, swallowing the fire rising in her throat. Letting her anger get the better of her would not resolve this—even if this argument was bordering on ridiculous. 'Niko, my job here was done the moment I gave my diagnosis. It's up to your team now to take care of Alexis—and they are far more equipped to do that than I am.'

An expression fluttered over his face, a glimmer of doubt that almost had her breathing out a sigh of relief. She didn't like the tension snapping into place between them. Of all the things they could fight about, this one didn't seem worth it.

'I don't like you being so dependent on outside funding. I've seen what it can do to people, how it warps their sense of duty,' he said after a beat of silence, his arms slackening at his side.

'Ah, I see where this comes from,' she said, as much to herself as to him. He was worried she was putting her profit and the funding of her research ahead of patient welfare. A crack appeared in her heart as she thought that, and disappointment seeped in through that tiny fracture. How could he think so little of her that this would lead him to lash out? Was he really looking at her and seeing someone like his father, who put his own profits in front of patient's well-being? Hadn't she shown her trustworthiness over and over again since she'd started here?

She willed her voice to remain steady as she said, 'You will have to trust me on this, because without outside funding, I can't continue my research. And without my research, we wouldn't have been able to save Alexis's life. Or any of the other lives all around the world that we already saved. Sure, a lot of my time is spent courting deep pockets, convincing them of my cause. It's not an aspect I enjoy, but it is a part of my work. I'm not stopping with that because...'

Niko stared at her for what felt like an eternity, his lips slightly parted as if he was contemplating his next words. His hand came up to his face, and he rubbed it over the stubble on his cheek. The noise filled the air, drawing attention to the quiet settling in between them.

'Because of what?' he asked, his eyes narrowing.

'You have to deal with your insecurities in a constructive way. Not dump them on me.'

Niko's eyes flared, and she almost immediately regretted those words. She needed time to compose her thoughts, not blurt them out with whatever emotion was currently the strongest in her. 'I'm sorry, what I'm trying to say—'

He halted her with a shake of his head. 'You don't have to worry about that. The Athena Institute has enough funding to keep you going. I didn't want to say anything until I knew for certain. But I got word from the real estate team here, and we can expand the west wing to make room for your lab,' he finally said, and rendered Camila speechless with it.

She stared at him, processing his words and searching his face for any indicator that this was a joke or some kind of misunderstanding. Because otherwise, what he was saying was that he had unilaterally made a decision that concerned her as a person *and* as a professional. It didn't fit in with the picture of Niko she had developed over their whirlwind romance in the last few weeks.

'I—what? Why would you extend the hospital for me? I'm not moving my laboratory here.' The thought alone was ridiculous. She was well established in Switzerland. Her entire team was there, working right now while she took this assignment. How could he even suggest that with such finality?

The line between his brows grew deeper. 'Why not? I'm in a position where I can give you the resources of the best cardiac hospital in Europe. You'll want for nothing, and with my backing, you can go further than ever without having to beg for so much in front of investors and medical press.'

'Beg?' It was the only word Camila honed in on, not even registering the rest of his sentence. Of course she would love to have the backing of the Athena Institute, and associating herself closer with it was one of the main reasons she'd come here. But she couldn't just take it because... 'I have *never* begged for anything in my entire life. Everything I worked for, I clawed together with my own two hands. *I* didn't get a hospital handed to me to do with as I please.'

She was on her feet now, meeting Niko's gaze with an angry stare of her own. 'And I may have considered this offer if you had presented it as such, not as a unilateral decision about my work.'

Niko sighed, his hand slipping up to his temple and giving it a rub. 'Isn't that what you wanted? You told me about all of the insecurities growing up, about having to scrape by to fund your work. I told you I would take care of it, of you... of you *both*.'

Camila's eyes grew wide, and her hand came down on her stomach. 'I know we haven't spoken about what we want to do. But me moving my work over here to work under you is not feasible. I've been working so hard for the last five years. I can't give you such control over me. What assurance do I have if we don't work out? I can't risk my entire career for...'

His eyes narrowed on hers when her words trailed off. 'Can't risk it for me? For *us* being a family? If you don't want to come here, what is your grand plan for this relationship? How do you see us playing out across half of Europe?'

'That...' Camila swallowed hard, trying to get rid of the lump in her throat. 'Neither of us have had this particular conversation. I don't know what I want, but I won't be strong-armed into a decision like that. Not when we both have been avoiding this topic.'

They had arrived at the point that Camila had hoped and prayed for would never happen. The place where her mother's words would become the unmovable truth. No matter how much stress and grief her constant toxicity had brought into Camila's life, she couldn't deny the truth that lay beneath her warnings.

Niko might not see it this way, but planning such a big thing without even consulting her was a first attempt of wresting control from her. She could never allow any man to do that. It had been the reason she'd never seriously dated anyone and had solely focused on her work most of her adult life.

'I'm not trying to control you, and the fact that you would think so shows that you don't trust me to stick around. To…stay when things get complicated,' Niko replied, his jaw clenched tight as he referenced how their conversation had started. He wasn't wrong. Camila was waiting for the axe to fall, because she couldn't comprehend how completely Niko had changed her life. How wildly in love she was with him and how, despite that, they didn't fit together.

He would never understand how she needed to be in the spotlight. Not because it pleased her but because her life's work depended on it. It would always scare him, and she would always wait for the day he would leave, because they always did. Her father had done that, too.

'I don't trust you to stick around,' Camila said, the words thick in her throat, like she had to convince herself they were true when she knew they weren't.

'And I can't watch you sell yourself out like that when there are other choices,' he replied, and Camila wanted to believe that she heard the same thickness in his words. That he, too, was struggling.

'Then maybe we were getting too swept up in the moment, enough to ignore compatibility issues. Maybe we just thought there was something because of our circumstances. Without realising that we needed more than our attraction to make this work.' That was the only explanation she had.

How else had they arrived at this conversation—reached this conclusion?

The crack in her heart widened when Niko nodded, a frown pulling at the lips she longed to kiss even now. 'Yeah, I guess so...'

And there it was. The end she had been summoning the moment she had let him come too close. The way her insides were tearing open, she would have thought this moment would tear her in half. But she needed to keep it together. *They* needed to keep it together. They still had to be in each other's lives for the sake of their child.

Camila took a step back, the walls of the office suddenly much nearer than they had been a moment ago. She needed to leave before all the feelings bubbling up inside her burst out in the open.

'We still have the appointment for the re-scan next week. I'll see you there and then we can discuss...next steps,' she said hurriedly, needing the words to leave her before she broke apart.

Niko moved closer to her, his hand stretched out as if to touch her, but he stopped at the last minute. The tip of his tongue darted over his lips and she could see him searching for the right words to say. But there were none. Nothing he could ever say would right anything between them. Because at the end of it all, they had simply got caught up in some attraction they shouldn't have—leaving them both with a burn to remind them.

There were things in this world that were un-movable truths. No matter how much Camila wanted them to be different.

They always left eventually.

CHAPTER ELEVEN

THE CORRIDORS OF the Athena Institute looked particularly grim today, enough so that Niko noticed. He would have to speak to the real estate team about that. Maybe they changed to a new cleaning company? Whatever it was, it looked…off.

He didn't stop to question that the change might be linked to the foul mood he'd been nursing for the last few days. Or that it turned even darker as he walked through the hospital towards his office. Everywhere, people were talking with their loved ones, and the hospital staff were bustling around, comforting patients, administering medications or simply helping them with a conversation and some quality time. Those were the things Niko valued, the changes he *wanted* to see in the Athena Institute. And it should fill him with pride to note them.

Yet he couldn't shake the cloud surrounding him. It felt like all eyes were on him as he walked through the corridors. Though why would they even bother to look? Did they know about the decision Camila and he made last week after the diagnosis of their patient? No one in the hospital even knew that they were together.

They had made the decision together, and he thought that would be comforting. Two adults deciding that they needed to change their relationship with each other, needed to…be something else.

'Oh my God, you really are a menace,' the familiar voice said way too brightly for this early in the morning as Niko shoved open the door to his office. 'You didn't even flinch.'

He walked up to his desk, dropping his briefcase on it before turning around and staring at his sister. She had her legs draped over the side of the couch, her head propped up by a few pillows so she could see him.

'I grew up with you, Eleni. You couldn't scare me even if you wanted to,' he replied, taking his seat and starting up his computer.

'Don't offer me a challenge you'll regret. You know how competitive I am,' she said, swinging her legs around and pushing herself into a sitting position.

Niko shook his head. 'And you know I'm a busy person, so what brings you here?' The sooner they got to the bottom of that, the faster he could get back to the things that mattered— this hospital. The *only* focus he should have in life right now until his child was born.

The thought brought a new wave of heaviness to his chest, and Niko pushed it away.

'You didn't come to dinner yesterday,' Eleni said, her dark brown eyes a reflection of his own and staring right at him.

He paused for a second, his thoughts catching up with him. Yesterday was Thursday? Somehow that had slipped his attention. 'I was busy with some things,' he lied, knowing that if he admitted to forgetting it, there would be a different conversation to be had.

'Too busy to text and let us know?' his sister asked, raising her eyebrows at him, and Niko frowned.

'By the time I realised I was caught up, it was already too late to call you.' That was technically true, seeing as he only remembered this second that he was supposed to be at dinner last night. It would be decidedly too late to call now.

'Right…' Judging by Eleni's quirked brow, he could tell she didn't believe him. Not that he put that much effort into his excuse, anyway. Things were too chaotic for him to spend time on appeasing his family. They would understand once he filled them in—which he didn't plan on doing until much later. Right now, he still had too many things swirling inside his head to give anyone a good explanation as to what had happened to him and Camila. How they had gone from living in their little bubble together, too afraid to move in case it burst, to deciding that maybe they were better off on separate paths. Paths that wound and turned parallel to each other but had enough space to diverge.

'Okay, so… I'll put this out there and then you tell me what you think. My big brother is not the mopey or surly type of person. But walking in here, I definitely got a lot of looks from your staff, and when I asked about it, a lot of them said you were in "a bad mood".' Eleni paused, levelling an inquisitive stare at him. 'Now, I know you're not someone who is in a bad mood. People who have just met you will *think* you're in a bad mood, but that's just your face.'

Niko frowned when she waved her hand in his general direction. 'Is there a point to any of this, Eleni? Or are you just here because you're feeling whimsical? I have a hospital to run.'

His sister sat up straighter at his words, tilting her head slightly as if she had noticed something only she could see in the room. She certainly made no attempt to tell him, so he asked, 'What?'

'Ah, when you said, "I have a hospital to run," some memories came back to me from a few years ago.' She paused, and he could see some uncertainty in the tight press of her lips. 'Father used to tell me that a lot whenever I would come by to talk to him about something.'

Niko stared at her as an icy shiver spread through his body. His eyes flared. He had said something that made him sound like his father? Both of the Vassilis children had their fair share of trauma thanks to Stavros, and one saving grace had been finding refuge in each other. He could remember the amount of times Eleni had called him in the middle of the night after a particularly bad fight with their father, who had never passed up an opportunity to make her doubt herself. If Niko was charged with carrying on the family legacy, then Eleni was the disappointment that he was never shy to point out whenever he could.

She knew how deep his own hurt sat and would never make such a comparison unless she could genuinely see it—and was worried for him.

He let out a sigh, his gaze dropping to his desk as he considered. 'Okay... I hear you. What's on your mind?'

Eleni looked at him, patting the space next to her on the couch with a tight smile and waited until he had sat down there.

'You weren't at the dinner yesterday. But Camila was,' his sister finally said, and the roaring in his ears was instant.

His pulse kicked up in speed at the mention of her name, his heart pushing against his sternum in a sensation he'd been fighting the last week—ever since he watched her walk out of this office.

Camila was still here? His eyes darted to the date on his phone. The re-scan to figure out her due date was tomorrow. He'd assumed she would be back in Switzerland by now, setting up a life completely independent from his. Were the next steps she wanted to discuss about how to handle their co-parenting between two countries?

'I see. Then you probably already have all the details about what happened?' he asked, finally understanding the presence of his sister in his office. She—and his mother—knew and they wanted to check in on him. Or tell him what an idiot he was. God knew he deserved that and was thinking it himself in the quiet hours of the night.

'Really, Niko? You think so low of her you truly believe she would unpack the demise of your relationship at the family dinner?' A stark line appeared between Eleni's brow as she glared at him.

'Of course she wouldn't, but I also know she didn't lie about my whereabouts, or you wouldn't be sitting here right now,' Niko replied, letting out a deep sigh as he realised he would have to explain himself. Which was hard to do because he didn't really know what had happened himself.

'So, when did you two break up? I assume this was a breakup because you didn't actually ever say you were seeing her. Only that she was having your child and… Well, to be honest, I'm not entirely sure about the timeline of your relationship.' The earnest puzzlement on Eleni's face was enough to make him laugh even through this darker moment in his life. He and Camila had fallen for each other so fast, Niko couldn't blame Eleni for the confusion.

'We didn't exactly take the *traditional* path with anything. Camila is far from what anyone could call traditional. From a far younger age than necessary, she's been in charge of her own fate. Not that that is relevant to our...situation.' Niko paused, taking a deep breath. 'We mutually called it off after a disagreement about the future. I wanted her to come and live here, and she said her work demanded she'd be in Switzerland. That she didn't want to move her base of operations to Athens.'

Eleni cocked her head. 'Okay, she is established over there. I can understand that. Did she say why she didn't want to consider moving?'

'She didn't want to give me this much control over her work and her life,' Niko said, remembering the words almost exactly. It had shocked him to his core to hear them, that she would even think he would use any part of their connection to control her. Even if he was the one funding her research, he would never have the audacity to go anywhere near it. It would have always remained her own choices whatever she wanted to do.

'Why would she think that?'

Niko shrugged. 'I told her the Athena Institute had enough funding for her research and that I would be more than happy to be part of it. I had already spoken with the real estate team to make some space for her lab, with plans and everything.'

Eleni's lips pressed into a thin line, the line between her brows growing deeper. 'You told her you would like her to join you here, talked together to real estate about what kind of space she needed, and then she pulled out?'

He blinked at his sister, then slowly shook his head. 'No... I spoke to the real estate team to set it all up for her and then I presented Camila with the solution to our problem.'

Now it was Eleni's turn to blink, and he had the bizarre feeling that they had somehow ended up speaking a different language. 'But...how can you set up her lab if you didn't ask her what she needed? Did you broach the topic of her coming to Athens permanently with her before or after you put the plans together?'

With each word from his sister, a chill starting at the base of his spine began spreading its icy tendrils through his body until it reached all the far-flung corners. He turned the words around in his head, trying to see it from angles he hadn't thought of before and...

'She's refusing to accept my help or to find any other solution to the problem we're facing. Maybe I could have gone about a different way with my offer, but she wasn't willing to give me an alternative, either,' he said, and almost flinched at how immature it sounded. Was that how he really felt, or were things inside him so messy that he couldn't separate things?

Judging by Eleni's huff, she had a similar train of thought. 'What's the problem you're facing?' she asked, zeroing in on the insecurity he'd been carrying around from the very start. The opinion about her when he'd first met her that had buried so deep inside of him, he couldn't get rid of it now. Not when he saw the confirmation of it in everything she did.

'I don't know if I can take the constant limelight that she requires to do her work right now. Getting funding from me seemed like an ideal solution to that requirement. She must truly *want* this kind of life, otherwise wouldn't it be easy to say yes. If she'd meet me somewhere in the middle…' Something about it sounded wrong. Niko knew it deep inside his chest, knew that there was something just…off about it. But even though he had been stewing over it since their conversation, he couldn't come to a conclusion. Everything was just too convoluted and messed up for him to make any sense.

'I think she might see it differently from her point of view,' Eleni said. 'It's possible she's doing whatever she needed to do so that the maximum amount of people could benefit from her research. Did you not see her as a caring physician while she was here?'

Now it was Niko's turn to huff. 'Yes, she was

caring—brilliant, even. But so was our father before... Anyway, I can't help but think that something along the path of success and notoriety pulled him down. How can I be certain of her when her path looks so similar? When she refuses to take up the offer that would pull her out of needing to ask anyone for money.'

'Brother—' Eleni leaned closer, putting a hand on his thigh and squeezing it '—I hope you understand that I'm saying this with all the love and affection I have for you, but you are so far off the mark, I don't even think we are on the same planet.'

Niko scowled at his younger sister. 'Have you and our mother already made up your minds about this whole thing last night?'

'No, but after Camila left, we had a good idea of what might have happened. And I think you are entirely too concerned about the past. You are trying to solve a hurt that has nothing to do with her. She's not our father, and her needing publicity to fund her research doesn't make her our father, either. At the end of the day, people all over the globe are benefitting from her research, and it will save plenty of lives, no?'

He only mumbled at that, unable to refute the truth in her words. He may not like how much Camila spoke to the press to get her name out there, but Alexis wouldn't have had his diagnosis by now without her help.

'I'll take your silence as an agreement. So, last question and then I will be out of your hair since I know you "have a hospital to run."' Eleni lowered her voice for the last sentence, mimicking his own tone. 'Has she requested an exorbitant contract fee for her collaboration here at the institute?'

That wasn't the question he had expected. What had her fee to do with…? His mind stalled as he remembered the conversation he'd had with Emilia. How blown away his senior cardiologist had been because—

'She did it for free,' Niko said, his voice hardly above a whisper, speaking more to himself than to his sister. 'We offered her a fee in line with what her seniority in the field warranted. But she turned it down… Said she found the case compelling, and she would much rather add the notes to her research than charge us anything for her help. Emilia said she hadn't even wanted to accept a paid hotel, but I insisted.'

A small smile spread over Eleni's face, as if she could see the puzzle pieces fall into place in his mind. Then she gave his thigh one more squeeze before pushing herself off the couch and grabbing her bag off the coffee table. 'I bet she didn't even once ask you for child support during her entire stay, either.'

She hadn't. Because this had never been about money for her. Niko had been the one to project that fear onto her whenever she did anything that resembled what he had learned to despise in his father. But while everything Stavros did had been about lining his pockets, the same couldn't be said for Camila. All she had done had been in the service of furthering her research to give more people a chance at a cure—not to make her a wealthy woman. She pursued fame as a means to an end. To save people.

'Wait, Eleni.' He stood, reaching out a hand to stop his sister. 'Camila… Last night—how was she? Do I…?' A lump appeared in his throat as the words formed in his head. 'Do I still have time to fix this?'

Eleni smiled at him, her hand wrapping around his and giving it a reassuring pat. 'You should talk to her' was all she said, leaving Niko alone to gather his thoughts—and make a plan.

The tears were never far these days, and Camila blamed most of it on the baby. Or the quiet. Or how the sun was bright on that day. Any excuse was better than looking inward and examining the grief wrapping around her heart.

They had agreed that this was the best decision for them. They had uncovered too many opposing forces in their relationship that they couldn't over-come. Despite that, Camila hadn't yet booked her flight back. She'd told herself it was because she wanted to attend the appointment with Daphne, though a part of her recognised it for the comforting lie it was.

Camila wasn't sure of her convictions any more. Would it really be such a big deal if she moved her operations to Athens? She'd never cared about where the money was coming from for her research, only that she got enough funding to keep going.

Every night she stared at her phone, at the last messages she and Niko had exchanged, thought about the words she had left unsaid. But even then, she couldn't force herself to click the Call button. Fear coiled itself around her in thick strands, rooting her in place and not letting her look back. Or move on. Camila was stuck in this between space, unable to free herself.

All she knew was that everything hurt without Niko. Even breathing was harder than usual, and a mixture of sensations rose within her as she braced to see him again today.

Though she noted with a glance at the clock that he was running late for the appointment. Not a good sign. He hadn't been late once in any of their professional settings. She'd wanted to believe that if it was about their child, he would be even more precise. But as the minutes ticked by without him appearing in front of her, the chill in her rose higher and higher, and by the time Daphne called her into the exam room, Camila felt like the floor was made of rubber.

Daphne seemed to notice, too, for her hand closed around Camila's arm as she guided her to her seat. 'Are you feeling all right?' the woman asked with a subdued expression.

'Yeah, it's just…' The pressure behind her eyes grew stronger and she blinked several times, trying to fight the tears from spilling. She tried to swallow the lump in her throat, but the stubborn thing remained lodged in there, forcing her to talk around it. 'It's been a tough week.'

Daphne smiled, reached out her hand and patted her thigh and then opened the cabinet next to her, retrieving a box of tissues. 'My patients tend to cry a lot—which I encourage. It's better to let it out here than keep it bottled up,' she said, and the encouragement woven into her words wasn't lost on Camila.

What was worse, she really wanted to spill her guts. Outside of Niko and now his family, she didn't know anyone here in Athens, and so she'd spent most of her time in her hotel room, contemplating all the choices that had led her to this moment. So often her finger had hovered over the Purchase button for a flight back to Switzerland, but something inside her had stopped her from going through with it.

'Thank you.' She reached out to grab a tissue with a shaky hand, dabbing at eyes that were still refusing to spill any of the tears fighting their way out.

Daphne nodded, then leaned back in her chair. 'I won't ask you how you are since I have a good idea. I'm sorry you two are struggling to come together.'

Camila nodded. 'I fear it's just me today, so we can start whenever.'

The other woman frowned at that, her eyes darting to the watch on her wrist. 'Mm-hmm, it is unlike him to run late. But I've also never known Nikolas to be someone to shy away from responsibility.' Daphne paused, the lines around her eyes softening as she looked at Camila. 'I hope I'm not overstepping. But why do you have so little faith that my son will show up for you?'

Camila almost flinched at that question, the bluntness striking straight at the hurt she still carried around. Her lack of faith in his commitment had been one of the main reasons for their breakup—with her not being able to get over the words of caution her mother had drilled into her from early on. But then again, he had left. She was here by herself, struggling to find any peace in their decision.

What else was there to say to that? The loneliness was biting, the prospect of having to go through this all by herself almost too much to bear. But hadn't her mother's words ultimately proved right?

'He's not here, and I just…had it in my gut that this day would come. My father left when I was young and my mother never got over that. Never let me forget that, either. Now Niko is asking me to give up everything I worked for to live here, when I don't even know if our relationship will work out. What if it doesn't and I'm left to his mercy because I gave so much of myself?' The words bubbled forth with no filter or restraint, and Camila was too sad, too tired, too everything to care any more. She couldn't hold it in, had no more fight left to pretend like she was okay. When the first tear slid down her cheek, she didn't wipe it away.

Daphne only nodded, listening to her words in silence until they had dried up and then let her shed some tears before she asked, 'Your mother taught you to be guarded?'

One tear slid down Camila's throat, creating a cold sensation that had her shivering, and Camila pressed the tissue against it. The phrasing shifted something within her, showing her a perspective she hadn't seen before. Guarded? Was that what she was doing? 'It wasn't easy to see her struggle, even if we didn't see eye to eye on many things. If nothing else, I knew I never wanted to be in this situation myself...'

The other woman frowned, cupping her chin with her hand as she leaned forward. 'What were the things you disagreed about?'

Camila took a stuttering breath, not expecting the questioning to go this way—or any questions at all. She hadn't come here to unload her problems onto Daphne, but with no one else in her life right now and her being so warm to her... 'She didn't think being a doctor was a suitable career for me, didn't care that this was what I wanted out of life. When I defied her wishes for me, when she lost her control over me, our relationship strained further.'

The memories were still painful to this day. Camila had worked hard to become a success because of the adversity she encountered from her mother.

With a deep breath, she continued, 'Things were still tense between us when she passed away, and sometimes things feel...unfinished. Like I didn't receive some critical information growing up and now... I feel lost.'

Footsteps sounded outside, taking Camila out of the moment as she strained her ears. But they walked past the closed door of the exam room and down the hall, leaving her just a bit more deflated. Despite the bone-crushing certainty that Niko wasn't coming, a part of her was still holding out—still hoping.

Daphne gave her a gentle smile, her hand crossing the space between them to pat her on the knee again. 'It sounds like your mother put some of her insecurities in you, and I just hope you won't suffer the consequences of it now so many years later.'

Camila looked at the other woman with drawn-up eyebrows. 'What do you mean?'

Daphne's gaze slipped down to where her hand connected with her knee, her eyes glazing over as if she was off in her own world. Eventually, she said, 'My ex-husband was a harsh man, especially to Nikolas. I tried my best to shield him from it, but there was only so much I could do once he reached adulthood. Sometimes he wanted to be just like his father and worshipped the ground he walked on. But when he tried to be his own person, find his own way…that was when things became tense between them. Stavros had planned so much of Nikolas's life without involving him, and when my son rebelled against it, he rejected his father and almost chose to be the complete opposite. But even to this day, he carries a piece of his father around with him—and it's holding him back, too. But it's the only thing Nikolas has left of him.'

Daphne's words floated around her, wormed their way inside her brain and into her battered soul. He carried a piece of his father around with him? Was that what had interfered with their relationship—old scars that had never properly healed? The truth of her words sank deep inside her, and the shock of them vibrated through her bones.

Had she been carrying the words of her mother because that was the only thing she had left of her? Words of caution she wanted to believe were well meaning but were heavy with her mother's own insecurities?

'He lashed out at me because he thought me advocating for my research with different medical journals would lead to a dark place...because he saw it happen to his father. But then I took that as confirmation that eventually he would leave, just like I've been told all my life he would.' Her hand came down on her stomach in an instinctual protective gesture as she yearned to shield her own child from anything related to that.

How could she have fallen into such a deep trap of her own mind? She sat up straight as the enormity of her mistake became clear in her mind. 'I need to talk—'

Footsteps sounded again, far more hurried than the last ones, and her heart flipped inside her chest because she *knew* those footsteps. Not even a second later, the door flew open, and Niko stepped in, hair wind-tousled and slightly out of breath.

'Sorry, there was an emergency—why are you crying?' He knelt down in front of her, taking her face between his hands and wiping the tears from her cheeks. The gesture was so intimate—so *ordinary*—as if they hadn't just spent a week apart, believing their relationship was doomed to fail.

'I...it's been a tough week,' she said, and surprised herself when a weak laugh came out her throat.

Niko's returning smile was weak, and Camila gasped when his grip around her face tightened and he pressed his forehead against hers. 'I'm sorry, Camila. That's all my fault. I overreacted, please—'

A faint cough had them both turning their heads. Daphne had risen from her chair and was looking at them. 'I'll give you a few minutes, but we still need to do the exam before my next appointment arrives,' she said with a pointed stare at her wristwatch.

When the door closed behind her, Niko turned back to her, and the pain in his eyes struck her in the chest. They stared at each other in quiet contemplation before Niko continued. 'I was scared, because the thing you're doing—I've only seen it turn out one way. But by assuming it would be the same for you, I wasn't giving you enough credit. Enough trust. I accused you of that when it was me who didn't believe in you.'

Camila shook her head even though his words were balm on her battered soul. 'I played my part in this. From the very beginning, I was just waiting for you to leave and the moment I saw even a hint of wavering, I took that as confirmation that you were exactly as I feared.'

Niko sighed, his gaze slipping down to where his hand grasped hers. 'I assumed too much, thinking that is what we wanted, but I didn't talk to you because…everything was so perfect. Much more than things have ever been in my life. I was scared that if I moved, if I said anything, it could all go away.' He paused, looking back up at her. 'But I know now I needed to be braver.'

'I could have said something as well, but I didn't.' Camila took a shaking breath, calming her racing pulse. 'I was also content in living in our cosy bubble without thinking of the future— of how we should do this together. I guess we both have some past trust issues to confront. But I don't want this to ever get in the way of how I feel about you. About…being a family with you.'

He lowered his forehead to their hands. 'Please forgive me for not being braver sooner.'

She slid her hands over his cheeks, tilting his face towards her. 'There's nothing to forgive. We are here now.'

Niko's smile was brighter this time. 'We both decided we should end it, so should we both decide that we…?' His voice trailed off, his inflection going up in an unfinished question.

Camila bit her lip, emotions rising in her chest as she picked up the meaning of his words. She nodded slowly and then smiled. 'We should.'

Niko pulled her into a tight embrace and Camila pressed her head against her chest—like she had done so often, knowing this would not be the last time. They were going to say it together.

The warmth of his body felt like a shield around hers and she didn't want this moment to end, wanted to draw it out forever. But there were some important things they had to say to each other.

Reluctantly, she pushed away from him and met his eyes with a soft smile on her face. 'I love you, Niko. I want to be with you and give this child the family neither of us ever had.'

'I love you, too, Camila. Wherever you want to take us, I will be there,' he replied, brushing the last tear from her cheek before pulling her into a kiss that she wanted to last a lifetime.

And now she knew it would.

EPILOGUE

A COOL BREEZE drifted into the room, and Camila shivered as she looked up from her computer screen. Her office looked exactly the same as it had in Switzerland, though the walls of the Athena Institute were far less insulated against the cold.

Two years on and she was still getting used to the various changes in her life—some challenging, most though far more enjoyable than she could have ever imagined. After many conversations throughout the pregnancy, Camila and Niko had decided she would move to Athens before the birth. Both Eleni and Daphne had been indispensable in those first few months, practically living with them as they settled into life as new parents.

Her phone lit up, and a big smile appeared on her lips when her eyes slipped over the background picture. Staring up at her with big brown eyes and a toothy smile was her daughter, Helena, sitting on Niko's lap, waving her arms along with the rest of the crowd around them. They had been invited to the Olympics to watch Alexis Theodorou take his chance at the gold medal—after many training sessions supervised by both his coach and Emilia Seo to ensure he was really up to the task. Working together, they had managed to give Alexis back the one thing that meant the most to him—a shot at the medal.

She had received a text from one of her researchers, but Camila made a note to answer it tomorrow, swiping it away for today. It was late, and she already had plans. Her research was still one of her top priorities, but now...now there were more important things in her life.

And as if her thoughts had summoned those important things, her door swung open and Niko walked in, Helena on his hip. The smile on his face was bright, his eyes alight with an amused sparkle. 'What?' Camila asked when she noticed it.

'Nothing,' he said with a shrug and plopped their daughter on her desk, who let out a delighted squeal when Camila wrapped her arms around her. 'I just like coming to your office.'

The hidden meaning of his words wasn't lost on her. He was glad they were sharing this life together, had twined their personal and professional lives into something that worked for both of them. It hadn't been hard, either. Letting go of control had been challenging, and trusting that things would turn out all right no matter what wasn't something Camila was used to. But parenthood had changed everything, had changed them, in ways she couldn't even count. All for the better, and she wouldn't have wanted to do even one bit without Niko.

She could have never imagined that life could be like this. Niko had grown into the role as a father with such ease, taking on a big part of Helena's care while she worked. Seeing them at the end of the day and hearing what great adventures they'd been up to sent her heart soaring to new heights.

'Are you ready to go?' he asked, his eyes gliding over the papers scattered across her desk.

'Yeah, let's go. I've been looking forward to this dinner all day,' she said, standing up with Helena in her arms.

Niko turned to her, lifting his eyebrows. 'Oh yeah? Anything special?'

There was a playful, suspicious lilt in his voice, and Camila laughed. 'Maybe I have some interesting things to tell you,' she said, a secretive smile spreading over her lips as she brushed her free hand over her stomach.

Niko's eyes flared wide for all but a second. Then he, too, broke out in a smile filled with mischief and secrets. 'That's so funny. I might also have an interesting thing to ask you,' he said, and Camila's lips parted in surprise.

'Is that why Eleni asked me to borrow some of my rings the other day? When she never before asked about any of my jewellery?' she asked, remembering the bizarre encounter with his sister.

But Niko only shrugged, and she knew he was enjoying this moment way too much. 'You'll find out at dinner' was all he said as he escorted her out of her office, and Camila breathed in his scent as his arm came around her.

It didn't matter what he had to ask. The answer would be yes.

It always was when it came to Niko.

* * * * *

MEDICAL

Life and love in the world of modern medicine.

 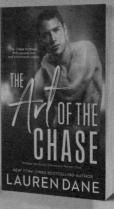

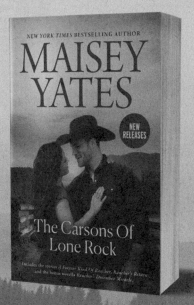

Subscribe and fall in love with a Mills & Boon series today!

You'll be among the first to read stories delivered to your door monthly and enjoy great savings.

WE SIMPLY LOVE ROMANCE

MILLS & BOON

—— JOIN US ——

Sign up to our newsletter to stay up to date with...

- Exclusive member discount codes
- Competitions
- New release book information
- All the latest news on your favourite authors

Plus...
get $10 off your first order.
What's not to love?

Sign up at **millsandboon.com.au/newsletter**